ADVANCE RAVES FOR **WARRIORS:**

"Spiritual heirs of the medieval knights, today's fighter pilots are the last true warriors extant in our uncertain age. Tillman captures their honor, skill, and courage perfectly in this excellent book." —Stephen Coonts

"This is an excellent book. Barrett Tillman puts you inside the fighter pilot's head and makes you understand what a warrior feels."
—Larry Bond, author of *Red Phoenix*.

WARRIORS
BARRETT ★ TILLMAN

BANTAM BOOKS
NEW YORK · TORONTO · LONDON · SYDNEY · AUCKLAND

WARRIORS
A Bantam Book / July 1990

Lyrics from "F-5E"
quoted by permission of Dick Jonas
and Enchantment Music Co.

Book design by Guenet Abraham.
Map design by GDS / Jeffrey L. Ward

Library of Congress Cataloging-in-Publication Data
Tillman, Barrett.
  Warriors : a novel / by Barrett Tillman
    p.   cm.
  ISBN 0-553-34881-7
  1. Israel-Arab War,—1973—Fiction. I. Title.
PS3570.I39W3   1990
813'.54—dc20   89-49444
                                                            CIP

Published simultaneously in the United States and Canada

Bantam Books are published by Bantam Books, a division of Bantam
Doubleday Dell Publishing Group, Inc. Its trademark, consisting of the
words "Bantam Books" and the portrayal of a rooster, is Registered in U.S.
Patent and Trademark Office and in other countries. Marca Registrada.
Bantam Books, 666 Fifth Avenue, New York, New York 10103.

PRINTED IN THE UNITED STATES OF AMERICA

BVG   0 9 8 7 6 5 4 3 2 1

Acknowledgments

MANY THOUGHTFUL PEOPLE—AVIATORS AND OTHERWISE—HAVE EASED my transition process from history to fiction. Among the first was David Ballantine, who thought enough of the original draft of *Warriors* to endorse it to his brother. Ian and Betty Ballantine accelerated the usual glacial pace of publishing negotiations, and Greg Tobin at Bantam has been an encouraging editor.

Additionally, grateful recognition is extended to those who contributed special knowledge or support, starting with the Champlin Fighter Museum in Mesa, Arizona. CFM is the finest institution of its type, and by happy accident it became the scene of meetings with pilots from Saudi Arabia, Jordan, and Israel. Lieutenant Colonel Jim Anderson of nearby Williams Air Force Base, who has since traded in his F-5 for a Boeing 737, was especially helpful with introductions and critiques.

Dick Jonas of Phoenix, a former fighter pilot himself and full-time balladeer, kindly allowed me to rewrite one of his songs. Also an Arizona asset is Jeff Cooper, the gunfighter's guru, who is the basis for small-arms doctrine.

Lieutenant Colonel Tom "Skip" Ostermann, an Eagle driver from Luke and Nellis, made valuable comments on current fighter aircraft, weapons, and procedures.

But the Navy also came through in fine style. Bob and Sally Lawson of *The Hook* magazine read the manuscript and provided a wealth of suggestions and advice. So did Captain Wynn Foster, USN (Ret.), whose knowledge of the A-4 Skyhawk and light attack aviation are golden.

Rear Admiral Paul "Punchy" Gillcrist, USN (Ret.), provided aeronautical charts and useful data on the Northrop F-20 as did Captain Phil Wood, USN (Ret.). Though the Tigershark never entered production, its private-enterprise origin remains deserving of thanks from every American taxpayer.

I could hope for no finer critics than Bob and Curt Dosé, Navy fighter pilots who have left indelible impressions on two generations of enemy airmen. Another tailhook aviator, Steve Coonts, was similarly encouraging.

Navy Fighter Squadron 143 responded quickly to a request for T-shirts of "The World-Famous Pukin' Dogs," who truly are *sans reproche*.

John Tillman provided a lucid explanation of nuclear physics while yet another jet pilot, Debra McCormick, lent a copy of the Koran and a knowledge of the Middle East.

As depicted herein, the geography and military capabilities of the region's nations are accurate to the extent known. The most significant departures from fact are the mythical Hovda and Balhama air bases in Israel.

Finally, those in the business know that there exist actual fighter pilots with callsigns mentioned in these pages. Neither too much nor too little should be made of that fact. But to the real Pirate and Devil—and to their fellow warriors with *noms de guerre* like Diego, Snake, and "the original Maverick"—this book is dedicated.

To set the cause above renown,
To love the game beyond the prize,
To honor, while you strike him down,
The foe that comes with fearless eyes;
To count the life of battle good
And dear the land that gave you birth,
And dearer yet the brotherhood
That binds the brave of all the earth.

Sir Henry Newbolt

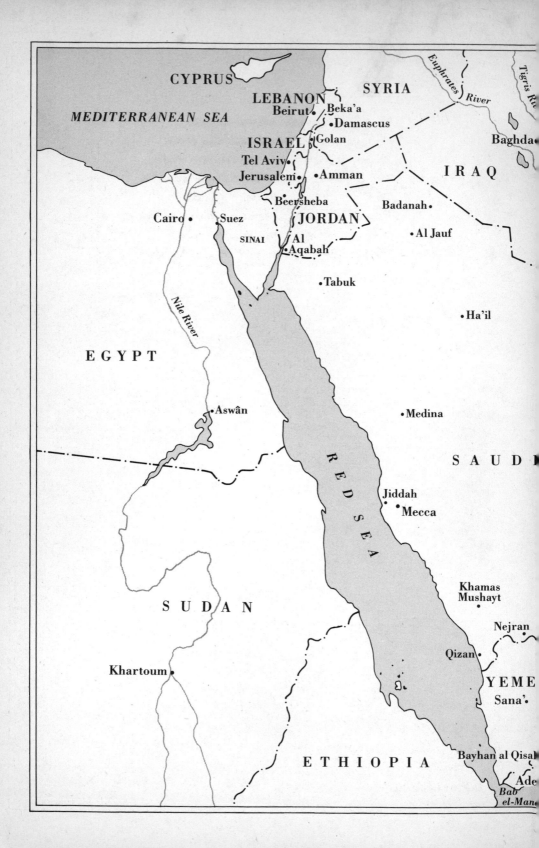

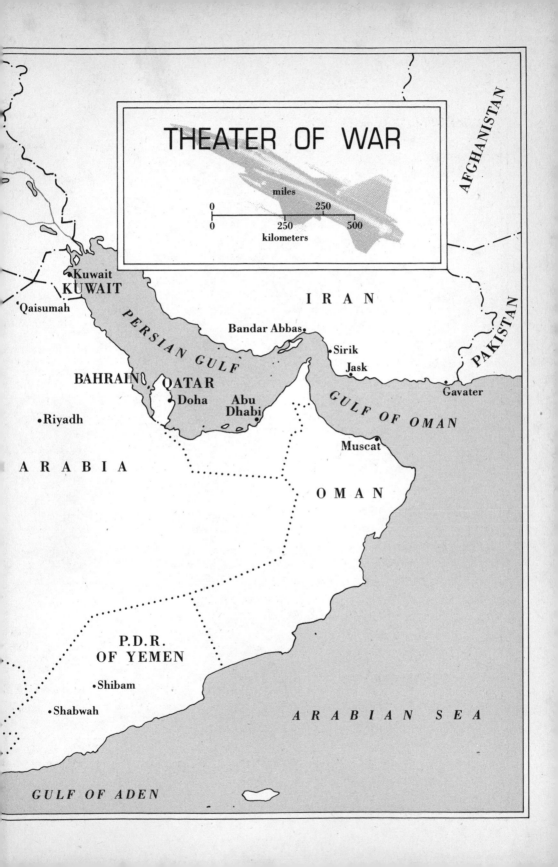

THEATER OF WAR

miles
0   250
0   250   500
kilometers

AFGHANISTAN

•Kuwait
KUWAIT

•Qaisumah

I R A N

Bandar Abbas•

•Sirik

Jask•

PAKISTAN

PERSIAN GULF

BAHRAIN QATAR

•Doha

Abu
Dhabi

•Gavater

GULF OF OMAN

•Riyadh

A R A B I A

Muscat•

O M A N

P.D.R.
OF YEMEN

•Shibam

•Shabwah

A R A B I A N   S E A

GULF OF ADEN

P R O L O G U E

WAR IN THE AFTERNOON

But we touched the heavens and found
them filled with a mighty guard and
shooting-stars; and we did sit in certain
seats thereof to listen; but whoso of us
listens now finds a shooting-star for him
on guard.

Surah LXXII.9

Chapter of the Jinn

1 ＝＝＝＝＝＝＝＝＝＝＝＝＝＝＝＝＝＝＝＝＝＝＝

DAY ONE
6 October 1973, 1405 Hours

MOST WARS BEGIN BEFORE DAWN. THIS ONE WAS DIFFERENT.

When the Klaxon sounded, a few of the pilots on alert at the Skyhawk base hesitated a single heartbeat before conditioned response hurled them into motion. The scramble was not wholly unexpected, for a recall still was in progress—ever since Israeli intelligence had determined that hostilities were imminent. After all, it was the tenth day of Tishri and most units were on partial stand-down for Yom Kippur, the holiest day on the Jewish calendar.

That combination of facts told thirty-seven-year-old Major Ariel Kadar that this was no drill.

Sprinting through the door of the ready room and into the hall leading to the hangar, Kadar overtook his young wingman. The squadron commander thumped the new lieutenant on the shoulder. "Come on, David. Don't let an old man beat you!"

The two pilots turned hard right into the covered alert pad housing their Skyhawk attack planes. Each was fully armed with 500-pound bombs and 30mm ammunition. With practiced ease Kadar was up the boarding ladder and almost mechanically plugging and strapping himself into the cockpit: torso harness fittings; G-suit lead, helmet with oxygen and radio plugs. In seconds he was starting his Pratt & Whitney J52-P8A engine, glancing across at the other jet.

Lieutenant David Ran was almost fifteen years younger than his commander and should have been a shade quicker. But he wasn't. Despite the unrelenting pace of training, which continued after he joined his operational squadron, much of the job still was new to him. As he lit off his own engine and saw the RPM and temperature gauges flick to life, he looked up. The boarding ladders had been removed, wheel chocks pulled free, and mechanics were signaling clear to taxi. Ran saw Kadar nod vigorously and the two Skyhawks taxied into the bright sunlight.

From the adjoining pad two more A-4s appeared, swinging behind the lead section.

During the fast taxi to the runway, the canopies came down and locked as each pilot silently ran through his pretakeoff check list. By the time they turned at the intersection onto the runway they were ready to go, and Major Kadar smoothly advanced his throttle as 9,300 pounds of thrust boosted his aircraft off the ground. All four jets tucked their tricycle landing gear into the wells and climbed for altitude.

It was exactly four and one half minutes after the siren had sounded.

Thus far not a word had been spoken. David Ran was only aware of the measured sound of his own breathing under his oxygen mask and the carrier wave in his earphones. He was the newest pilot in the squadron, but he knew his job and was proud that Kadar had chosen him as wingman. The CO had been flying Skyhawks for six years—ever since the first American-built A-4Hs had been delivered to Israel in 1967.

Ran looked over at his leader. It was typical of the man that his seniority counted for nothing in normal duty rotation. Even though Ariel Kadar was more devout than many Israeli pilots, he had passed up the chance to spend Yom Kippur with his family. The Day of Atonement was turning into something different this year.

In the lead aircraft, Kadar spoke with his ground controller. The airborne planes were given a westerly heading and told to investigate reported activity along the Suez Canal. *So, it's Sinai*, the squadron leader thought to himself. He knew the area well. It was only twenty minutes flying time from his base, and he had logged repeated missions over the sandy expanse. There had been frequent alarms since the Six-Day War—it was part of everyday life in the Israeli Air Force, or *Heyl Ha'Avir*—and consequently the nation's air arm was in a constant state of readiness.

Lugging a dozen 500-pound bombs westward at three hundred knots, the four Skyhawk pilots and the few other jets scrambled in the opening moments of the 1973 war unknowingly faced an unpleasant change of routine. Egypt in the west and Syria in the east had launched an unusually well coordinated two-front assault on the Israelis, intending to recapture territory lost in the 1967 war. The Egyptian assault was especially well executed, combining the cherished trinity of massive force, surprise timing, and overwhelming violence.

Reports varied, but on Day One between 500 and 800 Egyptian tanks crossed the Suez Canal at three points. The assault was supported by some 4,000 artillery pieces plus MiGs and Sukhoi fighter-bombers pounding the Bar Lev line of defensive positions which Israel had built parallel to the east bank of the canal.

That wasn't all. Egyptian planners knew the Israelis had placed explosive charges along the canal, ready to detonate in the face of an assault. Scuba divers had stealthily, skillfully removed or disarmed the explosives, and other commandos blew up Israeli radio and radar stations within reach of the waterway.

Almost simultaneously with the overture at 1400, the Arabs began jamming Israeli communications. It was a fully integrated operation, precisely the type of action most Israelis felt that no Arab nation was capable of executing.

Little of this was known to Major Kadar or his pilots on the first mission that afternoon. But as professionals they were prepared for most contingencies. They checked and rechecked their navigation, their aircraft instruments, and their armament switches. They activated their A-4s' radar homing and warning (RHAW) equipment. These "black boxes," as their American suppliers called them, were designed to provide advance warning of hostile radar tracking. The U.S. Air Force and Navy had learned hard lessons in the air war over North Vietnam. American involvement had only ended in January, so current information was available to the Israelis on Soviet-built air defense equipment. But some pilots of the *Heyl Ha'Avir* were disdainful. The Arab nations simply weren't capable of maintaining sophisticated electronics without extensive Soviet assistance. Everybody knew that.

With the canal in view well ahead from 14,000 feet, Major Kadar led his flight in a lazy turn to the left. He intended to swing down the east bank on a reconnaissance sweep, for he was authorized to attack any Arab unit displaying hostile intentions. Against that possibility, he double-checked his master armament panel.

David Ran looked to his left front, past his leader's Skyhawk. He noticed dust clouds along the canal and a vague milling activity on both banks. Abruptly he became aware of several things, each competing for his attention. Down to 12,000 feet, only a few miles from the waterway, he could see the aftereffects of an artillery barrage—by far the largest he could imagine. He saw formations of armored vehicles crossing west to east on pontoon bridges, and he heard an increasingly high-pitched scratching in his headset.

Ran's RHAW gear was quiet—no evidence of radar scanning. That much was encouraging, at least. Lingering dust clouds swirled into the air from shellbursts and tracked vehicles, making detailed observation difficult. But the flight had passed beyond the northern-most area of conflict and Ran noted his leader setting up for a diving attack on something below to the right.

Radio communication was almost impossible but each pilot followed his leader regardless; they knew the procedure by rote.

As Ran allowed the usual interval between his leader's roll-in and his own, he judged the target to be a cluster of portable bridges and waiting vehicles on the west bank. From this point it was a routine attack: one pass—put your bombs where they belong and get the hell out. So far nobody seemed to be shooting at them; perhaps they had caught the Egyptians by surprise.

Major Kadar's Skyhawk disappeared in an orange-black fireball. Small bits of debris lingered briefly in the sky, then were gone.

Ran absorbed the knowledge that his squadron commander—his friend—had just died. Then, not knowing what else to do, he pressed his dive on the portable bridging equipment and placed his illuminated sight reticle just short of the target. He made sure his wings were level, pressed the button on his stick grip, and felt his low-drag bombs kick off their racks.

After a brief wait to ensure that no bombs were skewed sideways, he began a steady pull.

Blue-green tracers flashed by Ran's canopy; somebody was tracking him with 23mm. The air bladders of his G-suit compressed about his thighs and abdomen. Instinctively, he grunted against the oppression of nearly six times the force of gravity as his nose came level with the horizon. More tracers and two twisting smoke trails drifted behind him. Realizing he was flying northwest—into Egypt—he rolled almost 90 degrees, pulled hard, and stomped opposite rudder to slew his A-4 erratically. Then he bent the throttle, exiting at thirty-five hundred feet.

The young pilot looked around, wanting to rejoin the second section. He spotted one Skyhawk and turned toward it. There was no sign of the number four man, and Ran feared the worst.

Four took off, two are coming back. That's no good. We've got to tell somebody what's happening. . . .

BACK AT BASE NOBODY KNEW MUCH MORE THAN WHEN THE duty flights had launched fifty minutes before. David Ran, now a combat veteran, unsnapped and unplugged himself from his aircraft and noticed the crew chief on the boarding ladder. Knowing the man's tacit questioning about the missing CO, Ran muttered, "He blew up. He just blew up."

The debriefing was a short one, for there were more missions to plan, brief, and fly. The squadron intelligence officer, hastily recalled from his home, was puzzled about lack of radar warning. It was known the Egyptians had SA-2 and SA-3 surface-to-air missiles across the canal, but their guidance frequencies had been determined. The jets' onboard RHAW should have detected the threat.

"You're certain there was no electronic warning?" the IO asked. He looked from Ran to the captain who led the second section.

"Absolutely," the senior flier said. "No indication at all. The first I knew was when the missile hit Ari's machine. I saw it too late to warn him. Besides, they were jamming our radios."

Ran leaned forward in his chair. A missile hit Kadar's aircraft? Ran had seen nothing but the explosion. But neither had he seen the number four Skyhawk go down.

The IO ran a hand through his thick dark hair. He expelled a breath and looked at the two pilots. "Well, we know two things. The enemy has a new guidance system that we evidently weren't aware of, and we know where the next mission is headed. You brief in five minutes."

By sunset David Ran had flown two more missions and his squadron had lost two more planes, though one pilot ejected safely. Meanwhile, Egyptian tanks pushed eastward from their three bridge-heads in increasing numbers.

DURING THE NEXT FORTY-EIGHT HOURS THE ISRAELI nation and its armed forces scrambled to compensate for the deficit of 6 October. There were the inevitable cries, recriminations, and how-could-this-happen agonizing. However, at air force headquarters the mood was more detached, if no less concerned. Late on the night of the sixth, a panel of senior officers reviewed the opening day's events and counted the cost. It was staggering.

The *Heyl Ha'Avir* had entered the war with some 330 frontline combat aircraft, of which 30 Skyhawks and 10 Phantoms had been shot down over Sinai and the Golan Heights. It amounted to 12 percent losses on Day One. Every man in the room knew what that meant. If the loss rate continued, Israel would be without an effective air force in one week.

Brigadier General Schmuel Baharov, head of air technical intelligence, took the floor. He was a balding, portly man in his late forties whose appearance belied an intellect bordering on genius. He had two passions in life: electronics and gardening. This night his flowers were the farthest thing from his mind.

"Gentlemen. The Egyptians have assembled a well-organized, self-supporting armored force with overlapping air defense. Their tank formations contain organic bridging equipment plus tracked missile launchers and antiaircraft artillery which moves as fast as the tanks themselves. Additionally, the enemy enjoys coverage within the envelope of fixed surface-to-air missile sites on the west side of the canal. This gives him antiaircraft protection from ground level to sixty thousand feet to a distance of some thirty miles."

Lieutenant General Natanial Abrash, director of operations, interjected. "Schmuel, we need to know about the lack of radar detection. My squadrons report almost no indication of electronic scanning, yet we're losing aircraft and crews to missiles and guns that must be radar-directed. What new equipment does the enemy seem to have?"

"I'm just coming to that. We've known that the Soviets provided SA-6 units to Egypt, but we had little indication they were deployed in such strength. Let me show you." Baharov turned on a slide projector and dimmed the lights in the room. Clicking the hand controller, the intelligence chief brought up the first picture. It showed a low-slung tracked vehicle with surface-to-air missiles on launchers.

"This is the SA-6, what NATO calls the Gainful system. It actually consists of two units; this one with the SAMs"—he clicked the selector—"and this one with the radar unit. We've determined that this so-called Straight Flush radar operates in continuous wave versus pulse mode. Not only that, it is capable of two frequencies. As you know, our radar warning receivers are calibrated to detect pulse radar. They can't pick up continuous wave at this time."

The screen changed to another image, this time a tank chassis fitted with a four-barrel antiaircraft gun.

"The Soviet ZSU-23-4 is similar to the Gainful in that it is mounted on a vehicle capable of operating with the fastest tanks. The weapon can be fired under local control or under its Gun Dish radar. The important thing to know in this case is that the radar is a much higher frequency than we can currently detect—up to twelve thousand megahertz or so. I don't have the actual figure yet, but I believe the Gun Dish frequency may be as high as sixteen thousand megahertz." There was an awkward pause as Baharov cleared his throat. "I expect to have that information for you shortly." He turned off the projector and brought the lights back up.

General Abrash sat back in his padded chair. "Well, we have discussed tactics since this afternoon, but frankly there's no easy cure. Ordinarily we'd send our airplanes in at low level to get under the missiles, but then we're exposed to antiaircraft artillery and small arms. It's what the Americans encountered over Vietnam."

Rolling his sloped shoulders, Baharov said, "I seem to have nothing but bad news for you tonight, but there's more. The Russians have equipped the Arabs with vast numbers of SA-7s. At least in the Egyptian units, there seem to be Grails down to squad level."

Baharov did not need to elaborate. The SA-7 first appeared in the Middle East in 1969. A hand-carried missile five feet long and weighing only forty pounds, it required no elaborate guidance radar. It homed on the hot exhaust of its target and, being completely passive, gave no warning to its intended victim. Grails could hit a jet from as far as four miles away.

Abrash, the director of operations, spoke again. "We'll concentrate on deception measures using chaff and flares until we can counter the electronic problem. Meanwhile, we're going to continue taking heavy losses." The general, who had flown in two wars, bit the end of his pencil. Almost to himself he said, "You know, I had a call from the army chief of staff today. He said his frontline commanders were reluctant to call for air support because they saw so many of our boys shot down."

No one in the room needed to respond. Such a thing had never happened in Israel's turbulent history.

DAY THREE
Suez Canal

The Phantoms came in low and fast from the north, parallel to
the east bank of the canal. The short overwater leg of their outbound
flight had been in two compact four-plane flights, but now, over
Sinai, they adopted combat spread. Modi Tal, the twenty-seven-year-
old captain in the lead F-4E, waggled his wings and the formation
smoothly broke into four two-ship elements.

Another captain leading the second flight had anticipated the
move and smoothly slid abeam of his own second section.

It was typical of the Israeli Air Force. The *Heyl Ha'Avir* lived by
the motto "Experience leads" and mere rank would not fill the
leader's slot. Far too much was at stake. The young captain had
flown more of these missions than anyone in his squadron.

It was Day Three and Israel was fighting on two fronts against
the most competent adversaries she had yet faced.

Captain Solomon Yatanahu, one year younger than Modi Tal,
had flown combat six years before under very different circumstances. The Six-Day War had gone entirely Israel's way from the
opening hour. He had actually regretted the limited opportunity for
combat. But this new war was entirely the opposite. Back-to-back
sorties, friends dead or missing, aircraft destroyed and damaged at a
terrific pace. Even MiGs over his home base—unheard of! And
though the *Heyl Ha'Avir* still was master of its enemies—in one
famous case two F-4s took off to engage a skyful of MiGs and shot
down seven—the flak and SAMs were deadly. Yatanahu had joked
with his radar operator that the desert camouflage paint on their new
Phantom was barely dry in time for this first mission. Seventy-two
hours previously it had borne the green tones of the U.S. Tactical
Air Command at Ramstein, West Germany. But not even U.S.
reinforcement could keep pace with the staggering attrition thus far.

Still, morale remained high. The squadron ready room bore the neatly lettered boast CEILING 80 METERS, a mark of professional pride. In order to destroy Egyptian tanks and avoid the heart of the air defense system, the Israeli pilots regularly flew at or below 250 feet, or 80 meters, altitude. It was hard enough in a high-performance jet making 400 knots or more on a training mission. Doing it in combat, retaining awareness of all that happened within shooting distance, called for skill and experience of exceptional order.

In the lead Phantom, Modi Tal shot a glance at his map. He didn't need it, for he'd flown almost a dozen missions over this area in the past two days. But he was too thorough, too professional, to wholly trust memory or habit. A gloved finger tapped the point on the canal indicating his run-in to the target. He spoke into his oxygen mask. "Estimate six minutes to initial point."

The "hot mike," continually open to his backseater, carried his words with electronic clarity. The response came almost instantly. "Concur." The radar operator, a twenty-two-year-old reservist, was backing up the pilot's navigation.

With a rock of his wings Tal indicated that the formation should split. Yatanahu led his flight to the southwest, pushing his throttles to accelerate ahead of the main formation and arrive from a different quadrant a few seconds before the lead flight, orbiting to intercept any Egyptian fighters.

The target was a ring of mobile antiaircraft batteries protecting a large Egyptian tank unit that threatened Israeli defenses east of the canal. Another formation, composed of six Skyhawks, was bearing down on the same target from the east and south. The F-4s would provide top cover from enemy fighters and attack the defenses while the A-4s went after the tanks. Assuming everyone's timing was perfect, the attack sections would hit from three directions in ninety seconds.

At 400 knots the F-4s were as fast as a .45-caliber pistol bullet at the muzzle. The ground ahead was blurred to a distance of more than 1,500 feet, so the pilots focused and refocused on more distant points. Their 250-foot altitude kept them in "ground clutter," the mixture of radar returns which diminished or ruined the effectiveness of Egyptian Gun Dish tracking units, but conventional flak and hand-held SA-7 missiles still posed a threat.

West of the canal, Solomon Yatanahu saw the sweep hand of his watch tick off the final seconds. He moved his twin throttles through the detent into afterburner and felt the J79-GE17 turbojets each kick in 17,900 pounds of thrust. Pulling the stick into his belly, he led his wingman in a full-power climb toward 15,000 feet, where they would briefly orbit to intercept any Egyptian aircraft attempting to break up the impending strike.

Thirty miles to the northeast, the main Phantom formation entered the target area. A carefully choreographed aerial ballet had just debuted as the mission commander held course and altitude. With precise timing, he swept into the outer fringes of the SAM belt, then popped up to 3,800 feet as he and his wingman released chaff and flares.

On the desert floor, patient Egyptian gunners and missileers watched the curtain rise in the preview of interim Israeli tactics. A similar routine was performed to the south, where the A-4s would appear in several seconds.

Tiny flickers of light reflected the sun as aluminum chaff—lengths of metal cut to match known radar frequencies—erupted by the thousands in the air. White-hot magnesium flares burst into existence, competing with the heat of jet engines and drawing off some of the missiles launched at the brown-and-tan camouflaged fighters. On each side of the target, Phantoms crossed one another's flight paths, adding more "hot spots" in the sky which might lure one or two SAMs from genuine targets.

The Gainful missiles—three to a vehicle—were unable to track fast, low-flying targets under these circumstances, and their threat was negated. But dozens—perhaps scores—of soldiers with shoulder-mounted Grails pointed their launchers skyward, acquired the green light indicating they were tracking a heat source, and fired. The desert blossomed with dust clouds as the SA-7s lifted off, crowding the flak-filled sky with lethal fingers groping for an unwary or unlucky victim.

The Phantom leader, seeing his countermeasures taking effect, noted the first white flashes in his peripheral vision as bombs exploded to the southeast. Good; the Skyhawks arrived on time. He turned back for another pass to assess the damage.

"MIGS FOUR O'CLOCK LEVEL!"

Captain Yatanahu whipped his head over his right shoulder in response to his wingman's call. Almost immediately he saw a camouflaged delta-winged shape bearing down on him. The Phantom pilot estimated its distance as two miles, closing fast. Not much time.

Yatanahu had 550 knots on his airspeed indicator. He pulled the stick into the right rear corner of the cockpit, stood on the right rudder pedal, and loaded almost seven Gs on himself, his radar operator, and his aircraft. With adrenaline surging and full concentration upon his adversary, he was hardly aware of the physiological effects of seven times normal gravity.

The MiG-21 had begun a countermove, curving to its left in an attempt to maintain position on the F-4. Yatanahu's momentum was too great to gain an angle advantage at this speed and distance so he momentarily stopped his turn, maintaining 135 degrees of bank. When he judged the moment was right, he continued his maneuver into an elegant barrel roll above, beyond, and below the MiG's flight path.

Yatanahu heard a garbled transmission from his wingman, who presumably was engaged with a MiG of his own. The captain was aware of his backseater's labored breathing on the hot mike, his favorable position relative to the MiG, and his parameters for weapons employment. He had already discarded the Sparrow option; he was too close for a radar missile and he wasn't convinced the electronic countermeasures the enemy had so unexpectedly developed wouldn't defeat an AIM-7.

Therefore, Yatanahu pulled into three-quarters of a mile of the MiG's tail, slightly offset to the left. His armament switch was selected for HEAT, and he heard the manic chirping in his earphones which told him his Sidewinder missile was tracking the enemy's hot tailpipe. Yatanahu pressed the trigger, and after a pause saw the AIM-9 surge past his left side. It arced toward the MiG and exploded in the engine's plume.

Instantly the Phantom pilot shifted his armament switch to GUN. He had a 20mm cannon in his nose and fully intended to use it. But the MiG-21 pilot chose that fortuitous moment to eject himself from his doomed fighter.

Yatanahu looked around, and his backseater anticipated his concern. "Two is rejoining at three o'clock." Two Phantoms had taken on three MiGs, destroying one and damaging another. Thirty-five seconds had passed. Yatanahu glanced at his watch and set a circuitous course for home. Whatever had happened with the anti-tank mission, he had done his job.

MODI TAL WAS PLEASED. HE HAD TIMED HIS WIDE TURN away from the target to allow much of the dust to settle, and now was screeching toward the southeastern corner of the armored pocket at nearly Mach 1. He wanted another pass to evaluate the results of the raid, which seemed to have been well executed. He counted at least eight vehicles aflame—either T-54 tanks or tracked missile carriers.

Several trip-hammer blows pounded the F-4E, sixteen in all. The Phantom rolled violently to the right, shedding parts as the aerodynamic forces tore at the ragged gouges left by 23mm explosive shells.

There had been no warning from the Gun Dish continuous wave radar. The Egyptian battery commander had shrewdly placed two vehicles beyond the obvious perimeter, camouflaged with sand-colored nets, and had obtained a firing solution on the speeding jet.

In the rear cockpit, the young reservist initiated command ejection without waiting for word from his pilot. At low level there was no time for corrective action, and as the stricken F-4 began its second roll both canopies came off. The rear seat fired, hurling the radar operator out of the Phantom one and three-quarters seconds before the pilot's seat rocketed away. The sequence prevented the front seat ignition from searing the backseat occupant, but it didn't matter. Both fliers were flung into the violent turbulence of supersonic air, and neither survived.

The battery commander saw the American-built fighter plunge to the ground and explode in a fireball of jet fuel. He was glad of his unit's success, but he was enough of a professional to know that one airplane in exchange for nearly a dozen armored vehicles was no bargain. The Israelis were learning fast.

North Arabian Sea

The four Vought F-8Js cruised effortlessly at 20,000 feet, deployed in combat spread. Each was armed with 20mm ammunition and AIM-9 Sidewinder missiles. Though the world's attention was riveted on events nearly 2,000 miles to the north, the aircraft carrier USS *Hancock* took nothing for granted. The four Crusaders on combat air patrol were proof of that. As "Hannah" approached the Gulf of Aden she came within range of several nations that wished no U.S. Navy warship smooth sailing.

One war had just ended—or at least American involvement had ended—and the thirty-year-old carrier was a veteran of that war. She had been on her eighth cruise to the Tonkin Gulf when ordered south at high speed with her escorts and fleet oiler. Now *Hancock*'s crew and Air Wing 21 wondered what role they might play in the new conflict in the Middle East.

Aloft in the lead F-8 was Commander John L. Bennett, skipper of Fighter Squadron 24. With three previous combat tours and a MiG-17 to his credit, Bennett was one of the most experienced fighter pilots in the U.S. Navy. At age thirty-eight he recognized that he was near the acme of his professional life. If fortunate, he might obtain one more flying tour as an air wing commander. After that, he did not want to think about it.

Bennett glanced at his fuel gauge, noting he had ample JP5 remaining. Engine rpm, fuel flow, tailpipe temperature all normal. Bennett's practiced scan took in his aircraft's vital signs in seconds and returned where it belonged—outside the cockpit. But he mused upon the events of the past few days.

Only days before *Hancock*'s task force had reached the strait separating Indonesia from Malaysia, Malaysia's strife-ridden government had declared the Strait of Malacca as its own. Foreign vessels transiting the waterway would have to pay a fee or be subject to attack. Reports of pirate activity only enhanced the tense mood, but Bennett smiled to himself. He was known in the fighter community as "Pirate," his tactical callsign.

The rear admiral leading the task force had passed through the strait at high speed without requesting permission or paying tribute. Instead, he kept at least one four-plane division of fighters airborne with armed Skyhawk attack planes ready to launch. The passage had been uneventful.

Now, orbiting 150 miles from the ship, Bennett considered the prospects of a clash with other regimes. From 20,000 feet he could see the Gulf of Aden adjoining Somalia, Ethiopia, and the People's

Democratic Republic of Yemen. Soviet-built MiGs would come out for a look at the "Yankee air pirates"—there was that word again—and VF-24 was ready for them. It had been five years since Bennett had killed a MiG, but constant practice had kept him ready. Besides, it wouldn't be the first time he had tangled with MiGs from a desert airbase.

Bennett rolled his shoulders and strained forward against his Koch fittings, easing the strain. He recalled the secret projects in the Nevada desert, "Have Drill" and "Have Doughnut." The Israelis had captured all manner of Egyptian equipment when they occupied Sinai during the 1967 war. Aircraft, tanks, missiles, artillery, and communications gear had been scooped up and sent to America for evaluation. Nine MiG fighters—a mixture of Type 17, 19, and 21—had been included, with a large supply of spare parts. U.S. Air Force and Navy pilots flew them almost daily for three years, evaluating every nuance of performance. Bennett had participated in that program, and what he did not know about the enemy aircraft was not worth knowing.

The test facility was spartan: a 15,000-foot runway with a prefab hangar and a couple of fuel trucks. All flying was timed to avoid exposure to Soviet satellites that passed over twice a day, and Bennett surmised the runway was bulldozed with sand when not in use. But the flying was terrific. Phantoms, Crusaders, Skyhawks, and other U.S. aircraft tangled in no-holds-barred hassles with the MiGs, pilots often switching cockpits to better appreciate each type's strengths and weaknesses.

Bennett knew that any pilot in VF-24 would give a year's flight pay to tangle with a MiG of any nationality or origin, for the Checkertails—like the rest of Air Wing 21 and the U.S. Navy—now were warriors without a war. Bennett felt that after Vietnam, protracted conflict was to no advantage. Short wars were the best. Just look at the Israelis.

DAY NINE
Ben Gurion Airport

Tel Aviv's airport had never been so busy. By 14 October almost constant traffic flew in and out, resupplying the Israeli armed forces, whose stocks of weapons, ammunition, and fuel had been sorely depleted. This morning, however, General Baharov, the IAF technical intelligence chief, anxiously awaited the unloading of several crates from the belly of a U.S. Air Force C-141. The crates contained neither missiles nor spare parts, though God knew how badly the *Heyl Ha'Avir* needed both.

The general's aide, Major Ephraim Bachman, was accustomed to the man's eccentricities. After all, geniuses traditionally are accorded some latitude in that direction. But the gardener with the Ph.D. in electrical engineering was not personally supposed to supervise forklift drivers.

"Quickly, quickly. That's it . . . straight back. Good! Now, take it over to the shed." The teenager driving the forklift glanced at the air force major. They exchanged knowing shrugs and smiled at one another as the intel chief continued badgering the line crew. "No, no, not like that! Where did you learn to drive, anyway? Here, let me show you."

At length Bachman diplomatically pried his superior away from the Starlifter's ramp and thereby restored a modicum of order to the harried logistics personnel. Opening one of the crates, the major removed some of the stuffing to expose the contents.

He stepped back, smiling widely. "There it is, Schmuel."

Probably in no other nation on earth did a major address a general by his first name.

The gray-haired officer leaned down, compressing his ample stomach against the green fatigue shirt he wore. He touched the electronic object with almost fatherly affection. "There you are. Just what we need, Ephraim. The ALQ-100. With this on our tactical aircraft we'll finally even the odds against the electronic threat."

The aide agreed. "I just hope there are enough of them."

Schmuel Baharov seemed not to hear him. Preoccupied with the self-protection jammer that could mean survival for Israeli pilots, he rattled off a litany of characteristics that his aide already knew by heart. "Not only does this device cover the X and S bands, but the L band as well. And it even has a built-in chaff dispenser."

With capability of detecting and jamming both missile and gunlaying radars, the ALQ-100 offered multipurpose protection for a fighter-bomber operating against sophisticated electronically guided weapons. The chaff dispenser was an added bonus, either replacing or augmenting dispensers already affixed to Israeli combat aircraft. The U.S. Military Airlift Command was providing as many as could be flown from the East Coast to Israel, but the routes and times were lengthy. Not many Mediterranean nations were willing to allow their airspace or bases to be used for the purpose of assisting the Jewish state.

Abruptly the general straightened up. "Yes, we'll get enough. And I'll tell you why. We lost eighty aircraft in the first seven days of this war. We may end up with more jammers than airplanes."

Gulf of Aden

HANCOCK WAS READY FOR A FIGHT, BUT IT HAD LITTLE to do with the ten-day-old Arab-Israeli war. Ordered to enter the Red Sea and steam northward to the near end of the Suez Canal, the U.S. task force anticipated problems with Palestinian forces on Bab el Mandeb, the former British possession at the mouth of the Red Sea. The strait measured only a few miles across, and artillery on the small island could engage any ship transiting the strait.

The United States informed Yemen that *Hancock*'s task force would exercise its right of passage through international waters. Consequently, when the lead destroyer entered the waterway between Yemen and Djibouti, twenty bomb-laden Skyhawks and eight hungry Crusaders were overhead. The message was not lost on local hotheads; the passage was uneventful.

The airborne planes were recovered before *Hancock* herself entered the Red Sea, for flight operations would be difficult in the confined waters of that body. Instead, an all-pilots meeting was called in the wardroom, where the task force commander's staff was to present a contingency plan drafted in response to orders from Washington. Some eighty aviators squeezed into the wardroom, fidgeting and jockeying for space. Clanlike, they sat by squadrons behind their respective skippers.

Bennett had a seat up front with a good view of the rostrum and regional map.

Stepping to the rostrum, a full commander shuffled his papers and looked around. Robert Tatum was a nonaviator—a "blackshoe" in fliers' parlance—but he was trusted by the admiral to handle an apparently unpleasant task. He let out a long breath and began.

"Gentlemen, the purpose of this briefing is to acquaint you with a contingency plan to deliver this air wing's aircraft to Israel."

Bennett leaned forward in his chair. He was conscious of almost complete silence behind him, contrary to the exclamations he would have expected.

"All forty-two A-4s and twenty-four F-8s are to be launched here," Tatum said, tapping the map, "about one thousand miles south of Tel Aviv. The route has been planned to remain in international airspace most of the way. But at the northern leg it will be necessary to overfly northwestern Saudi Arabia and part of Jordan." A murmur ran through the room, at once questioning and angry.

Tatum explained that the sixty-six carrier planes would land at designated airfields in Israel. Then, having taken a civilian suit and overnight kit, the naval aviators would don their "civvies" and board an airliner for New York.

Bennett glanced across the aisle at his opposite number in VF-211. They exchanged knowing looks. Contradictory thoughts rushed through their minds. *How do I down a couple of birds to keep a combat air patrol for the ship? Or How do I make sure I get in on this in case some MiGs come up to play?*

The pilots sat in awed silence for a moment. This was a veteran air wing, honed to a fine edge by seven years of combat over Southeast Asia. These men were warriors. They understood war, but they did not understand the rationale behind the plan. An aircraft carrier without aircraft was an overpriced transport vessel. Air Wing 21 had not sailed halfway around the planet merely to deliver its precious planes to another nation. Yet the aviators were to be deprived of their weapons. In a word, emasculated. The resentment was tangible.

But some, like Bennett, sensed an implied message. *Hancock*'s proposed reinforcement would amount to about 20 percent of the prewar Israeli Air Force, and it was axiomatic that no air arm could sustain a 10 percent loss rate for long. Bennett thought back to what had seemed the sweetheart deal with the MiGs in Nevada. Now maybe it made sense. Perhaps payment had been deferred.

After Tatum finished his briefing the squadron commanders got together. One Skyhawk CO said, "I can understand us giving the Israelis A-4s. They've flown them for years. But F-8s? Come on!"

The fighter skippers agreed. The *Heyl Ha'Avir* never had owned Crusaders. None of the Israeli pilots had flown the Voughts and there was no maintenance or logistic support in place to keep them operational.

Bennett summed up the situation in a sentence. "If they need F-8s that bad, they're really on the ropes."

DAY TEN
Sinai

At dawn on 15 October, jets bearing the blue Star of David lifted off their runways. With the new electronic countermeasures (ECM) gear, the Mirages, Phantoms, and Skyhawks had gained a large measure of protection from Arab tracking and fire-control radars, and the results showed. Daily aircraft losses had dropped to two or three—well within limits. But not even massive American replenishment could offset the staggering losses of the first week.

Lieutenant David Ran was as well aware of the shortage as anyone. He had seen squadron mates die and he knew how the ground crews slaved to keep remaining aircraft in commission. He was tired—tired in his bones—but he surprised himself with an unsuspected reservoir of stamina. A brief meeting with his diplomat brother Avrim told the story.

"Papa, you would hardly know David anymore," Avrim had told their father. "He's changed so much since I last saw him. There's still that shyness about him but he's also, well, so *confident*. I think he's learned a lot about himself these recent days. You know he's now a flight leader? Amazing." Avrim paused, uncertain whether he should tell his father what else had appeared in David's personality. Well, a parent is entitled to know. "Papa, there's something more. The war. I think he *likes* it."

David had been promoted to section leader, and while he did not like the war he found that he savored combat. It was a distinction that only warriors could understand.

Concentrating on the mission at hand, he frankly relished the prospects. Egyptian armored columns thrusting for Mitla Pass had outrun the coverage of their fixed SA-2 and SA-3 missile batteries. Now the narrow bridgehead afforded Israeli pilots a densely packed hunting ground.

Flying number three in the four-plane flight, Ran kept impeccable formation on his leader. The A-4s approached the target area at
300 knots and Ran checked his armament switches, then adjusted
the rheostat of his gunsight. He had developed a passion for
tankbusting and had told a former flight school classmate, "It's the
most fun you can have in an airplane."

More fun was at hand. The Skyhawks broke up to approach the
enemy armored column, two each from different directions. Anti-
tank helicopters hovered nearby, awaiting the cover of the jet attack
to make their own move against the Soviet-built T-54s and T-62s.
With other aircraft dedicated to chaff and flare dispensing, and still
more conducting standoff jamming of the higher radar frequencies,
the mission was a complex endeavor. But recent experience showed
that it worked most of the time.

From 8,000 feet Ran led his wingman down on the low-slung
silhouettes of Egyptian tanks. As usual, the sky erupted with flak
bursts, missile plumes, chaff, and flares. Ran went for a circle of
T-62s, jinking only slightly during his run. He felt bulletproof.

Tanks are built to engage their own kind, and therefore are most
heavily armored on the front and sides. They are most vulnerable
from above and behind, and Ran took advantage of that fact. He
arced around for a favorable angle on several of the forty-ton
monsters and initiated a fifteen-degree dive. Waiting until his slant
range was less than 2,000 feet, he placed the pipper of his gunsight
reticle on the hull of the nearest T-62 and barely stroked the trigger.

Eight 30mm shells left the muzzles of his twin DEFA cannon,
and six hit the target. They penetrated the 1¼-inch armor covering the
top of the Egyptian tank and destroyed it.

Ran instantly jockeyed stick and rudder to line up another and
fired a similarly economical burst. Flames and smoke erupted from
its engine compartment but Ran hardly noticed. He had learned what
every snapshooter knows: Once you have engaged a target, ignore it.
Just shift targets and shoot again—there is no time for sightseeing.

The two A-4s bottomed out of their runs and hugged the deck, scooting for safety behind every sand dune and depression. Ran had a brief image of helicopters launching missiles into the massed enemy armor. It looked like a good job.

Ran was eager for another pass; he felt sure of one kill and probably another. He had the best record in the squadron for rounds fired to tanks killed, as the *Heyl Ha'Avir* kept meticulous records on combat efficiency. David's armorers proudly boasted that their pilot was destroying one enemy tank with fewer than ten rounds of ammunition. His gun camera films were being shown as examples of how to do the job, and he was only getting better.

The flight leader pulled up at a safe distance and assessed the situation. He judged that the Egyptians were still preoccupied with results of the first attack and decided to risk another. A terse radio command told Ran what to do. The A-4s varied their roll-in headings from the previous pass and once more dropped into the seething caldron of missiles and flak.

A lucrative target offered itself in the form of a Gun Dish antiaircraft unit. Ran destroyed it in one pass while his wingman damaged another T-62. Both A-4s were down to sandblower altitude again when Ran felt a moderate *thump*. He thought it came from the rear of his aircraft. He scanned his instruments. Fuel state, hydraulic pressure, engine RPM and tailpipe temperature all registered normal.

Climbing back to altitude, Ran asked his wingman to look him over. The brown-and-tan Skyhawk dropped back and smoothly slid under Ran's tail, reappearing on the opposite side.

"You've got some battle damage to your stabilizer, but it looks all right. Any instrument fluctuation?"

"Negative." David thought he'd probably taken a near miss from a hand-held SA-7, but in flight there was no point speculating. After landing, the two fliers examined the torn aluminum of the Skyhawk's tail. Ran's wingman was in a chipper mood.

"You see what happens when you develop a reputation as a sharpshooter? People start shooting back."

David Ran turned on his heel and paced off to debrief.

THE 1973 WAR ENTERED ITS THIRD AND FINAL PHASE on Day Eleven. Two-thirds of the Egyptian and Syrian missile batteries were knocked out, freeing more Israeli aircraft for direct support of ground forces. Additionally, Iraqi and Jordanian forces were contained along the Golan Heights so the emphasis of Israeli operations shifted westward.

Suppression of Arab air defenses had badly affected IAF efforts. Though hundreds of sorties were flown daily, the early portion of the war required the large majority to be devoted to auxiliary tasks: flare and chaff drops, ECM and actual attacks on flak and SAM batteries. Now that had changed.

Captain Solomon Yatanahu explained the new situation in a briefing to his flight crews.

"Our tank forces are launching Operation Gazelle, designed to cut off the Egyptians in this area." He tapped a large-scale map with his pointer. "Bridging and bulldozer units are providing crossings over the Suez Canal in order to put our armor in the enemy's rear." Yatanahu smiled broadly. His fliers knew him as a determinedly cheerful leader, despite fatigue and losses.

"Boys, this is an historic moment. It's only the second time in Jewish history that we've crossed the Red Sea without getting our feet wet."

The aircrews shared the mirth. Yatanahu thought it was good to hear laughter again. After what they've been through, he thought, if they can laugh they can win.

DAY EIGHTEEN
USS *Hancock*

Commander John Bennett attended an intelligence briefing with the other squadron COs. The contingency delivery of F-8s and A-4s to Israel had been canceled because the situation was stabilized but the air wing "spy" kept the aviators up to date as a matter of course.

"Since the war started eighteen days ago, things have changed drastically," the intelligence officer began. "It's a weird setup, with Egyptian units on the east bank of the canal and Israeli forces on the west side. This armored column"—he pointed to Suez Town on his map—"has cut off most of the Egyptian Third Army. Everybody seems to be holding in place with the impending cease-fire."

Bennett leaned forward, chin in his hands. "When's the shooting supposed to stop?"

"Sometime tomorrow, evidently. I don't have full info on that, but my guess is that Washington and Moscow have reined in their surrogates and finally made them behave. That's probably what's behind this cease-fire in place, as confirmed by national reconnaissance assets."

Bennett smiled to himself. He liked to read for pleasure, and as a history lover he had acquired a regard for the English language as it was intended to be used. The subspecies called Pentagonese left him cold, even after sixteen years in the Navy. He knew perfectly well that "national reconnaissance assets" meant satellite photography, which, combined with radio monitoring from ships in the Mediterranean, provided a good picture of developing events.

The intel officer continued. "What this means is pretty obvious. The Israelis pulled things out of the fire by a damn narrow margin. We estimate they lost 50 percent of their frontline tactical aircraft in this war. Remember, it's lasted three times longer than the '67 war, with attendant heavier losses."

Bennett recalled the paper he had written at the Naval War College. Airpower was the key to the Middle East, and Israel could not afford a prolonged war. This current conflict, evidently headed for conclusion, was proof positive if further evidence were necessary. He reached in his shirt pocket, produced a notepad, and scribbled a few lines. John Bennett had certain opinions on the nature of airpower—attitudes not wholly in keeping with American policies. He was not sure what to do with his concepts, but he felt someday they might be put to use.

DAY NINETEEN
Sinai

The shooting on the Egyptian Front ended 24 October. However, clearing up the human and technological debris took longer than it had taken to produce the carnage. A few well-connected military attachés from nonbelligerent countries were able to examine the residue of combat, noting the effects of modern weapons for future reference.

Among those inspecting the battlefield around Suez was a Saudi Arabian Air Force officer, Major Mohammad abd Maila. He saw the charred, gutted hulks of trucks, tanks, and personnel carriers. He tasted as much as smelled the residue of burned rubber, diesel, and gasoline—and roasted flesh. It was not difficult for him to imagine the Israeli aircraft descending from the sky to destroy what had once been a powerful armored column. The screech of jet engines, the staccato pounding of antiaircraft guns, the high-pitched ring of armor-piercing rounds penetrating tempered steel.

Maila turned away from the wretched sight. He had excellent contacts in Riyadh, including well-placed members of the royal family. Perhaps he could spare his own countrymen some of what he had seen. Walking back to his jeep, the phrase echoed in his consciousness, *This must never happen again.*

PART ★ I

To steer an aircraft is nothing.
To fly it is difficult.

—French fighter tactics manual,
World War I

1

ANGER WAS EVIDENT IN HIS LONG STRIDE AND THE force of each heel on the sidewalk. But there was something else— embarrassment. He had not seen his friend in a long time, and to learn how a once-valued comrade had turned out was cause for embarrassment and anger. Pausing at the intersection, he unbuttoned his blazer and stepped off the curb. Both hands were thrust into his pockets, and the angry stride slowed to a more casual gait.

Damn, they were right, he thought. *All of them. Old John Bennett just can't stop tilting at windmills. You're not in the Navy anymore, Bennett. It's no longer your problem. Why can't you let it go? Dave only had a few hours, and you led him into another*

*argument and started the whole thing over again. Poor bastard only
wanted to see some old friends and have a drink, and you start
lecturing again on what's wrong with naval aviation.*

A brief smile creased Bennett's tan face. *God,* he thought to
himself, *it's true. They do breathe helium in Washington.*

It was an old joke in the operational forces that when a good
guy—somebody who understood what was important—got orders to
D.C., his personality changed. Damn, in a few months it was like
they gave him a prefrontal lobotomy. When you saw him next he
was mouthing inane ideas in Pentagonese.

These converts always seemed full of new buzzwords which, like
a bumper sticker, tried to pass for philosophy. John Bennett and
Dave Edmonds had been fighter pilots for twenty years; served
together in two squadrons. Both men enjoyed reputations as outstanding aviators; they had written the Navy's first tactical manual
for supersonic fighters. When pilots talked about the "super sticks,"
Bennett and Edmonds always were mentioned—like Lewis and
Clark or ham and eggs.

Today the questions always were about aircraft design, whether
it should be complex and capable of several missions or a single-
purpose, specialized plane. Because the political supporters of
complexity had prevailed, the results were extremely expensive
fighter planes. But Bennett and Edmonds had grown up in the least
expensive and oldest fighter in the Navy inventory, and the Vietnam
War had proven the validity of their arguments for simplicity. Their
Vought F-8s had outperformed every other fighter in the U.S. stable
in that long war, winning the highest kill-loss ratio.

But that was the shooting war, Bennett reminded himself. He
thought of his farewell speech to his squadron when he retired. "The
United States Navy, gentlemen, is an eighteenth-century institution
reluctantly being dragged into the nineteenth century." That had
caught the press's attention. So, with one foot in the grave, he
jumped in with both feet. He had told his junior officers that their

value as aviators would only become apparent to the U.S. government during the next war.

The reporters had lined up to pursue the retiring aviator's thoughts on the subject. They sensed a controversial quote, or at least a colorful one. "Tell us, Commander Bennett, does that mean you think there will be another war?"

The junior officers had braced themselves, knowing the skipper's reply. "Well, if we don't think there'll be another war, all of us are wasting a hell of a lot of the taxpayers' money." The base's public affairs officer had his hands full explaining that one!

It was a February evening in La Jolla, but the air was balmy with a gentle breeze off the Pacific. Bennett loved this small enclave carved into the California coast. He had raised a son and lost his wife here. The memory pained him again. The drunk driver had served barely a year in prison.

Inside his coat pocket, Bennett felt the engraved invitation to Dave's change of command ceremony. His friend would become captain of the carrier *Saratoga* on the east coast in a few weeks. Dave had specifically taken time to get together, despite a hectic visit to San Diego. Damn it, he was a good man. Old Dave had chased that MiG-19 right over Hainan into Chinese airspace and ran the bastard out of fuel. No manager or chairbound warrior would have done that, risking his career in the process. But the nagging doubt returned—what had Dave done to ingratiate himself to the power brokers in Washington? Maybe he had changed.

Or maybe, Bennett mused, *I've stayed stagnant while everybody else has progressed.*

Bennett loved the landscaped entrance to his apartment. It was a jungle of bent pines and well-tended flowers. He took in the simple beauty of the place, paying no notice to the figure closing on him from behind. A cultured Middle Eastern voice broke the silence. "I beg your pardon, Commander Bennett?"

John turned to face a man in gray trousers and expensive light-blue worsted jacket. The stranger carried himself with an air of dignity; of one accustomed to authority. His swarthy complexion was punctuated by a well-trimmed goatee. Bennett thought the Rolex on his left wrist must have cost $5,000. The gray-and-red tie was elegantly knotted and snugged to the perfectly starched collar of his dress shirt. This man had what soldiers called command presence.

The gentleman extended his hand and Bennett appreciated the firm grasp. This was a very self-composed individual, and Bennett's four-inch height advantage seemed to dwindle.

"My name is Safad Fatah. I am a Saudi Arabian diplomat. Could I please speak with you a few minutes?" The accent carried a trace of British influence—probably the result of an expensive education in England.

"What do you want to talk about?"

"Is it perhaps possible we could talk in your apartment?"

Bennett started to hedge but the Arab gentleman interrupted. "Please, Commander, it will only take a moment. I think you might find it most interesting."

Bennett unlocked his door, stepped back, and swept his hand inward, inviting the guest to enter. Fatah took in the apartment in a single glance.

"Please sit down. By the way, how did you know my name?"

Fatah rested his hands on his plump belly. "I have been in your country for the past five years. I am presently with the Saudi Embassy in Washington, and we obtained your address from some friends in that area."

Bennett's curiosity intensified.

"Can I get you something cool to drink? A beer perhaps?" Immediately Bennett realized his error. *Muslims don't drink alcohol,* he thought.

"No thank you, sir." If Fatah took offense he covered it admirably. "If you have a Pepsi that would be nice."

Bennett rummaged through his cluttered refrigerator. One of the women he occasionally dated was fond of Pepsi, and there were two cans left.

As he poured the soda into a glass, Bennett searched his memory. Whom did he know in D.C. who traveled in diplomatic circles? Feeling the warrior's suspicion of diplomats, Bennett kept his distance. He acknowledged the supremacy of civilian leadership over the armed forces, but he drew the line at meddling.

Bennett sat down across from Fatah and both men sized up one another. Bennett had removed his own jacket but the Arab sat impeccably clad with his coat still buttoned.

Barely sipping his drink, the Saudi leaned forward and his dark eyes fixed on Bennett's. "Commander, my government would like to discuss with you the possibility of a venture in my nation which would make use of your expertise. If it's agreeable to you, we would be pleased to have you as our guest in Arabia. If your schedule permits, we can set the meeting in Riyadh six days hence. I must leave this evening but I shall meet you upon arrival. We will, of course, pay all your expenses and we think you might enjoy a few days as our guest."

Bennett masked the confusion he felt. His face belied any uncertainty but his mind raced. "And what would you want me—"

Again Fatah smoothly interrupted. "Please, Commander, I cannot say more than I have. Everything would be made clear to you, but for the present would you please consider that I am not at liberty to divulge more information? My sovereign will explain everything to you in due course."

The Saudi's initial contact with Bennett was the result of a two-year effort Riyadh had invested in selecting the retired aviator. There was nothing about John Bennett the Saudis did not know; he even looked the part, as if cast for a motion picture. There were the clear gray eyes which could display disarming charm or icy rage. Women especially would see and be moved by those eyes, and

Arabs knew women as perhaps no other men on earth. The Prophet had given that knowledge to his people. Of that, Fatah was certain.

Bennett's cheeks were tanned and there were small lines at the corners of both eyes—testament to 5,000 hours aloft, many of them squinting into the sun in search of adversaries. The carefully groomed hair had a touch of gray now, but the overall impression was one of energy and vigor.

Following orders from his government, Fatah had selected the fifty-four-year-old retired naval officer after extensive screening.

Bennett's combat record, his writings on aerial combat, his reputation among his contemporaries and—most important—among his former students, were well known to Fatah. He knew of the man's marriage, the death of his wife, the fact that Bennett's son was enrolled at Arizona State University.

There had been difficulty obtaining a copy of the thesis Bennett had written at the Naval War College. It had been classified as secret, but the Saudis had obtained Bennett's document, plus several written by other prospective agents. Bennett's opus, *Airpower—Key to the Middle East*, had confirmed he was the man the Saudis wanted.

John Bennett at first said nothing as he considered the strange proposal.

The silence was broken when Bennett rose and stood with his hands behind his back. "Mr. Fatah, can you tell me if your government wishes to utilize my services in any way that could be detrimental to my country, or jeopardize my position as a U.S. citizen and a retired military officer?"

Fatah rose and looked Bennett square in the face. "Sir, I can assure you that is not the case."

There was a pause and Bennett strode to the window, staring at the blue Pacific. He said, "Mr. Fatah, I would be honored to be a guest of your king. I have made deployments to the Mediterranean and I would enjoy seeing the Middle East again. How long should I plan on staying?"

"Oh, I believe three days would be ample time for us to explain our proposal to you. I will have a car pick you up here at noon Thursday. Incidentally, Commander, is your passport current?" Fatah already knew the answer.

"Yes it is. What will the weather be like this time of year?"

"It is suitable for a lightweight suit and sports clothes." Fatah extended his hand and said, "Then I shall see you in Riyadh next week, Commander."

After the man left, Bennett opened a Coors and sat with his feet propped on the coffee table. His curiosity was aroused, and he felt sympathy for the cultured Saudi. The kingdom's days were numbered, he thought. The whole region was a caldron now, on a scale not seen in the past millenium. Iran's interminable war of attrition with Iraq finally had reached an uneasy settlement. Extensive blood-letting without significant gain by either side, severe economic disruption in the Persian Gulf with repeated attacks on third-party ships and ports—all these factors had forced a tenuous cease-fire. But the late Ayatollah and his successors had gained a victory of sorts. Despite the bitter religious discord between both nations, the cold-eyed Muslim priests in Tehran had reached an understanding with the Arab Socialist Baath party in Baghdad. Islam was slowly, reluctantly, uniting.

The year before, Lebanon's convulsions ended when the Syrian leadership was replaced by the spreading church-state doctrine of the mullahs. Press reports were ominous, for after the moderate Egyptian president and four ministers died in a mysterious plane crash, another bloody civil war was barely averted. The Libyans gleefully played a central role in fomenting turmoil in Cairo, and were suspected of sabotaging the presidential aircraft. It had taken decades, but the entire Islamic world seemed to be rallying under the green flag with star and crescent.

Nobody was naive enough to believe the Arab states would sublimate their individual differences for long; religious antagonism alone between Sunni and Shiite would guarantee lasting discord. But for the moment, the pressure was on the moderate Muslim nations.

John Bennett was aware of these facts. But he needed more information, a broader perspective. He set down his beer, grabbed the keys to his Mercedes, and headed for the library. In his methodical way he spent the evening building a background file, then he checked out a copy of the Koran.

The more he studied recent Middle East history, the more Bennett understood the rarity and importance of Saudi Arabia's relatively stable government. No other Arab nation of significant size had possessed a lasting hierarchy since World War II. There had been important efforts at pan-Arabism, most notably the short-lived Egyptian-Syrian alliance under Gamal Abdel Nasser. But the United Arab Republic, founded in 1958, fell apart within three years when the Syrian army broke with Cairo in resentment over Egyptian influence in Damascus.

Bennett read about the greater strife that followed. Anwar Sadat, perhaps the only genuine statesman in the region, was assassinated by radical army elements resentful of his accord with Israel. Iraq: plagued by coups and internal rebellion even before the war with Iran. Syria: successive governments toppled, then irretrievably mired in Lebanon. Jordan: perennial difficulty with the Palestinian population, open conflict with the PLO, and the festering matter of Israeli occupation of the West Bank. The list seemed endless.

But in Islam's holy book Bennett saw glimpses of what hardly could be missed by feuding Muslims themselves. The prophet Muhammad laid out a philosophy of life with strong appeal. Generosity and hospitality were extolled, as were attention to family and devotion to God. The Koran idealized strong, quiet men of action and commitment. If those qualities could be harnessed and directed under a unified leadership, the world would resound with their deeds.

Arabia

Barely twelve hours after takeoff from San Diego, the Saudi Air 747 was lined up with the runway lights at Al-'Aqabah, and the Boeing's tires scarred the runway with black rubber upon landing. Bennett was met by an elegantly robed Safad Fatah with a chauffeured limousine and driven to the palace. There the former naval officer was hospitably but quickly shown his elegant quarters and left to sleep off his jet lag.

Late the next morning Bennett awoke refreshed if not wholly recovered, still in awe of his surroundings. The room was more than sumptuous; it bordered on the decadent, he thought. He considered himself sophisticated and well traveled, but never had he stayed in such a room. Few Muslims would choose such surroundings; the opulence therefore must reflect their view of what infidels desire. *The shower and faucet handles must be solid gold. I don't know what these guys want,* he mused, *but they have the money to buy whatever it is.*

HOURS BEFORE BENNETT STIRRED THAT MORNING, KING Rahman had met with his principal military and civilian advisers. The meeting was solemn. The king, seated on an elaborately ornamented throne elevated above the floor, was noticeably ashen-faced. His ministers sat in a semicircle before him, and all took note of the monarch's pallor but none spoke of it. They did not need to. For as the 747 carrying the party from San Diego had passed the entrance to the Mediterranean at Gibraltar, a brief, violent assault had once more rent the Middle East.

The Israeli army, in a professionally executed lightning attack, had entered Jordan the night before. The invasion was justified by an announcement insisting the move was aimed at hostile guerrilla forces operating within that nation's borders. Israeli troops had occupied Amman in a matter of hours, supported by overwhelming air and artillery forces that smothered the defenses.

In Tel Aviv the prime minister announced that King Hussein was safe, en route to Cyprus with his family and senior advisers. The immediate fate of occupied Jordan remained uncertain, but it was unlikely the Israelis would withdraw anytime soon.

While few analysts agreed on a likely conclusion, most were quick to point out a long succession of events leading to the Israeli action. For several years Israeli public opinion had railed against the political leadership for its lack of action to increasingly violent resistance to Israeli domination of Gaza and the West Bank. Following the well-publicized riots of the late 1980s, Palestinians had gained wider global support, plus military aid from government and private organizations within Lebanon and Jordan. It was a descending spiral of violence: repression brought resistance and revenge bred itself in kind. Eventually the Palestinian *intefadeh,* or uprising, expanded beyond stone-throwing. It grew into selective terrorist raids, evolving as more arms and men became available. All too soon larger operations were conducted with supporting arms—often rockets and artillery from Syria and Iran.

The political chaos in Lebanon, coupled with Jordan's tenuous position between its indigenous Palestinian population and a need to show support for pan-Arabism, bred the cycle of violence. Bennett concluded that Jordan may have ceased to exist as a nation-state in much the way that Lebanon had degenerated.

With each Palestinian raid, with each Israeli death, the radical element of Israeli politicians gained increasing support from a disenchanted electorate. Consequently, the Likud party—spawned by the earlier hard-line Herut and Liberal parties—found itself ironically in danger of being portrayed as too moderate or even as ineffectual. Therefore, Likud could not afford to alienate the ultraorthodox segments like the Kach party, whose influence now exceeded its small numbers.

Eventually the fundamentalist, most nationalist Israeli politicians began insisting that Jordan was not a legitimate country, but a creation of the British. This viewpoint gained a 40 percent plurality among the electorate, and political pressure on the government became intense. Some observers predicted that Israel would propose Jordan as the long-awaited Palestinian homeland, thus skirting the sensitive issue of ceding Israeli-occupied land for that purpose. Bennett knew—in fact, had predicted—that some settlement of the Palestinian issue would be the only means of achieving a balance in the region, especially after the turmoil of the late 1980s. He was enough of a realist to know that peace in the Middle East was a pipe dream. But now it may be too late; the time for concessions to the Palestinians may have passed into history. Now they rode the wave of Islamic fundamentalism which seemed bound to sweep all before it.

Safad Fatah had hinted as much in his San Diego meeting with Bennett. The moderate Arab states, most notably the Saudis, stood to lose everything. All they could hope for was to hold what they already had.

The king had already met with delegations from Iran. Khomeini's successors were no less determined than the departed ayatollayh, but they were more pragmatic and had reestablished relations with Riyadh. The long, bitter war with Iraq had shown the folly of pitting Muslim against Muslim and flesh against steel. Now they called for a unified religious war—a *jihad*—which would once and for all destroy the Jewish state. The superpowers could do little more than observe the growing storm from the sidelines.

The Saudi monarch now sat on a tenuous throne, knowing that only the power of his oil and money could save him—if coupled with a precisely executed diplomatic scheme by men the quality of Safad Fatah. The Iranians were the key—maintain an accord with them, and the others likely would follow suit. But the king knew that the same men he had hosted over thick coffee and paper-thin wafers were capable of dispatching a team of suicidal assassins the next time.

Now, addressing his own ministers, the ruler of Saudi Arabia outlined the situation. Though his nation had not been directly involved in the many wars against Israel since 1948, the pattern of combat was well known in Riyadh. Every man in the room knew that no Arab army had seriously threatened the existence of the Jewish state since the Israeli Air Force had grown to early maturity in the mid-1950s. In the usually clear weather of the Middle East, and upon its barren deserts, no army could move on the few roads and hide from Israeli aircraft. Those roads had time and again been lined with the gutted, charred, rusting remains of trucks and armored vehicles.

John Bennett knew the facts as well as any Arab leader. It was the opening theme in his War College thesis which had brought him to Fatah's attention. Fatah had committed two paragraphs to memory:

The Middle East arena, from Suez on the canal to Tarabulus in northern Lebanon, is barely 400 miles. A jet aircraft covers this distance in less than one hour at cruising speed. At Mach 1 the time is barely thirty minutes. Thus, from Tel Aviv the radius of action for a supersonic aircraft puts it within combat in just ten to fifteen minutes.

Operating in clear weather, in terrain devoid of cities, forests, and even natural depressions in many places, a defending air force sits within easy reach of nearly all likely targets. Antiaircraft artillery and surface-to-air missiles may force the aircraft to pay a price for success, but success thus far has been denied the Arabs. Only airpower can defeat airpower, and at present the only thoroughly professional, world-class air force in the region belongs to Israel.

Fatah had underlined the crucial last sentence and quoted it when suggesting to his superiors that Commander Bennett was the man for the job.

JOHN BENNETT ANSWERED THE KNOCK AND OPENED THE double doors of his suite. There was Fatah, impeccably draped in a *mishlah* and the traditional *ghotra* headdress. *"As-salaamu alaykum,"* he said. "Peace be upon you." Bennett replied in barely recognizable Arabic. *"Wa alaykumu as-salaam.* And upon you be peace, Mr. Fatah."

"Well done, Commander Bennett," Fatah lied. "I am impressed. Come, we will go straightaway and I shall describe the protocol while we walk."

As Fatah escorted Bennett across the courtyard, Bennett noticed an uneasiness he had seldom known. A deep-seated feeling that this day could be the most important of his life was submerged beneath a seemingly cool exterior as Fatah briefed him.

"Commander, my king has instructed me to tell you that he wishes you to be completely comfortable and there will be none of the usual pomp. He wishes you to be informal, as he will be with you."

On entering the throne room they walked toward the king, who was flanked by his aides. Bennett was surprised to see the monarch dressed almost plainly in traditional garb, with simple accoutrements that belied his status. He was a man of medium height in his late fifties, with lively eyes and a winning smile. As Bennett approached, King Rahman rose from the throne and stepped forward, hand extended. The grip was firm, contrary to Arabic custom, and the king placed his left hand on Bennett's shoulder. *This guy is in the leadership business, all right,* the aviator thought. *Even looks the part: hair graying at the temples like people used to prefer in doctors, presidents, and airline captains.* But Bennett also noted the deep wrinkles above the brow.

Rahman guided Bennett to a semicircle of Western-style chairs around a gold-leaf antique table. A plain silver tray held seven cups and saucers. Seeming to materialize from thin air, two servants appeared and filled the cups with *gaoa*, a strong green coffee.

The king briefly introduced the other four men in attendance, as Bennett already knew of Safad Fatah's role as ambassador at large and family confidant. The American shook hands—far less firmly than had the king—with Generals Mustafa Halabi and Mohammad abd Maila, finance minister Tewfig al Aziz, and Dr. Fuad Hamoud, whom Bennett took to be another diplomat of some sort. The air force officers, crisp in their uniforms, showed the British influence and Bennett easily related to them. Aziz, short and balding, had a miserly look about him which Bennett thought ill suited the chief financier of Arabia. Hamoud was a cipher, a bearded man who said little but listened closely.

Following preliminary pleasantries about his comfort, the beauty of Bennett's California, and the world in general, Rahman motioned to the waiters. They replaced the *gaoa* with a highly sweetened tea, then disappeared. The king of Saudi Arabia set down his cup.

Game time, John, and here comes the serve.

The king leveled his gaze at the American and spoke in a precise Etonian accent. "Commander Bennett, I know you must be curious about our invitation to have you leave your beautiful San Diego and travel these thousands of miles to my kingdom. I have need of the services of a man of your capabilities and experience. Before I answer any questions, I would like to take a moment to tell you how we came to choose you. Please do not be offended if I tell you that we expended nearly two years and a great deal of money and influence to find a man such as yourself. In fact, I can say that we settled on four candidates for the mission I propose—two U.S. Air Force officers, a Royal Air Force man, and yourself. You became our first choice.

"We are completely aware of your exemplary service to your government. Your combat record, we know, made you among the most decorated airmen who flew during that terrible ordeal in Vietnam. We know of your expertise as a tactician, of your scholarly writings on the subject. We know of your reputation as a warrior. And we know of the loss of your wife, for which I extend my sincere condolences."

Bennett said nothing.

The king continued. "Your son is nearly grown and soon may marry." This caught Bennett by surprise. With a mischievous smile the monarch added, "In fact, dear sir, I understand you might soon be a grandfather." Bennett could not suppress an admiring smile. These people were thorough, and he appreciated that quality.

But inside, Bennett reeled. His first concern was that Paul's carelessness would offend Muslim sensibilities. Paul had told of two Saudis in his dorm at ASU. One of their female cousins had become pregnant out of wedlock, thereby making her guilty of fornication under Muslim law. According to Paul, the girl's parents had turned their home inside out until they found a picture of a young man. The girl would neither confirm nor deny that he was responsible. But the two Saudis said that less than two weeks later the boy in the picture was found on a Riyadh side street with an ornamental dagger in his back.

Bennett knew the story was plausible—the royal house had once shot a princess who married without permission, then beheaded her husband.

The king returned to the matter at hand. "Commander, the situation in this region has forced all the Arab nations to build a competent military to protect their individual borders. Simply put, we need a man to raise, train, and lead an air force for these defensive purposes. Can you tell me, sir, if you had unlimited resources of money and manpower, could you build a first-rate air force which could defend itself against an adversary skilled in the use of airpower?"

A chill shot through John Bennett. He suspected he might be setting himself up for loss of pension, passport, even U.S. citizenship. This was far beyond the consulting job he had envisioned. He would be an American national in charge of a foreign military force—in short, a mercenary. *Jeez, Bennett, you don't even subscribe to* Soldier of Fortune, he thought.

The junior Saudi general, Mohammad abd Maila, leaned forward. "Commander, I trained in the United States for part of my career. I am aware of the capabilities and limitations of various American aircraft—I fly the F-5 quite often still. If you agree to our assignment, we would guarantee you a free hand in the selection of pilots and procurement of aircraft. There are many questions we would have regarding this training and the best aircraft for our needs, but at present I believe we should stop and allow you to consider His Majesty's offer."

The king drew a gold cigarette case from his breast pocket and tapped the end of a Benson & Hedges against the case. Lighting the cigarette, he inhaled, blew a perfect smoke ring, and returned his gaze to the American.

"The general is correct." The king omitted the fact that Maila was a second cousin and lifelong friend. Some fifteen years before, then–Major Maila had been deputy air attaché to Cairo. "We should not ask you to decide here and now. Nor do we intend to. Commander Bennett, I can offer you an almost unlimited expense account to procure in large numbers the aircraft you select, to train the pilots and support crew, to provide you with any staff you choose, and to pay you the sums you decide appropriate for this endeavor. If you are not willing to take this assignment we can only say we have enjoyed your company, and we will make immediate preparations to return you to your home. All we ask is your discretion."

The king rose, and so did the others. "I believe we can end this discussion for the moment. Your head must be full of ideas and other questions. Commander, I should like you to be my guest for dinner tonight, and perhaps tomorrow you could let us know your decision. We are not asking at this time for any specific plan—only if you would like to train and lead this organization."

Bennett groped for a response, but the king raised his hand holding the cigarette. "I should explain one more thing. You would not be expected to lead this air force into battle. I pray such need will never arise. But I believe you are the man to make such a force ready for combat."

Washington, D.C.

President Walter Arnold left the cabinet meeting shaken by the disarray within his administration. Already there was outspoken division within his two-month-old cabinet. The United Nations had voted without dissent to condemn Israel for the invasion of Jordan and ordered immediate withdrawal of her troops. The United States had abstained, and the cabinet was angrily divided over whether the American delegation should have exercised its veto. Now the president was preparing to meet with a group of influential Jewish leaders who would urge him to treat the invasion as necessary to ensure Israel's security.

Arnold's razor-thin victory over his Republican opponent was attributed to a turndown in the American economy during the previous administration's final year. Huge deficits and balance-of-payments inequities, combined with OPEC's renewed strength, drove oil to nearly $30 per barrel. The result was another serious recession in Western economies.

Walter Arnold had been an outstanding U.S. senator with an inbred affinity for all the media—well-spoken, handsome, outgoing.

His strong grassroots support confounded the professional pols, who had been unable to knock him out of the primaries. But even some of his own party leaders—who had been shut out of the White House for nearly two decades—privately acknowledged he was not as strong a leader as the presidency required, and now his young administration faced its first serious foreign policy challenge.

Arnold asked for a background briefing on the Middle East situation before his meeting with the Jewish delegation, which included some major supporters and contributors to his campaign. The Israelis had done nothing to ease Arnold's task, though even he had to admit they were not bound by any such consideration. "Nations don't have friends, they have interests," Henry Kissinger had said. Now Walter Arnold was beginning to understand that ancient truth.

Public sentiment in the United States was running high against Israel. The invasion of Jordan seemed unwarranted to most Americans. With both military and political advisers on hand, the president settled down in the briefing room to prepare for the upcoming meeting.

Major General George Miller, the Army briefing officer, stood before the small audience. His two stars attested to his career success, despite an unimpressive appearance. Short and balding, sightly overweight, he looked more like a college lecturer than a warrior. In fact, he had never held a combat assignment. But his analytical ability, smooth style, and political savvy had won him his present position.

With three sentences of introduction, Miller repeated the litany of all military briefers. He identified himself, though almost everyone in the room was on a first-name basis with him, and stated the purpose of the briefing. The old formula: "Tell 'em what you're gonna tell 'em; then tell them, and finally tell 'em what you just told 'em."

This time Miller got straight to work. "Mr. President, as you will recall, previous terrorist attacks against Israel and Israeli targets outside the nation's borders have generated widespread sympathy for Israel and condemnation of the PLO. This has been especially true when third parties were harmed, including Americans. But now the terrorist leadership has shifted tactics. In fact, we have fairly good evidence that the PLO has destroyed at least two ultra-radical splinter groups which were planning bombings or suicide attacks in Europe. This change of emphasis indicates a more unified objective for the entire Palestinian movement. It acknowledges increasing understanding of the counterproductive results of terrorism in third-party nations, and it seems to indicate a better-defined goal."

The general adjusted his glasses, glancing at his notes. "From the Arab and Palestinian viewpoint, it makes more sense to concentrate all efforts against Israel rather than diluting their resources in scattered efforts elsewhere. This approach has the additional advantage of removing terrorist outrages from the headlines, thus focusing attention on Israeli colonization of the West Bank and the current operation in Jordan.

"The new effort began four months ago, shortly after the last major terrorist attack in Europe. You may recall that was the coordinated operation which timed the bombing of our embassy in Lisbon with the suicide commando raid on the El Al office in Amsterdam."

Walter Arnold nodded in recollection. Four Americans and three Portuguese had died in the Lisbon explosion. The Israeli airline office had been a repeat of the Rome tragedy of 1985, this time with nineteen dead, thirty-three wounded, four terrorists killed and two captured. The two actions had rebounded against the PLO faction, as an extended bill of credit for Israel which had been stalled in the senate had gone through two days later.

General Miller continued. "Beginning last October, small-scale military operations were conducted on the borders of Israel from

Lebanon by a fanatic Muslim army. The PLO denied affiliation, and while that's probably an exaggeration, it is clear that the aggressive group was acting largely on its own. The Israeli decision to enter Jordan was precipitated by increasing raids from across that border. In one three-day period in November, sixty-two Israeli soldiers were killed and twice that number wounded. The militant Likud party narrowly won a vote of confidence forced by the more radical politicians." Miller looked over his reading spectacles for emphasis. "Prime Minister Aloni and Defense Minister Shelkan share their views.

"Likud promised swift action to end the cross-border assaults, which in fact were no longer mere raids. The operations were supported by artillery and frequently by long-range rocket batteries. The objective of these assaults usually were Israeli military facilities, though on one occasion a kibbutz on the West Bank was overrun and occupied briefly. By the time the raiders were repulsed, some forty civilians had died. That was the first time the Arabs tipped their hand with more sophisticated weapons, since at least one Israeli helicopter was shot down by an SA-7 man-portable missile."

Taking in the summary, Arnold was concerned about both international and domestic factors. "General, who supported these radicals? Where did they get all of this hardware?"

"Sir, we have hard intelligence on logistics, advisers, and weapons from Iran, Syria, and Libya. Additionally, North Korean and Cuban assistance has been observed. Soviet participation was reported but hasn't yet been proven."

The president leaned back in his seat. "Thank you, General." Miller realized he had been dismissed, picked up his papers, and walked out. When the door closed, Arnold looked down the table at his press secretary.

"Jerry, let's face it. The Arab raids leading up to the Israeli invasion don't really matter anymore. We have to deal with the current situation. We have a carrier battle group in the Mediterranean but it can't really do anything, and I damn sure don't want it to!" He paused for emphasis, then looked at his aide. "How do you assess the public mood about what's happened in Jordan?"

Jerry Butler knew what his boss was getting at. "Mr. President, there is no doubt about it. The two recent cases of Israeli espionage in this country have hurt their cause. Things seemed to die down after the influence-peddling episode in the House Armed Services Committee last summer. But then the new antitank round was found crated and ready for shipment to Israel—"

"Yes, yes. I remember." Arnold's voice was harsher than he intended, but the recollection of those events still rankled. With practiced ease the president shifted into his modulated make-the-voters-feel-good baritone. "What I need to know, Jere, is how you interpret the country's mood right now. Forget the damn polls. What do *you* think?"

Recognizing the conciliatory tone, Jerry continued. "I was coming to that, sir. My point is, with recent examples of continued Israeli spying over here, not many voters will feel very sympathetic to their invasion of Jordan. Since you're asking me, Joe Average on the street is going to want us to steer well clear of supporting or even condoning what's happening in Jordan. Our national interests don't seem to be threatened, so why get involved?"

Arnold nodded assent. "All right, we'll have to deal with the anti-Israeli lobby as well as with the Jewish lobby. It means steering a neutral course right down the line. You understand?"

The press secretary nodded. "Yes, sir." *I sure do,* he thought. *It means walking the fence again. Remember the first principle of politics: Never upset a voter without a good reason.*

2

Riyadh

JOHN BENNETT LEANED BACK ON THE OVERSIZED PIL-
lows on his king-size bed in the luxurious suite. Hands behind his
head, he lay with eyes closed, recalling the dinner that had ended
only two hours before.

Bennett had dined with King Rahman and one of the children.
Queen Aishah was out of sight with her daughters and youngest son,
which Bennett knew to be the custom. The boy at dinner looked
about fifteen, spoke very good English, and seemed conversant in
aviation matters. Bennett had almost dropped the spoon in his soup

when the younger casually mentioned logging 200 hours in his personal Beechcraft Bonanza.

The evening was easygoing and pleasant. The king had pointedly avoided discussing business, preferring to compare notes on places both men had seen and known. Having made three deployments to the Mediterranean, Bennett was familiar with the area, though he allowed himself greater knowledge of Toulon and Naples nightlife than the sovereign. But Rahman had impressed Bennett with mention of a fourth-place finish at the Le Mans twenty-four-hour race "in my impetuous youth."

It had gone like that all evening. But just before adjourning, the monarch had drawn Bennett aside.

Holding Bennett's arm and leaning close, he had said, "One thing for you to consider before our meeting tomorrow. You are aware of the strength of the Israeli Air Force, both in type and number of aircraft and in quality of pilots. Now, assuming you have an unlimited budget to procure any number, any type of fighter, and the time to train young men to your standards, is it possible that this air force might match the Israelis?"

Bennett returned the king's level gaze. This was the tacit question which forced itself to his consideration during the morning session with the ministers.

"I need to know, Your Majesty, if you intend me to commit this force against the Israelis. You understand it could jeopardize my status as a retired American military officer."

The king said, "Yes, I understand that completely. And I want you to know, between the two of us, that I would not expect you to be compromised that way. But I will be honest with you, my friend. As events now stand, with the invasion of Jordan, anything is possible. I must know all the possibilities beforehand. As Safad Fatah has told you, we Saudis are likely to find ourselves in the middle before long. We may well have to fight our Arab neighbors as well as the Israelis. That is why

I need a highly professional, thoroughly competent air defense force."

Bennett's mind raced. Something did not fit here. He respected this man who ruled the desert kingdom, and very much wanted to believe him. "Tell me, Your Majesty. You already have a modern, well-equipped air force. Why not simply expand it along the lines you already have?"

A smile crossed the king's face. "Ah, Commander Bennett, please understand. The Royal Saudi Arabian Air Force bears the markings of my nation, but in a real sense it is not mine. The aircraft, the support, and most of all the maintenance, depends upon foreign sources. Your country's contribution is nearly over, with the military assistance group. Now with the political factors we face, both in Washington and in our own region, we cannot count upon an uninterrupted flow of matériel or advisers. For this reason I want an independent air force, directly under my control with an absolute minimum of dependence upon external factors.

"You will excuse me if I speak bluntly. The Jewish lobby in America is very strong. Every time the United States wishes to sell us equipment or provide advisers, your politicians are deluged with letters and protests. This despite the very well-known fact that *my* country has not gone to war against Israel since 1948. But if our military supplies are embargoed, I will have my Arab brothers to worry about—perhaps even more than the Israelis."

At length Bennett said, "I see your point, though I wonder if the 'Jewish lobby' is as important to American policymakers as purely strategic considerations."

Gripping Bennett's arm even harder, the king spoke in a soft, almost toneless voice. "I ask you, John Bennett. Can you build me a fighter force the equal of the Israelis'?"

There was a pause of nearly half a minute as Bennett gazed at the elegant candelabra on the table. Then, softly but clearly, he had said, "Given time, yes."

Now, reclining in bed, Bennett's thoughts turned from the evening's conversation to metaphysics. He was not much on classic literature but he was well read enough to draw a comparison. The potentially Faustian nature of his relationship with the Saudi king struck him with chilling intensity. *So here you are, Bennett. Satan leans on your shoulder and whispers in your ear, tempting you with the best offer a fighter pilot ever had, or hoped to have. In exchange for . . . what?*

Bennett inhaled and considered the prospects. To build a fighter force from the ground up, with a completely free hand. Select the people, draft the syllabus, choose the airplanes. And best of all, no bullshit, no bean-counters to answer to. Mold a completely professional organization along sound military principles unencumbered by ass-covering politicians and hand-wringing diplomats. *It's hog heaven, Bennett, and you'd be belly-deep in slop,* he thought.

The irony of the situation occurred to him. Perhaps it would take one of the world's underdeveloped nations to bring the jet fighter force to its highest development. A Muslim kingdom one-third the size of the United States, nine-tenths covered by barren plateau. The place didn't even have any rivers.

Over eleven million inhabitants populated this wide expanse, where still barely 30 percent of the total lived in cities. Though education was free, it was still widely ignored and the literacy rate only matched the ratio of the urban population. Life expectancy was under fifty years, and though Saudi Arabia was the world's second-largest oil producer, only 12 percent of the people worked in industry. Not much had changed since oil was found in the 1930s.

Bennett had researched the nation and the royal family before leaving San Diego. King Khālid ibn 'Abd al-'Azīz al-Sa'ūd had succeeded to the throne in 1975 following old King Faisal's assassination by a nephew. The present monarch had inherited the throne in a tempestuous family political squabble. Bennett regarded Rahman as a man on a tightrope with no safety net. He walked a narrow line between the conservatives in his own country and the ambitious radicals outside.

The monarch was right about his military situation. The Saudis still could not maintain a large, sophisticated air force by themselves. There were too many foreign strings attached, there was too much political favoritism ingrained in the existing forces. What the king wanted was a band of professional mercenaries who owed him complete allegiance, free of external pressures.

It kept coming back to the Israelis. Match them, and the Saudis could master any other opponent in the region. Hell, man for man they'd master any other air force in the world.

The Israelis were the global standard. They knew von Clausewitz chapter and verse. They trained hard and they fought to win.

Bennett thought of his cousin Mike, an electronics specialist on the USS *Liberty* in 1967. The Israelis had torpedoed the intelligence-gathering ship with PT boats and strafed her with jet aircraft. Later they said it was a mistake. They'd thought she was an Egyptian vessel flying the American flag. Mike had lost a leg but thirty-four of his shipmates lost their lives. He was still bitter—as much at the Johnson Administration for accepting the Israeli version as at the Israelis themselves. When *Liberty*'s captain was presented the Medal of Honor for his valor in remaining at the conn despite disabling wounds, the citation never even mentioned the identity of the "hostile torpedo boats and aircraft."

Mike's name for the attackers was specific and unprintable.

It came to Bennett in a sudden rush. He might have within his grasp a means of maintaining or even expanding American influence in the Middle East while perhaps preventing a recurrence of the cycle of disaster his country had experienced in the region. *Liberty* in 1967, Iran in 1979, Beirut, the *Stark* and *Vincennes* episodes during the 1980s. Each military crisis had resulted in unnecessary loss of American lives or a loss of prestige and confidence in American institutions. Now the Saudis, by seeking to strengthen their own hand, were offering him a chance to do more good for the United States than he ever had done while wearing an American uniform.

While on active duty Bennett had attempted to convince people in authority that the most important element in the fighter equation was the pilot; that a superior aviator usually will beat an inferior pilot, regardless of their respective aircraft. Superior equipment— within certain broad limits—only mattered at the top of the league, between evenly matched pilots.

It had been proven time and again, yet the decision makers of years before had opted for high-tech, highly "capable" aircraft that cost $25 to $40 million each. This, combined with an overriding concern with safety, actually led to a denigration of combat skill. Bennett thought of the Air Force colonel who said, "I'd hate to see an epitaph on a fighter pilot's tombstone that says, 'I told you I needed training.' How do you train for the most dangerous game in the world by being as safe as possible?" But the pilot was to become the lesser of the equation. Many budgeteers believed that computers and technology had rendered the human mind and hand obsolete. That was bad enough. But they also discounted the human heart.

Bennett fell asleep, feeling somewhat optimistic about prospects for "his" fighter force serving to enhance U.S. influence in the Middle East while perhaps deterring wider war. He slept fitfully until shortly before dawn, when he drifted into the deepest sleep phase. Usually he dreamed in those hours, though he seldom clearly remembered his dreams. Cynical about such things, he never attached any importance to them. But throughout his adult life one dream had recurred.

It had begun after an exchange program with the Marine Corps between tours in Vietnam. Bennett had ridden in the backseat of a Phantom on a night mission. But in the dream he seldom saw the evolution from the cockpit. It was as if he stood watching from an elevated platform as the attacking jet screamed down at him from the darkness. Sometimes the plane was an F-4, often a Skyhawk—usually delta-winged.

Bennett stood alone, watching the bright jet exhaust as the aircraft arced straight up, tossing its single bomb in a high parabola which was lost to sight in the night sky. He always remembered seeing and hearing the jet top out of its two-mile-high Immelmann turn, rolling right-side up and diving away until even the noise disappeared. The bomb never landed. Bennett wondered what would happen if the dream ever lasted to completion. He thought once or twice that if that happened, he might die. . . .

A high-pitched sound woke Bennett with a start, an eerie wailing piercing his ears. Momentarily distracted, he felt for the familiar nightstand by his bed. It was not there. Then he rolled over a notepad and he remembered. He was a guest of the King of Saudi Arabia and had been sleeping in the palace. The startling sound was an imam's call to first prayer of the day, when a silver thread first becomes visible in the dark.

Bennett checked the luminous dial of his watch: 0530. He tried to sleep again, to no avail. Rolling on his back, he placed an arm over his eyes. Exhaling, he muttered one word. "Damn!"

SAFAD FATAH ESCORTED BENNETT INTO THE ANTE-chamber before the morning meeting. The American learned that the men who had attended the previous day's conference would be present again. Entering the conference room, he was directed to a chair and the king entered moments later. All stood.

With a wave of his hand, Rahman spoke in English. "Be seated, gentlemen. This should not take long."

The king sat down and leaned forward, hands clasped on the polished table. "Gentlemen, last night at dinner Commander Bennett said that he believes what we propose can be done. Additionally, he received my assurance that we would not call upon him to jeopardize his American citizenship, nor his status as a retired U.S. officer."

Looking around the table, lingering upon his two air generals, the monarch continued. "The self-defense force which Commander Bennett would establish would be administratively separate from our existing air force. In matters of acquisition, funding, and policy, I shall make the decision as to which organization is to have priority in specific matters. That must be understood by all."

The air force officers nodded solemnly. Bennett hoped the king's words would pave over any rough spots with the Royal Saudi Arabian Air Force—the *Al Quwwat el Jawwiya Assa'udiya*. To Bennett, one of the attractions of the king's offer was elimination of just such bureaucratic infighting.

The monarch turned to Bennett. "Commander, you have had some measure of time to contemplate the offer. Will you accept?"

Bennett inhaled. *Here goes*. "Your Majesty, this is the greatest challenge of my life. I believe that I understand what is necessary to build a first-rate fighter force. And I have the aircraft in mind, the Northrop F-20 Tigershark."

The two Saudi generals looked at one another in astonishment. Bennett knew what was coming and quickly continued. "Sir, gentlemen, I believe I should explain my background and preferences. This may help you better understand how my opinions are formed.

"Most of my professional life, some three thousand hours, was spent in the Vought F-8 Crusader. It was a single-seat, single-engine fighter with mixed gun and heat-seeking missile armament. This configuration gave U.S. Navy pilots the highest kill-loss ratio of any aircraft employed in Vietnam. It is the configuration of most other successful fighters, from the F-86 in Korea up to the General Dynamics F-16 today. Because this type of fighter is relatively simple, it is reliable. You can fly more sorties per aircraft than most larger, more complex types. So it really doesn't matter how many aircraft you own, provided you can keep more than ninety percent of them flying all the time. At least, within rather broad limits."

The king was intrigued. "I see. You would rather have six aircraft which fly nine-tenths of the time than ten aircraft which fly half the time."

"Exactly. It is better from an operational viewpoint, and from an economic one."

General Mustafa Halabi interjected. "Excuse me, Commander. But we already considered the F-20 and rejected it as little but an improved F-5. It did not meet our needs."

Bennett was ready. "Yes, sir, I'm aware of that fact. And with all respect to the Royal Saudi Air Force, I stand by my choice. The F-20 began life as the F-5G but in fact is a completely new airplane." Bennett was directing his remarks where they counted—to the king and the financiers. "It was not bought by the U.S. armed forces and therefore never had a fair comparison with its competition. But it has many virtues: some similarity with your existing F-5s, easy to fly and easy to maintain, plus it has outstanding sortie generation rates with very fast turnaround times between flights. Considering your criteria, I think it's exactly what you need: competitive but economical."

"Your Majesty." It was the economics minister, Aziz. He had not spoken before. "This makes elegant sense to me. With your permission, I shall investigate this matter." The king nodded. "Mr. Bennett," Aziz continued, "how much would this F-20 cost us?"

"I believe, sir, the current price is around fifteen million U.S. dollars, about the same as the last production F-5s. But considering the current state of the American economy, well . . ." Bennett grinned. "Let us say, Mr. Minister, that you should find a buyer's market."

Aziz returned the smile.

There's a horsetrader if ever I saw one, Bennett thought.

The king was intrigued by this exchange. "Very well. Mr. Aziz will make the necessary contacts immediately. Commander Bennett, you needn't concern yourself with acquisition. We shall bring you into the picture with the manufacturer at the appropriate time."

"Yes, sir. If I may add something. Although the F-20 has not been procured by any of the U.S. armed forces, a foreign manufacturing contract exists. It is my understanding that the parent company is producing subcomponents for a consortium in Europe and Asia. I am acquainted with one or two middle-level managers of this program. Have I your permission to see them on a personal basis to better familiarize myself with the aircraft? Naturally, I would make no mention of our plans."

Looking around the table for comment, the king saw none. "As you wish. Now then, Commander, how much time would be required before an air force such as we want could be made operational? You understand we have saved much time already by beginning construction of facilities in our country as well as Bahrain, and we have identified or recruited young men for pilot training as well as maintenance personnel and a cadre of instructors who would work for you."

"Your Majesty, it would probably be in excess of three years. The U.S. armed forces believe it takes five years to produce a combat-ready fighter pilot. But our syllabus can be streamlined to address only the matters that count. Also, I believe you can support more flying hours per month than most nations.

"However, even after that time it would still require experienced leaders to take the force into combat. Your pilots would be as good as any in the world, and I believe they would fly perhaps the most formidable air superiority fighter ever produced. But leadership is the key." Bennett paused, knowing he was treading carefully across uncertain ground. "One possibility might be assignment of some experienced Saudi pilots to the F-20 program."

The king looked at his air marshal. "That is something we can discuss later. Please continue."

Consulting his notes again, Bennett said, "Your Majesty, we would need about a hundred and fifty frontline fighter pilots. That means at the peak of our power approximately a hundred and thirty aircraft. Taking into account that we will have some peacetime attrition, we need to begin training with forty or fifty two-seat versions of the F-20. I think we would be looking at the purchase of some two hundred total aircraft over a five-year period. Existing F-5Fs, the two-seat Tiger II, could provide lead-in training."

General Halabi raised his hand. "Your Majesty, a question please." Turning to Bennett, the officer asked, "By lead-in training do you mean operational training, sir?"

"No, sir. The biggest time saving is a shortened course with elimination of standard training requiring transition to two or three aircraft. I propose weeding out the candidates with a twenty-hour course in light planes—Pipers or Cessnas. Those who pass go directly to the two-seat F-20B."

The air force chief stiffened. "Is that possible?"

Bennett pressed his point vigorously. He spoke louder than he intended. "Definitely, sir. I'll explain more fully when I return with the complete plan. But the advantages are considerable—cost saving, time saving, and greater proficiency in the combat aircraft." It was obvious to all that Bennett felt passionately about his proposal. "You see, the F-20 will not depart controlled flight under any but the most abnormal conditions."

The king interjected. "We can discuss these details later, gentlemen. For now, Commander Bennett, we know you must study this situation more. How long would it be until you can present a detailed analysis?"

"Your Majesty, I think I can wrap this up—complete the work—in under two months."

The king glanced around the room again. "Very well. Commander, what shall we pay you for this five-year service?"

"Sir, I would expect to use American and British instructors, and as we noted perhaps some Saudis as well. The U.S. and British should receive from a hundred thousand to a hundred and twenty thousand dollars per year in order to attract and hold the very best men. There would have to be a schedule allowing them to return home periodically, as I do not envision families at the training bases. Most of the instructors would have three-year contracts. At the end of that time, a smaller number would have the option to renew for one or two more years. With flight instructors and maintenance supervisors, probably fifty-five or so in all.

The king and Aziz glanced at one another. Aziz gave an elegant shrug.

Bennett, you're playing with the all-time high rollers.

"Yes, that is fine," the king said. "But what of yourself?"

Bennett had spent part of the night considering that question. "Your Majesty, I ask nothing for myself." He paused. "However, as you gentlemen know, I have a son in college. I would like a trust opened in his name, to be administered by an attorney of my choosing. As for myself, full compensation for all transportation, accommodations, communications, and any other expenses related to this work."

The king said evenly, "And that is all?"

Bennett returned the level gaze. "Well, not entirely, sir. You see, I wish one more thing."

"Yes?"

"Your Majesty, I would like my name painted on one of the first F-20s."

The king, a worldly man, interpreted this odd request literally. "That is all? Just paint your name on the machine?"

Bennett glanced at the Saudi generals. They were both grinning and the younger one—Maila—flashed a thumbs-up. "You see, sir, that means it's my airplane. I'm the one who flies it."

A laugh escaped the monarch's lips. He pounded a hand on the table. "Very good, commander. We shall paint your name on the first F-20 we receive. But you won't mind if we borrow it from time to time."

Bennett's smile was ear to ear. "Not at all, Your Majesty."

The king rose, and with him all the others. He spoke briefly in Arabic to Fatah, who ambled from the room.

Fatah was back in a moment, carrying a small, elegantly wrapped box. He handed it to the king.

"Commander John Bennett, we wish to present you with this gift in appreciation of your visit. We would have given it to you regardless, but now I am even happier that I may send you home with it. Please open it."

Bennett fumbled with the wrapping, feeling embarrassed at the attention focused on him. As he opened the lid he withdrew a small green ivory figurine of a pregnant woman.

"Commander," the king explained, "this is a fertility symbol which was excavated near Jiddah in 1976. Artists tell me its design is dated to thirteen hundred years B.C. This one is not that old, but it is ancient. Legend has it that a man who owns this figure will meet a woman who will give him happiness and children. I pray that it will bring the companionship and warmth of a woman back into your life."

Bennett felt the lump rise in his throat and the moistness well up in his eyes. He glanced down at the green figurine and spoke in low, halting words. "Your Majesty . . . I don't think . . . I can't say what this means. Only, thank you."

AFTER BENNETT HAD LEFT FOR THE AIRPORT, THE KING sat smoking and drinking coffee with Fatah and the other civilian representatives who had attended both sessions.

"My compliments, gentlemen. You did your work very well indeed."

Fatah inclined his head. "Thank you, Your Majesty. We were confident he was the best candidate."

The king blew a smoke ring. "Yes, yes it was. Dr. Hamoud, well done. Have you any new insights into our air leader?"

The Lebanese psychiatrist set down his cup. "No, Your Majesty. Only reinforcement. We knew that Bennett's driving ambition is to prove his point about air combat. This is what separated him from the other three choices. They are equally well qualified—in fact, one U.S. Air Force officer is a retired two-star general. But Mr. Fatah and I had considered the possibility that Bennett might work for nothing. A man of conviction. This is his chance to vindicate his theories that have not been accepted by his countrymen. Now we have given him a golden opportunity and I am certain he will make the most of it."

"How does his psychological profile indicate future attitudes?" the king asked.

"Your Majesty, there should be no significant change. Especially once the machines arrive and Bennett becomes involved in training and flying. We have selected him at the most opportune time. He is alone and vulnerable. You saw the reaction when you presented him with the fertility symbol. Such men do not show emotion easily."

Hamoud licked his lips, warming to his subject. "Sire, when he asked for the trust for his son, I felt my analysis had been accurate. When he asked for his personal machine, I knew it absolutely."

The king turned to Fatah. "You will coordinate with Aziz. You may tell the other parties that our plan has begun, but secrecy is important. Their contributions will be needed in a few months."

"Yes, Your Majesty."

Tel Aviv

Israeli Intelligence occupied a twenty-one-story steel and concrete antenna-crowned complex on the outskirts of the capital.
Radio antennae allowed immediate communication with any field
unit while pulling in transmissions from many other sources in the
region—all part of the endless process of information-gathering and
analysis. In a secure space in this complex Lieutenant Levi Bar-El
slouched in his chair, reading dispatches from the day before. The
young man was a reserve officer from the port city of Ashqelon,
serving a full year of active duty based on his skills as a language
instructor.

Though Bar-El's khaki uniform was clean, with moderately shined
boots, it would not have passed an American drill sergeant's inspection. An almost studied informality had grown up in the Israeli
armed forces, and casual dress combined with longish hair presented a disarming picture to most military professionals.

The report which Bar-El carried to his chief's office seemed
insignificant. It involved the flight of a Saudi aircraft two days
before from San Diego, California, to Riyadh.

Israeli agents in Los Angeles had photographed the passengers
with 300-millimeter lenses. One they knew as an agent of the Saudi
military establishment who had visited several Southern California
defense contractors over the past two years. Two were middle-level
diplomats. There was a four-person party comprised of two college-
age princes of the royal family and their European girlfriends. And
another man was an American perhaps six feet tall, approximately
fifty years old, whom the operatives noted had carried himself with
military bearing. The field representatives could not identify him
yet, but they suggested following him upon his return. The apparent
extravagance of flying eight people in a jumbo jet was not com-
mented upon—the Saudis seemed to enjoy such displays from time
to time.

Since the American desk of Israeli Intelligence had thought the flight worthy of note, it had passed the data to the Israelis' Saudi desk of army intelligence. The two offices agreed on a coordinated surveillance and now Bar-El had to arrange for technical assistance from his chief.

Israeli early-warning aircraft would attempt to relay information when the 747 was en route to the United States. American satellite tracking equipment would intercept communications between the Boeing and ground controllers as it transited half the world's surface. Bar-El's other responsibility was to notify the operatives in Riyadh that Safad Fatah's guest would be leaving within the next day or so, and the departure time should be relayed immediately.

With his field cap tucked under one epaulet, Bar-El checked his watch in the hallway. His chief was a stickler for punctuality and the morning briefing was thirty seconds away. Bar-El counted down the seconds, then punched the access code on the key pad and waited for the light. When it came on, he turned the knob and walked in with six seconds to spare.

Over the Mediterranean

The huge jetliner cruised easily at 37,000 feet, leaving the Middle Eastern landmass twenty-five miles south of Beirut. Its westerly heading took it along Oceanic Route G2 parallel to the Cyprus coast.

The sun shone brightly off the blue water, and Bennett looked out the left side at the green outline of Israel. When you flew in this part of the world Israel looked like a child's geography book. It was green at the edges, but mostly brown in the middle. However, he knew that the coastal area was not the only productive region. The Israelis really had made the desert bloom.

Such an industrious, productive people, the Israelis. Bennett did not know any Israelis well, and nearly all his contacts had been military. He found their aviators of a uniformly high professional standard, though frequently hard-headed, even arrogant. But you had to hand it to them. They started from zero and built not just a world-class air force but that rarest of commodities in the Middle East—a lasting democracy. Bennett knew that no war had ever been fought between democracies. That had to be the way to peace, if ever it came.

Then Bennett's practiced eyes picked up the small dots at the 747's eight o'clock position. He did not know it, but the Boeing had reached the mandatory reporting point called Velox, seventy nautical miles out of Beirut where Route B17 crossed Route G2. Bennett did know that he was in international airspace. As the dots closed the range he recognized them as F-15s, and the blue Star of David on the white disk plainly stood out. He wondered if they were running practice intercepts.

Fascinated, Bennett watched the lead Eagle extend its massive speed brake and ease into position. The wingman remained back about a half-mile in echelon. The Israeli leader stabilized himself low and behind the port wing, settling about a hundred yards out. Bennett had the eerie sensation that the pilot's eyes were fixed on him.

The leader read the Saudi Air's registration letters and relayed the data to his ground controller. This confirmed the identity of the aircraft which intelligence wanted. The helmeted figure in the twin-tailed fighter raised his right hand in salute, made a sharp left turn, and resumed the lead. Simultaneously the two gray fighters lit their afterburners and pulled into a sixty-degree climb, doing a matched set of aileron rolls. They were stylish fliers.

Tel Aviv

The next morning Levi Bar-El entered the access code into the pad and again waited for the light. The door opened and an enlisted dispatcher handed him a two-inch-thick pile of messages from the previous night. The young officer found the one he was looking for near the bottom. It was from the Israeli Embassy in Washington, providing details of the San Diego arrival of the Saudi airliner.

Field operatives had followed the hired limousine from Lindbergh Field north to the community of La Jolla. In front of a small apartment building on La Jolla Village Drive they noted a nameplate: J. L. BENNETT. Nothing was known about him yet.

Two hours later another dispatch reached the intelligence collection center. It identified John L. Bennett as a retired naval aviator. Less than forty-eight hours after that came a complete background report from Washington. The man had made at least two recent visits to the Northrop Aircraft plant in Los Angeles.

John Bennett was put under discreet surveillance.

Then Levi Bar-El turned to his stack of other unfinished business. Most of it had to do with events in Jordan.

Over Central Jordan

Major David Ran led his four delta-winged Kfirs along the Al Ghadat Highway, keeping three to four miles north of the paved road. Antiaircraft gunners and missileers loved pilots who flew down roads, establishing an easy tracking solution for surface-to-air weapons. As a tactics development officer, Ran was well aware of the danger and thus kept away from the straight-line route.

Not that there was much genuine concern. Ran's flight was out to test a new cluster bomb on reported vehicles nearby, but the targets had fled. The various Arab forces inside Jordan seemed to have drifted away in the past week or so; Ran had only been fired upon twice in that time. He noted with satisfaction that the Israeli occupation of the country was nearly complete, so his recent combat data could be analyzed. Much had changed since David Ran flew Skyhawks in his first war. Now he was in line for a squadron of his own, and that very thought thrilled him more than the barren landscape rushing beneath him at 365 knots.

3

JOHN BENNETT SAT ALONE AT THE TAILHOOK RESTAU-
rant. Located off Harbor Drive, it provided a view of North Island
Naval Air Station, where two aircraft carriers were moored. He knew
one was the *Constellation*, number 64. She would deploy to the
Pacific in a few more weeks. The other ship was less distinct.
Bennett squinted and thought he made out the white numeral 61 on
the massive shape. *Ranger*, he thought. That's right. Pete Clanton
had been busier than a one-armed paper-hanger getting her back in
commission. The short, balding engineering officer was an over-

worked commander who collected Oldsmobiles. John recalled that
Clanton had about three dozen scattered between Norfolk and San
Diego.

Bennett had just set down his vodka and tonic when he was
startled by two hands on his shoulders and a high-pitched, loud
voice in his ear: "Check six, Pirate!"

Bennett turned to see a set of brilliant white teeth and an unruly
thatch of red hair. The face was slightly pockmarked—the kind of
skin which does not tan, but easily sunburns. Pirate, he thought.
His old callsign, the *nom de guerre* which all tactical aviators use.

"Ed Lawrence, as I live and breathe. They still let you out
without a leash?"

"How you doing, John?" They shook hands, warmly regarding
one another. They lived within fifty miles of each other but seldom
met more than two or three times a year.

Bennett waited while Lawrence ordered an iced tea with lemon.
Lawrence took a swallow, let it settle, and got right to the point.
"Okay, what's the super-duper secret, Skipper?" The redhead had
been Bennett's operations officer in VF-24 and consequently Bennett was still the CO.

"Just a couple of preliminaries, Ed. I suppose you're still flying
for the airline?"

Lawrence fingered his drink. "Yeah, I'm a copilot with enough
seniority to call most of my trips. Straight and level all week, don't
upset the passengers, arrive on time. All that good stuff. But on
weekends and days off I go bend it with the Reserves. I'm exec of
VF-301 now, and I enjoy the F-14 even with another body in the
cockpit. I'll tell you, though, I wish to hell you and I could strap on
a couple F-8s and go hassle again."

Bennett leaned forward, across the table. "Ed, maybe we *can*
bend it again. Not in Crusaders, but something even better." He
checked his watch. "In about forty minutes a man will show up
here. His name is Safad Fatah. He's a Saudi minister at large and

I've agreed to do a job for them. I need some help. Your kind of help. I need a good executive officer—somebody I know and trust. And I need an ass-kicking fighter pilot."

Lawrence's eyes grew wide with curiosity. "Well, don't stop now. Tell me more." He gulped half his drink.

"This job is about four or five years steady work. It'll pay between a hundred and a hundred and fifty grand per year, and it'll be exciting as hell. Other than that, unless you're on board I can't say much else."

Lawrence emitted a low whistle. "Judas Priest. Who do I have to kill?"

Bennett's gray eyes gleamed, his mouth suppressing a grim smile. "Don't ask," he said. "Actually, it's fighter pilot instruction, building an air force from the ground up."

Lawrence cocked his head, his eyes narrowing. He waved a finger at his old skipper. "Wait a minute. You're telling me some raghead sheikh is willing to pay me more than I'm making now, to fly fighters and teach people to do what I used to do for thirty grand?"

"That's about it."

"If that's the deal, I'm in." Lawrence pounded the table. "Miss, another round for me and my friend, please!"

Bennett waved away the waitress. Ed Lawrence was a teetotaler, one of only two Bennett had ever known in naval aviation. The first had been pretty much a washout. The redheaded fighter pilot sitting across from him may have been the best stick-and-rudder man he had ever known.

"Remember, Ed, these people are Muslims. If our guys go boozing on them, it's a quick ticket home. That's rule number one. . . ."

"Okay. What's rule number two?"

A smile creased Bennett's tanned face. "You remember what Deacon used to say?"

Lawrence thought a moment. "Oh, sure. Topgun instructor. Always came up with pithy sayings." He frowned in concentration. "Which pithy saying?"

"The one that goes, 'Never trust any pilot who would rather use a slide rule than kick your ass.' "

"Hot damn, this sounds too good to be true. Who else is involved? Can't be just the two of us."

"It'll probably involve forty or so flight and tactics instructors and maybe a dozen-plus maintenance, weapons, and avionics folks. That's why I started with you. The Saudis already have a list of prospective pilots. I need not only good sticks, but pilots who can teach. Masher Malloy and Bear Barnes and probably some Air Force types as well. Even some Brits."

"Sounds good. But where are the Saudis going to find enough pilots like that? There aren't many in my situation—unmarried, free to pick up and move. Not many airline captains or pilots with other careers will go running off to Arabia."

"Fatah's people have been very thorough over the past couple years," Bennett replied. "They've saved us a lot of time with groundwork, not just with instructors but with facilities over there. Most of the work will be done by the time we arrive."

Both men knew that the kind of talent they needed was rare. Instructor pilots with sufficient experience and willingness were few and far between. There were a few score in the Free World: men with combat in their logbooks, still young enough and unencumbered enough to uproot themselves for this type of challenge. Fewer still would be capable of living and working in a strict Muslim nation for years at a time.

Lawrence said, "John, what about your boy Paul? What does he know about all this?"

"I spent most of a weekend with him in Tempe last month. He's gotten a girl pregnant and they say they're going to get married. Well, I guess we all have to learn the hard way. At least he doesn't have AIDS. I told him I wouldn't stand in his way, but he couldn't count on me for help. I told him I'd be doing consulting work out of the country and probably wouldn't be around very regularly."

Lawrence fingered an ice cube. "Geez, that's rough."

Bennett leaned back. "Oh, it's not as bad as it might seem. I'm helping with his tuition and he has a partial scholarship. What I didn't tell him is that the Saudis are establishing a trust for him and the baby instead of paying me. It'll be administered by a family friend here in San Diego." Bennett glanced out the window again, looking at the two carriers. "What about you? When can you break loose from the airline and the Reserves?"

"Far as the line goes, I'll finish this month's schedule. That's less than two weeks. I can resign from the Reserves anytime."

"Is that going to cause problems, create bad feelings? I mean, it's mighty short notice."

The redhead shrugged. "In words of one syllable, who the hell cares? For twelve years I was an underpaid fighter pilot. Now I'm an overpaid airline pilot. I look forward to being an overpaid fighter pilot, the best of all possible worlds."

Bennett raised his glass. "Short war."

Lawrence clicked his glass against Bennett's. "Short war." The traditional warrior's toast.

At that moment a blond man in a business suit walked up to the table. "Excuse me, are you John Bennett?" Neat, professional man. Calm demeanor. *Oh, God,* Bennett thought. *Not FBI.*

"Yes, I'm Bennett."

The stranger reached inside his suit coat. *He's going to show me his damn badge. We're had. But I haven't done anything.*

The stranger produced a color photograph. "Do you recognize this, Commander Bennett?"

It was a green figurine of a pregnant female. "Why, yes. Are you—"

"Mr. Fatah sent me. He has learned that you and he are under discrete surveillance by some Middle Eastern people." The stranger's eyebrows rose suggestively. "I was sent to keep the meeting."

Bennett asked the man to sit down, conscious that the stranger had not offered his name. Bennett introduced Lawrence, who clearly wondered what he had stumbled into.

"Gentlemen, you won't see me again so names don't matter." He placed an envelope on the table. "Mr. Fatah is at the number on the envelope. You are to call him there from any phone except your home, Commander Bennett. The call will merely confirm receipt of the written instructions in this envelope. Any questions?"

The two fliers stared at one another, then at the blond man. "No, I guess not," Bennett said.

"Then we're done." The stranger stood up, glanced around in a casual fashion. "Oh, one thing. You can't shake these people on your own—they're too good. Just try not to let on that you know you're being watched. Fatah's people will handle things." With that, he walked to the bar.

Lawrence and Bennett cast wary looks around the room. Unless the Israelis were using grandparents or had rented a family of four complete with unruly children in the adjoining dining room, there were no shadowers. From what little he knew of discrete surveillance, Bennett was confident the shadowing team would not follow him into a public place. Most likely there were three or four individuals outside, forming a moving box around the subjects. Equally effective but less obvious. At least, that's how Frederick Forsyth described it in his novels.

Bennett got up and made a call from the pay phone. He returned in moments, rotating a forefinger in the air. The start-engines signal. Lawrence got up and followed him out.

Tel Aviv

Levi Bar-El's presentation at the daily intelligence briefing came toward the end. His main topic was the American naval aviator who had visited Saudi Arabia two months previously, but Bar-El had more current information this morning.

"Two days ago our people followed this man Bennett to a restaurant in San Diego. After about forty minutes he and another man, apparently who met him there, took the new man's sports car to another restaurant about seven kilometers away. Our people waited ten minutes after assuming position, then sent in a female operative to locate the subject. She did not see them."

Bar-El checked his notes. "The sports car remained in the parking lot, apparently to make our team believe the subjects remained in the restaurant. But now we believe that a van was waiting in the alley behind the building. It was seen there upon taking station but was gone a few minutes later. It was dark, and—"

"Yes, yes, we know the routine." It was the section chief, Colonel Chaim Geller. He liked young Bar-El, but noted the lad had a tendency to make excuses for field agents he didn't even know. A natural enough reaction, but one that would have to be trained out of him. "The question is, where are they?"

Bar-El swallowed. "We do not know for certain, sir. It appears they have left the San Diego area. Maybe they have left the country. We should know shortly."

Geller waved a hand. "Well, they handled themselves pretty well for amateurs. Apparently no outward signs of suspicion. No doubt the Saudis or their hirelings spotted our team. No real harm done. Now, who is the second man? Also an aviator?"

Relieved at the change of subject, Bar-El flipped the page of his folder. "Edward R. Lawrence. An airline pilot who retains a reserve commission as a full commander in the navy, second in command of a fighter squadron. We identified him by his automobile registration. According to our air force intelligence, he flew with Bennett during two tours in Vietnam. Lawrence shot down three enemy aircraft and became a tactics instructor like Bennett. Two of our people knew him during his duty instructing at the Navy Fighter Weapons School at Miramar Naval Air Station, San Diego."

"What do they say of him, Levi?"

Bar-El was pleased—double-checking with the air force had impressed his chief. "Sir, they say he is a pilot and nothing else. He seems to care only for flying. One of the types you need in a shooting war, but who does not do as well in peacetime." He glanced down again. "An accomplished flier, a good leader, and both our men agreed he was one of their best instructors." Bar-El smiled.

"What is it, Levi? Something else?"

"Well, naturally I didn't tell our pilots the reason behind this investigation. But one of them said that if Edward Lawrence was looking for a job, we should hire him right away."

The chief tapped a pencil on his desk. "Apparently somebody else thought of it first. I only wonder why they disappeared like that. It tells us they're aware of our surveillance." Geller bit on the eraser. "What's your estimate, Levi?"

Bar-El was not used to being asked what he thought—only what he knew. "Sir, I would have to say that probably . . ." *Think fast, Levi, they're testing you,* he thought. "Sir, it's only a guess, but perhaps the Saudis feared we would expose the men to their government." *No, no. They've done nothing wrong, and the State Department already knows Bennett visited Arabia, quite legally.* "The only other thing is—well, Colonel, are we planning a wet operation against them?"

The section chief returned Bar-El's wide-eyed expression with emotionless brown eyes. "No, of course not. We have two Mexican nationals who can do such work for us in that area, but there is no need. At least not now."

Bar-El realized the recent Israeli intelligence operations in the United States would make such a move politically impossible. And besides, far better to run an assassination operation outside the United States, if it came to that.

"But," Geller continued, pointing his pencil at the lieutenant, "I think you are getting warm. The Saudis may fear we would eliminate Bennett and Edwards. Therefore, they became overly anxious and moved the men too quickly." He nibbled the eraser again. "Whatever they're up to, we'll know of it soon enough. Keep me informed, Levi. Thank you."

Los Angeles

The morning after eluding the Israeli team in San Diego, the two aviators entered an apartment on Beverly Glen Boulevard. *Damned amazing*, thought Bennett. He'd never been in Beverly Hills before. "The Saudis thought of everything," he said as he and Lawrence inspected the furnished apartment.

Lawrence opened a cardboard box on the dining room table and emitted a low whistle. "I'll say they thought of everything. Check this out." He held up fifty crisp new hundred-dollar bills. "Let's go to Vegas and let this ride one time. Get in practice for Tailhook."

The annual Tailhook reunion at the Las Vegas Hilton was a landmark event in naval aviation. Only now living down its riotous early reputation, the symposium had become more professional. But still it was great fun.

Bennett laughed. "Hey, do you remember Tailhook '74 when Hoser McAllister disappeared Friday night? They didn't miss him till Saturday afternoon. Found him laid out in a closet, dead to the world with one bare foot and a toe tag. Even had his arms folded across his chest—with that lily in his hands."

The men found clothes in the bedroom, each bathroom stocked with toilet articles, and the refrigerator crammed with enough food for two weeks. There was even a rowing machine in one bedroom. Lawrence noticed the coffeemaker and began brewing a pot. "You notice, the Moslems didn't leave you any booze. By the way, when we get wherever the hell we're going, will the guys be able to drink or will they have to go cold turkey for a couple years?"

"We'll be based in Bahrain, which is pretty lax by Muslim standards. Actually, I think there's two reasons for that. One, it keeps us Yankee air pirates out of Arabia most of the time, and two, we'll be positioned to intercept hostiles from Iran if need be. But in Arabia the guys better get used to the 40-weight oil that passes for coffee."

The redhead flashed a white grin. "I always knew clean living would be its own reward. I'll be the only instructor who's not having DTs after a couple months."

Bennett said, "Like I always told you, I never trust a fighter pilot who doesn't drink. Actually, we'll have our own compound. I checked with Fatah, and Bahrain is a lot looser situation than Arabia. Our guys can hoot with the owls, and there's European women employed in Bahrain as nurses, dental technicians and the like." Bennett held up a warning finger. "But in Arabia, where we'll be spending a lot of time, it's the straight and narrow for all hands."

"You think that'll scare off many guys?"

"Some, I suppose. We'll just lay down the law. The rule is, anybody who takes one drink too many in Bahrain or who gets out of line in any way in Arabia gets a one-time warning. Especially if any of our students are around. A second time gets the offender a one-way ticket home."

"Fine by me. One thing I don't understand, though. I don't have my passport. How do I get out of Uncle Sugar and into the land of oil wells and camels?"

"Fatah said on the phone that this unexpected change of plans would require some innovation. I don't have mine, either. He's supposed to call in a couple days to fill us in. Meanwhile, we sit tight. We can use the time to lay some groundwork."

The next forty-eight hours passed more quickly than either man had expected. The more Bennett studied the situation, the more he was convinced the answer was men more than airplanes. Late the second evening he tossed his pen down and rubbed his eyes. A stack of papers testified to the work they had accomplished.

"You know, Ed, I've been thinking of the *Ticonderoga* cruise when we lost five pilots in the first twoline periods. You remember? We got replacement aircraft but no new sports until we got back."

Munching a sandwich, Lawrence said, "That was before my first tour, but I sure heard about it."

"Oh, that's right," Bennett said. "God, it all runs together sometimes. But the point still applies. Like the RAF in the Battle of Britain. Their problem wasn't so much Spitfires and Hurricanes. It was experienced pilots. Every civilian who got killed in London meant a load of bombs that should have been dropped on airfields. The Germans had the RAF on the ropes and switched from attacking airfields to cities."

Lawrence bit into his sandwich again, wondering where this led.

"Well, my point is," Bennett continued, "that nothing's changed today. Even with limited numbers of high-priced birds, it's a lot easier to produce a fighter plane than a proficient fighter pilot. It takes, what? Eight to ten months to roll out an airplane from the factory? It takes about five years to put a combat-ready pilot in that bird's cockpit.

"This is where we come in, why the Saudis really want us. They know they can buy airplanes almost anywhere. But producing world-class pilots is a much bigger job."

The phone rang then, the first time since they had entered the apartment. Lawrence picked up the receiver. "Hello."

"This is Safad Fatah."

"Oh, sure. Hi. This is Ed Lawrence."

"Ah, Mr. Lawrence, just the man I need to talk to. Do you still have your house key with you?"

"Yes. In my pocket."

"Splendid. Please leave it in the mailbox. And tell me where we may find your passport. It will be delivered today."

Bennett heard Lawrence describe the desk drawer containing his papers. Lawrence also asked why it had not been obtained before.

"Dear sir," said Fatah in a diplomatic tone, "if we had done that, it would have given our other friends time to trace you."

The redhead felt like a student asking what day it was at graduation. "Mr. Fatah, I need to make arrangements with my airline and the Naval Reserve. What's the situation?"

The response was immediate. "We have sent letters over your signature to all parties concerned. We shall handle any follow-up details for you on this end."

Lawrence was impressed. Like Bennett, he appreciated professionalism wherever he encountered it.

"Oh, one more thing. What about my Porsche? We left it at the second restaurant."

"Mr. Lawrence, we shall buy you another Porsche if needed. I will not stay on the line any longer. Tell Commander Bennett that you will be contacted before much longer, and I extend my regards."

The line went dead.

Lawrence left his house key in the apartment's mailbox that night. At 0800 there was a knock on the door. Bennett opened it, drowsily rubbing his eyes, and looked around. Seeing no one, he glanced down. There was a paper sack with Lawrence's passport and his own. *Funny, I didn't ask them about mine.* He paged through it. *They don't have a key to my place, or the code to my alarm system,* he thought. Then it occurred to him. This was not his original. It was completely authentic, using an official form. *But how did they get the photograph and the signature?*

Then he remembered. His photo had been taken shortly after arrival in Riyadh, and he had signed a letter of intent. Bennett smiled in appreciation. *These people are real pros*, he thought. *They didn't have time to duplicate Ed's passport, but they had mine ready to go, complete with forged signature. If the Israelis search my place they'll find my passport and figure I'm still in the country. Slick.*

Bennett knocked on Lawrence's door. "Flight quarters, Commander. I think we'll be gear-up in a little while."

Washington, D.C., the White House

President Walter Arnold was upset. In office barely four months and already his press secretary and two cabinet members told him the administration showed declining confidence ratings in the polls, especially where foreign policy was concerned. Secretary of Transportation Pamela Cousins had heard party pros who were comparing Arnold with Jimmy Carter—unfavorably. It was a hell of an attitude for a formal cabinet meeting.

"Well, damn it," Arnold said, "what the hell am I supposed to do? Everybody in the Middle East wants us to do something different. It's a no-win situation all around. You people have told me that one of the best ways to dent the trade deficit is to sell weapons abroad. You've also told me that if we sell to the Arabs, the Israeli lobby will scream its head off and there'll be editorials all over the country."

Secretary of Transportation Cousins thought, *Welcome to the real world, Mr. President.* There were those in the administration who said, only half-jokingly, that the five-foot-three blond was a better man than Walter Arnold.

"Mr. President, that brings us to the last item." It was Secretary of State Thurmon Wilson, a scholarly, balding political ally from Arnold's native Connecticut. "You are aware that last week the Israelis noted that several dozen American citizens, all believed to be ex-military pilots or mechanics, have traveled to Europe and Saudi Arabia. This seems related to sudden Saudi interest in a fighter aircraft called the F-20."

The president said, "Yes, I saw the memo. Do you think it's cause for alarm?"

"No, not yet." The New England accent cut through the heavy mood in the room. "But we'll have to make a decision pretty fast, the way they're pushing. They seem really interested in this plane. I'm sure Ben has details."

Benjamin Wake was Secretary of Defense. A self-made million-aire from a Florida electronics firm, he prided himself on keeping data under his white crewcut only slightly less efficiently than the computers his firm made. "Yes, I'm acquainted with the F-20. And frankly, this seems an answer to a prayer. It's called the Tigershark, designed by Northrop in Los Angeles, and it's a relatively unsophis-ticated piece of hardware. It's a single-seat, single-engine air superiority fighter based on Northrop's old F-5 Tiger. If we decided to sell the Saudis another airplane, that's the one. The Israelis can't holler too loudly because it's no match for what they're flying."

Arnold pursed his lips. "Then why would the Saudis want it? They already have some of our most advanced equipment."

"Yes, sir, that's right. But remember, they and most other countries which have bought the F-20 don't have the ability to maintain high-tech weapons without extensive support. I have a list of nations that currently fly the Tigershark: Malaysia, South Korea, Chile, the Sudan, and Morocco. Taiwan is almost certain to buy it, since Mainland China is off our backs now that F-20s are manufac-tured under license. A European consortium now builds the air-plane, mainly for export."

Wake sensed that the president was becoming sympathetic to his viewpoint. "Now, sir, you may remember during the Reagan Administration there was quite a flap about making exceptions to Third World nations. Most of them wanted our frontline equipment —F-15s and F-16s. Because we didn't buy the F-20 ourselves, others perceived it as inferior. Now that's changed, mainly because of economic factors. A Tigershark costs under half of what some other fighters run."

"Hmmm. What does State make of this, regarding the Israelis?"

Secretary of Defense Ben Wake interrupted. "Excuse me. But we know that the Saudis want simpler aircraft to supplement their F-15s and British Tornadoes." Wake glanced around the table. "You all remember how the Saudis bought billions of dollars of British aircraft when we wouldn't sell them more Eagles. No telling how many thousands of U.S. jobs that cost. Well, I think this is an excellent opportunity for us, Mr. President. The F-20 is far easier to maintain and to train pilots for than one with sophisticated electronics. Also, the Saudis are ordering Tigersharks without radar-guided Sparrow missiles. The Israelis can't complain too much."

"Why not? Isn't this F-20 still a potential threat to them?"

"Well, theoretically, yes. But with limited armament of guns and two heat-seeking missiles, the F-20 would be similar to the F-16, which we and the Israelis already fly." Wake pressed his point. "Remember, Jordan wanted F-16s and we refused so they bought Fulcrums from the Soviets. We've only been hurting ourselves by acceding to the Israeli lobby in Congress all these years." There, it was out in the open.

The president shifted his gaze to the Secretary of State. "Thurmon, what do you make of all this?"

"State has no serious objections, sir. In fact, I'm in favor of selling the Saudis or anybody else whatever they want to buy, within broad limits. Aside from economic reasons, it makes good political sense. The Saudis are the key to the whole region if we're going to maintain any kind of balance there. Especially now that Israel occupies Jordan. If we can keep the Saudis happy by selling some second-line airplanes, by all means do so. Anything we can do to maintain our presence and influence should be encouraged, especially with the growing Iranian fundamentalist movement."

Walter Arnold lightly tapped his fingers on the table, his mind already made up. "Very well. We'll approve the F-20 sale and put up no obstacles if the Saudis want to hire some former military pilots as instructors. But let's try to keep this as low a profile as possible." He looked around the table. "This meeting is adjourned."

Tel Aviv

Levi Bar-El braced himself for another grilling from Colonel Chaim Geller. *The man torments me,* thought the young lieutenant, *because he has no other diversion.* In truth, Bar-El recognized that the section chief was pushing a protégé's limits, forcing him to become more competent, less dogmatic in his thinking. Dealing with the recent Jordanian crisis saw to that. And right now Bar-El was ready for more "therapy."

"Ah, good morning, Levi. Sit down." Geller pushed a chair out from the table. "What do you have on our mysterious Americans?"

"Sir, we believe they are no longer in the U.S. Our covert team inspected Bennett's apartment and found nothing out of order. His passport was there, but because of the sighting in London we believe the Saudis provided him with a duplicate. Our people did photograph a strange object, however. It seemed odd enough to bring to your attention." Bar-El unclipped a Polaroid photo from the report and slid it across the table.

Chaim Geller examined the photo. The green figurine of a pregnant woman intrigued him. "It's not from North America, I can tell you that." Bar-El was taken aback. He knew almost nothing about his superior's outside interests and never would have taken the shrewd intelligence officer for an archaeologist or art historian.

"Well, no, Colonel. Our evaluation from the university is that the piece came from the Middle East—probably Arabia or Oman. It dates from about the tenth century B.C., but whatever the date, it is rather rare and therefore very valuable. Professor Mersky at the antiquities center said he had only seen six or eight such figures himself, and this one is in better condition than most."

The colonel handed back the photo. "Very well. What else?"

"Bennett and Lawrence seem to have been in London for several days, as I noted. But it is unlikely they will return to California anytime soon." The lieutenant checked his notes. "Lawrence's sports car was taken to his home and put in the garage. Evidently both Bennett and Lawrence have someone looking after things—watering lawns, paying bills, and so on. Bennett's son at Arizona State University seems to know relatively little, but doesn't appear overly concerned. Our contact thought it best not to press the matter. We'll monitor him on a regular basis."

Geller stood up and stretched. He wanted to go for a walk in the sunlight, but glanced ruefully at the paper stacked on his desk. "All right, Levi. I saw the report on the other American fliers, and I see there are two or three British pilots on the Saudi list. I've forwarded a memo to Air Force intelligence. Obviously, the Saudis are expanding their training cadre. The cabinet will want to know about this, and no doubt there will be concern. But for now, let's not draw hasty conclusions. The Saudis are in the middle of all this."

Geller noticed the mild look of surprise on the lieutenant's face. "Now don't misunderstand, Levi. Of course the Saudis wish us no good. But you want to develop your sense of objectivity in this business. Put yourself in their position. With Iran, Syria, and even Iraq and others becoming more unified under the Muslim radicals, a relatively moderate regime will be hard-pressed to remain apart."

Bar-El said, "It may be impossible for the Saudis."

Geller decided to play devil's advocate. "Let's say you're now the king of Saudi Arabia. What would you do to help keep your throne and guarantee your family's position and prestige?"

Thinking for a moment, Bar-El spoke carefully. "Well, I would try to maintain a balance, try to have it both ways. I would open channels to the fundamentalist Muslims while strengthening my position with the Western powers—the source of my military equipment and market for my petroleum."

Geller gave a decisive nod, his double chin outthrust. "Just so." He flexed his shoulder muscles. It was getting warm inside. "I'll make a prediction, Levi. We'll see relative calm—I said *relative* calm—for another couple of years. But once the Arabs have time to consolidate their gains and increase their political unity, we're in for one hell of a fight." The colonel smiled. "You're a fortunate young man. You're going to live to see some very interesting times."

4

Bahrain

"NOW THIS IS SOMEBODY WHO APPRECIATES OUR TAL-
ent," opined Ed Lawrence. Looking about him, he took in the
immaculate new facility on the Persian Gulf island, still not wholly
completed. "It's amazing what you can do when the head office just
says, 'Do it.' If this was in the States, the ink would still be drying
on the letter of intent."

Bennett said, "The advantages of a monarchy, my boy."

In truth, Bahrain was an independent state, nominally autono-
mous from Saudi Arabia. But Riyadh had long paid most of the little

nation's defense bills. Now, with establishment of the F-20 program, the king wanted his second air force built and trained here. It was near enough to Riyadh, but away from prying eyes and—if need be—closer to Iran to intercept unwelcome ships or aircraft.

The new compound inside the airport perimeter was solely for the American and British instructors. It included single-level apartments with a central swimming pool, lighted tennis courts, and a plush lounge. The latter featured elegant wood and leather decor, comfortable chairs, and a horseshoe bar.

Not yet completed was a gymnasium and a fifty-meter pistol range. Bennett intended to teach small-arms proficiency in order to create well-rounded warriors.

"Besides," he told Lawrence, "I like to shoot."

The Saudis had made startling progress in the three months since Bennett and Lawrence had arrived from London. British supervisors and foremen had ensured quality work. The combination auditorium and briefing room where instructor pilots and maintenance supervisors would meet, and where preflight and debriefings would occur, was ahead of schedule. Bennett recalled the king saying that much groundwork had begun even before instructors were recruited, and the time saving was substantial.

The academic buildings for student pilots and F-20 simulators were finished, and the sophisticated equipment was being installed. The General Electric Company had developed what Bennett and Lawrence considered an outstanding pilot-training syllabus for F-5 students in Tempe, Arizona. It was near Williams Air Force Base, where the 425th Tactical Training Squadron provided training in the Tiger II. A similar format for the Tigershark was intended for the Bahrain field. It featured individual study cubicles with color-coded course material—light colors for the early topics, growing to blue and black toward the end of the course. Thus, students progressed at their own best rate with increased comprehension.

The two naval aviators sat in the air-conditioned bar, reviewing their notes. The next day they would make their final presentation to the king and his ministers. Bennett flipped through his notebook marked INSTRUCTOR PILOTS.

"We're up to speed now on IPs. It didn't take Fatah's contacts as long to screen them as I thought it might. Do we have the maintenance billets filled now?"

Lawrence sipped an iced tea. "Yup, nailed down a former F-5 type who retired a couple years ago and got tired playing golf five days a week. He's sixty-one and about to climb the walls. Jumped at the chance to get his hands dirty again, though he's mainly a supervisor. He's supposed to arrive next week. Also filled out the armament section. Fatah's guys in London recruited a Royal Navy warrant officer who seems to know everything worth knowing about twenty-millimeter weapons. He retires next month."

"Good deal. Let's see . . . that puts us up to speed with forty IPs and twenty maintenance folks. The simulator and academic people are being handled by Fatah's contacts in the U.S."

Lawrence fished a crumpled letter out of his hip pocket. "Almost forgot. I received this from Masher Malloy—you know he's supposed to join us before long. It's interesting reading."

Bennett smoothed the creases and scanned a short article, apparently clipped from a West Coast newspaper. It quoted a Department of Defense spokesman who described the F-20 as "a less capable and therefore less threatening aircraft" than what the Israeli Air Force was flying. The spokesman took particular note that most of the Saudi purchase of seventy-five F-20s had been ordered without radar and, therefore, without Sparrow missiles. Scrawled at the bottom in barely legible handwriting was the note: "Can't wait to get my hooks on this second-rate bird. Check six, Masher."

"Check six" was one fighter pilot's way of saying "Take care of yourself" to another. It referred to the vulnerable six o'clock position directly behind an aircraft, the preferred position to launch an attack.

"You know," said Bennett, "I'm kind of sorry to see Masher leave the Navy. I've always been curious how long he could stay on flight status before they got rid of him. He must be the oldest lieutenant commander still flying. Like Admiral Rickover—they'd have to kick him out."

Lawrence barely swallowed a mouthful of tea without choking. "What I want to see is how he gets along in the land of Allah. Can you imagine a skirt-chaser like Malloy going without women for two months, let alone two or three years?"

"Well, he'll just have to make the most of his thirty-day leaves."

Jidda

The 737 jetliner paralleled the eastern bank of the Red Sea. Bennett could see, out the port side, several dust devils racing across the arid sand. As the Boeing landed at Jidda, the nation's administrative center, he reflected that the sacred city of Mecca was only a short distance inland.

Bennett folded up his working papers and stuffed them in his briefcase with his well-thumbed copy of the Koran. He carried E. H. Palmer's 1880 translation, still widely circulated, and referred to it whenever possible. Combined with reading regional history, Bennett had educated himself about the region's geopolitical and cultural relationships over the past few months—something Ed Lawrence largely resisted.

Sitting beside his friend, Lawrence tucked away the F-20B pilot's manual as the 737 taxied to the gate.

It was a short drive over blazing-hot tar roads to the small castle nestled on the cliffs above the Red Sea. A thick wall, ten feet high, surrounded the castle and Saudi soldiers patrolled the parapets. A uniformed sentry in impeccable khakis saluted as the chauffered

Mercedes slowed before the gate. Dark sweat stains formed half circles under each arm and a line down his shirt front.

"Poor bastard," murmured Lawrence. "That's about like standing guard in hell."

Unlike most American briefings, which arrayed the principals in front with the speaker behind a rostrum, the conference room featured a large wooden table about twenty feet long. Arranged around it were twelve chairs. The preliminaries were brief but cordial; King Rahman warmly greeted Bennett and made Lawrence feel at ease. Safad Fatah was his usual elegant, composed self.

The king sat at the head of the table, directing the Americans to the opposite end. Among the attendees Bennett recognized Aziz, the finance minister, and General Maila. There were only three air force officers among the participants, the reminder being introduced as financial and political ministers.

Bennett mentally ticked off that bit of information; it showed the king was keeping his promise about minimal contact—i.e., interference—with the established military forces.

Safad Fatah leaned over to speak quietly with the two aviators. "Gentlemen, I am asked to inform you that you should report to your embassy in Riyadh within the week. They have some procedures to follow and reports to submit to Washington. No need for alarm, I assure you. Merely routine."

Bennett and Lawrence made appropriate notes, then passed out photocopied documents for each person there. After a few more moments the king called the meeting to order.

"This presentation, as you all know, is the final briefing we will receive before actually beginning the F-20 program. Commander Bennett and Commander Lawrence have worked long and hard, and I fear we put them through some unusual procedures to get them here."

The two Americans glanced at one another. The sudden departure from California those months ago now seemed far away.

"As it turned out, our concern for their safety was unfounded, but we should remain vigilant and cautious. I trust our guests will understand that we were motivated solely by concern for their well-being."

Bennett lifted his right hand to indicate his appreciation.

Then the monarch began in earnest. "All of you have met Commander Bennett, but some of you do not know Commander Edward Lawrence." The king acknowledged the American, who rose briefly, then resumed his seat. "Commander Lawrence is an experienced warrior and fighter pilot instructor from the United States Navy. He will serve as Commander Bennett's second in command. Gentlemen, I have the honor to inform you that you are being granted equivalent positions of colonel and lieutenant colonel, respectively. We understand that your American citizenship does not allow you to hold rank in a foreign military, but within the confines of my kingdom and for purpose of authority you should find these titles sufficient to your needs."

Bennett, in his thorough way, had studied this potentially sensitive situation. He knew that Douglas MacArthur had served as a field marshal in the Philippine Army before World War II, and he personally knew veterans of the Flying Tigers and Eagle Squadrons who held military rank in the Chinese and British armed forces—clearly in violation of American neutrality, but with full knowledge and permission of the Roosevelt Administration. With that precedent, Bennett felt on safe ground. Bennett's attention was drawn back to the meeting when the king introduced him.

"Thank you, Your Majesty. We appreciate this significant honor. Now, gentlemen, a brief summary on the advisory personnel. We have forty instructor pilots under contract, following careful screening by Mr. Fatah's people and our own evaluation. Most of these pilots are personally known to us, except the British, of course. Seventeen are former U.S. Navy pilots, one former Marine Corps, and fourteen former U.S. Air Force. The remaining eight are from the Royal Air Force and Royal Navy. Of these forty, eighteen have combat experience, including two of the British from the Falklands War of 1982. All are well-qualified flight instructors and combat tactics instructors in jet aircraft. Each has been screened not only for professional competence, but for maturity and stability.

"The contracts provide for a pay scale averaging a hundred and ten thousand dollars per instructor annually, with thirty days off each nine months. All transportation and living costs will be absorbed by the Saudi government. The funds will be deposited in a Swiss bank account on a monthly basis, with a three-month advance upon each man arriving in Saudi Arabia. In addition, the government has purchased a million-dollar life insurance policy for each individual with Lloyd's of London." Glancing down, he continued, "Each contract runs for two years, at which time it may be renewed."

Bennett looked up from his notes, aware that he had the undivided attention of everyone in the room. "As for the maintenance and other personnel, their expenses will be met either by their employers such as Northrop and General Electric, or by the Royal Saudi Air Force in the event we bring current Saudi pilots into the program. It is our intention to push qualified individuals into leadership positions as fast as possible. The instructor pilots will remain airborne mission leaders and tactics advisers beyond the second year, but maintenance and support—the all-important aspect of an air force—could be fifty percent Saudi in less than three years.

"Now, we also have developed a third community which will have much importance in determining how fast the F-20 program develops. Mr. Fatah has hired two flight surgeons from the United States and a British psychologist and a Lebanese psychiatrist. These gentlemen have devised entrance examinations for the Saudi applicants, based upon a time-proven system which rates psychological, personality, and other traits. We believe this should allow the highest possible number of graduates per class—approximately sixty-five percent."

Bennett did not discuss the behind-the-scenes maneuvering that had led to this system. It had taken some hard talking to convince all the Saudis involved that applicants for the F-20 program—already a prestigious assignment before the first class convened—would be rated wholly on merit. As in many third world nations, military aviators largely came from the politically well connected upper class.

Bennett and Lawrence had bluntly told Fatah that not even royal blood would ensure a seat in the course. However, the number of well-educated Saudi males with 80 percent proficiency in English automatically meant that young men from privileged backgrounds would fill most of the classes.

Bennett continued. "Gentlemen, you all realize that the investment of this many of your brightest young people in this type of program will limit their usefulness elsewhere. The individuals we seek are high school graduates between eighteen and twenty-two years of age. They will be selected from only about six percent of your national population. This is the same ratio in most countries. Only this proportion is found in the general populace with the attributes necessary to become a successful fighter pilot. We are looking for youngsters in excellent health with perfect vision and superior motor skills. They must be highly motivated, willing to work long and hard toward their goal. As I noted, about thirty-five percent will not finish the course, but we can make good use of those who make it to the halfway point, provided they wish to do so."

General Maila interjected. "What uses do you foresee for such students? Would they remain in the F-20 program?"

"Yes, if they had aptitudes for maintenance or operations. But those who make it to the halfway point in Tigersharks will be fairly accomplished aviators. Their problems are likely to be spatial orientation in dogfighting or poor G-tolerance, things of that sort. If any of them want to fly less demanding aircraft, I would recommend transferring them to units better suited to their abilities."

Bennett referred again to his notes. "Mr. Fatah's organization has identified an initial group of nearly a thousand young Saudis who meet the eligibility criteria for age and education. Others will be similarly identified as each group of young males approaches age eighteen. Our first class involves sixty-five candidates, who already have begun extensive remedial English instruction. We expect this to continue for one month, with language tests at intervals throughout the academic and early flying portions of the syllabus.

"Preflight training stresses physical fitness, with emphasis on those physiological traits needed to withstand the high-G environment of aerial combat. Cardiovascular training will be stressed, as well as upper body development, which provides a sort of built-in resistance to blackout—up to a certain point. The F-20, remember, is a nine-G airplane. It will require a pilot in peak physical condition to fly it to its limits.

"Groundschool will last six months. The course outline and the methods are explained in your handouts. In addition to such topics as aerodynamics, mathematics, engines, and airframes, the students will have classes in the Koran and Arab history. Each barracks will be named for an Arab martyr or hero. We wish to impress these students—and they are at an impressionable age—that they are being groomed as warriors. Toward that end they will live under strict military supervision. They will learn the manual of arms and close-order drill to instill pride and discipline. But I hasten to note that as Lieutenant Colonel Lawrence and I have learned, this training must be tempered with encouragement. The students will be allowed to visit their families at regular intervals as well.

"We think that all sixty-five who begin preflight training probably will complete it. Normally only those who fall ill or cannot keep up academically will be left behind, but in many cases these individuals can fall back to the next class.

"Hands-on experience will come at the end of preflight when the students learn to start and run jet engines in a test cell. They will also learn ejection seats and desert and water survival."

Bennett stopped to sip his lemon-flavored water. "We envision a graduation ceremony at the end of six months, with all family members present. His Majesty has agreed to attend, but the publicity will be minimal. The event is mainly for the benefit of the cadet and his family, with two weeks leave at that time." He knew the next revelation would concern some of the men around the table.

Here goes, Bennett. Hang on. "We will start flying the cadets immediately in the two-seat F-5F. This is without prior instruction in propeller aircraft or training planes of any kind, although at first I had thought we might use other aircraft as lead-in training. Now I don't think that is necessary. The two-seat F-20Bs are being delivered at a rate sufficient to replace the F-5Fs before the first class is completed. Thorough simulator instruction can prepare the students for about seventy-five percent of the tasks they must complete in the air, but there is no substitute for actual flying. Since the Tigershark is practically stallproof and resistant to spinning, it affords a unique opportunity to save time and money in the training curriculum."

Bennett stopped to let the impact sink in. "Are there any questions?"

The senior Saudi general, Mustafa Halabi, raised a hand. "Colonel Bennett, I remember you mentioned this before. But is it absolutely certain this will work? Obviously, placing young boys in high-performance aircraft could involve great risk."

"Yes, sir, I am absolutely certain it will work. As you know, it's easier to fly a jet than a piston-powered aircraft. The key is training— thorough, intensive training until the students know each procedure reflexively. We'll keep the cadets flying with IPs longer than normal to be doubly certain of each boy's ability before he solos. The U.S. Navy conducted a similar program many years ago, starting a study group in two-seat Grumman Cougars as their first aircraft. There were no significant problems, and I can only assume that the entrenched training organization and manufacturers prevented the service from adopting the program."

Warming to his topic, Bennett pressed on. "There's another example, too. One of our Air Force instructors tells me that the Singapore pilots he worked with are among the best F-5 pilots anywhere. One of his students was twenty-two years old, had been flying the Tiger II since age eighteen, and had one thousand hours in it. I believe the Singapore syllabus involved preliminary instruction in propeller trainers, but it's been proven that the accelerated program really works."

Lawrence cleared his throat, gaining Bennett's attention. The redhead was letting his friend know that he was beginning to speak rapidly and his voice was rising because of the passion he felt for this topic. Bennett continued in a modulated tone.

"Our F-20 pilots will fly one airplane and one only in their entire careers, most likely. Their first fifteen flights will be in the front cockpit with an instructor in back. After basic airwork and about seventy-five landings they will go solo—one of the high points of their lives, I assure you." Bennett glanced down the table at the king and Fatah. "I might add that I've been assured we will not face the problem of fuel shortage which plagues many other air forces."

There was a ripple of laughter around the table.

"The post-solo stage will concentrate on navigation without electronic aids. As you know, most of our F-20s are being ordered without radar or navigation equipment. The value of this training will be apparent if the force is committed to combat. In today's world, electronic countermeasures can preclude navigation, communication, and many weapon systems. Our pilots will not know any such problem since their entire training will be directed toward visual navigation, radio silence in most cases, and gun armament with heat-seeking missiles. Many authorities say those days are over and apparently believe that only the most sophisticated aircraft and systems can do the job. However, we believe otherwise. In your country, with clear weather most of the year, with well-trained pilots flying simple, easily maintained fighters, we expect to match or beat any likely opponent.

"We expect that about five of the sixty-five students in each class will wash out during this phase of training. At the end of the formation-flying stage the student will have about a hundred hours, and here we expect our highest attrition from dropouts and wash-outs. Approximately ten students will be disqualified at this level, but as I noted they may be useful in other capacities.

"At this point, having flown approximately five thousand hours of instructional training, we can expect two or three aircraft will be written off or grounded from damage. Our procurement policy has taken aircraft attrition into consideration.

"The next phase is instrument training. Now, this is not because we expect to do much night flying. But the frequent haze over the gulf and heavy dust storms will require instruments. It is a demanding phase of flight and will stress the student to a considerable degree. If he can fly a high-performance aircraft alone, on instruments, he has what we Americans call the right stuff. Instrument flight is one of the greatest teachers of discipline, and a tremendous confidence-builder. We will continue instrument training at intervals throughout the syllabus. Probably this will involve two night flights per month.

"Subsequent stages include advanced formation flying, including tactical formations based on the American loose-deuce two-plane section. Next comes weapon employment. This is the portion toward which all prior training has been directed. Students will begin with air-to-ground gunnery, quickly progressing to aerial gunnery. There will be twenty flights in this syllabus, all in loose-deuce formation or four-plane flights. Inert Sidewinder missiles will be on board, and students will take turns attacking and defending against missile-equipped opponents. We expect to make heavy use of simulators in this phase, as it will be an excellent means of recognizing AIM-9 missile-firing parameters.

"Finally, tactics flights against a mixture of instructors and other students will put together all the cadet has learned previously. Frankly, this is the most dangerous regime in the entire syllabus, and we expect to lose some aircraft. Instructors will use a moderate degree of effort to stress the students and keep them from getting overly confident. By now the students will have some two hundred hours, and some nations have committed pilots to combat at that point.

"By the end of this final stage we should graduate forty to forty-five students of the original sixty-five. Properly led, they could give a good account of themselves in combat at this stage. But naturally we prefer greater experience before committing the F-20s to such a test."

Bennett paused to see if anyone had a question. He noted that he had kept the audience's wholehearted interest, so he pressed on. "Graduation ceremonies will be the most moving emotional experience of the young pilot's life. His family and friends will see him receive his silver wings and his commission as a lieutenant. Pay will rise to about a thousand dollars per month. He will have more freedom of movement and will be rid of drill and marching. I recommend a three-week period of leave, and the commissioned pilots would be eligible to marry. I do not recommend marriage prior to graduation. These young men will have their hands full just keeping up with the curriculum.

"Upon reporting back to base, the graduate pilots will begin to sharpen their skills. An eight-month period involving a hundred and sixty flights will be conducted entirely under combat conditions. Every takeoff, every landing, every briefing will be made under the assumption that hostilities are imminent. The same will apply to maintenance personnel. The pilots also will fight other types of aircraft—Saudi F-15s and Kuwaiti Mirages, for instance. Barring completely unforeseen problems, at the end of this eight-month period, our pilots in the F-20 should be able to defend Saudi airspace against any probable opponent. Frontline assignments will follow, with fifteen pilots and thirteen aircraft per squadron.

"We intend to plow back into the system about half of the outstanding Arab students to ease the instructor burden on our current IPs. This will be done on a rotational basis after we have identified those with talent and aptitude for flight leader and instructional duty. In this manner we will reinforce the self-sustaining concept for the F-20 program, building on each successive class."

Bennett gulped another mouthful of water. He was nearing the end of his first presentation, and knew his audience was intrigued by the program.

"In each of the first three squadrons there will be an American or British adviser who, though not officially the commanding officer, will possess nominal command. Lieutenant Colonel Lawrence will lead the first such unit, and over a period of time these leaders will be replaced by your own people. We will continue recruiting instructors as new classes are formed, and we expect to begin basic flight training every two months—sixty-five students each. At the end of three years there should be eight to ten operational F-20 squadrons, with a maximum strength of a hundred and thirty aircraft. By that point there is little question that your Tigershark pilots could defeat most air forces in the world, fighting against even odds. The F-20's in-commission rate should enable this force, if necessary, to meet or beat a larger enemy with a lower in-commission rate.

"At this point I should say a few words about the F-20 systems." Bennett glanced around, for he knew some men in the room would disagree with his proposal. "The Tigershark has a superb radar. It can distinguish buildings on the ground and even individual aircraft parked on a field from a considerable distance. But I do not intend to purchase many aircraft with radar." He raised a cautioning finger. "I'll tell you why.

"My own experience tells me that a well-trained fighter pilot can survive and win in combat without relying on radar. And because all major air forces now have powerful jamming capability, I'm convinced that the radar option will be denied both sides. That puts us back to square one. The battle will most often be decided by individual skill, training, and aggressiveness.

"However, to hedge our bets I'm recommending acquisition of radars in one-quarter of our aircraft. Selected students will be trained in its use—those most likely to become flight leaders. But the extra investment in training and resources would add nearly two years to our initial operational date if we were to go for one hundred percent aircraft and pilot radar capability. We can use low-cost part-task simulators for teaching switchology and radar technique, while our own radar-equipped F-20s—and maybe with help from some F-15s—should afford an adequate capability. But I stress again: In a major war neither side will have unimpeded radar. Victory will go to the side with the best-trained pilots who use their assets most intelligently.

"Finally, a word about maintenance. This is the overlooked aspect of military aviation, but it is the most crucial since all other factors depend upon it—training no less than combat.

"We expect a total of two hundred and fifty mechanics and other specialists to train under our maintenance instructors already on hand. We have identified sufficient other qualified people to expand the maintenance program at a rate equal to pilot training. Each student pilot class will have a parallel class of about thirty Arab mechanics graduate about the same time. In the beginning this will require pulling some of the existing Saudi mechanics off other aircraft—most notably the F-5 program, which, of course, is phasing out. Here again, we will return the better students to the system for use as instructors themselves."

Bennett paused and looked around the room. "Gentlemen, this concludes my initial presentation. His Majesty has told me we will break for lunch and resume the briefing thereafter."

There was complete silence. No one said a word—not the king, nor his air leaders, nor his ministers. Then Bennett caught Safad Fatah's gaze and the aviator recognized what he saw in the Arab's face; a wide-eyed realization. In this room John Bennett, American, had just laid down the key to the box containing the balance of power in the Middle East. "Tiger Force," as it would be called, could become a deciding factor in the future of this region.

Glancing about in concern, Lawrence turned to his friend and leader. He noticed that Bennett's hands were contracted tightly into fists. The redhead slid back his chair as if to rise, but did not, aware of the breach of decorum to stand before the king arose.

However, the movement stirred the Saudis. They slowly filed out behind their monarch and Bennett trailed after them. Lawrence matched him stride for stride, then could stand the silence no longer. "What's eating you, Skipper? I thought your briefing went very well."

Bennett walked a few more paces, then abruptly stopped. His gray eyes met Lawrence's. "I was just thinking. There was a French philosopher who said something I've never forgotten. He said, 'Be careful what you wish. It might come true.' "

Bahrain

Mild pandemonium was in progress in the Tiger Force auditorium. Men who had not seen one another in years grasped outstretched hands, shouted across the large room, or searched out old friends. Forty of the best fighter pilots on the planet were gathered to hear their commander brief them. But for the moment there were handshakes, loud voices, expressive hands, and laughter.

John Bennett walked among the men, greeting several and calling by name those he recognized. He particularly responded to those who once knew him as their squadron commander and still called him Skipper. Bennett warmly shook hands with Dennis "Masher" Malloy, late of the U.S. Navy's Fighter Squadron 143, and hailed George "Bear" Barnes, whom he had known during an exchange tour with the Marine Corps. Bennett also took note of a few others, recalling names and faces from the personnel folders. The second-tallest man in the room, after Barnes, was a former Air Force pilot with blond good looks—Tim Ottman. Bennett couldn't recall the man's callsign.

The Brits stood out from the crowd, both by dress and demeanor. Whereas most of the Americans wore well-used flight jackets, the former RAF and Royal Navy fliers were impeccably dressed in coat and tie or razor-creased tropical kit. Bennett made a point of greeting Peter Saint-Martin and Geoffrey Hampton, each sporting a regulation mustache.

Slowly the noise subsided as Bennett strode to the front of the auditorium and mounted the podium. Those who had never even seen a photo of the man instantly recognized his position. Anyone who had spent time in the military would describe Bennett's posture with the identical term: command presence. Bennett himself thought of the phrase as he looked out over the audience. Occasionally he told intimates that every leader has to be part entertainer. Some leaders are frightening entertainers, others are personable entertainers. Bennett could be either.

"Gentlemen, welcome. My name is John Bennett. Callsign, Pirate. I'm a fighter pilot." This elicited a ripple of enthusiasm and a scattering of applause from those who knew him. "Each of you can call me by my first name—Colonel." Laughter rolled across the audience. It was a familiar gambit, but a welcome one in this strange setting where so much was unfamiliar. It was also to be taken seriously.

Bennett allowed the response to die out, then continued. "This is a great opportunity for us and, I might add, a lucrative one."

A chorus of agreement washed over him. A couple of fliers

shouted, "It's about time!" Most of these men had pursued other careers but their first love was pushing a fighter plane to its absolute limits, outmaneuvering another man similarly motivated and similarly equipped. No other part of their existence so absorbed them. Bennett knew that, for some, this was a last hurrah. A last time to bend the airplane and see the other man out in front, to know that you were better than he. The feeling in the air was electric.

"Guys, I won't keep you here too long today. I know most of you are just getting settled in. But we're here to build the best air force in the world. It'll be a small one, but the product we turn out will be the finest on earth because you will make it so."

Bennett paused, wondering how much to pursue this line of thought. He decided on a short diversion. "We've all been to pretty much the same places and done pretty much the same things. I guess in a way that makes us special. Certainly it makes us different. I like to think that we know how to do what the admirals and generals and budgeteers wanted us to do—but usually wouldn't let us."

This brought a staccato rush of endorsement for the sentiment.

Bennett continued. "Well, the Saudis have given us the best chance we'll ever have to prove our point. We're going to make the most of it. By the time we're done, the bean-counters will know they missed a bet when they held us back. We're going to push our concept just as far as it will go—burning lots of gas, shooting lots of ordnance, and yanking and banking till hell won't have it." There was a smattering of applause. "In fact, I hope that at the end of two years—certainly four—we'll all be so damned tired of flying that we'll be glad to hang up our G-suits."

Bennett knew he had made his point. "I'd like to introduce Lieutenant Colonel Ed Lawrence. He answers to Devil on the radio. He's my exec and in charge of instructor training. Ed, stand up."

Lawrence raised himself from the front-row seat and waved laconically.

"Colonel Lawrence will distribute the schedule tonight. You'll begin groundschool day after tomorrow, after your jet lag wears off. Certain of us will take the role of students both in the simulators and upstairs, with two flights in each phase. My feeling is that by the time we each have about fifteen hops we'll be up to speed and ready for our first students. Most of the F-20 two-seaters have been delivered, and we'll have the first single-seaters in a couple more weeks.

"Now, this is important, so listen tight. Here in our compound and among ourselves we'll have the informality we're used to. But outside the compound, and especially among the young cadets and Arab officers, we *must* maintain a military bearing. One breach of etiquette means a warning and loss of a month's pay. A second time, even for a different offense like boozing or skirt-chasing, and you're gone with the wind, gentlemen. No appeal, no exceptions." He paused to let that sink in. Then he continued, with a lighter tone to his voice. "I've been reading the Koran as time allows, and that combined with close contact with the Saudis has shown me a few things." He paused to glance at his notes.

"The Muslim religion is a warrior's religion. Death in battle is exulted. One *sura* says it all: 'Prescribed for you is fighting, though it be hateful to you.' The faith is characterized by extreme fatalism, and this trait must be handled carefully when dealing with your students. Many Arabs believe that when your time is up, there's nothing to do but accept the decree of God. *Inshallah* is a phrase you'll hear often. It means 'God's will.' Naturally, this attitude does not go well with military aviation. You must impress upon these cadets that they can *never* give up, never quit trying.

"Another phrase you'll hear a lot is *mafi'misula*. It's the Arabic equivalent of *mañana*, meaning 'no problem.' There's a widespread tendency to let things slide, to go around them rather than solve them. It's a cultural difference we will have to deal with, firmly but tactfully. Westerners are far more direct than Arabs, who always want to exchange pleasantries first. Similarly, briefings and debrief-ings tend to be extremely lax in Arab air forces because it's impolite to praise one person over another, let alone to imply criticism. Consequently, you must *always* seek to balance your debriefs with something positive, to keep encouraging the students at every stage of the syllabus.

"We've arranged briefings to better acquaint you with Arab philosophy. But there's room for optimism. The students we're getting are barely more than kids, so their minds are relatively open and I'm assured there will be a minimum of culture shock. But get this: We're receiving the cream of this country's crop. I guarantee, if you produce for these boys, they'll break their hearts trying to please you.

"Overall, just one thing to remember tonight. The Arabs will respect strong, quiet men who lead by example. Polish up your Gary Cooper impersonation and you won't go far wrong."

Bennett looked around the room. He was confident he'd made his point. "All right. Last one to the bar buys the first round."

Colonel Bennett made sure he was the last to place his order.

Washington, D.C.

Secretary of State Thurmon Wilson was angered by the Israeli ambassador's suggestion that some obscure retired naval officer might be breaking the U.S. Code. Wilson pressed the button of his desk phone and asked his secretary to put him through to the Secretary of Defense.

"Ben, good afternoon. The Israeli ambassador just left my office in a huff about some of the U.S. citizens under contract to the Saudis. You recall it was discussed at the cabinet meeting last time."

The defense secretary listened to Wilson's New England accent with controlled petulance. *Oh, Christ,* he thought. *The Israelis again.* "Yes, I remember. We decided there was no harm in the arrangement."

"That's right," Wilson said. "But the Israelis seem especially interested in one man, apparently the leader. He's a retired Navy commander named John L. Bennett." Wilson spelled the name. "He's from the San Diego area. The Israelis seem to know a lot about him, and they suggest he may be in violation of U.S. Code."

"In what way?"

"Employment by a foreign military power, which technically could define him as a mercenary. But that's the broadest possible interpretation. If some lawyer wanted to push it, he'd make a case against every instructor or civilian tech rep we have outside the country. It wouldn't stick, of course, but that's the theory."

Benjamin Wake interjected. "Did the ambassador make reference to the Saudi F-20 buy?"

Wilson paused, uncertain of the aircraft designation. "Is that the airplane we discussed previously?"

"Yes, it's designed by the Northrop Corporation. Long ago we gave permits for export to most of the friendly third world countries and it's also in production abroad. It's called the Tigershark."

The Secretary of State remembered Tom Wolfe's description of the macho appellations given to combat aircraft: a mixture of sharp teeth, cold steel, cosmic warlords, and evil spirits. "Yes, that's the one. The Israelis are trying like hell to slow down the Middle East exports. They're lobbying heavily in Congress, you know."

Wake knew where this conversation was leading. "I know. But do you know how many people are employed by that company? The president said last week that with our balance-of-payments deficit and with the unemployment in Southern California, there was no way we could reduce foreign military sales. It's politically as well as economically unfeasible."

"So what about this Bennett character?"

"I just wondered if your Navy people could check up on him. You know, give me something to show the Israelis and prove we're trying to cooperate."

The defense secretary inhaled, held his breath, and closed his eyes. *Just what I need—another project.* "Thurmon, what the president said about national economics also applies to geopolitics. The Saudi organization that Bennett is building gives us leverage and political influence we may need badly in that region. Especially with the way things are going with the radical Moslem states."

Wilson decided on a direct appeal. "Can't you just go through the motions? Give me something to throw the Israelis and show our good faith."

"All right, Thurmon. I'll have one of my people get back to you in a couple of days. But I can tell you right now, we can't tell you any more about this guy than the Israelis already know. Christ, they probably can tell you what toothpaste he uses."

"Well, thanks. I appreciate it. Do you have any suggestions about the Israelis' concern regarding the Tigershark?"

Wake's tone was that of a schoolmaster lecturing an earnest but dull student. "You can tell them exactly what we said in the cabinet meeting. The Saudi versions have no radar so far and no radar-guided missiles. That makes them less capable than almost anything the Israelis already are flying. After all, that's why we approved the bird for export."

"Yes, well, thanks again, Ben. Always good to chat with you."

Tel Aviv

Lieutenant Levi Bar-El felt his cheeks redden in embarrassment. His chief and other intelligence executives had been polite, but he had been lectured on the importance of a sense of perspective, of establishing priorities. His section chief had hinted at that very topic not long ago, he recalled. But Bar-El had pressed right along, sending up smoke signals which had made their way to some very nervous politicians, already edgy about the international reaction to Jordon. He hadn't violated military etiquette, and he had only nudged the borders of military-diplomatic propriety. Now he realized that the people he talked to had in turn spoken to others.

"Lieutenant—" the colonel had begun.

Levi knew right then he was in trouble. Ordinarily Chaim Geller used first names.

"I agree with you that the foreign pilots and the new aircraft are a matter of potential concern. But you have other projects more pressing. Therefore, please do not allow the Saudi situation to become an obsession. Remember, we have the finest air force on earth. No matter how many American and British instructors the Saudis hire, our fighter pilots will handle the situation."

Still, Bar-El could not shake a sense of premonition. He knew that a good intelligence officer developed a sixth sense, and more often than not it proved accurate. He had studied the official color photograph of the man named Bennett, concentrating on the man's gray eyes. They held . . . what? Dedication, tenacity? That, surely, but something more. Bar-El inhaled. He wondered if the colonel had used the very word to describe this man. Obsession.

5

Bahrain

JOHN BENNETT APPROACHED THE SLEEK FIGHTER WITH his helmet tucked under his left arm. He wanted time alone to preflight the aircraft by himself, for in the two weeks since his briefing to the king and the Saudi ministers he had been too busy for his obligatory visit to the U.S. Embassy in Riyadh. But today he would fly an F-20—his F-20—to the capital. Bennett noted the name elegantly painted on the canopy rail; the king was as good as his word.

The weather was warm, even at 0700, and Bennett perspired _₁er his Nomex flight suit, G-suit, and torso harness. The ambient temperature was heightened by a hot wind. But he hardly noticed. He stood beside the two-seat Tigershark, aware of his heart beating slightly faster than normal. He savored the smells of the aircraft—a heady mixture of jet fuel, hydraulic fluid, and rubber. Almost self-consciously he glanced around to see if anyone was watching. He was supposed to be a detached professional, and such men aren't expected to be sentimental about the tools of their trade. *That's what the groundlings think,* he mused. *But they don't know, not unless they're aviators.* It was a point of pride that the U.S. Navy produced *aviators* while almost every other service in the world merely produced pilots.

God, it had been good. The sights, the aromas, the feelings all came rushing back. Sensations half remembered—or half forgotten—from his youth. Bennett had been out of the cockpit more than a decade, but many things had not changed. The tension of the G-suit around his thighs and abdomen, the good tightness of the gloves, even the irritation of a helmet pressing one's ears and forehead, and the flesh creased by the oxygen mask. Girding for battle. He imagined warriors had always felt these things, since the days they wore animal skins or chain mail.

But there was more. To impart to young men the skills that only a few ever master. To do something in his own nation's interest in this critical part of the world, Bennett felt an urgency and a newfound sense of excitement and anticipation beating in his chest.

"You look real tactical this morning," Ed Lawrence shouted.

Bennett turned, his reverie interrupted, to watch the redheaded flier waddle toward him.

We all look slightly ridiculous, he thought. *Like disembodied junction boxes, with our G-suit leads and oxygen hoses and radio cords dangling.* Which was exactly the case. Until a jet fighter pilot was fully plugged into his machine, he was simply an independent flight system, useless without his airplane.

"It's great to be getting back in the air, isn't it, Skipper?"

Lawrence ran an affectionate hand along the F-20's fuselage much as Bennett had done.

"Well, I've read the manual a few times through and you'll recall I did okay in the simulator."

The F-20 simulators still were being installed but Bennett had exercised his rank and qualified ahead of most pilots on the schedule. The Saudis would be the first third world country with flight simulators that showed the world outside the cockpit. They were tremendously expensive but invaluable for accelerating training. The computer-generated imagery which allowed students to experience earth and sky as well as the instrument panel previously was limited to nations which produced the systems, such as the United States, Britain, and France. One of the new simulators, with the academic software which went with it, cost almost as much as an "economical" jet fighter.

Bennett climbed into the front seat while Lawrence strapped, hooked, and plugged himself in the back. Lawrence already had twenty flights in the two-seaters and had overseen initial checkouts of two other instructors. As more aircraft arrived, that pace would accelerate.

Lawrence keyed the intercom: "All right, boss, you've got it. Let's fire up this hummer and get going."

Bennett glanced in the rearview mirror. He saw the exec's old helmet with three yellow stars representing his MiG kills over North Vietnam. Just like old times. *Now all we need is a flock of MiGs,* Bennett thought. He shrugged involuntarily. *Be careful what you want—it might come true.* After start-up Bennett smartly saluted the line chief and taxied to the active runway.

The hot sun radiated shivers of heat from the concrete as Bennett lined up on the centerline. Holding the brakes, he advanced the throttle to 80 percent of full military power. The Tigershark strained against the brakes like a hungry predator, and Bennett's legs trembled slightly from the pressure on the pedals. Satisfied the

General Electric turbofan engine was performing normally, he released the brakes and pushed the throttle into afterburner.

Though the F-20 weighed 15 percent more than the F-5, it possessed 70 percent more power. Seventeen thousand pounds of thrust were ignited as raw fuel was pumped to the TF-404's afterburner section, and 15,000 pounds of Tigershark rocketed off the runway.

Bennett was elated. He let out an involuntary war whoop as he was shoved back in his seat. Hauling the stick back, he kept the airspeed below landing gear limits, flipped the circular knob on the left of the instrument panel, and felt the wheels lock into place. Then he pushed the nose down to almost level, allowing the little fighter to accelerate. In seconds he had 400 knots on the airspeed indicator. He began an abrupt three-G pull-up and watched the altimeter reel off 5,000 feet before he could count it.

Bennett came out of burner and continued a less dramatic climb. He wanted to settle down and get his bearings before sampling the F-20's performance in other regimes. He made slight, deft movements of the control stick, performing four-point aileron rolls, left and right.

"Not bad for somebody who's almost eligible for social security," Lawrence rasped from the backseat.

Keeping the nose level, Bennett selected afterburner again and let the wickedly beautiful Northrop accelerate to 600 knots. Then he rotated the nose to 60 degrees above the horizon and sustained the climb to 40,000 feet. He came out of afterburner, marveling at the F-20's thrust-to-weight ratio.

Bennett keyed the mike. "Judas Priest, Devil, what have you got me into?"

"Uh, I sort of thought it was the other way around, Skipper."

"Well, considering my advanced age, and the fact I've been out of the saddle for ten years, this one-point-one machine takes some getting used to."

The F-8 Crusader they had both flown in Vietnam had almost as much thrust as the F-20's engine, but the Crusader weighted 25,000 pounds combat-loaded for air-to-air. That meant its thrust was about 70 percent of its takeoff weight. The Tigershark, like most other new fighters, had ten percent more thrust than weight—on the order of 1.1 to 1.

For the next thirty minutes Bennett knew again the wonder of high-performance flight. He rolled, pulled the aircraft through a six-G turn, and felt his body weight increased to over 1,000 pounds by the force of gravity. He flexed his abdominal muscles and grunted through the M-1 maneuver, which helped delay the onset of grayout. His G-suit inflated and gripped his extremities as if in a giant vise, keeping more blood in his brain than would be possible otherwise. It also allowed him to maintain vision longer, but inevitably the gray fog at the periphery of his sight grew larger, and twice he blacked out completely.

The old bod ain't what it used to be, sport. But damn . . . ain't this grand! The high side of fifty isn't so bad.

After a half-hour of remembered exhilaration, Bennett turned over control to Lawrence. As IP, the redhead contacted air traffic control and activated his flight plan to Riyadh. Bennett pulled out a notebook and reviewed air traffic control procedures as well as topics for his meeting at the U.S. Embassy. Glancing to the north, he saw a huge sandstorm developing and made a mental note. He would have to be sure the extra canopies and windscreens he had ordered were en route. Flying through blowing sand, Plexiglas became pitted, with reduced visibility in just a couple of years.

Bennett shoved his notebook back in the map case. *To hell with paperwork. I'm gonna fly.*

In the backseat, Lawrence felt the stick wobble in the familiar "I've got it" signal, and turned loose. Up front, Bennett tapped his gloved fingers on the controls, softly humming "Back In the Saddle Again."

Claudia Meyers entered the chargé d'affaires office in the U.S. Embassy and sought out a volume on the shelf. She found Title 37 U.S. Code and methodically searched through it. Leonard Houston, the chargé, had been called away and asked her to cover his appointment this afternoon. Claudia frequently covered for her superior, and in moments she found the section she wanted. She read it twice and marked it. There was no problem, but the procedures had to be observed.

Ordinarily the State Department would not have sent the daughter of a Jewish father and Catholic mother to a position in an Islamic nation, but Claudia Meyers was accustomed to breaking precedent. She had been programmed early for success, and attendance at a Catholic school with very high academic standards had prevented her from taking on a strictly Jewish identity.

Claudia's language ability had won her a succession of positions and the admiration of her superiors. She had learned French at home and was professionally fluent in Arabic. Though religious observance was not part of her upbringing, a shrewd early career move had brought her competency in Hebrew. Thus, she was well suited for Middle East assignments.

Her Anglicized surname, changed three generations ago from Meier, her creamy complexion, and her blond hair belied her more immediate heritage. From a distance she looked a decade less than her actual age of thirty-eight. Only closer could one see the tiny laugh lines either side of her hazel eyes.

There was another reason she was here. Claudia Meyers had requested Riyadh. She knew the Saudi capital was only growing in importance, and she had calculated three years ago that this would be a good career move. Having served in State for almost fifteen years, she had enjoyed the life-styles of Washington and Paris. Now she tolerated the medieval attitude toward women, which still included slavery, in exchange for experience.

Claudia picked up the dossier on Houston's desk and flipped through it again. She gazed at the official photograph of the former naval officer with the usual background of the American flag. He was dressed in a dark blue uniform, wearing the hat featuring what military men called scrambled eggs, and he bore six rows of decorations. She scanned the bare facts of the man's career, which she assumed had been successful by military standards. A fighter pilot, apparently, one of the glamour boys.

Claudia was not fond of military men—overbearing, egocentric macho types, mostly. She had dated a few embassy guards and attachés over the years and two or three had been charming. At least they were preferable to overbearing, egocentric wimps who populated most of the world's embassies. But on the whole, she found the talk of "force structures" and "tasking" deadly dull. There had been no man in her life since she had left the United States and arrived in Arabia, and she did not expect to search for one at the expense of her career.

The intercom buzzed. "Mr. Bennett to see you," said the receptionist.

As the door opened Claudia stood up and crossed the floor to meet her visitor.

John L. Bennett had changed into a lightweight summer suit with a yellow shirt which offset his tan. Claudia appraised him at a glance: five feet ten, graying hair, well built. They shook hands and he was impressed with the strength of her grip. He noted the Phi Beta Kappa key on the simple gold chain around her neck. Then he thought of the three yellow stars on Devil's helmet. *We all keep trophies*, he thought.

Bennett appreciatively observed Claudia's willowy frame and her beautiful legs. He decided that men would remember her bearing, her manner, and her husky voice rather than her face.

Claudia was unprepared for Bennett's cheerful nature. She wondered if he was always in such a good mood. The tan, the startling gray eyes, and the strong white teeth made a favorable impression. When she released her grip and invited him to sit down, she noted the creases on his face and across the bridge of the nose.

"I flew in from Bahrain," he said, taking a chair.

"Yes, I know." What was he getting at?

"Oh, I noticed your look at my face. I saw the same thing in the mirror when I was changing. The oxygen mask has to fit tight and it always leaves a mark for a little while."

"Then you didn't come by commercial airline?"

"Oh, no. I'm a fighter pilot. We hate to leave the driving to somebody else."

Claudia relaxed more. Bennett's comment provided a logical entry to the business she had to discuss with him. She was a firm believer in first impressions, whether good or bad, and Bennett made a good first impression. His easygoing manner, his infectious smile, and his appearance combined to put her at ease. Claudia was conscious of an immediate attraction to this man. He was not at all what she had expected of . . . what? A mercenary?

Mr. Houston had implied that the meeting with Bennett was more to placate the Israelis than to conduct actual business. Edward Lawrence was meeting with the U.S. air attaché while Bennett saw Claudia, so clearly State was covering the bases in response to pressure from elsewhere. But Claudia found she was enjoying the session.

From experience, she had expected Bennett to be defensive in discussing his dealings with the Saudis or to present a blustering facade. But he did neither. Instead, he answered her questions with a directness that she found refreshing.

"Commander, I've reviewed the facts of your contract with the Saudi government and there is no problem. I merely wish to confirm our understanding of the situation."

"I understand, Miss Meyers. Go right ahead."

Claudia folded her hands on the desk and learned forward. She was a student of body language and noted that Bennett leaned toward her as well. "You are helping the Saudis build an air defense force which—if you'll excuse the expression—will be separate from but equal to their existing air force. Is that correct?"

"Yes, that's right." He briefly explained the king's concern about maintaining the sophisticated aircraft already on hand, and their vulnerability to foreign embargo of parts and mechanics from the West.

"What do the Saudi Air Force leaders think of this situation? Aren't they likely to be jealous of you and your people?"

"That's one of the things Ed Lawrence is discussing with the air attaché," explained Bennett. "But I can tell you that the king has guaranteed my organization a free hand, clear of rivalries and intraservice politics." Bennett thought for a moment, wondering how far to carry his discussion with this diplomat. *What the hell*, he thought. *If she's any good at her job she'll already know the facts.* "I would not have taken the offer under any other circumstances. You see, service politics is one reason I retired from the Navy. I don't want to fight that battle again—in any language." He laughed, then added, "With any luck, I won't have to do so. *Inshallah.*"

Claudia shared the humor, secretly surprised and pleased that the aviator possessed a knowledge of Arabic philosophy. But there was something of the hunter about this man. In a strange way—new to her—it was an appealing quality.

Much to her surprise, after the interview Claudia noted that she had spent ten minutes more than the thirty allotted with Bennett. His grasp of regional politics and the importance of maintaining American influence in the region drew her increasing attention and admiration.

She escorted Bennett to the door and shook hands before leaving. Conscious of the pressure in his grip, she said, "I expect you'll get to Riyadh fairly often. Maybe I'll see you again."

Bennett's gaze held hers and she felt mild anger when her eyes lowered despite herself. *Two strong personalities, Claudia,* she told herself. *That could mean trouble.* Then she said, "Have a good flight back."

Bahrain

"These kids have come a long way in six months," Ed Lawrence said. "But do you think they're going to make fighter pilots?"

John Bennett glanced down the ordered rows of cadets. They wore neat khaki uniforms devoid of insignia except for the collar pins of the duty officers. Duty officer was a rotational assignment in each fifteen- or sixteen-man section in the first class. The duty allowed the instructors to gauge each cadet's leadership potential.

"We'll know soon enough," Bennett replied. "At least we weren't excessive in our estimates for preflight."

Lawrence agreed. Of the sixty-five students in Class One, all but two had finished the six months indoctrination and groundschool, though two more were being held back for Class Two because of marginal English fluency. Some of the others were borderline in mathematics and navigation, but overall the quality was high. The IPs expected forty or more to win their wings.

The Saudi drill instructor bellowed the order in the manner of drill instructors from time immemorial. The cadets snapped to attention, saluted the reviewing stand, and momentarily remained still. Their uniformly high state of physical fitness was evident from tensed muscles, even beneath their clothes. Preflight had invested heavily in cardiovascular development with running, step tests, and weight lifting. Even swimming was emphasized.

Now, Bennett reflected, these youngsters were in the best condition of their lives. He knew they would need that advantage to meet the challenge before them.

At the dismiss order, the students broke formation and were overcome in a sea of congratulatory shouts and gestures. Friends, family members, and cadets of the two newer classes crowded around to offer good wishes.

The two Americans walked into the shade of a pavilion after standing in the Arabian sun for the previous half-hour. They had wanted to make their presence conspicuous for the graduating cadets but neither was wholly acclimatized to the forenoon heat. They accepted iced tea from the waiter and found an unoccupied corner.

Lawrence downed half his drink in one gulp. "You know, Skipper, if you want to leave for a couple weeks I'm glad to fill in."

"Yeah, I think I will, Ed. I sure appreciate your taking up the slack. I guess I still feel guilty about not being there when Paul married his girl. Now that I'm a grandfather I really should go see the kids."

General Mohammad Abd Maila walked over, immaculate in dress uniform. He had been involved with formation of the F-20 program from the start but maintained a discrete distance from administration of the force. Both Americans regarded him as a friend of Tiger Force, yet wondered at the man's apparent inability to perspire. Offering his hand to Bennett and Lawrence, he said, "Gentlemen, my heartiest congratulations. I saw the scores of your first graduating class's academic tests. Seventy percent are above our target median. I really must have our training people consult with you."

"We'll be right happy to oblige," Lawrence said.

Bennett winced. *The guy talks like a Hollywood cowpoke. Who'd guess he grew up in Seattle?*

"General, I will be returning home to visit my family during the next two weeks. As you know, this class will be on leave for that period. Colonel Lawrence will supervise the preflight stage for the next two classes in my absence."

The Saudi turned to examine the youngsters. "Tell me, have you identified any of these young men as outstanding leaders?"

"Yes, sir, we certainly have. Two in particular. Rajid Hamir and Ahnas Menaf. Both are bright, well-motivated young men with excellent attitudes. They're extremely anxious to learn but they show maturity and self-reliance among their classmates. I would say they're the natural leaders of this class."

General Maila flashed a smile. "I am most pleased to hear of it, Colonel Bennett. You probably do not know, but Rajid Hamir is a nephew of Safad Fatah. I've known the family most of my life. I agree, the boy has much potential." He saluted crisply and walked away.

Lawrence looked at Bennett. "Did you know the Hamir kid was related to Fatah? I sure didn't."

"No. But it doesn't surprise me. Safad wouldn't want to give the impression to anyone that his nephew carried extra favor with us. It wouldn't have mattered if we'd known, of course, but I'm glad for Fatah's sake. He must be proud enough to pop his vest."

The redhead finished his iced tea. "That's ol' Safad's normal condition, from what I've seen."

"I wouldn't let the gentleman hear you say as much."

Bennett pondered the two cadets, both near the top of the class academically, both with considerable potential, but each so different temperamentally. Rajid, at nineteen, was shy almost to the point of being introverted. Studious and serious, he went out of his way to help classmates with academics. That alone made him popular.

Ahnas Menaf was two years older, more confident in himself. Unlike 99 percent of Arab men, he had no mustache, but with a demeanor approaching debonair, he was admired by the younger cadets for his image. Bennett knew from academic records that the lad had ability. Time would tell whether the image fit the man.

. . .

BENNETT CAUGHT THE COURIER FLIGHT TO RIYADH
that evening. He had made a dinner date with Claudia Meyers; he
had allowed just enough time to be with her before his departure
for Rome and on to the States.

When Bennett arrived at Claudia's door she was fully prepared
to go. He admired that about her. Each time he had called upon her
in the previous six months—twice at the embassy and once at her
apartment—she had been prepared. No shuffling of schedules, no
role-playing delays to make him wait and demonstrate his desire to
meet her terms.

They took a taxi to a nearby restaurant but Bennett declined a
full meal. "I'm reading up on jet lag. It says you're not supposed to
have much protein when traveling. Which is kind of tough on a
confirmed steak-and-potatoes man."

"Surely they'll feed you on the plane."

"Yeah, I think so. By the way, I had to get an earlier flight to
make connections for a nonstop from New York to San Diego. I
leave ninety minutes earlier than planned."

"Oh . . . I had hoped we'd have more time." Her voice said as
much about her disappointment as her words.

Bennett was pleased to know their rare visits meant as much to
her as they did to him. A brief, awkward silence fell upon them
as they studiously scanned their menus. Each felt that the other
wanted to say more. Bennett had just screwed up his courage when
the waiter approached to take their order. Claudia rattled off a
long string of Arabic with obvious ease and the waiter bowed, then
left.

Claudia smiled across the table. "I ordered for both of us. I
hope you don't mind."

"Not a bit. Thanks. This is still new to me, you know. I don't
get out very often—"

"Neither do I." She glanced down, then returned her gaze to Bennett. "It's awfully difficult for a single woman to develop a social life outside her profession here. I knew that when I came, but the reality of life in a Muslim country still can be a cultural shock to a Western career woman."

Bennett wondered if she was as lonely as he, and decided she probably was. It was one more thing they had in common, aside from the growing physical attraction between them.

They discussed embassy gossip, regional politics, and Bennett's son. Claudia recalled a previous reference to Paul, and listened with interest as the aviator related his not entirely satisfactory story of the young man—a premature marriage and a child.

Claudia was relaxed enough to ask a personal question. "How are they going to get along like that? I mean, marriage is hard enough at any age, let alone in college. But with a child as well . . ."

"I've arranged a trust for them, only to be used in emergencies. They don't even know about it. My attorney will notify them should the need arise. I guess it's best for Paul and his wife to have to make it on their own. If they do succeed, their marriage will be stronger for it." He paused, gathered his courage, and looked into her hazel eyes. "Claudia, have you ever considered marriage?"

She blinked, hesitated an instant, then felt relieved. *Now we're getting somewhere.* "I don't mind telling you I've had two proposals, John. I turned down both of them. The first was in college, the second a few years ago, from another foreign service officer. Neither would have worked. The first time, I was at UC Berkeley and got caught up in the excitement of the political activism, but we were too immature for marriage."

"I have a hard time imagining you as immature."

Claudia suppressed a smile. "Well, all right. *He* was too immature, caught up in radical politics. If he knew I'd defected to the establishment he'd demand return of the Che Guevara poster he gave me."

"And the second guy wanted you to join him on a hardship post in Sierra Leone, right?"

"Not quite. We were both in Washington at the time. But our careers were competitive. It just wouldn't have worked." She shot Bennett a sly glance. "How about you? Ever think of remarrying?"

"Not seriously. After Elizabeth was killed in the car wreck I had my hands full raising Paul. He was in high school at the time and a little wild. He needed all my attention."

"That's about what I'd expect of you." Her tone was both admiring and sympathetic. "But surely there were plenty of eligible ladies in La Jolla."

"Oh, sure. I was out of the Navy by then but I still knew lots of women. Cruise widows we call them, wives whose husbands are at sea. Actually it was a pretty tame arrangement. I'd help them with repairs around the house and they'd fix me dinner once in a while."

Their meal arrived and Bennett cautiously tasted his entrée. It was a rather bland mixture of vegetables with small portions of meat which he seasoned to his own taste.

She said, "Go ahead, silly. It's safe. It's lamb stirred into a mixture of herbs and vegetables. I'd tell you the name but you'd never remember it. Just trust me that it's what a traveler needs."

Half joking, half serious, Bennett said, "I don't remember what the Koran says about mixing cuisine. Guess I'll have to read up on it during the flight home."

Claudia leaned her chin in one hand, regarding Bennett with increased interest. "I wouldn't have picked you as a student of religion."

"Well, normally I'm not. But when I was asked to consider this job, I studied a synopsis of the Koran and have read most of it in translation. I'm just trying to see things from the Saudi viewpoint."

"What do you make of the writings of the Prophet?" Claudia was on firm ground—she had read the Koran in Arabic twice. All one hundred and fourteen *suras*.

"Most of it's pretty heavy going. For me, anyway. The organization makes no sense, if I understand it right. You know—the short, easily read *suras* last, which I think were written first. And the imbalance between the Meccan and Median revelations. No wonder it took Muhammad twenty-one years to get all of the text. He must have hardly known which parts came in what order."

Claudia smiled. "Remember, he was beloved of God. When he was gone—"

"Yeah, 632 A.D."

"When he died in June 632," she went on, "the *suras* were written from memory and organized by the caliph Uthman, who had scholars prepare a definitive version. Enough people knew the writings by heart that it could be done."

They continued discussing the holy book until it was time to leave. Claudia realized Bennett's interest in regional politics had led him to an understanding of the rift in Muslim doctrine: the Shiites believing that only direct descendants of Muhammad, through his daughter Fatima, could lead Islam; the Sunnis adopting a case for individual merit, much as tribal leadership was decided. Though Shiism was the decided minority in the Arab world, it was the dominant sect in Iran. By contrast, Iraq's population was nearly evenly divided while most other nations—Egypt, Syria, Jordan, and Saudi Arabia, to name the more prominent— were Sunni.

Conversely, Bennett was impressed with Claudia's detailed knowledge of the historical Koran: the comparison between Biblical figures described in the Old and New Testaments—Noah, Moses, Abraham, and Jesus. It occurred to him that the three great religions spawned in this volatile region had as much in common as they had to dispute.

Bennett escorted Claudia home and stepped inside just long enough to kiss her decorously on the cheek. But he felt her press close against him and her hand went to the nape of his neck. He wrapped his arms around her, their mouths met, and he felt her lips part in the beginning of a long, delicious kiss. Then he turned to go.

"John." He glanced over his shoulder. "I pray that you have a safe trip and a wonderful reunion with your son. *Fii amaah illaah.* Go in the care of God."

"Masaa' il-khayr," he replied, touching her cheek. Claudia laughed appreciatively before closing the door. "Good evening" was more a greeting than a sign of leaving, but it mattered little. John Bennett offered possibilities that Claudia Meyers had not considered in years.

Jidda

The morning after Bennett's flight left for Rome and New York, Safad Fatah met with two other Saudi officials. He was very un-Arabic in his direct manner.

"Our pilot training program is proceeding on schedule. The first class completed preliminary instruction this week, and two more classes have entered the same phase. It appears we shall have our hundred and fifty F-20 pilots in barely two years with the rapid curriculum."

Tewfig al Aziz, the economics specialist, expressed cautious concern. "That is as we expected, it is not? But how long will it take until all of those pilots are qualified for combat? And what about the maintenance personnel?"

Fatah raised a placating hand. "The instructors still insist that each pilot should have two to three years experience beyond post-graduate training. That is, after the eight months following graduation from flying school and commissioning as officers. I do not dispute that claim. Nor do I take for granted the quality of our support people. Clearly, we must continue to rely upon our contract foreigners for quite some time. But the important thing is, we should have adequate numbers of trained Saudis in flying and maintenance positions to tide us over. If relations are broken with the Americans in eighteen months, we can draw upon our own resources for pilots and many of the technicians."

Aziz shifted his tiny coffee up. "Very well. What then about the additional aircraft?"

"That is why I wished to meet so soon. His Majesty has asked me to report on our options to lease or purchase the machines currently held or ordered by other nations." He looked to the third man.

Ali Abd Musad was a forty-nine-year-old retired air force officer who had been a Saudi attaché to Ankara and Rabat. Fatah had chosen him two years before for a long-term project which, in fact, might never come to fruition. But in the meantime, if the need arose, Musad's exceptionally fine contacts could prove invaluable.

"Our options are good to excellent," Musad said. "As you both will recall, the Turks were willing to appear reluctant to accept two squadrons of F-20s, insisting they preferred more advanced aircraft. This in turn caused Washington to offer favorable terms in exchange for Turkey accepting the Tigersharks. Since the U.S. extended trade credit in order to allow the Turks to complete the agreement, it is satisfactory to all concerned. Deliveries are scheduled to begin later this year, but Ankara has made it clear the F-20s are only an interim measure. Once economic conditions permit, the Turks will press for F-15s. Under that condition, we have applied to be the ultimate user in a contingency, but should an emergency develop we shall buy the Tigersharks in any case."

Fatah allowed himself a moment's admiration of the man. Musad had been an indifferent pilot but had shown an exceptional capacity for Machiavellian politics. His behind-the-scenes contribution to his nation's defense far outweighed his service in the cockpit two decades ago.

Aziz caught Fatah's attention, pursuing Musad's line of thought. "We have assured Ankara that our purchase of the aircraft will be at least eighty percent of the contract price. But since the Turks will not be paying in full anyway, the arrangement actually could be profitable for them. They will continue to fly their Phantoms and other machines, so there should be little attrition among the F-20s should we need them."

Fatah wrote a memo on his notepad. Without raising his eyes, he said, "Good. Now what about the Moroccans?"

Musad leaned back, at ease and confident. "That situation is even better. The end-use certificate specifies that those F-20s may only be transferred or sold to a nation already flying the type. It's different from the Turkish contract, since there exists the possibility that Greece might buy some Tigersharks. Between Turkey and Morocco, we can maintain a twenty to thirty percent reserve for our own F-20 force. And I have established contacts with both air forces—and perhaps the Sudan or South Korea—for extra spare parts in the event of an embargo."

Still writing, Fatah asked, "And what is the projected U.S. reaction if we exercise these options before an arms embargo? That is a possibility we must consider."

Musad's face was passive, in contrast to Aziz's. "I should say it depends upon relations between the Americans and the Israelis at the time. You may have heard that Israel provided Skyhawk parts to Argentina during the Falklands War, and Phantom parts to Iran in order to keep the pressure on Iraq. Neither exchange, to my knowledge, was approved by Washington. Yet there was almost no criticism."

"But you know the Jewish influence in America." Aziz's voice had a brittle edge. "It is endless, there is no bottom to it."

Musad was about to reply that he could not blame any nation or group that acted from self-interest. It was the way of the world. Fatah looked up from his notes. "Yes, that is so. The Israelis can do almost anything they wish where the U.S. is concerned. They can spy on Americans, they can lobby against American interests in the U.S. Congress. They have even killed Americans with impunity." He looked over the top of his bifocals. "They cannot produce oil for the Americans. But we can."

6

THE INTELLIGENCE OFFICES WERE NEVER EMPTY.
Staffed around the clock every day of the year, they operated
smoothly as each eight-hour shift alternated or—increasingly—
overlapped. Colonel Chaim Geller flexed his legs, walking down the
hall. It had been a long day in a long month. The occupation of
Jordan continued to require much of his time, even with reduced
military activity in that unhappy land.

Moving past the cubicles on either side, the once-sunburned
archaeologist pondered his dissipating tan. He seldom got outdoors

during daytime anymore. The shift had changed two hours ago and, working overtime, he noted with mild surprise the lamp on young Bar-El's desk remained on. Looking closer, he realized the reserve lieutenant was still there.

"Levi." The young man glanced up. "Here I thought we had said good-bye hours ago. Your active duty ended this afternoon."

Levi Bar-El shifted slowly in his army issue chair. Geller realized his protégé ached as much as himself. "Oh, yes sir. You know how I'm obsessed with this Saudi case." *I'm leaving today*, he thought to himself. *No need to be diplomatic. Not until next year.*

The section chief walked over, peering at the papers on the desk. He could not suppress a pleased grin. "By God, Levi, you may not be entirely objective yet, but you're hell for persistence." He made a special effort to pat the lad on the shoulder. "Something new?"

Holding up a report, the lieutenant said, "Our friend John L. Bennett was in America for almost two weeks and now is en route back to Arabia. Evidently the graduation of his first class from groundschool allowed him a short vacation."

Geller scanned the related papers from the file. "It seems they're serious about building this F-20 force. Well, for better or worse they'll probably have time to make it operational. I've not revised my estimate of six months ago."

Bar-El stretched his arms, slumped back, and mussed his curly black hair. "I remember. You said a relatively quiet two years or more. The Air Force staff thinks they will have to deal with these Saudi F-20s eventually."

The colonel dropped the file on the desk. "At least there's time to make plans. The Islamic fundamentalists still have to sort out their internal problems, consolidate their gains, and try to decide how to take us on. I believe their newfound unity has bought us a breathing space. If in fact they are consolidating their national and religious objectives to apply mass against us—"

"The correct procedure," Bar-El interjected.

A teacherlike wave of the finger. "You're learning. But if they are in fact consolidating and planning along those lines, it will take much effort in Iran, Iraq, Syria, and Lebanon."

"So you think they'll continue harassing us, building their military strength, and working diplomatically as well."

Geller said, "Absolutely. The imams must know by now they cannot afford another major loss. But some of them are dogmatic enough to think twice about dealing with the Soviet infidels. It may take time to overcome that attitude about unbelievers, especially after Afghanistan. But eventually pragmatism will win. Next time they'll choose the proper moment and try to do it right."

Bar-El scratched his head. His eyelids felt heavy. "Then what can we hope for in the meantime?"

There was the faintest trace of a smile at the corners of Geller's mouth. "I myself would prefer a miracle. A change of human nature. But lacking that, you know sometimes miracles are the product of a lot of hard work."

Bar-El's face was expressionless. Sometimes he did not understand his chief at all.

"More bickering among Sunni and Shiite, perhaps even some shooting along the South Yemen border." An eloquent shrug. "We'll just have to wait and see."

Bar-El cocked his head to one side. The colonel thought he looked just like a curious puppy. "Do you mean we—"

"Levi, Levi, my young friend. Surely you realize I mean nothing. And in our line of work, even nothing can be highly significant. You've heard the phrase 'negative intelligence.' " The colonel winked, then heartily clapped Bar-El on the arm. "Enjoy yourself in Ashqelon, and save some fish for me."

Levi Bar-El stared at the retreating form of his section chief, pondering the myriad meanings of mere words.

Bahrain

Ed Lawrence rapped on the door at 1030 hours.

"Come in."

The redhead opened the door and stepped into John Bennett's three-room suite. Lawrence noticed the unmade bed, baggage piled in one corner, and a Browning Hi-Power pistol disassembled on a newspaper on the floor. Bennett emerged from the bathroom, dressed in khaki shorts, a white T-shirt, and sandals. "Hey there, Ed."

"Welcome back, Skipper." They shook hands. "Two weeks passes pretty fast, doesn't it?"

"Sure does. Actually, I got back late yesterday afternoon. Went straight to bed, and I'm still catching up on my jet lag."

"Yeah, I heard Masher and a couple of the guys saw you drag in here. Figured you'd hole up and recuperate." Lawrence sat down in the vacant chair. "So tell me. How's it feel to join the geriatric set?"

Bennett sprawled on the bed and rested his hands behind his head. "Ed, I have a granddaughter. Six pounds fourteen ounces at birth, now up to about ten pounds. She's going to have gray eyes, I think." He smiled widely and Lawrence saw the twinkle of pride in his friend's own gray eyes.

"How are Paul and his bride doing?"

"Oh, pretty good. Paul's decided to major in engineering, and I told him electronics would be a good future. So I expect he'll go for an EE. His wife's been working at a day-care center in Mesa so she has a good handle on children. I'd say they're doing all right. No gravy, but all right."

Lawrence pointed at the disassembled pistol. "New shootin' iron, I see. Nine millimeter—thought you were a .45 man."

"I am. But .45 ammo's tough to get in quantity in this part of the world. So I looked up a buddy of mine in Phoenix. He's a naturalized South African gunsmith. I told him what I needed and he worked overtime to modify this Browning." Bennett picked up the receiver and handed it to Lawrence. "See, he's enlarged the thumb safety and polished the feedramp. The trigger lets off at about three and a half pounds. Also, he installed high-visibility sights."

Setting the frame back on the paper, Lawrence asked, "Why the concern with ammo? Couldn't you bring a couple boxes of .45 for your Colt?"

Bennett lanced his exec with his best instructor's stare. "How many rounds of twenty mike-mike did you fire in banner gunnery?"

Lawrence was perplexed. "Hell, I don't know. Must have been thousands and thousands with all those gunnery detachments to Yuma and everywhere. I remember Hoser McAllister got frustrated on his third or fourth hop and burned out all four barrels one time, trying to saturate the banner in one pass."

"Yeah—that's why they call him Hoser." Both men laughed.

Bennett pressed his point. "Okay, you and I and every other F-8 driver burned up case-lots of ammo in practice. But how many rounds did you fire in combat, air-to-air?"

"Exactly two hundred eighty-three, on my second MiG. So what's the point?"

"You just answered the question, sport. Getting proficient with a handgun or rifle's no different from aerial gunnery. You shoot a lot more in practice than in combat. So instead of trying to bring a few thousand rounds of .45 ACP here, I got a gun to match the local situation. The Saudis can supply all the nine millimeter I can use."

"You really expect a shootout?"

"Well, I'll put it this way. If I don't have a shootout, I'm paranoid and healthy. If I *do* have a shootout, I'm prescient and healthy. The operative word is *healthy*." He grinned, knowing he had made his point. "Besides, it'll make a good impression on the cadets to see the head honcho taking his turn on the pistol range. Now, how are things shaping up for the flight program?"

"Real good. The first class started F-20 academics yesterday. We're sticking to the modified GE syllabus, alternating between classroom lectures and do-it-yourself study with the display consoles. We'll start giving indoctrination rides next week. Keep their interest up."

"Good deal. Are the IPs up to speed on the schedule?"

"Affirmative. A couple guys have questioned the accelerated pace of flight training but they seem to buy the reasoning."

Bennett had expected that. He recalled his own early instruction at Pensacola—the days lost to marginal or poor weather in the gulf climate, the remedial or make-up flights just to stay current. He and most of the Navy-trained instructors had periods when only ten or twelve flights were possible in two months. But Arabia's clear weather allowed flying almost every week of the year, provided it was scheduled early enough in the morning.

Lawrence got up to leave. "I'll tell the guys you're back aboard. We can get together with the different class IPs for lunch, dinner, and an evening session. I'll set it up for today and tomorrow." He walked to the door. "Oh, by the way. Did you see your lady diplomat when you came through Riyadh?"

"No. I called but she was out at some meeting. Why?"

"No reason. Just some lecherous snooping. You going to see her regularly, do you think?"

Bennett was mildly irritated; Lawrence had a way of making one's personal matters his own. Bennett wondered if it was because the exec had so few close friends himself. "I expect to see her again. When time allows."

"She's quite a bit younger than you, isn't she?"

"As a matter of fact, she's about sixteen years younger. We get along together despite such a vast age difference." His voice was tinged with irony. It also said, *Proceed with caution*.

Recognizing the danger signal, Lawrence flashed a brilliant white smile and a big thumbs-up. "Outstanding." Then the door closed behind him.

THE NEXT SIX MONTHS PASSED QUICKLY. THE FIRST class began dual instruction in the F-20B, flying in the mornings and continuing academics and physical conditioning in the afternoons. The second class of cadets completed indoctrination and ground school, and there was another ceremony when the preflight stage was completed.

Bennett was immensely gratified at the young pilots' progress. Ahnas Menaf, one of the standouts from Class One, was the first to solo. His instructor, Tim Ottman, said the last four of the scheduled fifteen presolo flights were unnecessary. "I won't say the kid's a natural," Ottman had told Ed Lawrence, "but he catches on real quick, and he retains what he learns." The IPs in each section held a solo party for the students to mark the event. It was a relatively sedate affair by Western standards, but Bennett and Lawrence knew it reinforced morale among the Saudi students.

The F-20 program seemed to be proving Bennett's theory: Military flight training could be far simpler, less expensive, and more efficient than most air forces allowed. But Bennett did not intend merely to monitor the students' progress, nor rely wholly on the observations of his instructors. He kept his finger on the pulse of the budding Tiger Force, and he knew the best way to do that was by flying.

GEORGE BARNES WAS A SIX-FOOT-THREE FORMER MA-rine corps aviator; a pleasant giant who tipped the scales at 225 pounds in fighting trim. His size and build had earned him the nickname "Bear." It had been his radio callsign from the day he reported to his old Phantom squadron. As the sole Marine among the IPs he was constantly beset by cheerful insults from the Navy and Air Force pilots. But to Barnes, 39 to 1 meant even odds.

Sitting in the operations office, tapping the eraser end of his pencil in time with "Semper Fidelis" on his portable tape recorder,

Barnes seemed lost in thought. He was gazing out the window to the flight line and did not see Bennett walk in from the opposite side of the room, across the counter.

"Hi, Bear. Still listening to mood music?"

Barnes glanced up. "Hello, Colonel. Yup, guess it's in my blood. I think I was eleven years old before I realized 'The Marines' Hymn' wasn't the national anthem."

"Sure, I remember now. You're second-generation jarhead."

Bear straightened in his chair. "Damn straight. My daddy retired as a master gunnery sergeant."

Leaning conspiratorially across the counter, Bennett whispered, "Listen. I wouldn't want this to get around, but I applied for the Marines myself back in Pensacola."

Bear squinted suspiciously. "Oh?"

"Yup. But when they found out my parents were married I was disqualified on the spot." Both men laughed. It was an old joke, probably as old as the Corps.

"All right, Skipper. What can I do for you?"

"I got caught up with my paperwork and figured I'd combine a proficiency flight with a look at how one of the cadets performs. They're all soloed now from Class One."

Bear reached back to the wall, pulled a clipboard off the rack, and scanned the pages. "Once an ops officer, always an ops officer," he said with a moan. He had the operations desk this month, an assignment held in rotation by those IPs not yet flying with students full-time. "Sure, you could put in some time with one of the boys in an extra hop. You'll have to make it clear it's not a checkride. A lot of these A-rabs get real skittish about that sort of thing." He put down the first clipboard and thumbed through the aircraft availability chart. Two-seat F-20s still were arriving, and the allotment was not yet filled. "I'm not sure there's a B model available right now. Maintenance is busy with the new birds, checking them out."

"Well, my lad, how about 001? You remember—the bird our employer, His Highness in Riyadh, so kindly purchased for my sport and amusement? Last time I flew her, she still had my name on the canopy rail."

Barnes bowed and touched his forehead. "I hear, your magnificence, and I obey. I'll have the wrenchbenders put 001 on the ramp for an 0630 launch. Any particular student you want to fly?"

"Anybody who's not slated for academics. I want to fly with at least three students per class from now on. Which section is free in the morning?"

Barnes flipped through yet another clipboard. "Second section is off. The section duty officer is Halid; alternate is Hamir."

"Good. I'll take Rajid Hamir. I hear good things about him."

Bennett walked into the ops office at 0545 next morning, already dressed in flight suit and boots. He carried his G-suit, torso harness, and helmet bag, preferring not to wear them until ready to fly.

Rajid Hamir was already there, scratching earnestly at his paperwork on the table provided for flight planning. He rose when Bennett entered, and stood at attention.

"Good morning, Mr. Hamir. Ready to fly?"

"Yes, sir. I am preparing the forms now."

Bennett smiled, setting his baggage on a chair. "You know, about the time I got out of the Navy, we said that you couldn't fly until the paperwork equaled the empty weight of the airplane. I like it better here, where all we need is a flight plan and takeoff data."

"Sir, I am computing the takeoff roll and weight-and-balance figures."

Bennett looked over the student's shoulder. The flight plan was complete, with each square neatly filled in. Noting the youngster's circular computer, Bennett sat down and tapped Rajid's calculator watch. "You go ahead and finish the density altitude, but I'll show you its effect when we're airborne."

Density altitude was especially important to flying in the Middle East. In hot climates, basic physics dictate the amendments to the law of gravity. The molecules in warm air expand apart from each other, contrary to cold-air molecules, which crowd together for comfort. Consequently, hot air generates less lift than cool air because the molecular density is not as great.

This phenomenom is called density altitude. An aircraft taking off from an airport at 1,100 feet above sea level, with a temperature of 115 degrees Fahrenheit, uses the same length of runway as during a standard day at over 5,000 feet. But not only takeoff is affected. Every flight regime—climb rate, dive recovery, turn radius—is similarly affected.

Fifty minutes later the two-seat fighter was airborne, tucking its tricycle landing gear neatly away and accelerating into the cooler upper air. Flying in the front seat, Rajid demonstrated what he had learned thus far: turns, climbs, and descents. Bennett noted the boy's movements usually were smooth and precise. There was little tendency to overcontrol, despite the Tigershark's sensitive boosted controls.

"All right, Mr. Hamir. I've got it." Bennett wiggled the stick in the instructor's cockpit to indicate he had control. "You remember what we learned about density altitude? Well, watch your altimeter. We're at fourteen thousand five hundred feet, straight and level at three hundred fifty knots. Ordinarily the airplane will complete a split-S in about five thousand five hundred feet under these conditions. Here we go."

In one fluid movement Bennett rolled the Northrop on its back and pulled the stick into his stomach. The little fighter plummeted downward, recovering into level flight on a reciprocal heading from its entry. "What does your altimeter say?"

"Seven thousand six hundred feet, sir."

"Correct. That was a three-and-one-half-G pull-through, and we lost about seven thousand feet. So you see the effect of density altitude, even up here in cooler air." Rajid's helmet bobbed up and down, indicating comprehension.

"Very well," Bennett said, "take us home."

Rajid looked over his left shoulder, clearing himself for the port turn. He reefed it in tighter than the standard-rate turn he had been taught.

Bennett was pleased. *Kid likes to pull Gs. Outstanding.*

They entered the traffic pattern on a forty-five degree angle into the downwind leg. Rajid lowered gear and flaps, set up his approach speed, and hit his turning points for base leg and final within fifty feet of prescribed altitudes. "This will be a touch-and-go," Bennett radioed.

The tower acknowledged.

Rajid's touchdown was within the first third of the runway, slightly right-hand tire first. He let the mains settle on, allowed the nose to settle slightly, and advanced the throttle. Lifting off, he accelerated into a nose-high attitude, retracted gear and flaps, and turned left onto the crosswind leg.

Bennett shook the stick again. "I've got it this time. I'll show you something about this bird's slowflight characteristics. Now, what controls airspeed?"

Rajid thought for two seconds. "Pitch and power."

"Right. If you have zero pitch, or angle of attack, what happens?"

"You fly faster. For the same throttle setting you fly faster. If you reduce power you lose altitude."

Bennett turned onto the downwind leg, leveling off at pattern altitude. "Now, you know that you can maintain a steady rate of descent at a given power setting with a certain pitch angle. Like you do on final approach to landing. But you can also fly slowly while maintaining altitude with a bit more power."

Rajid just nodded, uncertain where this was leading. Bennett had discussed the situation with Rajid's instructor, being careful not to upset the boy's training. Now he demonstrated his point: Anyone can fly fast. It takes an *aviator* to fly as slowly as possible.

"Mr. Hamir, I'm pulling the nose up thirty degrees. We'll start to settle at this reduced power setting, won't we?"

"Yes, sir. Unless we add more throttle."

"Exactly right! So here we go." Bennett carefully jockeyed stick and throttle until the F-20 settled into a nose-high attitude, maintaining level flight. "We're doing about a hundred and thirty knots, and I'll see if we can keep that speed all the way down." At each ninety-degree turn he lowered the nose slightly, avoiding the natural tendency to bleed off airspeed in the corners.

"You see there? By leaving the throttle alone, we're controlling our airspeed and rate of descent with pitch. If I set this up right, we'll maintain this rate of descent onto the numbers."

With the nose cocked up, the Tigershark came around on final with the gear and flaps still retracted. Bennett extended the wheels and flaps immediately after rolling out on final approach, adjusting stick and throttle to compensate for the increased drag. He maintained the nose-high descent almost to the runway lip, flying the airplane onto the white-painted numbers well below normal landing speed.

"Now, Mr. Hamir, why do you suppose anybody would want to do what we just did?"

"Well, sir, to land as short as possible."

"Right again. But your training has told you never to fly low and slow near the ground. It's dangerous, and accounts for a lot of landing accidents."

"Yes, sir." They turned off at the first taxiway and headed for the ramp.

"So what do you make of this demonstration? Am I teaching you bad habits?"

Rajid was quiet for a moment. "Sir, I believe this is an exercise to build proficiency."

Bennett liked what he was hearing. *Good lad.* "And all the students will learn to do this. It's unlikely they'll have to land that short on any runway, but knowing you can do it makes you more comfortable in the airplane. Just don't do it on your own yet—you'll get to it in a few more flights."

Bennett walked away from the F-20 and the quiet young Arab, feeling about as good as a flight instructor can feel.

Riyadh

The door opened and Bennett caught his breath. Claudia wore a knee-length yellow silk dress, her legs outlined against the thin fabric. Her long hair fell free, unrestrained by the ribbon she normally wore. It was the first time Bennett had seen her in anything but a conservative business dress.

She greeted him with a quick hug, then led him to her small dining alcove for coffee. Bennett decided the apartment was much like its occupant: organized, direct, stylish. He had only seen as much of it as was visible from the doorway twice previously, most recently several months ago when they had dined together before he had left for the States.

They sat down and Claudia poured some coffee. Handing him his cup, she looked him squarely in the face. "You flew in with a fighter plane again?" He noticed a peculiar expression on her face, a jesting tone in her voice.

"Yes, I delivered our maintenance supervisor for a meeting. Why?"

Claudia suppressed a girlish giggle. "I was just thinking about the first time I saw you. The marks on your face from the oxygen mask. They're not as noticeable this time."

He leaned far across the table, his face within six inches of hers. "Maybe you're just getting used to being around fighter pilots." He could smell her perfume again. Their noses touched.

Claudia leaned back. "I guess you're flying more often now."

Bennett said he was and she caught the gleam in his eyes. This was obviously a man committed to his work. He told her about his flight with Rajid and about some of the other students. The first class was now into its formation-flying stage, and the second had just started dual instruction. The pace was accelerating.

After a time Claudia suggested they move to the large sofa in the living room. The afternoon shadows were lengthening outside. They sat close to one another and Claudia leaned casually against the padded couch. "John, we've known each other for, what? About eight or ten months?"

He thought for a moment. "Yes, about ten."

"I was just thinking. Even though we haven't seen each other very often, I can talk to you. And I hope you don't mind a personal question about your work."

"Not at all."

"I know, or at least I've met, a lot of military people. I go out with some of them on occasion but I don't date anyone regularly. But in your case, I just wonder why you'd want to go back to doing the same thing you did for twenty years. I mean, coming all the way to Arabia and starting an air force when your family is back in the States."

Bennett thought a moment. "This is actually a lot more than just a job, Claudia. I've thought a lot about what kind of person I am to run off halfway around the globe when my son was getting married and I was becoming a grandfather.

"I'll put it this way. Being a fighter pilot, a professional warrior, isn't just something I do. It has more to do with who I am. It's not even a life-style—it's, well, an identity."

"I hope you didn't think I was being critical," Claudia said.

"No, no. I'm plenty critical of myself. But maybe it's programmed in my genes. Maybe I had no choice—I had to be a warrior."

Claudia looked perplexed. "You mean Robert Ardrey's *Territorial Imperative* and all that?"

"Well, not exactly. But some of my relatives might agree. You see, my family is from Florida, and we've always had military men in the clan. My uncle was a Navy ace in World War II—that made a big impression on me. But my great-grandfather was the real influence. Great-Granddaddy Bennett was a wealthy plantation owner who also taught mathematics at the college level. He wasn't obliged to go to war—"

"You mean the Civil War?"

Bennett put on a stern face and spoke with an exaggerated Colonel Culpepper accent. "No, ma'am. Ah mean Th' Wah of South'n Independence."

Claudia laughed.

"Anyway," he continued, "the old gentleman went into debt to form and equip his own artillery unit. He had no military training but he was damn good at it, and by war's end he was a colonel in command of a regiment. When I was a kid I read some of his letters that my grandfather had kept. It didn't fall into place until years later, but some of Great-Granddaddy's comments came back to me.

"In 1864, after almost three years of war, the old boy wrote his wife that he was actually enjoying himself. I wish I could remember the exact phrase, but he said that leading men in battle was the grandest feeling he ever experienced." Bennett turned somber. "When the South surrendered, it broke his heart. He died a couple years later."

Claudia leaned closer. "And you feel that way about leading men into battle?"

"It may seem peculiar, but I've always distinguished between combat and war. There's a difference. I don't know of anybody who likes war, or the causes of war—greed, envy, ambition, or just plain stupidity. But I wish I could feel the way Great-Granddaddy did about his war. Vietnam was mine—four combat deployments in seven years. For most of us, victory was simply surviving. Down deep, I suppose I regret that my war wasn't as . . . satisfying as some others." He had almost said *as fun*.

Claudia gave him a tight-lipped look. But her eyes revealed a willingness to understand him. "So, you're vicariously living your misspent youth all over again, here in the pay of the king of Arabia."

"There may be something to your analysis, professor." He touched her hand. She did not move it away. "But mainly, this offer lets me continue to do what I think I do best. And some of the friends of my youth are here. It's not exactly the same as when we were in our thirties, of course, but I know this: Any professional fighter pilot would trade his front-row seat in hell to be with us."

Claudia's professional instincts took over. "What effect do you think your air force will have in the region?"

"It's hard to say; I just don't know." Bennett concentrated hard on his thoughts. "Maybe the F-20 force, if it's allowed to grow to maturity, can help stabilize things. If I make some contribution to the Saudis, maybe they'll be able to help moderate the harsher Arab states. They've done it in the past. I hope the king will be able to use his money and influence on some of the radical governments in the area. Especially those that want to throw the Israelis out of Jordan. I know things have been pretty quiet there, but it can't last indefinitely."

Bennett was voicing thoughts he had seldom expressed. "I really hope, though, that Tiger Force—that's what we're calling it now— can prevent the involvement of U.S. forces in this region. We've seen it for so long, Claudia. The '67 war, Beirut, *Stark,* and *Vincennes*. On and on. Americans get killed over here because of ill-defined goals or just bad luck. I saw that sort of micromanagement up close in Vietnam and I want to help prevent it from happening again."

"Obviously, State shares your sentiment, as do I. But you know,

John, the king really is becoming a captive of the Muslim radicals, and he remains in power only because they haven't organized to unseat him. The moment he becomes of little use to them, with his influence abroad, you can bet his regime will fall." She lowered her voice without realizing it, continuing in an almost conspiratorial tone. "I'd have to deny I said this, but there's evidence the king is serving as a back-channel intermediary between some U.N. committees and the Arab hard-liners. Everyone seems to hope there'll be a negotiated settlement leading to Israeli withdrawal from Jordan."

Bennett pressed her hand. "Do you think there's a chance?"

The hazel eyes lowered and the blond head shook ever so slightly. "No, I don't."

Bennett looked off into space for a moment, then turned to her again. "All right, young lady, fair is fair. Now let me ask you a personal question."

"Okay."

"What's a good-looking girl like you doing on a day like this with an old fighter pilot like me?"

Claudia licked her lips and John thought it must have been a nervous reaction. "At first it was curiosity. As I said, I've known lots of military people in my career. But you were different. I guess you described the difference yourself. You are a warrior. Most of the others—attachés and embassy guards—just wear uniforms.

"Then, as I got to know you more, I found there was more depth to you than I thought. Probably that night before you returned to the States, when we discussed the Koran. That's when I decided you were more than an airplane pilot. You were somebody I wanted to know."

Outside, the capital city was gathering itself for the late afternoon ritual. Imams called the faithful to prayer from the minarets for one of five daily prayers which devout Muslims always make.

Claudia rose. "We've been sitting too long. We could dance if you like." She knelt beside her stereo and flipped through several albums. Finally she selected one, set the record and tone arm in place, and turned back to Bennett. She held out her arms. "Here we go."

Bennett stepped toward her. "What's the song?"

"You'll see."

They met in the middle of the room, pressing close together. As the first strains washed over them, John closed his eyes. "Oh, wow. You can pick 'em." They began to move.

"I'd almost forgotten 'Moon River,' " he said. The languorous strains filled the room with a pleasant dizziness. Bennett pressed his face close to Claudia's, savoring the silky texture of her blond hair and the fragrance of her skin.

He spun her around and they danced in silence. . . .

It was evening when Bennett quietly slipped from Claudia's bed. Without disturbing her sleep, he padded from the room and picked up the phone on her desk. After a short delay he talked to the Saudi sergeant who was to have met him this evening. He left instructions to be picked up at the embassy at 0830 next morning. Then he eased himself back into bed, pressing close to Claudia and thanking Whomever had smiled on him.

P A R T ★ I I

Death was our new trade. We
were training to be professional
killers

—Brigadier General Chuck Yeager

Yeager, Bantam Books, 1985

7

Bahrain

THERE WAS A NOISY CHATTER AS THE FORTY INSTRUC-
tor pilots settled themselves in the auditorium that night. They
arranged themselves comfortably among the cushioned seats with
folding-arm writing platforms. Each IP occupied two or even three
seats to accommodate himself, his texts, and his notepaper.

Colonel John Bennett strolled down the aisle, pausing occasionally to exchange a word with one of the fliers. Then he climbed the
podium and tapped on the microphone. In moments he had everyone's full attention.

"Gentlemen, I know you've been over this material before, and I know a lot of you are tired from flying two hops today. But it's important that we review this phase and coordinate our syllabus on vertical maneuvering. As you know, the F-20 is ideally suited to fight in the vertical plane, and we want to impress the students with that fact from the beginning. You guys whose students haven't reached the tactics phase can benefit from this discussion and file it for later reference."

A mustached flier with flaxen hair raised his hand. Bennett nodded to him. "Peter?"

"I don't wish to seem provincial, old man. But when it comes to combat maneuvering, one only wants a bit of viffing to get the job done. Works every time."

This sparked laughter in the ranks. Peter Saint-Martin, one of the British instructors, had flown Harriers much of his career. *Viffing* was derived from an acronym for "vector in forward flight" —adjusting the jet nozzles of the "jump jet" to move vertically or laterally without banking the aircraft. Peter had shot down two Argentine helicopters in the Falklands, matching the helos maneuver for maneuver.

Bennett dimmed the lights from his console, focusing the men's attention on the screen behind him. "Here you'll see the basic syllabus for this phase," he said. "It's the same material as written in your instructor's booklet."

He picked up a pointer and ticked off the maneuvers each student would have to master. "The cadets are now familiar with offensive and defensive maneuvers in the horizontal plane. You guys report that nearly all of them are proficient in these matters, and they understand the theory of energy management."

"Good, maybe they can explain it to me." This brought a chorus of laughter. Bennett wasn't sure, but it sounded a lot like Tim Ottman, the wisecracking Air Force veteran.

In jet fighters, inertia or momentum is characterized as energy—

high airspeed or altitude which can be converted to energy. The objective of a pilot is to "manage" his energy state, lest he find himself at a disadvantage. However, there are times when he desperately wants to reduce his energy, forcing an opponent behind him to overshoot and therefore become vulnerable.

A Navy pilot spoke volumes when he said, "Nothing is true in tactics."

"You've dealt with lag pursuit and displacement rolls," Bennett continued. "This, of course, is the logical introduction to the vertical maneuvers we'll be teaching in this next phase. Be sure you emphasize to your students that we're dealing with identical concepts here, but we're moving them from the horizontal into the vertical. We want to strive for consistency at this phase, so it'll all come together for the students later on. Basically, we're indoctrinating the cadets without telling them so. Eventually they'll make the discovery themselves, and that means they'll have learned the lesson. I know that's how it worked with me!"

The red-and-blue ribbon diagrams projected on the screen were familiar to everyone in the audience. As in most military services, red lines signified the enemy, blue meant friendly. The lag pursuit and displacement roll diagrams showed how an "energy fighter" could overcome an "angles fighter," despite the latter's better turning ability. One used airspeed (energy) to turn out-of-plane from the opponent, timing the maneuver to arrive inside the radius of his turn at a favorable position to shoot. Like so much in aerial combat, it was a simple concept which was difficult to employ without substantial experience.

Bennett poked his pointer at the items he wanted to stress.

"High yo-yo, low yo-yo, and vertical rolling scissors. You should stress that with the high thrust-weight ratio in our airplane, our pilots are cutting their armory by at least half if they ignore the vertical performance. There's a natural tendency in young studs to hang in there, pulling the big Gs in a wrapped-up turn, trying to 'macho' it out with the other guy. Repeat that a turning fight may be okay in a one-on-one situation, but when there are other bogies around, they're going to become the meat in the sandwich in a level turn. They'll bleed off energy and get low and slow, and that's nowhere to be."

Bennett discussed a few points relative to each maneuver, then quickly reviewed what he had covered. Ten minutes later he brought the lights up and asked for questions. There were none, which is what he expected.

THE NEXT MORNING TIM OTTMAN WAITED FOR HIS SEC-tion of five students to gather in the briefing room. The husky, blond New Yorker draped his six-foot frame over a writing chair and nonchalantly exercised a bright yellow yo-yo as the cadets filed in. The toy caused some querulous glances and one or two amused grins.

"Good morning, gentlemen." Tim's distinct New York accent—which Masher Malloy insisted on describing as a speech impediment—took some adjustment for the Saudis. Ottman was always careful to speak deliberately, a habit cultivated years before as an F-15 instructor at Luke Air Force Base.

"Sit right up front where you can see clearly."

The IP continued working the yo-yo up and down, occasionally flipping it straight out at waist level before reeling it in. Once he was certain the Saudis' attention was focused on the yellow spool, he began his introduction.

"Gentlemen, this is a yo-yo. I don't know why it's called by that name, but it doesn't matter. As you see, it goes up and down." He hadn't stopped manipulating the toy since the students entered the room. "But it does other things, too. Allow me to demonstrate."

Ottman stood up and paced back and forth. With practiced ease he let the string out nearly full-length until the yo-yo rolled along the floor. "This is called walking the dog," he explained, strolling behind it. "You can call Rover back with a flip of the hand." Ottman whistled to the yo-yo, retrieving it while calling, "Here, boy. Heel." It was a masterful display of skill. And of education. Ottman knew that the best way to teach any subject was to entertain the student.

Placing the toy on the desk, Ottman said, "You might wonder what all this has to do with fighter tactics. Well, before long you're going to be yo-yoing yourself, in an F-20. You'll use your vertical performance to go almost straight up and straight down—almost like the gadget I just demonstrated."

Ottman turned on the slide projector and focused the light on the screen at the front of the room. He flipped to the first slide. "This is the purpose of what we call the high yo-yo. It's to prevent you from overshooting your opponent. You're turning with him, maybe forty degrees off his tail but inside his turn radius. You're overtaking him because of excessive speed, and in a couple of seconds you'll slide outside and lose your advantage. If you stay in a level turn with him, he's going to start beating you."

Ottman advanced the slide carousel. "So here's what you do. Instead of continuing to turn in his plane of movement—horizontally— you roll wings-level and pull up. Not a lot of pitch-up, but enough to turn out-of-plane." The slide showed the attacking fighter climbing above the bogey, which continued its turn. "What you're doing is equalizing your forward movement with his. Your climb stops the rate of closure and prevents you from making an overshoot." He flipped the selector again.

"Now, with both of you at about the same rate of forward movement, you are high in his rear hemisphere. While he continues his turn, you are gaining separation from him. You have room to play with. You roll into him, maintaining your arc across the top of his turn. But don't get hasty." He advanced the slide tray once more.

"This is the hard part," Ottman said carefully. "Timing is

important. When you get the separation you want, you regain the energy you expended in your pitch-up by diving to the inside of the bogey's turn. How hard you pull depends on what you want to do. If you're going for a guns pass, you commit slightly ahead of him to pull deflection. If you want to kill him with a missile, you go for the high-percentage shot and lag him a bit—let him extend farther out so you finish close to his six o'clock, well within firing parameters."

Turning off the projector for a moment, Ottman spoke directly to each student in turn. "There are a couple of common errors in playing the high yo-yo. You want to avoid excessive pitch attitudes up or down, because that will throw off your timing when you commit into him. There's a tendency to begin the maneuver too late, when the overshoot is well developed. But"—he held up a finger to emphasize the point—"once you're nose-high in his rear hemisphere, the range will open fast, allowing him to extend away from you for separation. In that case, you've prevented an overshoot but you've gained nothing. You have to start over again, without your initial advantage. So remember, the timing and degree of pitch-up will determine how well your yo-yo works."

The IP turned on the projector again. "I'm not asking for questions yet, gentlemen. This is just an introduction to these maneuvers. But I want you to remember that the yo-yo can work low as well as high." The next slide showed the attacking fighter losing position to the bogey. "Now, in this position, you can use a low yo-yo to increase your closure and angles advantage. That is the opposite of what the high yo-yo did for you, but the principle is the same. By rolling low into the other man's turn, you get a gravity assist by going downhill. When you reach approximately the same heading as his, you can pull up, under his tail, by cutting the corner across his turn. This has the additional advantage of masking you from view. He's likely to get nervous and wonder where you went. If so, he may ease off his angle of bank to look for you. While he's doing that, you can gain position on him.

"A point to remember: Don't plan on winning the fight with a single yo-yo, either high or low. It's unlikely you'll gain proper position *and* closure rate simultaneously in one evolution. If you get greedy—if you try for too much too soon—you stand a chance of depleting too much energy or of allowing the other guy to gain separation. Then he can take it away from you. So here is the rule of thumb. Two small yo-yos, either high or low, are safer than a single big yo-yo. Conduct the fight in stages, maybe starting with a low yo-yo to close the range, followed by a high yo-yo or barrel roll to gain a better angle. Of course, if you're in a good position to kill him after your first move, don't waste time trying to sweeten up the shot. Usually quicker is better when you have the choice—it lets you get back to scanning the sky around you."

Ottman continued his introductory lecture for another forty minutes. He described the intricate arabesques in detail—vertical rolling scissors, displacement and lag rolls, almost everything the student pilots had done in the horizontal. But now they stood their previous world on end and contemplated the offensive use of the Tigershark in the pure vertical. The third dimension was becoming real to them.

"There's something else I want you to think about," Ottman added. "Up to now you've been concentrating on outmaneuvering an opponent, to get in position to shoot him. But if you play it right, and with a bit of luck, you won't have to engage in a prolonged hassle. Your aircraft is tremendously agile." He yawed the F-20 model's nose rapidly side to side. "You can point and shoot as well or better than any fighter now flying. Master that, with forward-quarter missiles, and you'll be way ahead of the game."

The blond IP set the model down. "You are going to work on each of these maneuvers," he concluded, "starting with a couple of simulator sessions to learn how the bogey should appear to you when things are done right. For now, though, remember the most important thing: Your airplane flies just as well straight up as it does straight and level." He glanced at his watch. Two or three minutes remaining. He produced his yellow toy again.

"Now, gentlemen, who wants to master the yo-yo?"

Washington, D.C.

"Mr. President, halfway into your term, your job rating from the American public stands at barely fifty percent approval. What do you make of that?"

Walter Arnold squirmed slightly in his chair. *Damn it, stop fidgeting*, he told himself. *Makes it look like you're cornered*. Which he was, in a sense. He had granted a rare one-on-one interview to Trudy Willard, much to the delight of her network. But Arnold's decision had been based on his perception of the TV journalist, an old hand around the White House. Christ, she'd gone on-camera to report Carter's concession in '80 with visible tears in her eyes. She was supposed to go easy on liberals. Jerry Butler, the presidential press secretary, had said as much.

"Well, I'll tell you, Trudy," Arnold began, recovering his composure. "That means I'm holding my own. It's almost identical to my victory margin in the last election."

Nicely done, Mr. President, conceded the interviewer to herself. *But I'm not the fluff peddler you expected, am I?* Actually, both individuals were getting what they wanted: Arnold proved his accessibility and Willard could stick another feather in her bonnet.

"I'd like to ask about the Middle East, Mr. President. What can you say about the continuing crisis in Jordan?"

That's more like it, my girl. "There's cause for both encouragement and alarm there, Trudy. Encouragement because at last, after two years or so, the various parties are talking to each other. But I see cause for concern because the Israeli forces in Jordan are coming under increasing harassment from the unoccupied areas. It's still a tense situation, and we're working hard to keep everybody talking to each other . . . ."

Bahrain

"Who's the honcho in the robes?"

Ed Lawrence pointed toward a throng of Saudis showing considerable deference to a man in flowing *mishlah* and *ghotra* with the traditional *jambia* curved dagger at his waist. Bennett glanced to his right, squinting in the bright sunlight. "That, my boy, is our employer of these past two years. King Rahman of Arabia."

"Oh, yeah. I remember he promised to award wings to the first class. But it's still hard for me to ID people in their native duds."

Bennett groaned, glancing around to be sure nobody overheard his exec. Occasionally Bennett had seen the king in immaculately tailored business suits, contrary to the monarch's predecessors. Acknowledging Rahman's temperament and need to balance himself between two poles—tradition on one hand and racing events on the other—Bennett admired the man's sartorial versatility.

More than 200 people occupied the seats and covered bleachers arranged on the flight line. Most were there to see their sons, brothers, cousins, and nephews graduate from pilot training. But no Saudi women were present—some things just didn't change.

Others represented the embassy community—predominantly Arab and Western diplomats and attachés. Though low-key throughout the previous two years, the F-20 program had drawn much professional interest. Now that the first class was graduating, there was speculation as to how the assets would be employed. People had picked up Bennett's phrase, Tiger Force. He had designed a patch and had his personal aircraft repainted. Now 001 sported a wicked shark's mouth on the nose and glaring eyes around the gunports.

The two Americans walked to the pavilion reserved for IPs and maintenance staff near the announcer's platform. The instructors wore their Nomex flight suits with brand-new name tags standardized for a more orderly appearance. Velcro-backed Tiger Force patches flashed their orange and black colors from the left shoulder; orange ballcaps and polished black boots completed the outfit. It wasn't entirely regulation, but it looked more uniform than the hodgepodge of U.S. Air Force, Navy, and British gear the IPs had worn previously.

As the announcer asked the guests to take their seats—speaking alternately in Arabic and English—the forty-one graduating cadets stood to attention by their chairs. Bennett reflected on the composition of the class. His estimate of two-thirds completion had proven surprisingly accurate. Over the previous two years, including preflight, twenty-four of the original candidates had fallen short.

Also gone were three of the original instructors. Two had found the prolonged regimen in an Islamic culture too confining and had backed out. The other withdrew owing to family problems back in the States. Replacements were quickly found from Safad Fatah's pool of alternate applicants.

The accident rate had been within limits, considering they were taking fresh students and putting them in a frontline fighter from the first day. The airplane was uncommonly forgiving and the engine superb. Five F-20s had been lost in two years. One of the single-seaters had suffered a disconnected throttle linkage and the engine had gone to idle power. The pilot had no choice but to make a controlled ejection; he'd been rescued unharmed. Another had gone down with its student pilot during a solo aerobatics flight. Judging from witnesses' report, the young man had initiated a split-S from too low—he evidently misjudged the density altitude. Two losses were attributed to GLoC—the unavoidable G-induced loss of consciousness present in all modern fighters.

Two months previously, during a tactics flight for dissimilar air combat training, a two-seater had collided with an F-15 Eagle. Both aircraft were destroyed; the Saudi Eagle pilot was killed. The IP in the Tigershark's backseat ejected with minor injuries but the student was badly burned by jet fuel which ignited on bailout. Several other students washed out of the advanced phase, having proven they could fly the airplane but were poorly adapted to a high-G environment. Two of these were retained when offered the chance to recycle as maintenance officers.

The remaining tigers had done well—most of them uncommonly well. And God, did they push the airplane! There had been several minor scrapes, but the students learned from their mistakes. Each was wiser for his errors.

Having established a baseline of evaluation criteria with the first class, the IPs expected to do better with the second. The next batch, graduating in two months, probably would produce forty-three to forty-five pilots—enough for three full squadrons. Two squadrons would be formed from Class One, with the overflow being diverted at first to instructor and maintenance-engineering slots. From these men would come the future leaders of all eight to ten Tigershark squadrons. In the meantime, senior Saudi pilots from F-5 units were transitioning to F-20s, though the IPs would remain closely affiliated. The king and Fatah were concerned with retaining the independence and "purity" (the word was Fatah's) of Tiger Force.

The band struck up the Royal Saudi Anthem and everyone stood during the short instrumental. Then the announcer—a gifted twenty-year-old linguist from the second class—called the spectators' attention to the left front. Six F-20s started engines in succession and taxied in formation to the end of the runway. Lawrence glanced at Bennett, and they exchanged wry grins. Masher Malloy, looking uncharacteristically regulation, arched his eyebrows and rolled his eyes suggestively. Tim Ottman raised one hand, his fingers crossed.

Bennett whispered to Lawrence. "How much practice did you say the guys put in?"

Lawrence raised the fingers of one hand.

"Five hours?"

"Five flights."

"Sorry I asked."

At almost the last moment, Safad Fatah had passed along the king's "suggestion" that an air show be part of the ceremony. The IPs had already planned a formation fly-by, but the Saudis wanted something more. Against their better judgment, Bennett and Lawrence had assembled an impromptu aerobatic team of six instructors.

Fortunately, there were four experienced air show pilots on the staff: Bear Barnes had been the lone Marine on one Blue Angels team; an Air Force pilot named Brad Williamson had flown with the Thunderbirds; and two British pilots were veterans of the RAF's spectacular Red Arrows. A U.S. Navy and Air Force man were selected as solo pilots. It had not been possible to work up a really quality routine in the limited time, with instructor duties thrown in.

Geoffrey Hampton, the precise Briton who had been a contract Jaguar pilot for Oman and the senior Red Arrow, was designated team leader. He had worked out a twelve-minute routine which minimized formation aerobatics and stressed the F-20's performance. There had been time for just one full rehearsal, including the announcer, before graduation day. Now, huddled at the end of the runway, the team heard Hampton key his mike.

"Brakes off—now." Four Tigersharks accelerated together, lifting off and shifting smoothly into diamond formation. The two solos made a section takeoff fifteen seconds later, occupying the crowd's attention while the four positioned for the first pass.

The show was routine as military flight demonstrations go—but impressive nonetheless. The Tigershark's performance was dramatically illustrated as the first soloist flew across the field in landing configuration at 140 knots. His partner overtook him from behind at 450 knots, lit the afterburner, and rocketed into a series of vertical rolls almost out of sight.

The first solo pilot had positioned himself for a low pass at Mach .92. Many of the spectators never had experienced the phenomenon of near-supersonic flight, and the effortless grace of the Northrop's passing—split seconds ahead of its own sound—prompted murmurs in the stands.

There followed a demonstration of the F-20's low-level maneuverability. The second solo pilot screeched over the field at 510 knots, lit his afterburner, and rolled into a vertical bank. Pulling a constant six Gs around the turn, he made two circuits—720 degrees—then climbed straight up. He was joined overhead by his partner, awaiting the diamond four.

As the six jets touched down and taxied to the ramp, knowing glances were exchanged among the IPs. *Whew—we got away with it!*

Bennett picked up a valise and walked to the announcer's stand. He arrived just in time, as the young Saudi announcer was sticking to the schedule his notes required. Mounting the platform, Bennett looked at the crowd. Standing behind him were the students, arrayed in perfectly ordered rows.

The announcer briefly introduced Bennett, then handed him the microphone. Addressing the king, Bennett spoke slowly and clearly for the benefit of all present. "Your Majesty, it is my privilege to present to you the graduates whom we honor today. These young men have worked as hard to earn their wings as any pilots I have known in any nation. We, their instructors, are immensely proud of them."

The king, striding forward, seemed to glide in his elegant robes. He warmly shook Bennett's hand and, in precise English, said, "Colonel Bennett, your organization also is honored this day. You have completed the training of the first class on schedule, and we acknowledge the second and third classes which will graduate later this year. You gentlemen from the United States and Great Britain have accomplished all that you set out to do. I have no doubt that your professionalism will be admired by all those present today."

Bennett recognized the latter statement as a mild rebuke to the doubters who insisted the accelerated schedule could not be accomplished. The king now regarded Tiger Force as his own, and no one could deny that the program had succeeded. The first class had achieved the equivalent of more than two and one-half years work in barely two, including indoctrination and preflight.

The instructor for each section of students stood by the rostrum as the announcer called each name in turn. Flanked by his IP, the student watched as the sovereign picked a set of wings from the large felt pillow and pinned them on the khaki uniform. A hearty handshake, a few heartfelt words in Arabic, and the young man stepped off the platform as a commissioned officer.

Bennett took a moment to speak to most of the students. He made a special point of talking to Rajid Hamir and Ahnas Menaf. Each had been identified as potential leadership material. Menaf, more self-confident than most, was among the best stick-and-rudder men in the class. He would go directly to work in the instructor's class, ready to pick up the third class late in its syllabus.

Bennett naturally warmed to Hamir. Clasping the twenty-one-year-old's hand, he could not conceal his pride. "Mr. Hamir— Rajid—you can be proud of yourself. You've done very well in training and I think you'll have a fine career."

The young man smiled shyly, blinking back the emotion he felt. He introduced his father and brothers. Bennett was surprised when Rajid mentioned his fiancée. There had been no previous indication the young man intended to marry. Eventually Bennett added it up: The marriage had been arranged when the couple still were children. He did not realize such things still were done. *Well, live and learn*, Bennett thought. "Congratulations, Rajid."

"Thank you, sir. She will be a good mother for my sons and I hope she will be happy as a fighter pilot's wife." Rajid looked left and right, then leaned close. "Even if it may not be what she hoped for."

Bennett thought better of pursuing that line of conversation. "You know that after your first squadron tour you'll return as an instructor if the force needs to expand."

"Yes, sir. I am pleased with both opportunities."

"Lieutenant Colonel Lawrence and the other IPs selected eight of you for that duty. We have warned everyone against overconfidence; there's still eight months of operational training in the squadron, and flight leader upgrade. But pilots like you and Mr. Menaf—excuse me, *Lieutenant* Menaf—will be the basis of Tiger Force's future. It's a big responsibility, Rajid. But you can handle it."

IT WAS LATE AFTERNOON BEFORE BENNETT AND MOST of the IPs could disengage from the reception and displays. Two F-20s, including 001, were available for inspection while student pilots from Class Two took turns answering the litany of questions. Bennett had just untangled himself from the French air attaché to Saudi Arabia when Lawrence tapped him on the shoulder.

"Somebody's looking for you."

"Is that good or bad?"

The blue eyes sparkled. "Oh, I'd say good—very good." He pointed to a corner of the hangar. "Close enough for a visual?"

"Affirmative."

Claudia only recognized Bennett as he drew near. She had never seen him in flight suit and ballcap—somehow he seemed to belong in those clothes, in this place. She extended her hand.

Bennett resisted the urge to hug her. It was not permitted in public. "Claudia. I'm really glad you could make it. I got your note."

"It was uncertain until almost the last minute. But Mr. Houston had to represent the ambassador so I hitched a ride." She shifted her glance. "Do you know Colonel Mallon? Glen, this is John Bennett."

The Air Force officer shook hands with Bennett. "Sure, we've talked a couple of times at the attaché's office. You've done a fine job here, Commander." An earnest smile. "Wish I could trade my desk for one of those F-20s."

Bennett appreciated another airman's discomfiture with a ground job. "Don't you get to fly?"

"Not nearly enough. I was an Eagle driver at Langley, long ago and far away. Sometimes I beg a ride with the local sports, but it's not the same." Bennett liked Glen Mallon.

The attaché glanced at Claudia and set his lemonade on a tray. "I'd best mingle with the politicos. See you both later." Bennett decided Mallon would have to take an F-20 ride soon.

"Can you stay for a while, Claudia?"

Her voice was low, almost conspiratorial. "I arranged to stay for two days. The others are leaving tomorrow morning. I'll have to write a report on the trade mission here, but I can do that from memory. Besides, the embassy feels guilty about asking me to postpone my vacation. I planned to spend my fortieth birthday with my parents but we're short-handed."

Bennett had almost forgotten—9 October was two days away. "That settles it, then. You'll have your birthday cake here. The IPs and some maintenance guys are celebrating graduation tonight. Can you come?"

"Are women allowed? I mean, how much mingling can you do?"

Bennett laughed. *Mafi'misula.* No problem. We have our own compound here. It's a lot more relaxed than in Arabia. As long as we keep the animals in the zoo, there's no sweat. We're even allowed booze—with British bartenders. In fact, there's quite a few British girls as well—plus Irish, New Zealanders, and some Europeans. Nurses, mostly. Health care is a big item here."

Claudia seemed relieved. "So I wouldn't be the only woman?"

Bennett leaned close. "You are the only woman for me."

"You know that's not what I mean." Her face reddened.

"All right. There are a few wives, too, mainly Brits."

"Okay, I accept. You'll have to pick me up. I can't go unescorted, you know."

"It's a deal."

THE HORSESHOE-SHAPED BAR WAS CROWDED WITH SIXTY flight and maintenance instructors and a few guests. The noise level was tolerable, not quite drowning out the attempt at harmonization of four pilots who occupied the jukebox corner.

> *He's flown the Foxtrot Two-Zero*
> *From L.A. to Riyadh and back.*
> *There ain't a fighter that flies in the sky*
> *He's afraid of or that he cain't hack.*
>
> *They taught him to fly down in Texas,*
> *Sent him to Nellis Air Patch.*
> *Got an airframe to mark, it's called Tigershark*
> *And the plane ain't been built she can't match.*

Bennett edged his way to the bar, ordered iced teas for Claudia and himself, and guided her by one arm. They stopped briefly to talk with Peter Saint-Martin and his wife Lynn, a tall brunette from Buckinghamshire. Then Claudia noticed the squadron badges adorning the wall. Intrigued, she walked over to inspect them. Each represented the donor's previous units, most being enamel mounted on shield-shaped wood backgrounds.

It was an impressive display. Claudia noted the 64th and 65th Aggressors from Nellis. There was the red-starred insignia of the Navy adversaries, the Bandits and the Cylons, and the mailed fist of the Challengers. There were the Silver Eagles from Luke and their partners, the Triple Nickel of the 555th Tactical Training Squadron.

And from Topgun and the Air Force Fighter Weapons School. One and all, artists in the realm of aerial combat, teaching it to the new sports or duplicating the opposition.

Bennett let Claudia take in the collection, silently pleased that she found it interesting. She turned to him. "It's fascinating, so colorful. It's almost like medieval heraldry."

"Some of it is taken directly from legitimate heraldry, like VC-13." He pointed to the gold fleur-de-lis emblem of Navy Composite Squadron 13.

> *He'll taxi up into your saddle,*
> *Turn on his M-39s.*
> *He'll blow you to hell with a twenty mike-mike shell,*
> *Safe up his guns and fly home.*

Claudia walked down the hall, drawing appreciative glances from the mostly male celebrants. She looked at another panel, then leaned closer. "My God," she exclaimed, "this can't be for real." Bennett moved to look over her shoulder. He laughed aloud.

Claudia was puzzled. "What's funny about that? I think it's disgusting. 'The World-Famous Puking Dogs.' What does that mean?"

"That's VF-143. And it's a long story."

"Well, I don't understand. I mean, what kind of group would actually choose an insignia like that?"

Bennett placed a reassuring hand on Claudia's shoulder. "I'll whistle up somebody who knows the story." He looked around the room, then motioned to a group of pilots seated around a table. "Hey, Masher. Come here a minute."

A short, slightly built man in Nomex flight jacket stood up and casually strode over, beer in hand. Claudia noted the jacket was well used, emblazoned with several patches. The name tag with the stamped Navy wings said MASHER MALLOY, FIGHTER PILOT.

Bennett made the introductions. "Claudia Meyers, this is Dennis Malloy, known to one and all as Masher. Dennis, this is Claudia. Behave yourself."

Claudia and Malloy shook hands and regarded one another. Masher had been seeing a leggy Irish governess named Beverly, but she was not present that evening. The little aviator looked Claudia up and down for a long three seconds. A direct question was forming in his mind when he sensed his commander's purposeful gaze.

Flustered, Claudia noted that the man's startling blue eyes darted from her face to her bosom and back again. Apparently he was not going to continue the conversation on his own.

Bennett said, "Masher, I was telling Claudia about One Forty-Three's nickname. You were in the squadron; how'd it begin?"

The query startled Malloy from his preoccupation with Claudia's chest. "Oh, the Pukin' Dogs. Well, it all started a long time before I reported aboard, but the original idea was to have a griffin as the squadron emblem." He sipped at his Coors, as if concentrating on the details with difficulty. "One of the junior officers was supposed to make a papier-mâché centerpiece for the commissioning. But he wasn't too good with papier-mâché. He got the griffin's wings all right, but the head sort of drooped and the mouth was open too far. They ran out of time and couldn't do it over, so they had to go with what was ready.

"Well, one of the wives walked in, took one look, and said, 'Jesus, it looks just like a pukin' dog.' And that's what One Forty-Three's been called ever since."

"Thanks, Masher." Bennett's tone was one of dismissal. With a last soulful gaze at Claudia, the little flier walked back to the table to rejoin his drinking buddies.

Claudia's expression showed bemusement. "Are they all like him?"

Bennett chuckled softly. "A few, a few. But one of the first things I learned in this business is that a man's personality on the ground may have nothing to do with his flying. Masher's an example. He's a good pilot, but an even better instructor. Upstairs he's all business. Down here, he's real loose."

Next morning a quarter to seven,
They sent him to fight once again
Against a Foxtrot 15, turns tight, fast, and mean
And they said there's no way he can win.

Well, he set up in the front quarter
At a fairly respectable range.
Hit the disappear switch, rolled out at Deep Six,
And the Fox 15 went down in flames.

The couple found a table with two vacant chairs and sat down. Bennett introduced Tim Ottman, who gallantly rose and seated Claudia. She smiled at him, taking in the handsome six-footer. *Well, maybe there* are *some gentlemen among fighter pilots*, she thought. Soon they were deep in conversation.

"Claudia, I guess you haven't met many guys like these." He gestured around the room. "Tell me, what do you make of us?"

Claudia giggled, shaking her head. "Well, I admit I've never been exposed to so many . . . different—"

"You mean screwy," Ottman said.

". . . so many different and entertaining people at one time. You guys seem to have so much fun together."

Bennett hadn't interrupted, preferring to let Claudia get to know some of the IPs on her own. Now he said, "Well, we do enjoy one anothers' company. After all, we have a lot in common."

Claudia finished her tea. "Yes—you're all crazy."

"That's part of our charm," Ottman insisted. "For instance, most people would think it's crazy for anyone to want to die at age forty-eight. But I think there's something to it. Probably the best thing that could happen to any of us would be getting killed in action at forty-eight."

Claudia's face registered disbelief.

"No, I mean it," Ottman said. And she almost believed him. "Look at it this way. You're still at your peak mentally, and most of us are in reasonable physical condition at that age. But in another couple years . . ." He snapped his fingers. "You're on the way out, kid. It's a long slide from there."

Claudia glanced at Bennett, seeking reinforcement. He winked at her. "Listen to the next verse."

> *He wanted to die as a legend,*
> *So he climbed it up seven miles high.*
> *He aimed it straight down, drove it into the ground,*
> *Screaming "That's how a fighter should die."*
>
> *He died with his G-suit and boots on,*
> *With a throttle and stick in his hand.*
> *He'd never been beat by any fighter he'd meet*
> *And the legend, it outlived the man.*

Bennett and Claudia spent the rest of the evening mingling with other instructors and guests. Claudia was pleasantly surprised to learn she had mutual friends in London with the Saint-Martins and Geoff Hampton. She also had a discussion with Ed Lawrence.

"You've known John a long time, haven't you, Ed?"

"Yup. Twenty years or more."

"Has he changed any?"

Lawrence thought for a moment. "Not much. Pirate always was a lot of fun to be with—real dependable. You get to know a lot of people in a career, but there's only a few you really trust. I'd trust John with my life. In fact, I have done just that."

"Do you think he's happy here?"

"Yes. I know I'm happy here, doing what I do." He hesitated a moment.

"What is it?"

"Claudia, you and I are different kinds of people. Ordinarily we wouldn't have much in common. But John is what we have in common. I'd say he's been happier than I've seen him in years. Since he met you."

Claudia squeezed his hand. "Thanks, Ed. I'm pretty happy, too. It's the best birthday I could hope for."

8

CLAUDIA SPENT THE NEXT TWO DAYS WITH BENNETT, mostly in the Tiger Force compound. The other guests had departed and the IPs for the graduating class were given leave. The couple were left mainly to themselves, which pleased them both.

Bennett devoted most of one day showing Claudia the academic area: classrooms and individual study cells. "Here, sit down at the console. I'll show you how easy it is to fly an F-20."

He tapped out the entry code on the keypad and the full-color screen showed the Tigershark's instrument panel. "You see," he began, "the directions are printed in white for this phase, and yellow for the next. Everything is color-coded from first to last in ascending order. The higher you get into the syllabus the darker the colors."

"That way you always know where you are in the program," Claudia said.

"Correct." He leaned over her shoulder, allowing one hand to rest on her back while he punched in the next lesson. "This sequence shows you how to start the F-20. It's a tactile screen, touch-sensitive, so you activate the switches in the proper order. You won't hear the engine start unless you do it properly."

Bennett had Claudia touch the appropriate switches, including the plastic safety covers. At each movement the screen showed, in animation, the covers lifted or the toggles activated. Immediately the whine of a jet engine was discernible. "There you go, you just lit off an F404 engine."

Claudia looked up. "Why, that's the most logical teaching system I've ever seen. Did you devise it?"

"Not hardly. This is a General Electric project, first used in their F-5E training center near Phoenix. The Saudis contracted for this facility from GE's simulation and training division."

Running her fingers over the console, Claudia said, "This must do a lot to speed up training. Is it one of the reasons you put the first class through so fast?"

"This and some other innovations in the flight syllabus. The advantage to this individual study cell is mainly psychological. In a classroom you have the teacher up front and he asks Student A a question. Well, Student A may not know the answer. Neither may anyone else, but the others look at A and think, 'Boy, what a dumbell.' This system here allows each student to progress at his own pace, so he retains much more of what he learns."

Later Bennett put Claudia in one of the F-20 simulators for a few minutes. He had the engineer start the program for takeoff and he showed her how to hold the stick and throttle. She made an erratic takeoff, overcontrolling as most beginners do. Bennett cautioned her to keep the nose above the horizon and flipped the landing gear lever for her.

"Okay, continue your climb and level off at ten thousand feet." He tapped the altimeter while leaning on the cockpit edge.

Claudia was stunned by the full-color panorama of the world "outside" her cockpit. As Bennett coached her through some turns, she overcontrolled again and the computer-generated imagery slanted crazily. "I feel a little dizzy."

"That's normal. This simulator can almost make you airsick. Level off for a minute." Claudia moved the stick less dramatically than before, and the imagery settled down. "Now, let's say you're going to strafe some point on the ground. That hill over to the left. Turn toward it and lower your nose."

Claudia shoved forward on the stick, aiming at the top of a rounded hill. Bennett saw what was coming. "Don't push it too far. Remember, you're at 95 percent power."

Too late, Claudia realized she was too steep. She gasped audibly, pulling hard on the stick. The scenery tumbled, then the screen went blank. "What happened?"

"Darling, you bought the farm."

"Well, any landing you can walk away from . . ."

Bennett helped her out of the cockpit, catching her arm when she slipped. "Gosh, I'm still dizzy," she said. "That thing is *too* realistic!"

THAT EVENING BENNETT SUGGESTED THEY HAVE DIN-ner in the club. Claudia preferred to go out, but he insisted. When they walked in, decorations already were in place. A large banner hung across the bar mirror: HAPPY BIRTHDAY, CLAUDIA! Several IPs were there, notably less boistrous than the night of the graduation party.

Claudia turned to Bennett, grasping his arm. "You rat! You set me up for this."

He smiled at her. "Actually, you can blame yourself. I wasn't going to say anything, but you let it slip to Ed at the graduation party. He and Masher set this up."

Lawrence walked over and kissed Claudia warmly on the lips. "Happy birthday, hon. The Big Four-Oh."

Claudia regarded him through slitted eyes. "So, you're the security risk."

Lawrence said, "Hey, I only acted on available intelligence. You know—loose lips sink ships? Besides, somebody *else* provided the specifics about age."

Claudia glanced at both fliers, feigning petulance. "Oh, there's that handsome Tim Ottman. I think I'll let him buy me a drink."

For the next two hours Claudia savored being the belle of the ball. The fact that she was almost the only woman present did not bother her in the least. She was accorded a combination of fraternal attention and the respect due the colonel's lady from a cheerful band of warriors. Partway into the evening she realized with a start that she—a career diplomat—actually was enjoying the company of such men. True, some of the courtesy being lavished upon her was attributable to the fact that many of the pilots had not talked to a woman—any woman—in several months. But she felt comfortable, accepted, and warm.

Bennett allowed the others to entertain Claudia, preferring to sit back with Peter Saint-Martin. Peter lit his pipe, settled comfortably, and took in the scene.

"You know, boss," he began, "we've had the women here only a day and a half or so. They'll be gone tomorrow. But I can't help noticing almost a brother-sister relationship among our bachelor or unattached IPs and the few wives—and your Claudia. I've seen it before. As men will do on lonely outposts without women of their own, they begin to focus their love and longing on those present. Some chaps believe it can only lead to conflict, but I disagree. At least, it doesn't have to."

Bennett regarded the former Royal Navy flier with new esteem. "Peter, I never figured you for a sociologist."

"Armchair sociologist, you might say." He puffed aggressively at his pipe. "Most men are loath to do anything improper in the presence of a woman who simply expects respect. As you know, when men live for long periods without the company of women, one of the first casualties is language. I've noticed that our chaps have minded their manners all evening."

The Britisher sat in silence a few more moments. "There's a dichotomy at work in our business. Men can engage in the worst form of behavior—killing and being killed—and be better at it when deprived of the presence of women. That's because in every society I know of, the promise of woman is of life and birth, of love and compassion. Things not synonymous with war. You see, it's almost a given that to prepare men for war they should be removed from the presence of women. Our instruction and training has to take place away from the female's basic goodness and civilizing influence. That's why war is possible."

Bennett leaned forward, clasping his hands on the table. "I think I agree with you, Peter. But what about the trend of more women in the armed forces?"

A decisive shake of the head. "Can't work, old man. Runs contrary to our civilization. Oh, I'm not saying women can't shoot as well as men or fly as well—we both know better. But I've never seen a cow in a bullring." He knocked out the ashes in his pipe. "You may have read Kipling. 'The female of the species is more deadly than the male.' Some say that females of any species are more dangerous, but read Kipling carefully. The females only become lethal in defense of their children or to feed them. Women will kill, certainly. To preserve their young. And I for one think that's an admirable quality."

Toward midnight, when the cake and ice cream and beer were gone, most of the men had drifted off. Masher Malloy, obviously picking his time carefully, approached Claudia with a small package.

"Miss Meyers, I'd sort of like you to have this. As a birthday present. It's been with me for quite a while and . . . I, ah, I just want you to have it."

Claudia opened the package, set down the wrapping, and held up the gift. It was a once-dark-blue T-shirt emblazoned with the black and white emblem of Fighter Squadron 143. Claudia laughed aloud, genuinely pleased, and held it up to her shoulders. The shirt hung barely to her hips. "Why, thank you, Masher. I'll think of you every time I wear it." She leaned down to kiss his cheek.

Slightly flustered, the little fighter pilot made an uncharacteristically quiet withdrawal.

Bennett drove Claudia to her hotel and walked her to her room. As they stepped inside she turned around. "Excuse me, John. I'll be right back." She went into the bathroom and closed the door.

Moments later the door opened. Bennett, sitting on the couch, looked up and gasped. Claudia wore the Pukin' Dog shirt. And nothing else. She turned around twice, a wry grin on her face. "Do you think Masher would approve?"

"I know damn well he would." Bennett took a deep breath and stood up. "Claudia . . ."

She stepped close to him, put her hands on his chest. "I know we've both been doing a lot of thinking about each other, and our lovemaking has been wonderful this past year or so. But I want to be closer to you, John. I'm forty years old and I really don't have anything but my career. Now I find I want something more. I want there to be an *us*."

He held her tightly. "So do I, Claudia."

The blue T-shirt fell to the floor.

In the C Ring of the Pentagon, Major General George Miller shuffled his papers, organizing visual aids and data for his next presidential briefing. It was no simple task, especially where the Middle East was concerned. The increasingly complex web of alliances, plots, and feuds cut across not only national borders, but political and religious lines as well. It tended to become very confusing, most notably when longtime antagonists began behaving in a distressingly friendly fashion toward one another. The increasing Arab unity was perpetuated by Israel's continuing occupation of Jordan.

Miller was too experienced a briefer to allow such things to bog him down. He called across the room to his aide, Colonel Robert Kaufman. They were alone in the room.

"Bob, did CIA confirm the data from Tel Aviv?"

Kaufman looked up from his map preparation. "Yes, sir. Not only based upon Israeli information, but there's confirmation from the Brits as well."

Miller penned a note on his first draft of the presentation. As he updated material over the rest of the evening, it would be added, modified, or deleted according to requirements. The final version would be typed less than one hour before President Walter Arnold's briefing.

George Miller sat back in his chair, raised his glasses, and rubbed his eyes. "Bob, come over here and park it for a minute. I want to brainstorm this thing."

The intelligence colonel poured himself a cup of decaffeinated coffee and sat down at the table. "Well, sir, the evidence is pretty conclusive," Kaufman began. "The Israelis, probably with some support from the Omanis and even from the Brits, are supporting guerrilla bands inside Yemen. There's a clear pattern of operations against South Yemen over the past several weeks. That much is indisputable. Raids have occurred."

Miller said, "Sure. But why? What could the Yemenis hope to gain from all this? All they may succeed in doing is upsetting South Yemen and starting a real firefight."

"That is one risk," Kaufman conceded. He tapped the file marked TOP SECRET and flipped the pages. "But it's been proven that South Yemen is intent on exporting revolution, as the old saying goes. My guess is that the government in San'a wants to show the People's Republic of Yemen that it can't have things both ways."

Ever the devil's advocate, Miller said, "Okay, I'll buy that as far as it goes. But let's play the intel game. Who really stands to benefit from border clashes between the two Yemens?"

Kaufman smiled. "Gotcha, chief." He waved a professorial finger. "Israel and Oman."

"All right, we're on the same track. But why? The president will want to know."

"Everybody in the spook business knows the radical Arab states have settled most of their differences over the past couple of years. With the Ayatollah dead, Iran has become a lot cozier with Iraq. In fact, we know that Israeli intelligence predicted it would take about that long to consolidate things. Now the Israelis are looking for a way to further destabilize the situation—give 'em more time to prepare for whatever's coming."

"And Oman?"

"Simple. South Yemen's hostile to Oman, too. Internal dissent, protests, support of opposition groups. It's a marriage of convenience between Muscat and Tel Aviv. By helping each other, they further their respective aims in the region."

Miller jotted down the salient points for inclusion in his briefing. Like a careful professional, he would be sure to distinguish between hard intelligence and that which was supposition and opinion. But all considerations would be available should the president wish a more detailed analysis.

Glancing up from his writing, the general explained, "I'm adding a reference to previous Israeli dealings with Arab nations through back-channel and third-party means. You recall their sale of Phantom parts to Iran during the war with Iraq, and they even advocated that we sell military hardware to Kuwait after the Brits copped that huge deal with the Saudis." Miller shook his head in wonderment. "At least ten billion dollars worth! The president asked recently how many U.S. jobs that would have meant. I heard the Labor Department estimated four-hundred thousand. No wonder Arnold's willing to buck the Israeli lobby. If he could get back some of that foreign trade, the labor unions would elect him king.

"Okay," Miller said, "so much for the poetry. Now what about actual operations in Yemen?"

Kaufman checked his papers. "Press reports, intel, and info from attachés in San'a are pretty much in agreement. Company-size operations in some spots, shooting back and forth across the border, and more recently South Yemen has launched air strikes along the border, which is ill-defined."

"Any aerial combat?"

"Evidently not yet. There's only been a couple of quick hit-and-run affairs. But it seems the South Yemenis have used Saudi airspace to make an end run. If the Saudis get involved, I imagine that would suit the Israelis just fine."

Miller stared at Kaufman's coffee cup. "It sure would."

Bahrain

The DeHavilland 125 taxied to a stop and the engines were cut to idle. As the vacuum-cleaner sound wound down, the business jet's door opened and Safad Fatah descended the steps. He was closely followed by Mohammad Tuqman, a specialist in foreign affairs.

Bennett greeted the two ministers at large and showed them to the waiting limousine. He turned around in the front seat to talk to them during the short drive to the Tiger Force operations office.

"Mr. Fatah, arrangements have been made as you asked. Colonel Lawrence is occupied with scheduling for the third class but he will attend our conference. I've also arranged for two of our prospective squadron commanders to be there."

Fatah nodded. "You have selected ranking Saudi pilots to lead the F-20 squadrons, then?"

"Yes, sir. We coordinated with air force headquarters, and we've agreed with Riyadh that two experienced F-5 pilots will perform those duties as soon as they finish the transition phase to Tigersharks. It doesn't take too long."

"That is good," Safad said. "We do not have very long."

Minutes later, the two Saudi ministers seated themselves in the operations office. Joining Bennett and Lawrence were Major Ali Handrah and Major Mohammed Jauf, who would command the first two Tigershark squadrons in due time. But the current crisis had caught them unprepared for operations. Both men knew they were there to listen.

The ops office was clear of everyone but the four Saudis and two Americans. It was an austere, businesslike room. Navigation and weather charts hung on the walls, with aircraft status boards and pilot training rosters neatly arrayed. The only nonfunctional item readily visible was a sign over the door: EXCEL OR DIE.

Safad Fatah came directly to the point. "Gentlemen, you must be aware of the situation with Yemen and South Yemen. I fear it is not improving at all."

Bennett said, "Yes, sir. I understand there's been border clashes recently. Sounds like the South Yemenis mean to stir up more trouble."

Mohammad Tuqman interjected. "Worse than that. They are

involving us. South Yemen troops and aircrafts have crossed our borders to attack their neighbor."

The Americans were familiar with the situation. The two countries had border disputes dating from at least 1934. South Yemen—formerly the British crown colony of Aden—was perhaps the poorest nation in the region. The British had closed their naval base in 1967 and, despite severe differences following British departure, the YAR, Yemen Arab Republic (usually called Yemen) and the People's Democratic Republic of Yemen (usually called South Yemen) attempted consolidation. The effort had violently been curtailed in 1978 when both presidents were killed in a two-day upheaval. In South Yemen a pro-Soviet Communist, Abdul Fattah Ismail, seized power by military coup and executed his predecessor. Ismail may have ordered the death of the YAR president as well. However, Ismail's regime was toppled by an even more radical element seven years later.

Ed Lawrence leaned forward. "Excuse me, Mr. Fatah, Mr. Tuqman. But I know the borders in that area are not well marked. Is that part of the trouble?" He visualized JNC-35, the jet navigation chart for the area. Most of central Arabia was uncharted, the section a blank white space on the map. Navigation warnings were printed along the unmarked Yemen border.

"Just so," Fatah replied. "That part of the peninsula is sparsely populated and the boundaries have never been properly defined. Much of the terrain is rocky desert. But clearly our sovereignty has been violated. Again and again."

Tuqman waved a bony finger. "And there is much to evidence that South Yemen is causing trouble in Oman."

Tiger Force knew about Oman. Long ruled by a despotic, incompetent sultan, the nation gained more enlightened leadership in 1970 when the sultan's son displaced him. British aid helped suppress rebels aided in part by South Yemen, but Britain closed its base on Masira Island in 1977. The government remained relatively unstable, and defense was directed almost exclusively by British officers, though Israeli assistance had been reported. Bennett and Lawrence knew some of the RAF pilots flying Omani Jaguar fighter-bombers.

Though he guessed what was coming, Bennett asked, "Where does Tiger Force fit into all this?"

Fatah reached into his briefcase, compressing his paunch as he leaned over in the chair. "These are reports of South Yemen violations of our airspace. I also appended a status report on the People's Democratic Republic Air Force." He handed the documents across the table.

Bennett and Lawrence already were acquainted with the PDRY air arm. They maintained current files on all military forces in the region as a matter of course. Flying MiG-21s, Sukhoi 22s, and one squadron of fast MiG-23s, the South Yemenis were looping north into Arabian airspace by staging from bases at Shibam and Seiyun 150 miles east of the YAR border. By approaching Yemen from the northeast, they had eluded detection until almost the last moment and caught their opponents by surprise. Through human and satellite sources, it was known that the Soviets operated SA-2 and -3 missile batteries in South Yemen, and Cubans were believed leading some of the MiG and Sukhoi fighter-bomber formations.

"Would you like us to patrol that area?" Bennett asked.

"Yes. Our diplomatic efforts have had no effect," said Fatah. "As you know, we have only minimal contact with Marxist regimes, as a matter of faith."

Bennett clasped his hands, leaning forward. He fixed each Saudi with an intent gaze. Speaking softly, he said, "Mr. Fatah, Mr. Tuqman. You realize that Tiger Force is not fully operational. Our first class is nearing completion of its first six months of squadron formation and the operational training that goes with it. But neither squadron has been expected to be combat-ready yet. That's two months away, with Majors Jauf and Handrah slated to take command."

Fatah nodded. "Colonel Bennett, Colonel Lawrence, we recognize that it probably would be necessary for some of your instructors to provide . . . advice . . . during this period."

"Do you mean flight lead, sir? Tactical leadership?"

Fatah regarded the two Americans. "His Majesty takes a personal interest in your safety. As American citizens, none of your instructors could possibly cross into foreign airspace." His dark eyes flashed.

Lawrence said, "We don't mind taking on this job; in fact, it'll give our people some good experience. But why not use the regular Royal Saudi Air Force? You have F-15s down there at Nejran and Khamis Mushayt, two hundred fifty to three hundred fifty miles from the Yemen border."

Bennett interrupted. "Unless you need fighters closer to the borders. Smaller, less complex airplanes that don't need the ground support equipment of the Eagles." He tapped the chart on the table. "We could stage Tigersharks to these smaller strips and react a lot quicker."

Bennett glanced at Majors Handrah and Jauf, who surely would be involved in the upcoming operation. He winked conspiratorially at them. They self-consciously grinned in return.

Lawrence fidgeted in his chair. "Mr. Fatah, we're self-contained for the most part, and we don't need many mechanics. From what we call a cold start, we can be airborne in sixty seconds." The redheaded flier warmed to his subject, envisioning the situation and mentally licking his chops at the prospect of combat.

"In ninety more seconds we can be at thirty thousand feet. That means if we get word of bogeys, we can be at altitude in two and a half minutes from the go signal—"

Fatah held up his hands, as if to fend off the verbal torrent. "Gentlemen, please! You do not need to convince me." He smiled through his goatee. "Your enthusiasm is gratifying, and the reasons you state have been made by our air staff in Riyadh."

Then the mirthful tone was gone and his voice became more serious.

"But, my friends, there is more to this situation than you know. You have always been forthcoming with me, and I can do no less." Fatah's gaze settled on Bennett. "In truth, you are being tested. There are those who would not be disappointed if your Tiger Force failed. That is, I believe, why this assignment has arisen at this point. Those who envy your relationship with His Majesty realize that your pilots are not fully trained yet."

Bennett returned Fatah's gaze. "Safad, my boys can handle this job."

The minister nodded and sat back. "I assumed so. But remember, palace politics are at work here. If you had refused this mission, or if you fail, your influence would suffer."

"Then we won't fail." It wasn't a boast; merely a statement.

Lawrence interjected. "Well, who's on our side? Will we have any support at all?"

"That is what we are here to discuss," Fatah replied.

"We'll need airborne radar," Lawrence said. "There's a good ground-control intercept station at Khamis Mushayt, but it's almost useless for targets below ten thousand feet. The mountains interfere too much."

"Please prepare a list of what you need," Fatah smoothly responded. "Anything within reason will be supplied."

Lawrence managed to hold back a smile.

Bennett asked, "Gentlemen, when would you want some F-20s down there, and how many?"

"We estimate a dozen fighters would suffice, one squadron's worth. In, say, three days?"

Bennett said, "Yes, sir. We'll meet with you tomorrow with a preliminary plan."

Walking back to his quarters after the meeting, Lawrence rubbed his hands together. "Put the saddle on the stove, Mother. We're ridin' the range tonight."

THAT EVENING THE BRIEFING ROOM WAS QUIET—NOT tense, but definitely attentive. Lawrence had spoken to some of the IPs from Class One and selected three besides himself—all of them unmarried—who were willing to take on the assignment. Now Lawrence and Bennett explained the setup.

"We've decided to share the wealth," Lawrence began, "and we'll have two four-plane flights from Orange Squadron and one from Black." Each F-20 squadron carried a color designator within Tiger Force. It bore no relation to the Royal Saudi Air Force designation, but was used by the F-20 pilots and IPs as an internal identity, a morale-builder. The first two squadrons were traditional tiger colors. The next three, from Class Two, would be White, Red, and Green. Green was Muhammad's color.

Lawrence had chosen these men well, Bennett thought. There was always a tacit pressure on military aviators—an unspoken expectation to accept any proposition. "Never turn down a combat assignment" was a watchword in the profession. Bennett knew that few of the forty IPs would in fact refuse potential combat, but he wanted to be certain. The men sitting before him were warriors.

"You guys know the background," Bennett said. "The Saudis are concerned about protecting their airspace from intrusion by any party. They're trying to walk a tightrope in the Middle East, and they no more want to encourage a fight than to appear to run from one. That's why they've decided to confront the South Yemenis."

He studied the IPs' faces. Masher Malloy seemed edgy, fidgeting in his seat, but Bennett knew it was excess energy. Geoff Hampton, the former Red Arrow, was the soul of composure. Bennett would have preferred Peter Saint-Martin, who had combat experience, but he was married. The USAF delegate was Tim

Ottman. Lawrence had been careful to select one man from each community besides himself.

Bennett smiled at the recollection of Ottman's oft-stated explanation of the 1973 Paris Peace Accords. "Here I was, fresh out of training, up to speed in the F-4, and they called off the war. Well, you know why. The MiG drivers mutinied. They said, 'Oh, no, Ottman's coming! Quick, sign the damn paper!' " Well, now perhaps Tim would have his war.

Masher Malloy raised a hand. "Skipper, what about ROE?" Rules of engagement always were a sore point.

"I'm coming to that. This is supposed to be a show of force. We cruise a couple miles abeam of any unidentified gaggle and one of the Saudis raises them in Arabic. The ROE are clear from then on. If the bogeys ignore an order to leave Saudi airspace, or if they don't reply, we turn to engage. If they bug out, let 'em go. There's no hot pursuit over the border into Yemen."

Malloy squirmed. "Geez, I've heard that tune before."

Bennett pinned Malloy with a stare which made the little flier uncomfortable. "Just remember, this isn't our fight. It's not even our air force. Riyadh makes the rules. Clear?"

Bennett continued. "Otherwise, it's pretty lenient ROE. If the bogeys turn into you, fight's on. If they attempt to gain a rear-hemisphere advantage, you fight. And for damn sure, if they shoot first, you shoot back."

Consulting his notes, the CO continued. "We'll cover this tomorrow and again with the pilots before you head south. What I want to emphasize is your relationship to the Saudis. Each of you has flown with most of the fifteen studs we'll be using from Class One. You know most of their moves, their strengths and weaknesses. We're in a ticklish situation because, though we're senior to these boys, we're not really their commanding officers. One of the Saudi majors has wrangled permission to go along, but it's understood Ed will run the show for this limited time.

"We'll run this exercise zip-lip as much as possible. It's a good opportunity to test our radio discipline. It should be a non-ECM environment, so you can call sightings and breaks as needed, but let's use this first opportunity to impress the young sports with emcon. We should be able to run any intercept under complete emissions control because we won't be radiating."

This drew a few chuckles; most Tiger Force aircraft had been ordered without radar.

"Each of you will be flying section lead in your flight. This will give the Saudis good experience, and will allow them to handle the challenge transmissions to the Yemenis. Those should be the only calls any of you make, except an emergency, before you have to engage. We've decided to follow up the Arabic challenge with English. If there's no reply after that, expect the worst."

Lawrence broke in, a wry smile on his face. "Of course, we could try hailing them in Spanish. Word is some Cubans are calling the shots with those folks."

Hampton spoke up. "John, any more word on how long this may last? We'll need to plan for resupply to the staging fields."

"Nothing on that yet. But I imagine if there's one or two good hassles, and they lose a few MiGs or Sukhois, things will settle down. At any rate, plans are being made for F-5s to take over the sector patrols as soon as possible. At visual distances it'll be hard to tell one of them from an F-20."

Ottman chortled. "Good idea. Make 'em respect *us*, then terrorize 'em with something that looks like us."

"That's about it," Bennett said. "You'll have info on your radar controllers before you leave—E-3s staging out of Khamis Mushayt. You can arrange procedures with them when you arrive.

"One more thing. Be sure to go over loose deuce again with all your pilots. You'll be flying in rotation; an alert flight, a backup flight, and an off-duty flight during daylight hours. With four Saudis per flight, one of them also will be off duty. But you guys will be on the board full-time. So don't take anything for granted. Reinforce the fundamentals. And stress that selection for this job doesn't replace the training syllabus. Even if some of our studs come back with scalps on their belts, they'll still have two months of operational training to finish."

Lawrence noted slightly puzzled expressions on one or two faces. "It's psychological, guys. We need to keep the Saudis from developing overconfidence. If we give special treatment to a couple of pilots who bag MiGs, it could cause morale problems later on."

Masher Malloy interjected. "That's fine by me, Skipper. But, uh, what if one of *us* gets a kill? I don't suppose there's a bonus, is there?"

Bennett leveled an earnest gaze at Malloy. "My boy, you'll have the satisfaction of knowing you did your duty for the king."

Tudmur, Syria

The twin-engine transport bearing Iraq's green triangles on its wings braked to a smooth halt on the ramp at Palmyra Airport. As soon as the turboprop engines wound down the door opened and the Syrian honor guard came to present arms. The Antonov 26 became center stage in the third act of the day's drama, while the Syrian army band struck up Iraq's "Anthem of the Republic" as the Baghdad delegation deplaned.

Previously the same band and honor guard had welcomed similar arrivals from Tehran and Tripoli.

Some 120 miles northeast of Damascus, Tudmur was remote enough to hold a meeting of Arab military officials without undue attention from outsiders. For despite their ingrained differences, the Muslims had two things in common: an abiding hatred of Israel, and a special interest in the future of Jordan.

9

Bahrain

JOHN BENNETT AND ED LAWRENCE STOOD BY THE NOSE of Lawrence's fighter. It was barely daylight, and the air was pleasantly cool. The two friends occupied a few moments with small talk, but soon an awkward silence fell upon them.

Lawrence glanced again at the luminous dial of his watch. "Well, it's showtime." He shifted his feet. *There's nothing worse than times like these,* he thought. Intimate friends want to say things to one another but somehow The Warriors' Code prohibits it. Best fire up and get going.

Bennett extended his hand. "Normally I'd say 'Good hunting, Devil.' But now I'm showing my age. All I can think is, take care of yourself and bring the Tigers home."

"Pirate, your halo is showing. Don't worry about us. We'll be fine." Lawrence gave Bennett an extra-hard squeeze of the hand, then turned and scrambled up the boarding ladder.

Bennett stood back and watched the now-familiar preflight process. Crew chiefs jumped down, withdrew the ladders, and motioned the long, graceful aircraft onto the taxiway. Lawrence's jet led the procession, canopy still open, red running light strobing from the fuselage. The exec tossed an ultraregulation salute at Bennett, who merely waved.

Bennett stood motionless, watching each of the streamlined dark shapes glide past. When Tim Ottman's flight taxied by, Bennett waved again. Then he flipped a sharp salute to Rajid Hamir. His heart pounded a little harder as he thought of Rajid's young fiancée.

In minutes the fourteen Northrops were poised at the end of the runway. Two by two, they made section takeoffs. Climbing sharply, they accelerated in astonishing climbs to make best use of the early-morning air which would provide economical cruising for the 730-mile flight to Khamis Mushayt.

Bennett turned and walked back to the line shack. He felt let down, almost sad, and he did not quite know why. He had taken every precaution possible. The C-130 with spare parts, Sidewinder missiles, 20mm ammunition, and a skeleton force of mechanics had left during the night. It should arrive at Khamis Mushayt well before the fighters. Communications, accommodations, and several contingency plans had been arranged. Even two spare Tigersharks had been allocated, just in case maintenance problems unexpectedly cropped up.

Why do I feel so . . . unsettled? I've seen men off to combat before and I didn't feel this way. Maybe it's the difference between leading men and sending them.

My God, I miss them already. It's going to be a long wait.

■   ■   ■

ONCE SETTLED ON COURSE TO THE SOUTHWEST, ED
Lawrence rocked his wings. The three flights of four planes each,
and the spare section of two, adopted loose deuce formation. It was
doctrine in Tiger Force to fly every mission under simulated combat
conditions: open intervals to fighting formation, minimal or no radio
transmissions, constant vigilance.

From long experience Lawrence knew that his wingman was
half turned in his seat, almost facing the lead F-20. Lawrence
himself was oriented toward his partner. Some pilots preferred to fly
with their left hand on the stick, leaving the throttle untouched
in combat spread. But in any case, the orientation allowed each
flier visually to clear the area behind his friend's tail—especially
important in the jet age, with rapid approach speeds and air-
to-air missiles drastically reducing the time to spot and call out
an attack.

Lawrence's visored eyes scanned the sky around him, moving in
a boxlike pattern perfected by thousands of hours aloft. His scan
registered the two cathode-ray tube displays in his cockpit, took in
his fuel state, and returned to the outside world. Fighter pilots were
always thinking fuel, for they were professional managers of that
precious commodity.

Cruising at Mach .82, the F-20's fuel flow was about 2,300
pounds per hour while the Tigershark made nearly eight miles a
minute: 450 knots at 35,000 feet. Within 110 miles of destination,
the pilot could pull the throttle back to idle and glide at 250 knots,
burning only 200 pounds of fuel per hour. Thus, the last 110 miles
would consume merely 80 to 90 pounds of JP4 during the 25-minute
descent. That was normal fuel flow in a turbofan fighter being flown
like an airliner. But a fighter plane is for war, for killing other
aircraft. And in combat it uses fuel in an ungodly manner. The F-20
could fight for two minutes 400 miles from its base and return with a

safety reserve, or cruise nearly 2,000 miles on the same amount of fuel.

Lawrence felt calm, confident, and slightly hungry—a predatory hunger. It was the kind of hunger the toughest cat on the block feels. A fight was coming. He could feel it.

THE NEXT FOUR DAYS WERE FULL BUT UNEXCITING. Settling in at Khamis Mushayt, arranging for rotation to Nejran and advanced fields, the Tiger Force personnel adjusted to the routine. They were taken with the stark beauty of the Empty Quarter, the Ar *Rub Al Khali,* but even more so with Nejran. Seeing the pure desert oasis for the first time from the air, Tim Ottman was enchanted. The beautiful village of mud structures, with an ancient castle surrounded by dates and palm trees, was straight out of a fairy tale. *Now I've really been to Arabia,* he thought.

The F-20 pilots met with the crews of two Saudi Air Force E-3A AWACS planes, which would provide airborne warning and control. Ed Lawrence and the other instructors were impressed with the airborne controllers—sharp young men who would monitor Saudi airspace for intrusion from South Yemen and direct F-20s to intercepts if necessary. The two AWACS would stage out of Khamis Mushayt, alternating missions daily.

The two forward fields, southeast of Nejran, were suitable for Tigersharks and F-5s but were not yet adaptable to larger aircraft requiring more support. Most of the pilots were confident of a confrontation with the Yemenis; some earnestly wished for it. Only a few recalled Bennett's warning: "Be careful what you want. It might come true."

Based on Lawrence's schedule, a four-plane flight of F-20s patrolled the Saudi-Yemen border once or twice a day at irregular intervals. There was no discernible pattern to the patrols—predictability is a sin to a dedicated warrior. Varying patrol times, patterns, and altitudes, the Tigersharks trolled impatiently, letting the South Yemen radar get a good look at them.

While the airborne flight made its seemingly random passes up and down the border, the second flight sat runway alert at one of the forward fields. Hangars were available, so the pilots and mechanics were spared the worst of the Arabian sun. These four fighters could be airborne in one minute, ready to reinforce the airborne flight in perhaps ten minutes, depending on the scene of contact. The third flight remained at Khamis Mushayt, rotating forward every third day to allow one of the others a rest.

At dusk on the fourth day Lawrence discussed the situation with Major Ali Handrah, one of the prospective squadron commanders. They were relaxing over lemonade in the small building allotted Tiger Force at Khamis Mushayt.

Theirs was a courteous, professional relationship, devoid of warmth. Bennett had warned his exec against any word or action which could be interpreted as overbearing or superior. Unofficially Lawrence outranked Handrah, but the American also was a foreigner in the pay of the king of Arabia.

"Major Handrah, I've been thinking about our patrol patterns. What would you think if we fly farther inland for a couple of days? Give the appearance that we're not as concerned anymore. It might help defuse the situation if we show the Yemenis that we're working into a routine attitude, with more or less predictable schedules." But his words belied his intent.

The Saudi set down his lemonade. Lawrence knew the officer's orders were to observe more than command. He also knew Handrah was expected to establish a sense of discipline in his young pilots; if Riyadh wanted a show-the-flag mission, the youngsters' high spirits should not lead elsewhere. If the intrusions could be ended without a fight, so much the better.

Handrah said, "Yes, Colonel Lawrence, I agree. Your suggestion is in keeping with our orders. Perhaps the Yemenis will realize we intend to keep patrols in this area. There have been no more intrusions since we arrived."

Lawrence's plan went into effect the next day. In conferring with the airborne controllers from his staging base, he learned that MiGs out of Shibam had caught the new pattern. For the next two days they flew much closer to the border—wherever it was!—thus taking up the slack to maintain closer contact with the F-20s.

Then, on the eighth night, YAR guerrillas struck an army compound twenty miles inside PDRY territory. Tiger Force immediately got word from Saudi intelligence, and Lawrence laid plans accordingly.

The South Yemenis reacted the next morning. But the MiGs and Sukhois avoided Saudi airspace, crossing directly into YAR territory to bomb and strafe two guerrilla compounds. Ed Lawrence bristled with anticipation, trolling as close to both borders as he dared during the raid. His Saudi student leading the flight played it straight, and returned to the advance base upon reaching "bingo" fuel state.

"I'll be a sad sack." The redhead tossed his helmet down to the crew chief and slowly unhooked. "We could see some contrails but that was all." He viciously unsnapped the koch fittings of his torso harness. "Shee-it."

Lawrence arranged for the third flight to join him while Tim Ottman's four planes, plus one spare, took the next patrol. The IPs agreed that they should have full strength available now that things might be heating up. There was still a good chance Lawrence's "restrained" patrol pattern might entice some MiGs over the border.

Southeast of Nejran, 0640 Hours

At the advanced field an ordnanceman stood beside Lieutenant Rajid Hamir's wingtip, flashlight in hand. It was the ninth day of the operation; something would have to happen soon or the operation would be called off. When the F-20s started engines the young Saudi airman watched for a thumbs-up from the pilot, indicating the Sidewinder missile on each wing was activated. The armorer then shined the flashlight on the AIM-9's seeker head, visible behind the thick glass in the nose. By moving the light laterally and vertically, the "ordie" saw whether the thermoelectrically cooled homing system was functioning normally. Such was the sensitivity of the infrared seeker that its eye followed the heat of a mere flashlight.

Developed by the U.S. Navy in the 1950s, the Sidewinder was simplicity itself. It mated the then-new seeker and warhead to an existing rocket motor, and the original models cost $800 apiece. The current versions, with a front-attack capability, ran over $100,000 but they were deadly effective. British Sea Harrier pilots in the Falklands War scored an 80 percent kill rate with their AIM-9Ls.

Rajid Hamir led his wingman off the runway moments after Lawrence had landed. The second section, led by Tim Ottman, was only seconds behind, followed by a spare. Keeping low, Rajid checked the position of the other three aircraft and keyed his microphone button.

In rapid order came the responses: one, two, three clicks. All four pilots had checked in; their radios were functioning. There was mild jockeying as each F-20 took turns flying a mile behind its partner, double-checking the tracking tone of its missiles. Satisfied that each aircraft was fully operational, Rajid detached the spare with a waggle of his wings and set course east-northeast at reduced throttle. In one-mile spread the two sections adopted loose deuce and waited. No one had spoken a word since takeoff.

Over the Yemen Arab Republic, 0715 Hours

Captain Julio Martin Cordoba led his four Sukhoi 22Ms outbound from a wadi in the Yemen desert. He had made a surprise follow-up attack on one of the guerrilla bases across the border from South Yemen. The Cuban pilot had shrewdly figured that the YAR "terrorists," accustomed to one bombing at a time, would not expect a second attack moments after the first. And he had been right. The guerrilla camp had just begun to stir, with enough of the smoke and dust settled to allow good visibility from above, when Cordoba's flight arrived.

It had been a well-executed attack. The Su-22s—NATO callsign "Fitter"—had struck from north and south, almost simultaneously. Glancing down, Cordoba doubted that many of the terrorists had survived this time. He was not new to the game. He had flown in Angola years before.

Leading his reassembled formation northeasterly, Cordoba had plotted a return course which described an arc tangent to the claimed Saudi border. Thus, he avoided a reported YAR antiaircraft missile battery which had fired on MiG-23 reconnaissance flights recently. He knew from radar reports over the past week that Saudi fighters had never crossed into Yemeni airspace. Besides, MiG-21s would be airborne to screen his flight during his return along the border.

Over Saudi Arabia, 0717 Hours

Ninety miles away, a Saudi captain peered intently at his radar scope in the airborne AWACS. One of his companions monitored the South Yemeni fighter-direction frequency, noting that radio discipline was typically poor for Soviet-trained air forces. With a highly-structured command-control system, the MiGs relied on instructions from ground controllers for almost every phase of flight, down to dropping external tanks and arming missiles.

The Saudi captain placed his cursor on the MiG blips, providing an electronic memory for consultation anytime later. He already had a good idea of the direction and speed of both Yemeni formations.

The geometry was coming together. From its God's-eye view the E-3 radar plane scanned the three groups of aircraft crowding the Saudi-Yemen border area. The Sukhois were headed to a point very near the boundary—perhaps upon it—and the MiGs were converging toward that point from the east-southeast.

The four F-20s, on direction from the airborne controller, turned hard right. Rajid and Tim Ottman took their wingmen in startling climbs, splitting to a five-mile separation between sections. Rajid heard the controller call, "Bogeys on your nose, twenty-eight miles at sixteen thousand." Rajid gave his mike button a quick click to acknowledge.

Shabwah, People's Democratic Republic of Yemen, 0719 Hours

"Where did *they* come from?" The duty controller sucked in his breath. He stared a moment longer at his scope, hardly believing the abrupt appearance of the small blips in Saudi airspace. The Yemeni officer shouted over his shoulder into the darkened hut. "Comrade Colonel Sorokin! Look at this!"

Colonel Kirill Sorokin was a forty-eight-year-old air defense specialist assigned—semi-permanently, he ruefully thought sometimes—to the People's Democratic Republic of Yemen. He had performed similar duties all over the world, and surely the pest hole he now occupied belonged right at the bottom of the list. Hotter than Hades, thousands of kilometers from anywhere with precious little comfort, there was not even much liquor to ease the burden. "Serves you right for being so good at your work," his superior had said. Some system, which rewards competence with misery, Sorokin thought.

Flinging aside the blackout curtains separating his small office from the control room, the Russian took in the esoteric data contained on the radar scope in just a few seconds.

"Damn it to hell!" he shouted.

The controller visibly flinched. He was well acquainted with the colonel's temper.

To Sorokin it looked as if the Saudis intended to cut off the Sukhois at the border. He yanked the headset off the controller and pressed it to his ear. He did not know the tactical callsign of the MiGs, and there was no time for formality. "MiG flight! Heads up! Interceptors closing on you from the north. Select afterburner and arm your missiles."

Sorokin had played this game many years before, in the air defense center in downtown Hanoi. Seeing a developing opportunity, he relied on the Cuban, Cordoba. *He's experienced*, Sorokin thought. *He'll follow orders without hesitation.*

The Russian ordered the lead pair of Sukhois to come hard left, dashing into Saudi airspace. The lead section had Atoll air-to-air missiles while the other Su-22s had been armed solely with bombs and rocket pods. Cordoba would have expended his ordnance and should be down to fighting weight on fuel. The MiGs were to hook right, enveloping the Saudis in a two-pronged aerial pincer. Though it was a hasty decision, it could work if timed properly.

Over Saudi Arabia, 0720 Hours

Rajid eyeballed the four MiG-21s on his left quarter, watching them close at a combined rate of some 1,500 mph. He heard Tim Ottman call, "I'm high." Noting the four 21s were flying a "welded wing" formation, with each wingman almost wingtip to wingtip on his leader, Rajid pulled in toward the nearest section. His armament display panel showed the right-hand Sidewinder was selected.

The AIM-9 missile had a forward-quarter capability, with enhanced sensitivity in the infrared seeker head which detected even the aerodynamic frictional heat generated by a high-speed aircraft. Rajid heard the warble of the tracking tone in his earphones, and for an instant he marveled that all his training was being put to use.

Then he called "Snake!" and pressed the trigger.

It was a low-percentage shot, with only a marginal chance to score. But the MiGs were forced to break formation to evade the missile, immediately putting the Yemenis on the defensive. They had not had time to fire any missiles of their own. The nearest two MiGs split from one another and Rajid pressed his attack on the wingman.

Circling overhead like a lethal shepherd watching his flock, Ottman alternately tracked the second pair of MiGs and tried to follow the engaged Tigersharks. *So this is combat,* he mused. *Funny, it doesn't feel much different from practice.*

Acting on doctrine, Rajid called, "I have it."

His wingman pulled up to cover the fight, turning to place the lead MiG off his nose. When the second 21 broke hard right to defeat the missile, Rajid had held his course, passing on a reciprocal heading to the 21's belly side. He could have continued his turn, using the F-20's superior maneuverability to gain an angle when both fighters came around the circle. But that would prolong the fight. He recalled Colonel Lawrence's dictum: Don't waste time trying to sweeten up the shot. Kill the bogey soonest.

Instead of turning, Rajid pitched into a high yo-yo immediately after passing the MiG's tail. Pulling up, he quarter-rolled to keep his opponent in view through the top of his canopy, arcing onto his back.

Straining against the G, forcing himself to keep the MiG "padlocked," Rajid felt an odd sense of detachment, almost as if he were a spectator of this combat rather than a participant. *I've been here before*, he thought, *in practice and in the simulator. I'm going to win!*

The frightened Yemeni pilot reefed hard in his four-G turn, almost as much as his MiG-21 could sustain. He had difficulty keeping the Saudi in sight above him, and hoped to throw the Northrop outside his turn radius. But by continuing his level turn he gave the Tigershark a predictable path to anticipate the conversion, and it did not take long.

Pulling hard behind the 21, sensing the fuzzy grayness at the periphery of his vision, Rajid waited until his nose was approximately aligned with the MiG's. He recognized that he had a bit more separation than he needed, but he was well within the Sidewinder envelope. He had a favorable angle off the tail and took off some bank to reduce the G on his airplane. Hearing the tone again, he called the shot.

FROM OVERHEAD, OTTMAN SAW THE SECOND 'WINDER come off the left rail, fly unerringly to the MiG, and explode. There was a bright flash in the sky.

"Yeah!" Ottman shouted in his oxygen mask.

The MiG-21 disgorged a cloud of dirty orange flames, with hundreds of tiny metal fragments in its wake. Instantly the canopy came off and the pilot's seat rocketed from the cockpit. The remains of the aircraft plummeted to the desert floor.

Seeing his wingman hit the ground, the MiG leader elected to disengage. The camouflaged delta-winged fighter reversed its turn, no longer sparring with Rajid's wingman. The F-20s' ROE said no hot pursuit, but the second MiG section remained in Saudi airspace. Ottman keyed his mike: "Orange Lead, this is Three. Two bandits still in a level turn with me, coming around upsun right now."

Rajid rapidly scanned the sky, hoping to silhouette the MiGs above him against the high, thin overcast. The glare bothered him. "No visual, Three."

"Lead from Two. I have the bandits." Lieutenant Hasni Khalil had good eyes.

"You have it, Two."

Khalil slid out abeam of Rajid as the two easily traded the lead. Moments later Rajid saw them, also noting Ottman's section arcing upward to position itself beyond the bogeys. The MiGs were trapped.

"Orange Flight, this is Sentinel. Two bogeys at twenty-two miles, closing from southwest." The AWACS was doing its job.

Ottman cursed to himself. Damn Sukhois—he'd almost forgotten them. "Lead from Three. I'll take 'em."

"Ah, roger, Three."

Ottman rolled over and took up the heading. His wingman moved out abeam, expertly anticipating his move. With a visual on the Sukhois at six miles, the two F-20s began working for position.

Over the Undefined Border, 0722 Hours

The Su-22M is a large single-seat fighter-bomber, as big as a Phantom. Though it has variable-geometry wings, it cannot turn or accelerate with lighter aircraft but it has powerful armament and Mach 2 speed. Julio Martin Cordoba led his Yemeni wingman to engage the Saudis with air-to-air missiles and, if necessary, the seventy rounds in each of their 30mm cannon. Granted position for a gunnery pass, the Sukhois might have done some harm. But against alerted, aggressive Tigersharks the Fitters stood little chance.

Colonel Sorokin sized up the tactical situation displayed in blue-green light on the scope before him. He was not aware of the term, even though he understood some aviation English, but he called for a bugout. "Cordoba! Hostiles ahead and above you. Get out of there, now!"

The Cuban already recognized the setup as a no-win situation. He called for a disengagement, executing a crossover turn the moment he saw the F-20s zoom-climb for the perch.

BEFORE THE SUKHOIS COMPLETED THEIR REVERSAL, Ottman and his wingman were on the way down, cutting the corner and closing in on the big fighter-bombers. He could see the yellow-white glow of the afterburner on the right-hand Fitter, momentarily wondering if the turn was offensive or defensive. He briefly thought of the ROE, then decided the Yemenis were staying to fight.

When the Northrops rolled out they were best positioned against the right-hand Sukhoi. Its partner had made a less radical turn, bleeding off less airspeed, and thus gained better separation from the threatening F-20s. Ottman settled into an easy bank, almost on G, at one and one-half miles. "Four, do you have a tone?" Ottman wanted to give the Saudi the shot if possible.

He heard the carrier wave, then a slight pause. "Negative, Three." The disappointment was audible in the boy's voice.

That was what Ottman actually had hoped for. He heard the death rattle chirping in his earphones, knew his starboard missile was tracking the right-hand bogey, and depressed his mike button. "Snake!"

Accelerating through Mach .88 at 1,200 feet, the big Sukhoi had no hope of evading the missile. Ottman's 'winder detonated close to the tail as the active laser proximity fuse induced a slightly premature explosion.

THE ASTUTE YOUNG CAPTAIN IN THE E-3 FOLLOWED the headlong chase southward. The F-20 answering as Orange Three was too close to the demarcation line; he should be warned. "Three, this is Sentinel. Recommend you break off."

Ottman was in no mood for unsolicited advice. His easygoing demeanor on the ground was ruthlessly shoved aside as his professional fangs came out and his armament system sequenced to the port rail. With a discernible overtake on the Sukhoi, he regained missile tone and fired again.

The Sidewinder took the tail off the Su-22, which rolled violently before searing a long, greasy smear on the shale floor. Ottman had a glimpse of the enemy pilot's seat ejecting from the doomed aircraft as it rolled inverted.

Orange Three and Four pulled up, cleared one another, and called the Sentinel. "No bogeys remaining this side of the border," came the E-3's reply. "RTB."

Ottman acknowledged. "Returning to base." Then, "Orange Lead, do you copy?"

Rajid's voice came through. "Roger, copy. We're five miles in trail." A slight pause. "Orange Two has a kill."

Ottman's adrenaline surged. He pulled into a near-vertical climb to cruise altitude, rolling gleefully all the way. He had not known it was possible to feel so good.

Southeast of Nejran, 0749 Hours

A small crowd was gathered at the staging base as Orange Flight taxied in. Spectators noted empty missile rails on two of the fighters, with gunpowder streaks on a third. There were cheers, grins, and thumbs-up all around. Mechs and pilots hauled Rajid Hamir from his cockpit and bore him upon their shoulders, chanting, "Ra-jid, Ra-jid!" The young man smiled his shy smile and grabbed extended hands on either side.

Five minutes passed before Lawrence restored order. Masher

Malloy's flight was due back, and the reserve flight had been brought to ready alert. Lawrence got to Rajid just as Tim Ottman broke through the crowd.

The big New Yorker was exultant, and not only for his own success. He stalked up to Rajid and pounded the youngster on the shoulders with unintended force. Then Khalil was dragged into the circle, grinning after his gun kill. Ottman locked both Saudis in his beefy arms, squeezing their necks painfully.

"I'm so goddam proud of these guys I don't know what to say. Ed, you shoulda seen it. We took on six bandits and bagged three!"

Lawrence could tell Ottman's blue eyes were misting over.

After the debrief, Lawrence picked up the phone. He called the communications office at Khamis Mushayt and sent a message for Bennett:

> First blood for Tiger Force. Splashed two Blue Bandits
> and one Fitter. All tigers home. Details to follow. Love
> and kisses, Devil.

Less than an hour later came the reply, radioed in by the teletype operator:

> Sura 8:17. Pirate.

There was a scramble to find a copy of the Koran. One of the Saudi mechanics produced a volume and translated. Amid a crowd of onlookers he flipped to the Chapter of the Spoils and read, "Ye did not slay them, but it was God who slew them; nor didst thou shoot when thou didst shoot, but God did shoot, to try the believers from Himself with a goodly trial; verily, God both hears and knows. There, verily, God weakens the stratagem of the misbelievers."

■ ■ ■

MASHER MALLOY WAS DEAD.

Lawrence called Bennett the morning after the engagement with the news. As often happened, there was not much information. Bennett knew from the tone of Lawrence's voice that the redhead was upset, but the exec maintained his composure. He had been through this before.

"All we know for sure is that he augured in from over twenty grand," Lawrence explained. "We'd had hydraulic troubles with one bird, and since Masher's flight was on rotation, he decided to test-fly it. Besides, you know how he liked solo aerobatics."

"Sounds like oxygen trouble."

"I don't know how else to call it, John. He made no transmissions after checking the airplane and systems. The E-3 had him the whole flight. There's been no other excitement along the border so they had no trouble tracking him."

Bennett well knew the pattern. Nobody could say how many times aircraft on a routine flight failed to return because of some small malfunction, a tiny oversight which grew to tragic proportions in moments. Most flights in tactical aircraft require 100 percent oxygen above 18,000 feet—the level at which the atmosphere is half as dense as at sea level. Apparently Malloy had succumbed to oxygen starvation.

"Okay, wrap it up down there as fast as you can, Ed. Is your relief still on schedule?"

"Affirmative. We're due back day after tomorrow."

Bennett realized with a pang that Masher had never mentioned any relatives. He leaned back in his chair, hands over his eyes. A soft whisper escaped his lips. "Damn."

Secretary of Defense Benjamin Wake was in his office by 0700, reading message traffic from the night before. His early arrival was typical of the man, for his tireless energy and astute business sense had made him a computer millionaire early in life. "You don't get rich without getting up," he liked to say.

Scanning the summaries on his desk, Wake stopped abruptly and reread one report from the U.S. air attaché in Riyadh. The originating office told him that State also must have the information. That meant he'd be hearing from Thurmon Wilson again. The Secretary of Defense pressed a buzzer on his desk console and seconds later Major Emory Kirn, USAF, stepped into the luxurious office.

Wake waved the Riyadh report aloft before Kirn could speak. "Major, what else do you have on this Arabian episode?" Kirn was responsible for tracking such messages, and he cordially hated the job. He yearned for his comfortable old B-52 back at Fairchild.

"Nothing yet, Mr. Secretary. I knew you'd want more data so I've requested amplification. Apparently the combat occurred day before yesterday, so we should know more by noon."

Wake leaned back in his overstuffed chair. "What do you think, son? This is hearsay evidence, with no confirmation on U.S. personnel directly involved. Doesn't even mention the source of the report." Wake flipped the paper aside.

"Well, sir, it might be embassy gossip. Or it might be a Saudi officer bragging about their F-20s. You know fighter pilots."

Wake smiled in appreciation of the sentiment. "And I know the president. He'll want details ASAP. Keep on it, Major."

Bahrain

Three days later Claudia arrived on a courier plane for the memorial service Saturday morning. Friday is the Muslim sabbath and not all the Saudis could have attended then. She would return to Riyadh on Sunday evening.

Claudia was surprised to find she seemed to take Malloy's death harder than his friends did. She had expected the pilots to be more subdued, if not actually depressed. But upon entering the IPs' club she found an almost exuberant atmosphere. She began to understand that these were men accustomed to sudden death among comrades. Bennett escorted her to a seat and ordered her a drink.

Lawrence came in just then, wearing his flight suit. Spotting Claudia, he walked over to her. He leaned down to hug her and she squeezed his neck.

"Oh, Ed, I'm so sorry."

"I know, hon. I know." He sat down.

Bennett walked up, drinks in hand. "Hi, Ed. Can you join us for a minute?"

Lawrence shook his head. "Naw, I just stopped by to let you know everything's set for the service."

"You're leading the formation, right?"

"Yes, with one student from each class."

Claudia asked, "Are there funeral arrangements in the States?"

The two aviators exchanged meaningful glances; neither wanted to speak. Claudia looked from one to the other. Finally Bennett put his hand on hers. "Claudia, his plane exploded on impact."

"Oh." It was barely audible.

The memorial service was a short one. Most of the IPs plus many of the Saudi pilots and maintenance personnel attended. Flying had nearly shut down for the afternoon, and Bennett's brief remarks were uninterrupted. Standing in the shade of a hangar, the assembly bowed heads for a short prayer and sang the "Navy

Hymn" from photocopied pages. Most of the IPs knew the words by heart.

Claudia recognized the haunting tune and listened carefully to the words. She shivered involuntarily at the phrase "Hear us when we lift our prayer for those in peril in the air."

Seconds later four F-20s swept overhead, deployed in the World War II "finger four" pattern. As the formation passed the runway intersection at 1,000 feet, the lead aircraft—second from the left— abruptly pulled up in afterburner. Ed Lawrence executed an immaculate series of vertical slow rolls as the three Saudis maintained level flight. There was a gap where Lawrence had been: the missing man formation.

Claudia tightened her grip on Bennett's arm.

The wake—Claudia didn't know what else to call it—was more lively than she expected. But she felt the need to talk quietly with Bennett, and they found a corner where their privacy was respected.

Bennett sensed Claudia's uneasiness. Holding her hands in his, he got her talking about what she knew best. "Honey, I'd like to know what you think will happen in the region now."

She thought for a moment. "I can't speak officially, of course. But there's no doubt the radical Muslim states are preparing for something. My personal opinion is, it's probably too late to avert war. After all, that's why the king organized your Tiger Force. But what will make it especially hard on Israel is that the Arabs seem to understand diplomatic as well as military power now. They still remember the effect of the '73 oil embargo."

Bennett squeezed her hands. "There's no chance of negotiations?"

She shook her head decisively. "No, I don't think so, John. Not as long as Israel occupies most of Jordan. Remember, King Hussein declared himself out of the West Bank issue before the occupation, leaving the PLO as the Palestinian voice. As long as that matter remains unsolved, there's not much chance for peace."

Bennett softly pinched her arm. "That's not a very optimistic statement from a nice Jewish girl."

"*Half* Jewish." Claudia smiled but her voice had an edge. "And remember, there are still some Israelis who think the way I do. However, the current government has a no-compromise frame of mind. Most Israelis honestly feel they can't give up any territory. They want a buffer zone around Israel's border."

Deciding there had been enough shop talk, Bennett led Claudia to the small dance floor. Pressed close together halfway through the song, he whispered, "Hey there, lady. Can I give you a lift to your hotel?"

She regarded him with a twinkle in her hazel eyes. "Sure thing, sailor. If you're going my way."

PART ★ III

The beginning of all war may be
discerned not only by the first
act of hostility, but by the coun-
sels and preparations foregoing.

John Milton

Elkonoklastes, 1649

10

TEL AVIV, Aug. 1. (Special to Mideast News Service)
—Despite a period of relative quiet in the Middle East
over the past 12 months, various military authorities
anticipate a continuing growth of tensions in months to
come. Few serving officers or defense ministry spokesmen in the region were willing to speak for the record,
but nearly all those queried believe that conflict between Israel and the Arab bloc may occur in the near
future.

Israeli sources cite the continuing buildup of Soviet-
supplied forces in Syria, Iraq and Lebanon as a matter

of concern. In turn, Arab sources point to Israel's prolonged occupation of Jordan as reason for smoldering tensions.

Aside from sporadic incidents in Jordan, the largest military clash during the past year occurred last August. Responding to South Yemen intrusions into their airspace, Saudi F-20s intercepted a PDRY formation and reportedly shot down three fighter-bombers. Border incidents between Yemen and South Yemen have tapered off since then, with no further air combats in the region.

However, reports persist that a number of conferences have been held by Muslim military planners in the past several months. Details are not available, but informed speculation has it that Syria, Libya, Iraq and perhaps Iran are drafting contingencies for military action should negotiations fail to gain a settlement in Jordan. Most neutral observers feel that Tel Aviv would be hard-pressed to meet a combined Arab offensive with Israel's forces thinly spread throughout Jordan.

Diplomatic contacts agree that Saudi Arabia holds the swing vote among Muslim nations. Thus far Riyadh has steered a neutral course but hard-line Arab states have been lobbying the Saudis for a more active role in settling the Jordanian situation.

Washington, D.C., 1 August

Thurman Wilson handed Avrim Ran a paper plate containing a hot dog, potato salad, and baked beans. The Secretary of State's elegant Georgetown residence, all brick and ivy, seemed an incongruous setting for an American-style picnic, but Wilson knew how to play to an audience. State's intel on the Israeli U.N. ambassador was quite thorough, and Wilson had noted the genuine grin on Ran's face despite the overcast sky.

Ran had learned to enjoy most aspects of life in America and traveled as widely as his duties in New York permitted. Outdoor barbeques, the Grand Canyon, and even horseback riding all appealed to him. Which was exactly the reason Thurmon Wilson had invited him to this "informal" meeting of their two families. Ran chuckled inwardly. Who but Thurmon Wilson would wear a tie to a picnic? The man was absolutely transparent.

And, the Israeli discovered, his American colleague didn't have much patience today. After exactly thirty minutes of polite conversation Wilson maneuvered Ran into the kitchen, away from their wives and Ran's young children.

"Avrim, I needed this time alone so we can discuss the Middle East situation without interruption. It's going on three years since the occupation of Jordan"—Wilson was careful to phrase the accusation as passively as possible—"and there's no settlement in sight. The president is terribly concerned, and he'd have asked me to talk to Ambassador Palnet, but Shlomo of course is unavailable." Ran nodded, recalling that Tel Aviv's ambassador to the United States remained hospitalized in Israel, recovering from a coronary. "You're the senior Israeli diplomat in this country right now," Wilson continued. "I want to ask you to communicate this administration's deep concern—privately, of course."

Ran blinked in surprise. This was old business to him. "Of course, Thurmon. You may rely on it. But surely you know that little has changed. Our forces remain firmly in control, and the civil unrest has subsided tremendously." He stopped to gather his thoughts. He did not want to promise what he could not deliver. "And our third-party negotiations through U.N. relief agencies and the Saudis seem to be making headway."

"That's just the point," Wilson insisted. "Israel isn't dealing directly with those who matter—the Jordanians. Their government in exile on Crete has been reduced to almost observer status in the back-channel discussions."

Ran made no comment, so Wilson pressed the advantage. "As for the Saudis, I don't think we can rely on their good offices indefinitely. They could get dragged into a war with their neighbors or succumb to internal radicals. Just look at that air combat with the Yemenis a year ago. And it's no secret that Syria and Iraq are planning something—maybe in concert with Iran. Avrim, we know as well as you do about the military buildups on Jordan's borders. This whole issue has helped unite what previously was a pretty fragmented Arab world."

Staring into space through the kitchen window, Avrim Ran thought of what another war would mean to his younger brother David, now leading a squadron of his own. *Maybe he'd welcome it.*

Ran started out the door to collect his family. "I'll pass along your concerns, immediately. Oh, and Thurmon . . ."

"Yes?"

"Thanks for the hot dogs."

Riyadh, 3 August

The air-conditioned conference room was starkly pleasant in contrast to the broiling heat outside. The royal family already had moved to Jidda, the summer capital, but a series of military conferences in Riyadh were necessary.

Tiger Force was slated for the second day, as part of an overall air force briefing. Accelerating events had pressed a carefully drafted contingency plan into effect throughout the Saudi military, and the F-20 squadrons figured prominently. Bennett sat across the polished table from Safad Fatah, noting the immaculate tiled floor and ornate high ceiling with marble columns along the walls. He was still somewhat surprised that he had been invited to attend the full session, but perhaps Fatah had something to do with that. The entire region was gearing up for war, and Bennett thought it unusual that a foreigner would be allowed to attend all the briefings. However, over three years of close affiliation with King Rahman and his ministers had earned him a trusted place.

As General Mustafa Halabi completed his presentation, Bennett looked again at the large-scale map on the wall. Scattered in an arc through northern and eastern Arabia were new airstrips either nearing completion or well under construction. They fit into a plan which Tiger Force IPs had helped formulate months before, and now Bennett would explain the integrated plan in which they were featured.

Bennett was careful to acknowledge the tacit trust inherent in his very presence. He knew it was unusual. "Your Majesty, gentlemen, I consider it a rare honor to attend your conference. The confidence expressed in me, and by extension in all our instructors, is deeply appreciated, and I hope we continue to earn your trust."

Bennett went on. "As most of you know, Tiger Force has reached its status of eight fully operational squadrons. Counting the Saudi pilots turned back into the training program, we could form another F-20 squadron with just a few transfers from remaining F-5E units." The Tiger II had been partially phased out of the Royal Saudi Air Force over the past year, but the little fighter's ease of maintenance endeared itself to the defense hierarchy. With acquisition of F-15s and more recent large purchases of Tornado fighter-bombers from Britain, the Saudis' maintenance situation had increased in difficulty, but F-5 mechanics easily switched to F-20s.

Bennett pulled a standard rescue mirror from his pocket and tilted it back and forth. "Most of you are familiar with these signal mirrors. The light from one of these can be seen for forty miles or more on a sunny day." The mirror had a hole in the reflective paint on the reverse side, allowing the user to align the mirror on the ship or aircraft searching for him. This put the light beam on target. Then, with a simple motion of the hand, the mirror was flashed to attract attention.

"The early warning system we've devised is an adaptation of one that General Chennault used in China during World War II. Clear air and unlimited visibility in the desert will allow us to use mirrors like this as a foolproof communications system. It cannot be jammed or deceived by any electronic means, and if the user is assigned a Morse Code authenticator, the signal cannot be duplicated by an opponent unless he knows that day's signal. Since a full-scale conflict in this region undoubtedly would involve electronic counter-measures by one or both sides, this means of air-raid warning could be crucial."

Bennett took a sip of water. "We intend to establish a net of between four hundred and five hundred fifty watch posts in three tiers from north to south across the upper portion of the country. It is preferable to use Saudi army personnel in two-man teams for at least part of this network, since they already can handle radio equipment and could be readily trained to identify aircraft and handle basic mirror signals. However, I'm told that certain segments of the Bedouin population can also be trained in this role.

"This system, if required in the face of radio jamming, could provide about twenty-five minutes warning of the approach of hostile or unidentified aircraft. With the F-20's rapid response time, that is more than enough to scramble, detect, and intercept an incoming raid. Since our signal outposts include positions on the Sinai front, it would be nearly impossible for . . . intruding aircraft to outflank our system in daylight." He had almost said *Israeli aircraft*, though Arabia had to be cautious of some Muslim neighbors as well.

Turning to the map, Bennett said, "Now, as you have already heard, a series of outlying fighter strips is well under construction. Each will have underground provisions for fuel, weapons, and some maintenance facilities. At least three will have sheltered bunkers for command-control use and a few protected hangars."

He added a few explanatory notes, then asked for comments or questions.

The king immediately spoke up. "Colonel Bennett, I believe this plan contains a fine balance between simplicity and sophistication. But tell me, what provision is there for long-range engagement of enemy aircraft with your squadrons?"

Bennett noted the visible effect of the king's choice of words. *Your squadrons.* He did not know whether to be pleased or concerned with the implications, but the regular air force officers seemed content to let him alone.

"Your Majesty, we are reconfiguring many of our two-seat Tigersharks with the radar and Sparrow missile system. Each aircraft can carry two AIM-7s on detachable underwing pylons. After discussing the matter with some of the officers present, we have tentatively decided to add two or three such planes to the existing squadrons. We therefore hope to provide a full range of intercept possibilities, day and night." Bennett considered whether or not he should hammer the old nail again, and decided to hit it once more. "The history of aerial combat in nearly every theater of action in nearly every war is consistent, sir. About seventy percent of all shootdowns are made in clear-air conditions against alerted opponents. We see the radar missile not so much as a killer, but as a means of gaining an initial advantage. By forcing the opposition to evade the standoff weapons, we gain time for favorable maneuvering to pursue the combat with heat-seeking missiles. And, if necessary, with guns."

The king rubbed his chin. "That is well, Colonel Bennett. So much for our northern flank. Have you anything to add about possible concerns from the south and east?"

"Well, sir, I might refer you to our friends in South Yemen. Some of them are qualified to comment on the capabilities of Tiger Force."

This brought a ripple of laughter around the table, even some polite applause. The monarch allowed himself a tight smile and tapped his palm on the tabletop for emphasis. Bennett beamed with pride, but quickly returned to the matter at hand.

"As for concern about Iranian action from across the Persian Gulf, that has been a factor in our planning from the start. You will recall that we established our primary base at Bahrain with just that possibility in mind. And I'm glad to say that there has been no additional problem from either quarter."

Safad Fatah spoke for the first time during the day-long session. "Your Majesty, if I may interject." He had the full attention of everyone at the table. "The Iranian question is well to be considered. There has been much diplomatic activity in recent months, all at the highest levels. The government in Tehran has been feeling us out, apparently as part of an overall plan to bring the Muslim nations together under a unified banner." He paused to let that point sink in. "We know that communication between Syria and Iran has been especially active along these lines, and it would be folly to ignore the portent of such action."

Bennett glanced around, noting the sober faces. *So we're still at square one*, he thought. *Nothing's changed. The Saudis still are walking a tightrope between their Western economic partners and their radical Arab neighbors.*

The king stared at the polished tabletop for a few heartbeats. Then he said, "Thank you all for your efforts. This meeting is adjourned."

Bennett passed a word with his friend General Maila, who finally had found time to check out in the new F-20C. They talked shop for a few moments before Bennett walked outside. He met the first two Tiger Force squadron commanders, Majors Handrah and Jauf, near the message center. All three men were to return to Bahrain that afternoon. Bennett intended to use the next few hours to see Claudia for lunch; they had much to discuss.

As the limousine pulled away from the curb, Bennett glanced across the street. "Driver, could you please pull into that space up ahead?" The Saudi corporal immediately came to a stop. "Excuse me just one moment please, gentlemen," Bennett said to Handrah and Jauf. "I need a word with the air attaché."

Bennett had glimpsed Colonel Glen Mallon, the Air Force delegate to the U.S. Embassy. One of the maintenance supervisors had asked Bennett to pass along a report to the attaché's office, and this unexpected opportunity would save time later on. Time for Claudia.

Climbing from the rear seat with his briefcase, Bennett sprinted through traffic, barely dodging a kamikaze taxi, and hailed Mallon. The colonel stopped when he heard someone call his name and turned from his companion, another Air Force officer. Mallon turned toward Bennett, recognized him, and raised a hand in greeting.

Not quite to the opposite curb from the limousine, perhaps twenty-five yards diagonally up the street, Bennett felt the concussion a split second before the sound engulfed him from behind. He staggered forward, pushed by the force of the explosion, and fell. He caught himself with one hand on the curb, badly scraping the palm.

Bennett's survival instincts took over. He flopped face-down on the sidewalk, covering his head with his hands. For an instant he was back at Da Nang that night in 1968, sweating out a weather divert from Yankee Station while the North Vietnamese launched a rocket attack. The sound, the smoke, and flames, even the debris raining down upon him, all seemed the same. Risking a look, he raised his head and peeked over his shoulder. The limo was aflame, its ruptured gas tank feeding the blaze while thick black smoke boiled up.

Mallon had ducked at the sound of the explosion. Then, quickly recovering his poise, he saw Bennett on the curb a few yards away. He sprinted to Bennett's side. "John! Hey, John. Are you all right?"

Bennett was too stunned to respond. Both men looked back across the street. Thirty yards away lay the burning wreckage not only of the limousine but of two other parked vehicles. Several passersby had been knocked down, and Bennett knew at a glance that some of them were dead.

Tel Aviv, 6 August

Colonel Chaim Geller relaxed in his chair, an archaeology book propped open on his knees. Frequently he spent his lunch "hour" this way, though he seldom had sixty minutes to eat anymore. There was so much for Israeli intelligence to keep track of in the region that everyone worked overtime at least three days out of six.

Geller thought of the report from Riyadh and pondered its meaning. He also thought of young Levi Bar-El, now assigned to field intelligence with a parachute regiment. The eager youngster had declined the option to return to his previous position. Bar-El couldn't stand being a deskbound warrior anymore. Well, the boy's ability with Arabic and his call-up to active duty pointed in that direction. The section chief wondered whether Bar-El would ever hear of the latest event concerning the enigmatic Mr. Bennett.

Nearly all Tiger Force intelligence now went directly to the *Heyl Ha 'Avir*. But the car-bomb death of two Saudi Air Force majors, their chauffeur, and five civilians was of interest to other intelligence communities. By cross-checking a variety of sources, the story had come together with only a few gaps.

This Bennett was a lucky one, all right, Geller mused. Had the American air attaché not been on the street at the same time, Bennett certainly would have died in the car with the others. The natural question was, who and why?

Geller was miffed but not surprised to learn Israel was suspected by the Saudis. Ordnance specialists confirmed the C-4 explosive had been of U.S. manufacture, which to the outside world meant the Israelis could be involved. The section chief knew better and was reminded of the old professional dogma: Never assume the obvious without good reason.

"Whom do you suspect?" the director of diplomatic intelligence had asked the colonel that morning.

"Abraham, I'd lay even money it's the Yemenis or the Iranians."

"Explain."

"The F-20s delivered a one-sided defeat upon the South Yemen Air Force a year ago. We have known, as you are aware, that most of the instructors are Americans. This bombing could shape up as revenge, pure and simple."

The director tugged at his jowls. "Yes, I agree that is possible. But Iran?"

"Things get complicated there. Just a moment." Geller spun his chair, reached for a folder on his desk, and turned back. "We have strong evidence that high-level diplomatic discussions have been going on between most of the Islamic fundamentalist states and many of their more moderate neighbors. The link seems to be this man." Geller pulled a photograph from the folder.

"Ah, my old friend from Damascus!" The senior man's voice almost sounded jovial. "Ali al-Badran." He handed the picture back to Geller.

"Correct. He's probably the most skilled Arab diplomat, certainly the best and most experienced Syrian—"

"And he hates the very thought of Western devils conducting business in Arab countries. It's one of his ideological ties to the old Khomeini regime. That gives him credibility with the new clique in Tehran, which feels it has to pay lip service to the ayatollah's policies."

Geller tossed a little salute to the older man. "Very good, Abraham. You should consider a career in the intelligence field."

"Maybe I will someday, after I've finished digging up ancient civilizations." Archaeology was their common passion. That and the preservation of Israel. "So you think the Iranians and perhaps Syrians want to kill the head of this separate Saudi air force as a precautionary move?"

Geller shrugged his round shoulders. "It's one possibility. But I'll tell you one thing for sure. I wouldn't want to be in that American's shoes with two types of fanatics after me."

"I understand he's overseeing construction of more advanced airfields in northern Arabia. Is that a threat to us?"

"It could be offensive or defensive, depending upon how the fields are used. It's not for me to interpret, thank God. That's the kind of interpretation which leads to unwarranted assumptions, which leads to unnecessary action, which leads to war." He inhaled deeply. "Let's pray that the politicians don't reach the wrong conclusions."

His partner concurred solemnly. "Amen to that."

Washington, D.C., 7 August

President Walter Arnold settled into his chair for the National Security Council briefing, aware of the officers and civilian aides deferentially waiting behind him. Nearly all had remarked in recent months how his appearance had changed. Three tough years in office had left their mark on the president's face; his tan was long gone, deep lines accented his eyes and mouth, and the trademark silver-gray hair was almost completely white.

The staff and aides took their seats as the chief executive sat down. It was a larger meeting than normal, for the pending crisis in the Middle East had expanded in scope and complexity. Arnold believed in diversity of opinion right up to the point when he made a decision. He had once told his chief of staff, "No historian is going to write about me what they wrote about Kennedy—bad advice from bad advisers. By God, if I make a mistake of the Bay of Pigs magnitude, everyone with me is going to take the heat, too."

As he had for nearly every week in the previous three years and more, Major General George Miller stood before the president to update the global military situation.

"Mr. President, there has been no indication of further overt action on the part of Arab air forces in the past several days. However, there is a high level of diplomatic activity among the Iranians, Syrians, and Iraqis, with lower levels of consultation with other Arab states. This includes meetings of the Syrian ambassador-at-large, Ali al-Badran, with traditional moderates from Saudi Arabia, Kuwait, and the Emirates."

Arnold knew this pattern had existed for at least several months, probably much longer. "Okay. What about Egypt and Jordan?"

Miller was ready for that question. "The Jordanian government continues to exist in exile, if you will, but of course without exercising much influence as to what happens there. We believe that return of Israeli-occupied Jordan to the Jordanians will be a cornerstone of any proposed settlement.

"As for Egypt, there is nothing to suggest the current fundamental regime will change its attitudes anytime soon. Cairo's geopolitical stance is somewhere between Riyadh and Tehran—not as extreme as the Iranians but certainly not as moderate as the Saudis. That was to be expected after the previous government fell."

Miller flipped a page on his chart and pointed to military dispositions. "Mr. President, there has been movement of Egyptian antiaircraft units into Sinai." The pointer tapped out positions beyond the Suez Canal. "Intelligence photos show that they are remaining stationary at present, and in fact are part of a planned combined arms exercise. But their location could be ominous. These are relatively new units of considerable versatility. Each tracked vehicle contains a twenty-five-millimeter gun and two each short- and medium-range SAMs. They are deployed in battalion strength, and they can keep up with the fastest battle tanks."

"Is that mechanical fact significant?"

"Yes, sir. At least it could be. You see, if motorized infantry with tanks were to suddenly drive eastward across Sinai, they would have to take their antiair forces with them. By prepositioning such units, they gain a time saving."

"Why couldn't the Israelis knock out these units? That would prevent the tanks and infantry from advancing, wouldn't it?"

"Mr. President, these SAMs have terminal guidance which could be passive—acting upon heat or even noise of the target. They would not be easily defeated. You'll recall the serious losses the Israelis had from Egyptian SAMs in '73."

Arnold did not know the figures, and in fact did not care. But he did know that dozens of Israeli aircraft had been destroyed or seriously damaged by the belt of surface-to-air missiles during the Yom Kippur War. Only extensive U.S. electronics gear and replacement aircraft and parts had kept the Israelis flying in sufficient numbers. Arnold did not intend to oversee another situation in which American aid to Israel incurred economic retaliation from the oil producers.

"All right," Arnold said. "We have definite diplomatic activity among the Arabs, apparently for the purpose of establishing unity among the Muslim states. And we have possible military activity aimed at Israel from Egypt. What about other military cooperation?"

"I was just coming to that, sir." Miller flipped his chart again. The new page showed operating areas in Syria and Iraq. "Combined exercises have been held in these vicinities with Syrian, Iraqi, and reportedly some Iranian units. Our reports indicate a high degree of coordination between ground and air forces with good communications and control." This was new information, and its significance was not lost on those in the room.

"What this amounts to," Miller summarized, "is the possibility of Arab preparation for a combined offensive against Israel. This kind of alliance—political and military—has never been accomplished before. If it continues at current levels, the Israelis will be in for the fight of their lives."

"I assume the Israelis are as aware of all this as we are."

"Oh, yes, sir. In fact, we have confirmed some of our data with Tel Aviv."

Arnold perked up. "With Tel Aviv . . . Any chance they're feeding us some of this info just to gain sympathy?"

Miller was surprised—the president did not usually subscribe to Machiavellian theories. Perhaps three years on the job had taught him to consider more arcane and less apparent motives—even with longstanding allies.

"We considered that possibility, sir. All our data has been independently confirmed."

"How soon might such an Arab alliance move?"

Miller glanced at the intelligence representatives. "The Arabs have all the hardware they need right now, sir. And they have a very large manpower pool—much of it combat-experienced. This is especially true of the Iraqis and Iranians. Additionally, the Israelis are overextended in Jordan. They really can't keep the lid on there and fully defend their homeland at the same time."

Arnold rubbed his temple with one hand, his eyes closed. There was a long silence before he looked up again.

"General Miller, thank you. As usual, you're right up to date on things."

Surprised to be dismissed so abruptly, Miller walked offstage. He still had more to say.

The president turned to the NSC staff. "Gentlemen, ladies, we're entering a difficult period. We simply cannot allow ourselves to be forced into choosing sides in another Arab-Israeli war. The economic and diplomatic considerations are too great. I'll pursue this discussion at the cabinet meeting tomorrow."

Walking to his limousine, Arnold strode out of earshot of his Secret Service escorts. Grabbing his chief of staff by the arm, he hissed, "See what Wilson and State can do. By God, we give the Israelis three billion a year, never see most of it again, and they perpetuate this situation despite us. I *hate* being in the middle like this. It just isn't fair!"

The chief of staff stopped in his tracks, watching the briskly striding figure of the President of the United States. The staff director pondered the wisdom of sending Arnold the speech by Henry Kissinger years ago. "Nations don't have friends. They have interests." Of course, the present situation was not fair. What's that got to do with anything?

Riyadh, 23 August

Claudia Meyers knocked on the door of Bennett's hotel room. The door swung open, a tanned hand reached out, grasped her forearm, and pulled her inside. The door slammed shut.

They hugged each other tightly for several minutes. At length Claudia said, "My God, I'm tired of living on letters and phone calls." She squeezed his neck. "You feel so *good*."

He touched her cheek. "We do have a lot to talk about, don't we?" They sat down on the bed, and Bennett moved a black zippered bag to one side. Curled up with one another, they talked.

Bennett said, "All right, here's what I'm thinking of doing." He looked directly into her hazel eyes. "War's coming. No doubt about it. My boys are ready, and I can't do much more. I'm thinking of asking to be released from my extended contract, going back home with you and setting up a house in California or Connecticut or wherever you like. What do you say?"

She returned his gaze. "Is that a proposition, sailor?"

He grinned the white grin she loved. "Consider it a proposal, Claudia. I've been thinking along these lines for quite a while. Now I want to marry you."

Her voice seemed small in the room. "Okay."

That afternoon they made love and made plans. The main concern was how to accommodate their different work and responsibilities.

Bennett said, "I can probably wrap things up in less than sixty days. If necessary, Ed can take over for me. We're down to the basic requirements of twenty-eight IPs now, including one for each squadron, since basic flight training is winding down." He tickled her ribs and she wriggled away. "What about you?"

"I'll put in for termination of my position here right away. I'm senior enough that it shouldn't be too difficult, especially since I've been at this station so long." She edged closer to Bennett, grasping his near hand to prevent more mischief. "I'd like to finish my full twenty years with the State Department, John. If I got a Washington posting could you tolerate that for a while? It would only be another couple of years."

The disappointment showed on his face. "Oh, lord. Georgetown cocktail parties, small talk with the temporary acting deputy undersecretary from Lower Slobbovia. You'd really subject the man you love to that sort of thing?"

"Yes. If I was the woman he loved."

"Ouch." He raised his hands. "Okay, I surrender. But old John B. is going to look awfully funny in a tux. Besides, how will I communicate with anybody? You know fighter pilots can't talk with a teacup in one hand. It takes two, baby." He parodied the gestures common to aviators describing two aircraft engaged in a close dogfight.

Claudia laughed appreciatively, then turned serious. "What do you think you would do for two years or so in D.C.?"

He wrapped his arms around her. "I've never been a house husband. That seems all the rage these days. You know, send you off to work each morning with a healthy, nutritious lunch in your bag. Have a nice dinner waiting when you come home after a hard day with the Bulgarian ambassador."

Claudia kissed his cheek. "That's a lovely thought, but for some reason I don't quite buy it. Really, what would you do?"

"I think I'd like to write a book about my time here in Arabia. I might not be able to find a publisher, and I couldn't describe some things, of course. But the people I've worked with, especially the students, they're the real story." He warmed to his subject. "I wish you knew some of these kids like I do, Claudia. Doggone, so many of them are really terrific young guys. It's like Chuck Yeager said. You fly with all kinds of pilots from all over the world and there isn't a dime's worth of difference among them. Training and experience are what matter.

"I don't mean to overstate this, but in a way Tiger Force has been my family. I raised these kids, most of them from teenagers. I'm really going to miss them. And most of the IPs, too."

"That reminds me," Claudia said. She got up to fetch her shoulder bag and pulled out a worn blue T-shirt. Returning to the bed, she sat down beside Bennett. "I've kept this but I don't really know what to do with it. What do you think?"

Bennett fingered the familiar garment. "I think you should keep it. Masher would like to know that you still wear it."

Claudia slid under the covers and nestled close. "What do you think will become of the others?"

"Oh, most of them will go back to what they did before. Airlines, reserve flying, commercial instruction. Some will just become beachcombers."

"It won't be the same for them, will it?"

Bennett inhaled, thinking of Ed Lawrence. "No, it won't. You know, in the business we talk about being warriors, of being entirely job-oriented. No bullshit, stick to the basics. Beyond that, we talk about the pure warriors. Well, Ed's the only really pure warrior I know anymore. And it's not a cheery prospect."

She laid her head on his chest. "Why not?"

"Because he really is pure. He's never been married, has no outside interests. Flying and fighting are all he knows and all he cares about. He's very good at it, but there's not much else for him besides sport flying. I worry about what might become of him. There's nothing sadder than a warrior without a war."

Claudia ran her finger around his lips. "Maybe we could adopt him. At least have him to dinner or occasional weekends." Her face turned serious. "John, what's the attraction of combat? I get the feeling that some of you actually enjoy it."

He thought for a moment. "Yes, some of us do. I think of the Marine recruiting slogan way back when. 'Nobody likes to fight but somebody has to know how.' That's strictly public relations. The plain fact is, most of the really good fighters do love to fight. A lot of us just enjoy the hell out of flying the airplane, but Ed and his type are beyond that. The airplane isn't a vehicle—it's a weapon."

"What makes men like that?"

"Ego. Remove ego or self-respect from the human equation— they're both related—and you remove war." He stroked her back, concentrating on his line of thought. "I believe that implicitly. And it's the biggest factor overlooked in discussions of the causes of war."

Claudia moved her head to his shoulder, and he savored the touch of her hair on his skin. "I never told you, John, but you scared me *and* attracted me when we met. There was something about you that was . . . well, it was dangerously appealing. And I've noticed it among your pilots. They respect you, but I think a lot of them are a little frightened of you, too."

He chuckled. "That's what I hope for. Keeps 'em alert."

Bennett rolled over and nibbled on Claudia's ear. She inhaled sharply between clenched teeth. "You *know* what that does to me."

"Affirmative. Let's take a bath before dinner."

THEY ADJUSTED THEIR LEGS TO ACCOMMODATE ONE another in the tub. Claudia reached for a bar of soap, unwrapped it, and rubbed it between her hands. Then she leaned forward, lathering his chest and shoulders. Her eyes twinkled as she playfully rinsed the suds from his body by splashing water on him.

In turn, he picked up the bar and applied soap to her breasts and back. Then came a scratching noise, faintly heard, from the door.

Claudia began to ask a question but he silenced her with a raised hand. He heard the sound again and knew it was not a key. He knew everything he needed to know, and his adrenaline surged.

With a silent curse, Bennett leapt from the tub and sprinted eight steps around the corner to his nightstand. He knew he had made two mistakes: He should have taken the black bag with him to the bathroom, and he should have closed and locked the bathroom door. He heard the main door open as he brought the Browning Hi-Power up from the bag.

Bennett heard Claudia scream as a metallic tinkling filled the narrow hallway around the corner. He heard the sound of copper-jacketed bullets striking porcelain and enamel. Keeping low and kneeling, he braced his left forearm against the edge of the wall and centered his front sight on the intruder's upper torso. One glimpse told the story.

The entrance door was open and the gunman had stepped inside to his left, without silhouetting himself. He had pivoted right when he saw the open bathroom door, fired a long burst into the tub, and was swinging back left. The muzzle of the silenced Ingram MAC-11 came toward Bennett, slightly high.

In the next instant Bennett squeezed the Browning's three-and-one-half-pound trigger and the sharp-nosed, armor-piercing round smashed through the intruder's sternum. Without hesitation, Bennett lifted the auto pistol and sighted on the man's forehead and the next round shattered the cranium. The body collapsed backward against the vanity mirror and slid to the floor, twelve feet from the Hi-Power's muzzle.

Two rapid heartbeats later another form appeared against the backlighted hallway. Bennett's loading sequence was armor piercing backed up by hardball, and he fired two quick rounds into the center of mass. The second man, also armed with a silenced MAC-11, staggered forward and—perhaps from reflex—triggered a burst which went into the wall near Bennett's right rear.

The terror, the lethal pressure, and the semidarkness combined to ruin Bennett's sight picture. He lost the competitive sharp image of his front sight and fired his next round at the assassin's head. It was proper procedure—what the South Africans called the Mozambique Drill. But the sight alignment was off, and the man took a grazing hit in the neck.

Slumping to his knees, still trying to bring the submachine gun to bear, the man strained toward his target.

Bennett was momentarily upset by his failure to stop the fight with two good hits, and he thought of his .45 back home. But then there was a clear and angry mind at work behind the Browning's sights. The reduced distance made sights seem hardly necessary but he forced himself to focus on the front ramp. Then he squeezed the trigger.

It was over. Bennett thought of a reload, but estimated he had fired six rounds; the magazine still held seven. He felt an ephemeral sense of exhilaration, followed by disgust at the unpleasant substances on the walls and floor. Then he thought of Claudia. But he was disciplined enough to order his priorities.

Scrambling to his feet, Bennett checked around the corner and found it clear. He jumped over the cadaver at his feet, slammed the door, and locked it. He turned and threw both Ingrams on the bed, noting a lock-picking kit had fallen from one man's pocket.

Claudia.

He knew what he would find. She lay in the tub, up to her chin in red-dyed water. She had taken ten .380 rounds in the chest and abdomen from that one long burst.

Bennett slumped on the bed, suddenly cold. He huddled into a sheet. Violent emotions tore at him from different directions. Delayed fear, the heaviness in the arms, the raspy dryness in the throat. But there was more: anger, remorse, a numbing sense of loss.

A loud pounding on the door brought Bennett's senses back to the immediate. He glanced around, noting the familiar blue T-shirt on the floor. Picking it up, he held it to his cheek. And that is how they found him, sobbing softly to himself.

Bahrain, 26 August

When John Bennett returned to Tiger Force, Ed Lawrence was the sole person on hand to meet him. It was contrary to the group of IPs and students who normally were present as a mark of courtesy and respect.

He looks ten years older, Lawrence thought to himself as Bennett came down the stairs of the commuter jet. The exec noted his friend's haggard appearance—especially the circles under the eyes and the slumping posture. Lawrence walked toward the man the students called "King Tiger." Now he resembled neither.

Bennett held out his hand. "Hello, Devil."

"Welcome home, Pirate." Then Lawrence put his arms around Bennett's shoulders.

Bennett unwrapped himself and smiled grimly. "Let's have a drink."

The redhead said, "I think even Allah would approve."

Seated in Bennett's quarters, Lawrence filled him in on recent events. "You wondered why the Saudis were including you in all the air force planning, remember? Well, I talked to Rajid and a couple of others from Class One. You know there are about five thousand princes in this country?" Bennett nodded. "Well, we have our share flying F-20s. I guess it's still a case of not what you know but who you know that counts. Because it looks like our guys, the Saudi pilots, used some of their influence. After Handrah and Jauf were killed in the car bomb, our tigers told Saudi HQ they didn't want any more outsiders as squadron COs. They wanted us, the IPs, to fill the gaps."

Bennett showed interest. "That could mean trouble in our relations with the Saudi Air Force."

"That's what I thought," Lawrence said. "So I took it upon myself to propose a compromise, subject to your approval. Some of our sports are CO material—Rajid, Menaf, a couple of others from Class One. What say we recommend them for the slots?"

Bennett thought for a long moment. "They probably will be okay with more experience. But if it comes to shooting . . ."

"Yeah, I know. But this seems a good way of us keeping an even strain with both sides. At least, it may be the best we can get."

"You know, Ed, I didn't really know we had that kind of loyalty from these kids. I mean, I'm really pleased that's how they feel, but I'd have expected they'd want their own people."

"I discussed it with Peter and Tim and some of the guys. You know what a philosopher Peter is. He says it makes sense. The oldest of our first pilots still aren't twenty-six. The youngest of the last graduating class are between twenty and twenty-one. Hell, we raised these studs from pups. I guess it's natural that they look to us for continued leadership."

Lawrence poured more Jack Daniels over the ice in Bennett's

cup. "John, do you feel like talking about Claudia? I'm a pretty good listener."

Bennett inhaled deeply and slowly let it out. He closed his eyes for a moment. "Yeah, it might help."

"Any idea who the shooters were?"

"The Saudis said both had Lebanese papers. That may or may not mean anything. Apparently one of them was a mercenary connected to a Christian militia outfit in Beirut years ago. I was told that a lot of those people went free-lance."

"If they were Christian militia, that means Israeli support, doesn't it?"

"Yes. The Saudi investigators are convinced of it but they wouldn't discuss sources beyond the Beirut connection."

"Wow. Then the timing means—"

"The timing probably means the Israelis have planned preemptive strikes against airfields in reach of their Jordanian positions. That's how I see it. Decapitate Tiger Force and follow up with attacks into northern Arabia. But there's just one thing wrong with that."

"Yeah," Lawrence interjected. "They haven't hit us."

"Right. And it's not like the Israelis to telegraph their punches."

"So what do you think?"

"There's another theory that the Yemenis might have been behind it—a revenge thing. But I'm inclined to think it was Israel—maybe an unauthorized operation of some sort. There might have just been a slip-up and the assassins hit too early. One of the investigators said there's evidence they waited outside my hotel for most of the day, maybe expecting to hit me in the street. They might have gotten tired of waiting and decided to come in shooting."

Lawrence said, "What do you want to do about it, John?"

"I want to kill whoever's behind this. But I can't afford a vendetta." He took off his shoes. "I'm gonna turn in, take some sleeping pills, and get some rest. I'd like 001 ready for an 1830 launch tomorrow. Can you set it up for me?"

"Sure thing. No problem." He slapped Bennett on the shoulder. "Goodnight, pardner."

Walking to the operations office, Ed Lawrence knew exactly what his friend had in mind. "He's got a world of hurt inside him," the exec told Bear Barnes. "Now he wants to take it upstairs and leave some of it there."

11

TEL AVIV, Sept. 1—Israeli and Arab warplanes twice clashed over occupied Jordan today, in the largest Mideast air battle of recent years. As many as forty fighter jets may have been involved in the dogfights, resulting in the destruction of perhaps a dozen or more Syrian and Iraqi planes and an unspecified number of Israeli U.S.-built F-15s or F-16s.

Official accounts from Tel Aviv and Damascus were incomplete or contradictory, with no comment yet from Baghdad. However, military sources indicated that eight or nine Syrian MiGs were downed in the early-morning clash and four Iraqi jets about two hours later. Syrian spokesmen admitted that "a number" of their planes had not returned from a reconnaissance sweep over eastern Jordan, but claimed destruction of "several" Israeli warplanes. A carefully worded Israeli communique said that all its pilots were "accounted for" after each combat.

Unconfirmed reports stated that crippled Iraqi French-built Mirage fighters landed across the border in Saudi Arabia. Sources said it is unlikely the Saudis granted permission for such emergency landings, given Riyadh's effort to remain uninvolved in heightened tensions since Israel occupied most of Jordan more than three years ago.

Today's action was the first direct clash between Israeli and Arab aircraft since Tel Aviv's move into Jordan.

Bahrain

That afternoon the instructor pilots seated in the briefing room were more subdued than usual. They had been called to the meeting on short notice, and several still wore flight suits from their training flights. Tim Ottman and Bear Barnes speculated that the Saudis wished to renew their contracts. Others, like Geoff Hampton and Brad Williamson, adopted a wait-and-see attitude.

Lawrence and Bennett strode down the aisle and took the stage. There was immediate quiet in the room. Bennett asked that the doors be locked, though this had never been done before.

"Gentlemen, good afternoon. I'm sorry to call you here on such short notice—I intended to do some flying myself." Bennett was dressed in his Nomex flight suit with the Tiger Force patch on the right side and the Tigershark patch sewn on one shoulder.

"Early this morning there were two large hassles over eastern Jordan. One involved Syrian MiG-23s and the other apparently had more MiGs plus Iraqi Mirages. We don't know the full story, but it seems to have been quite a shootout, with losses to the Israelis as well as the Arabs. It's suspected but not yet proven that Iranian pilots were involved in at least one of these incidents."

A murmur ran through the room.

"Evidently the first combat was the result of Syrian overflights of Jordan to assess Israeli strength and dispositions. This has happened before, but has never been answered with such a hostile reaction. What makes this morning's events of interest to us is the fact that at least two Iraqi aircraft entered Saudi airspace to avoid pursuit by the Israelis. One Mirage was shot down barely on our side of the border. The other, already battle-damaged, landed without permission at one of our advanced fields." He paused to allow the gravity of that news to sink in. "This means we can expect attention from the Israelis almost anytime."

Bennett had expected a vocal response to this news. Instead, there was dead silence.

"I've been on the line to Riyadh several times since noon. This could well begin the direct involvement of Tiger Force, and all Saudi Arabia for that matter, in combat with the Israelis. They'll see our forward strips as a threat, offering assistance to other Arab aircraft. And they may decide to come after us, even though F-15s are patrolling the border to try and head off other Iraqi or Syrian intrusions.

"Consequently, I've reached an agreement with Safad Fatah and the Royal Saudi Air Force command. Each of you will be paid the balance of his existing contract, with a release from obligation to complete the tour, effective today. Mr. Fatah said to regard it as a bonus for a job well done." He paused, knowing that the audience awaited the other option.

"However . . ." Bennett let the word float for a moment, "if any of you should choose to remain with Tiger Force in the capacity of a planner or flight leader, you will be welcome. The legal implications will be explained in writing. I'm not saying you can have it all your own way because we don't know how the State Department might interpret it. But there's precedent which allows U.S. citizens to serve in the armed forces of foreign nations as long as those nations are not engaged in armed conflict with the United States. We don't have a full reading from London on this point—not yet."

Tim Ottman raised his hand. "Boss, what are you going to do?"

Bennett had anticipated the question. And he had decided that he would hold his counsel, preferring each man to decide for himself rather than follow the CO's example. "I've not made up my mind yet. You should decide what *you* want to do without considering anybody else's decision."

Peter Saint-Martin asked, "How long do we have to decide?"

"Riyadh needs to know by noon, day after tomorrow. That means I'd like a written decision from each of you by 2100 hours tomorrow." He looked around. "See you then."

Bennett knew there would be many transatlantic phone calls in the next several hours. He and Lawrence had already gone down the list of remaining IPs. They identified three who almost certainly would stay, and perhaps three more. Lawrence was already committed.

"Don't act hastily, Ed. You ever think about going home and picking up things again?" Bennett already knew the answer.

"My God, John," Lawrence had replied, "don't you get it? There's a war just around the corner. I *am* home." After an uncomfortable silence Lawrence had asked, "What about you?"

Bennett stared at the floor momentarily, then leveled his gaze at the redhead. "I'm staying."

■   ■   ■

NEXT DAY AT NOON, WELL AHEAD OF FATAH'S DEAD-line, Bennett and Lawrence met with the three other IPs who had decided to stay. Bennett looked around the room, checking off the motivation and capability of each pilot.

He had known that Bear Barnes would stick, and he had been equally confident of Geoff Hampton. Brad Williamson, the former Thunderbird, was a surprise. Bennett knew that Williamson had a family in Ohio and could get a slot in a Reserve F-16 squadron without difficulty. *Well, never mind,* Bennett thought. *Maybe he needs the extra money.*

Bennett went over the pertinent federal laws, just to reinforce the Americans' legal status. "According to Title Thirty-seven U.S. Code, Section Nine-oh-eight, Subsection A, Congress consents to retired members of the armed forces and members of the reserves— that's us—being employed by foreign governments provided the Secretary of State approves such employment. We're already covered, since State approved the Saudis' original request for us under this provision. We are acting on the assumption that as long as we don't hold military rank, we're not in violation. Technically we're civilian employees advising the Saudi government, despite any honorary titles. Whether we're called to account later on is uncertain."

Bear Barnes spoke everyone's mind. "With what the Saudis are paying, it doesn't much matter." There were nods of assent all around.

Bennett glanced around the room. "Bear is remaining as head of Tiger Force operations. As such he'll remain here, but may fly out to the staging bases as necessary. I'll be here part-time, spending the rest of my time at the fields and coordinating with Riyadh. Ed, that means that you, Brad, and Geoff will be de facto squadron commanders, but operationally you'll be flight leaders."

The exec stood up. "Suits me fine. I want to take two flights from Black Squadron out to the strip where the Mirage landed. If there's any activity tomorrow or the next day, it'll be there."

Bennett looked up at the eager redhead. "All right. Coordinate your departure with Bear. Geoff and Brad, you're with White and Red Squadrons, respectively. Rajid has taken over Orange and Ahnas Menaf fleeted up from IP to lead Green. Former F-5 COs are running Blue, Yellow, and Pink. Rajid and Ahnas are good flight leaders—that's the biggest step on the road to command, as you guys well know. But when you're working with them keep an eye open. They have a hell of a lot to learn in a short time."

Lawrence strode toward the door. "I'm gone. Good hunting, guys. Bear, I'll check in regularly."

Bennett was mildly upset with his friend's hasty departure. But there were other matters to attend to. "Bear, I'd like you to schedule a meeting with the two of us and the maintenance folks sometime tomorrow afternoon. We'll probably receive some of the birds from Turkey and Morocco before this is over, and I expect they'll have a lot of deferred maintenance."

That evening, before going to bed, Bennett looked up Tim Ottman. They sat in Ottman's room for half an hour, and the instructor thought that Bennett seemed even more withdrawn than when he had returned from Riyadh and Claudia's death. At length Bennett produced a thick folder from his briefcase. He handed the manila envelope to Ottman.

"I'd like you to take this back with you," Bennett said. "It's a summary I've compiled of our training syllabus, selection process, academics and flight grades, and debriefs on the combat down by the border."

Ottman's eyebrows went up. Flipping through the pages, he asked, "Anybody's name in here I might recognize?"

Bennett gave a tight grin. "No, nobody's names. Your secret is safe. What I want to do is ask you a favor, Tim. Sometime, when this is all done, I know goddam well that the managers and bean-counters will return to form. They'll start talking complexity and sophistication again. They'll come up with buzzwords like 'self-escorting' and try to make one airplane do everything.

"Well, you know and I know that it can't work. You build a thirty-five-million-dollar airplane that'll fight air-to-air and drop bombs, but the pilot doesn't have enough time or funding to train for both jobs equally well. He gets jumped inbound to the target, has to jettison his ordnance to survive, and even if he bags one or two MiGs, the opposition has won. Our guy is prevented from bombing his target."

Ottman said, "Boss, you're preaching to the converted."

"Old habit of mine." Bennett tapped his fingers together, as if in time to an imaginary tune. "Look, what I want you to do is hang onto this file. Put it away somewhere safe, make a duplicate copy. Then someday, when I'm gone and they start pushing more complex birds on the guys, you can show them in black and white what we've done. Our doctrine works, our training works, and our airplane works. I tell you, Tim, I'd give anything I have left to fly the 20 in combat. But that's not my job." He paused to catch his breath. Ottman noted with surprise that Bennett's eyes were misting. "Will you do that for me, Tim?"

Ottman extended his hand. "Count on it, Skipper."

Bennett gripped the proffered hand, then was gone.

Tim Ottman had trouble getting to sleep that night. Bennett's phraseology worried him. *When I'm gone. Anything I have left.* Though he was not a religious man, Ottman said a short prayer. He asked that John Bennett find peace of mind.

Northern Arabia, 3 September,
0735 Hours

Early next morning two Israeli RF-4C Phantoms streaked southeast across the Jordanian border into Saudi airspace. The reconnaissance aircraft had orders to photograph several of the advanced airfields now that Saudi F-15s no longer were flying standing patrols. The Eagles' replacement by Tigersharks was not yet known to the Israelis.

Still, this was to be a quick mission—in and out in minimum time, minimum exposure. One pass at each target, taking oblique photos to evaluate the type and nationality of aircraft on each field.

Assigned to each recce bird was a four-plane flight of F-15s. Trailing the RF-4s at two miles, one flight of Eagles crisscrossed 10,000 feet above the Phantoms, which would make their runs at 8,000. The other Eagle flight was deployed by sections, one upsun of the RF-4s, the other on the opposite side.

Saudi radar had tracked both flights over Jordan before they crossed the border. Reaction time had been calculated by the Israeli planners, who estimated the Saudis could not intercept before the photos were obtained and the mission was egressing back into Jordan. But from the moment of radar warning, Tiger Force had sprung into action.

A call to Black Base had Ed Lawrence's squadron airborne less than two minutes after the alert sounded.

Lawrence flung his second section out to his left at a range of six miles and sharply banked his own fighter to the northwest. Streaking across the barren desert at 2,000 feet, his wingman was in right-hand loose deuce at a mile and a half. Up to his left at 4,000 was his second flight. Lawrence had decided to keep his planes low even though the F-15 had a good lookdown-shootdown capability.

He gambled the Eagles would rely on ground-based radar in this limited-war scenario, hoping to surprise any Saudi pilots searching for airborne emitters—because "That's what I'd do in their shoes."

Lawrence pumped his control stick slightly, inducing an up-and-down motion of his nose, and four pairs of hands activated armament switches. Lawrence armed his left-hand Sidewinder and moved his gun selector to CHARGE. A reassuring hard *thump* reverberated through his Tigershark as 20mm rounds were driven into the chambers of his two M39 cannons.

Ed Lawrence still had twenty-fifteen vision, and at twenty-five miles he saw the flicker of sunlight from a canopy. Moments later he made out the distinctive smoke trails of the closest Phantom's twin engines with the range down to ten miles. Briefly he wished he had been able to deploy his other two flights to circle behind the Israelis and cut them off. But there was too much sky to cover all the possibilities. He put the idea out of mind and prepared to engage.

Black Lead made a slight right turn to offset and, at five miles, pulled hard in a climbing left turn. Belatedly, the Israelis visually acquired the second section and started a nose-down hard left turn. Lawrence keyed his mike, partly from long habit from hundreds of mock combats, partly to give the familiar call for morale's sake: "Fight's on!"

The exec put his gunsight reticle on the lead Eagle. Tiger Force had adopted a West German nonradar sight, capable of switching from the standard 30-mil circle-and-center pipper to the funnel-shaped sight he now used. Both were gyro-stabilized to provide lead computation, and Lawrence selected the latter, wide at the top for minimum range and narrow at the bottom of the funnel to indicate maximum range on a standard-sized tactical aircraft.

When the Eagle's forty-three-foot wingspan filled the narrow portion of the reticle, Lawrence fired his port Sidewinder. The AIM-9 streaked off the rail and headed for the big McDonnell Douglas fighter from the one o'clock position. Lawrence's minor angle advantage from his first turn was not decisive, but it was a start.

The Eagle, already in afterburner, pulled up abruptly to defeat the missile. Lawrence used the seconds thus gained to pitch up, roll almost 180 degrees, and follow the maneuver from his opponent's belly side. Invisible to the Israeli pilot, Lawrence allowed himself to drop back slightly in a lag pursuit. When the Eagle pulled over the top, the Tigershark was 1,500 feet astern at five o'clock.

Lawrence heard his wingman, Badir Qurat, call, "You're clear," and accepted the estimate as a matter of faith. He rolled out, momentarily at normal G with wings nearly level, and pressed the trigger.

"Guns!"

The big shells, three-quarters of an inch in diameter, hammered into the twin-tailed fighter from almost directly astern. Pieces flew off the wing and fuselage as the Israeli rolled inverted and pulled into a six-G split-S. Lawrence was right behind, hearing the voice of his wingman under heavy G, almost unintelligible. Lawrence estimated that the young Saudi was engaged with an Eagle himself.

What would I do in this guy's position? Lawrence asked himself. He came off the throttle and pulled up briefly, then pitched back down to regain his spacing. Sure enough, the F-15's huge speed brake behind the cockpit was deployed and the orange-white glow of the afterburners was gone. The Israeli had tried to force an overshoot. But now, with reduced energy the Eagle could not shake the F-20 locked firmly at its six o'clock. Lawrence placed his gunsight carefully and, in the minimum time available, triggered another burst.

Mortally hit, the Eagle rolled violently and the canopy came off. Out came the seat as the pilot ejected.

Lawrence took no time to savor his victory—he had done this before. Instead, he blinked the sweat from his eyes, checked his tail, and selected afterburner. In the F404 engine's tailpipe raw fuel was sprayed into the red-hot exhaust gases from the main engine and reignited. The normal 2,300 pounds per hour fuel flow which produced 450 knots airspeed rocketed to 60,000 pounds per hour— enough to propel the jet at Mach 1.3. But Lawrence wanted acceleration more than pure speed; he remained nose-level long enough to regain his energy state, then pulled up to rejoin his wingman.

The redheaded flier called, "Black Two, I'm free." Craning his neck hard to the left, he discerned two small dots at his seven o'clock, slightly high. In seconds he was through a vertical reversal, accelerating back into the fight.

The radios came alive with pilots' excited voices as missiles trailed smoky fingers through the clear air. Lawrence's wingman was turning with an F-15, neither gaining nor losing. It was no place to be in a multibogey fight—it left a pilot vulnerable to the unseen bandit outside one's periphery. And remaining in a level turn would bleed off airspeed.

As Lawrence crossed over the engaged fighters, Black Two saw him. Badir pitched up, calling, "You have it, Lead."

Lawrence cut across the circle, arcing downward to initiate a low yo-yo. But the Eagle driver was sharp; he recognized the setup, lit his burners, and rocketed upward. Caught nose-low, Lawrence could not match the climb in time to engage. He called his wingman to rejoin and they turned in place back toward the initial contact, accelerating rapidly.

Abruptly Lawrence heard, "Black Lead! Break hard right, now!"

Without thinking, Lawrence wracked the little Northrop into a seven-and-one-half-G starboard turn, climbing slightly. His vision grayed, he lost the color of the outside world, and a fuzzy narrowing of his sight accompanied the abrupt draining of most of the blood from his head. He caught just a glimpse of the nose of a cannon-firing F-15 attacking from three o'clock, now dangerously close.

"Where'd *he* come from?" Lawrence muttered aloud.

The exec intended to pitch up, covering his wingman who would engage the F-15 in a level turn, but there was no chance. With ungodly speed the Eagle continued straight ahead, accelerating through the speed of sound. Lawrence heard a garbled transmission from Black Five, his second flight leader; something about the Israelis disengaging.

Checking his fuel state, Lawrence decided he could remain in the area several minutes longer. He reformed his flight, gratified they were all present, and turned northward, hoping to head off any bogeys which had been delayed near the airfields in that quadrant.

Moments later Lawrence caught a fast-moving shadow on the ground, moving from right to left. He identified it as an RF-4. Calling, "You have it," he went high to allow Black Two to engage. But Lawrence was cautious; he knew the Israeli fighters never would knowingly leave a recon plane unescorted. He deployed his second section, Black Three and Four, then upsun to watch for the Eagles which must still be around.

In Black Two, Badir dropped behind the Phantom, tickling the Mach to keep pace, and settled down at about two miles range. Lawrence glanced down from his perch, mentally urging the kid to shoot. The Phantom was booming along in burner, offering a beautiful heat source from the two big engines cooking away. Lawrence depressed his mike button to speak when Two's first 'winder flashed off the rail. The RF-4 began a break turn just as the missile exploded.

The Phantom kept flying. Apparently the AIM-9 had detonated just outside lethal range—fusing problems, Lawrence surmised.

Seconds later Black Two fired again, this time remembering to call "Snake!" His starboard missile flew to the target and exploded against the white-hot heat source from the RF-4's J79 engines. The Phantom emerged from a dirty black cloud, nosed down, and hit the desert floor. Lawrence had not witnessed the ejection but he saw at least one parachute.

Ten minutes later seven F-20s landed at Black Base. Lawrence scrambled out of his fighter and ran down the parking line, noting that Black Seven was missing. The exec grabbed his second flight leader. "Where's your section lead?"

The young Saudi rolled his eyes. "He didn't rejoin. Eight called him down about twelve miles northwest. Didn't you hear the call?"

"No." Lawrence was skeptical; he prided himself on knowing what happened in every phase of a fight. Turning to the missing pilot's wingman, he asked, "What happened, Ahmed?"

"An Eagle hit him with a Sidewinder. He ejected, sir. I believe he is all right." Lieutenant Ahmed Salim was visibly shaken.

Lawrence pulled off his helmet. Turning to the line chief, he said, "Call the helo guys. Ahmed, you go with him. Give them the coordinates. And tell 'em there's at least two Israeli drivers out there somewhere."

The mechanic said, "We'll refuel and rearm immediately, but you should know that Six has damage. Looks like twenty-millimeter hits in the tail."

Lawrence nodded curtly, swearing under his breath. He rounded up his pilots and got a preliminary report: two kills, one loss, and one damaged. He cast an icy gaze at his pilots. "We'll debrief this in detail later. But we could have done better." Then he strode off to send an initial report to John Bennett.

Bahrain, 0850 Hours

The communications officer handed the message to the leader of Tiger Force a half-hour later. Bennett read it twice, then folded it and put it in his pocket. He resolved to move his interim headquarters to Orange or Black Base as soon as communications could be established and secured. The airfield construction program, including the primary base at Hā'il, had been started none too soon.

The message read:

> Two Black flts engaged two RF4, eight F15 at 0740
> hrs. Hostile mission: recce our fields. One RF4 es-
> caped, presumed photos Orange Base. Our claims: one
> F15 conf, one RF4 conf. No prob, one dmgd. Our

losses: one F20 shot down, pilot OK, one dmgd.
Poor radio discipline. Will do better next time.
Devil.

Black Base, 1830 Hours

That evening Ed Lawrence conducted a thorough, critical debrief. He was unsparing of everyone, including himself.

"I should have seen that 15 before he was in range and gunning," he began. "Probably he was getting out of Dodge at the speed of heat, saw us close aboard, and tried for a quick setup. Fortunately, Badir saw him just in time, and what began most likely as a quick tracking pass turned into a snapshot." Lawrence postulated that the lone Eagle had been trying to catch the RF-4 which Badir shot down. "The Israelis are real pros; they wouldn't leave a recce bird dangling like that if there hadn't been a mix-up."

Then the Tiger Force exec dealt with other aspects of the combat. "You guys can't take *anything* for granted, especially when fighting pilots the caliber of the Israelis. You have to think all the time. The only things a fighter pilot has going for him are his hot hands and his cool head. The minute you stop thinking, you're dead." He speared Black Two with a stare. "Badir, you were in a level turn with that F-15. You were holding your own temporarily, but eventually he'd gain on you. The 15 has a large wing area and its fuselage is a lifting body. We can't fight that way and expect to come home. You guys are trained to use your vertical performance, so use it properly."

Then Lawrence stressed his favorite subject—radio discipline. He was clearly disappointed. "There was too god—" He caught himself, refraining from swearing. "Too much chatter up there. We've trained this outfit to fight zip-lip from start-up to shutdown, but that went right out the window the minute the BBs started flying. I know it's hard to shut up in a fight. But somebody's life will depend on it someday—maybe yours."

Lawrence consulted his notepad, though it was hardly necessary. He had flown in so many multibogey hassles as both a participant and instructor that he could predict the problems of almost any combat with uncanny accuracy. He turned to his second flight leader, Lieutenant Ahmed Salim. "Ahmed, you guys apparently upset the RF-4's first pass at this base. While you tangled with his escort he had to reposition and make another run, which I think is the reason we caught him egressing. But you lost one bird and brought another back with holes in it. What happened?"

Salim had experienced a bad scare that morning. Two F-15s had separated him from his wingman midway through the fight and neatly scissored him when he tried to evade in a hard descending turn. His second section had broken up the Israelis' offensive scissors but the section leader had been bagged in the process.

The Saudi squirmed in his seat. "Their second flight was split by sections. When we engaged the lead pair, the second got an angles advantage on us. We didn't see them in time."

Lawrence knew the mistakes would be absorbed and were unlikely to be repeated. "Okay. I'm trying to whistle up some F-15s from Riyadh tomorrow for dissimilar ACM. We're likely to tangle with Eagles again and I want to be ready."

Dissimilar air combat maneuvering was mock combat against a different type of fighter than what one flew oneself. Since both Israel and Arabia flew Eagles, dissimilar ACM was possible.

"If the Israelis come at us again, they'll bring F-16s as well," Lawrence said. "I think that little hummer is going to be our main opposition, so we'll hassle among ourselves as well. With the F-20C's improved leading-edge droops we can match the 16 better than we could before. But you guys remember: You win or lose the fight up here"—he tapped his head—"as much as here," and he tugged the seat of his pants.

Secretary of State Thurmon Wilson arrived at the White House on time for his two o'clock meeting with the president. The Marine guards saluted and opened the door as the Connecticut-born diplomat briskly walked up the steps and disappeared inside. He was alone, which was rare at meetings with the chief executive.

Wilson had requested a private session with Walter Arnold ever since the White House chief of staff had passed along the president's plea to "do something" in the Middle East. The secretary admitted to himself, if not to anyone else, that he could do precious little to influence events in that broiling arena. United Nations efforts, the third-party Saudi contacts, even military maneuvers, all had failed to alter the hard-line Arab attitude. As for the Israelis— *Well,* Wilson said to himself, *they go their own way. As always.*

Arnold greeted Wilson warmly and showed him to a comfortable chair in front of the president's Oval Office desk. They got right down to business.

"Thurmon, you know how concerned I am about the situation between the Israelis and the Arabs. We have serious political and economic matters at stake, and we're being lobbied like never before from both sides. On top of that, the mood among the public in this country is clear. Americans just won't support our getting involved in a big way when our direct interests aren't threatened."

The president spread his hands in a gesture of futility. "If we keep supporting Israel, the Arabs and their oil cartel are likely to take it out on us. But if we moderate our support of Tel Aviv, the Jewish lobby here will raise holy hell. And not only that, we'll run serious risk of alienating other allies in the region—especially the Saudis. A lot of Arab governments already wonder how much they can trust us to keep our word." Arnold stopped abruptly. He thought of the way Congress had cut off aid to South Vietnam—how the ARVN had run out of ammunition that spring of 1975. And there had been the vacillating support of the Nicaraguan Contras before they too lost American aid. Senator Walter Arnold had voted to suspend military shipments in both instances.

"Mr. President, I'm afraid I don't have anything to cheer you up," Wilson replied. "I didn't phone just to issue a status report. I wanted to tell you of new evidence we've developed through neutral sources in Damascus."

Arnold was visibly upset. He did not need more bad news. "Who's neutral in that country anymore?"

"Well, this comes via the French Embassy. And we're checking with the Swiss in Tehran. But it appears the Muslim states are finally getting it all together. You recall the Syrian ambassador at large who's been conducting his own shuttle diplomacy over the past year or so? Well, he seems to be producing results. Syria, Iran, Iraq, and Libya, plus Egypt to a lesser extent, are presenting a united diplomatic front. We don't know about the Saudis yet— they're trying to stay on the fence. But evidently the others are issuing an ultimatum sometime this month. The Israelis withdraw from Jordan and cede the West Bank as a Palestinian homeland, or else."

Walter Arnold's reply was simply, "Or else . . ."

"Or else a full-scale war. And this time the Arabs have enough muscle and unity to make it stick. There have already been joint military planning conferences and joint exercises, you know. At least three high-level meetings have been held in Syria and one or more in Iran."

"Judas Priest."

The Secretary of State inhaled deeply. "And that's not all, Mr. President. They mean to play hardball. If we or any other Western power provide arms or other material support to Israel in the event of hostilities, there'll be an immediate oil embargo."

"You're certain of this information?"

"As sure as we can be right now. All we have to do is wait until the announcement in a week or so."

Arnold was ready to grasp at any straw. "But Thurmon, what about our U.N. initiative and the Saudi contacts with the hard-liners? At one time it looked like something might be worked out."

Wilson's gaze dropped to the floor. Then, raising his eyes to the president, he said, "I don't think those meetings were ever held in good faith. Based on available evidence, they were a smokescreen to keep us off balance. Like Japan in '41."

Arnold sat back in his chair, his eyes closed. *Why would any sane human want this job?* he wondered. He looked at Wilson. "Well, at least an embargo wouldn't hurt us as much as it did in '73. We've enough stocks to last quite a while. But, Christ! Within two months of election!"

The diplomat punched his left palm with his right fist. "I seriously doubt the timing is coincidental, sir." He leaned forward, emphasizing his next point. "Undoubtedly the Israelis already have this information. We can talk to their ambassador again, but I know damn well what he'll say. Tel Aviv calls the shots, and the present government is in no mood to negotiate. It'll be even less inclined to accede to Arab demands that Israel withdraw from Jordan and the West Bank."

The president glumly settled his chin in his hands. "Thurmon, what do you think would be the result if we supported Israel in another war?"

"Aside from the economic and political problems it would pose, there's also the terrorist threat. We don't know for certain, but presumably that's something the Iranians and their friends have discussed. They'd love to blackmail us into doing nothing. It'd be awfully hard to take that kind of political heat in this country."

"We should discuss this with Ben Wake and Defense," Arnold said in a flat voice.

Wilson nodded agreement. "Yes, of course. But nothing's really changed, you know. The Joint Chiefs are unanimous in their view that direct combat in support of Israel would not guarantee success, and undoubtedly would bring severe repercussions, as I just noted. Plus there's the domestic consideration. More American lives lost in the Middle East to no direct gain by the U.S." Wilson shrugged. "Imagine how that'll play on Main Street."

"So you think the best policy is hands off? Don't support Israel?"

For the first time in the meeting, Wilson smiled. "That's where an old lawyer can do some good, Mr. President. I recommend that we adopt a neutral stance, offering to continue mediating the situation. It keeps our contacts open to the Arabs and the Israelis, and to their supporters over here."

"All right, I'll buy that. But if it still comes to war, then what?"

"Frankly, Mr. President, I'm in agreement with Ben and the JCS on this one. I don't think our support or intervention would significantly change things. It would only get a lot of young Americans killed in a conflict that many people would regard as not in our national interest." He let the point sink in, sensing he had scored with a sensitive topic. Then he added, "Which reminds me. I have a report that yesterday the Saudi Air Force was engaged in a skirmish near the Jordanian border with some Israeli aircraft. This followed air battles the day before between the Israelis and some Syrians and Iraqis."

"Yes, I remember," said the president.

"It's not confirmed, sir, but apparently American and British pilots were involved. They're part of this Tiger Force the Saudis set up a few years ago."

Arnold's jaw grew slack. "You mean Americans might actually be in combat with Israelis? How is that possible?"

"It's possible, sir, because we bent over backward to keep our presence and influence in Arabia after the British grabbed that huge defense contract. I've checked the law on this point, and there's room for argument both ways. But so far the U.S. advisers in this organization have not broken any laws."

"Obviously, we can't let them continue there."

Wilson raised a cautionary hand. "I'm not so sure. The Saudis regard these people very highly and want them to stay. If we insist on pulling them out, there's no guarantee they'll come. They might simply turn professional mercenaries and all we'd accomplish is alienating the Saudis. Right now, I think we need credibility in Riyadh a lot more than we need to rein in a few cowboys."

President Walter Arnold let out a long sigh. "Okay. Keep me informed."

Tel Aviv, 5 September

"Well, there it is," said Chaim Geller. He plopped the two-page document down on the desk of his air force liaison officer at the intelligence complex overlooking the city. "There's no doubt that at least one American pilot was involved in the combat with our F-15s? These radio transcripts prove it, I suppose."

Major Eli Ashkiron of the *Heyl Ha'Avir* scanned the printout. "We didn't expect to get a complete voice intercept, Colonel. The F-20s are using minimum radio transmissions, and only in the heat of battle. But what this paper doesn't show is the individual's accent. He is definitely American, not British. Our linguists say he probably comes from the western United States."

Chaim Geller filed away that very useful bit of information for future reference. *As if knowing his place of birth will help us win an air battle,* the section chief thought. "I take it that all the transmissions that were monitored were in English?"

The major said, "Yes, including the Saudis'. That only reinforces our suspicion that the foreign instructors are still flying with this . . . Tiger Force." The officer, though a professional, had difficulty keeping the spite out of his voice. "Colonel, will our diplomatic people make a protest over this? I cannot imagine we would let American and British citizens actually fight for the Arabs without raising the matter in Washington and London."

"I don't know, Eli. That's up to the politicians."

IN THE FOLLOWING TWO WEEKS JOHN BENNETT AVER-aged barely five hours sleep per night, logging almost twenty-five hours in his beloved 001. The two-seat Tigershark with the grinning mouth and leering eyes painted on the nose was a familiar sight at the outlying fields as well as Riyadh.

Maintenance and support facilities had to be provided at the forward bases, and provision had to be made for regular resupply. Existing fields were used as primary bases, with staging fields farther out. Wadi al Qalībah, 120 miles inland from the Gulf of Aqabah, was the most westerly. Others spread across the north to the east: Tabuk, with two preexisting strips only 60 miles from the Jordan border; Al Jouf "old" and Al Jouf "new," some 120 miles south of the line; and Badanah "old" and "new," 125 miles from Jordan and merely 40 miles from Iraq.

Tiger Force's main base in central Arabia was northwest of Hā'il, 300 miles south of the Jordanian border. Here Bennett expected to conduct the crucial F-20 operations, and he spent considerable time at the facility. He had drafted plans long ago for this base: parallel runways a half-mile apart to minimize bomb damage, underground fuel tanks, second-level maintenance facili-ties, and prefab housing and administrative buildings. The king had been as good as his word; the Hā'il base would be operational within the month.

Bennett also had consulted with the Saudi air force command on how best to defend Arabian airspace. He proposed a plan which would force the Israelis to fight the air battle in Saudi airspace, denying them the opportunity to inflict attrition over their own ground. In this manner, Arab pilots who ejected would be available to fight again. Israeli aircrews bailing out would be lost to Tel Aviv. And Bennett knew that, more than aircraft, tanks, or weapons, Israel above all valued her sons. As much, he thought in those bitter moments, as he had valued Claudia.

The Turkish and Moroccan F-20s trickled in, ferried by Saudis as the Northrops became available. Tiger Force also made arrangements to take on two squadrons worth of Jordanian F-5 pilots. Bennett, recognizing their worth, knew the value of keeping a military organization intact. The Jordanians had flown together for years. British-trained, supported by an air-minded monarch, they were among the finest of all Arab pilots. Though displaced three years previously by the collapse of their government, they remained proficient and motivated. Bear Barnes and a few of the Saudis from Class One oversaw their transition to F-20s.

Bennett's main problem in Riyadh was convincing some top-level Saudis that Tiger Force actually could fight the Israelis to a standstill. He had anticipated the Arab attitude, but its depth always surprised him. Confined as he had been to the task of building Tiger Force, with its high morale and professional competence, he realized with a start that the mystique of Israeli invincibility worked a strong influence on Arab minds. One hasty meeting in the Riyadh air ministry was typical.

The discussion started easily enough when a colonel in the Saudi operations office complimented Bennett on Tiger Force's showing against the Israeli F-15s. Bennett's response was unexpected. "Actually, Colonel, we don't regard that action as very successful. We broke even, discounting the RF-4C."

"But surely such a result must be considered a victory for us," the Saudi insisted. "It is most unusual for any Arab nation to fight the Israelis to a draw."

Privately, Bennett conceded the point. How many times had Arab forces, their air arm quickly beaten, suffered devastation that only a modern army can receive from an effective, unopposed air force? Miles of burning tanks, trucks, and artillery pieces tossed about the desert like abandoned toys, the rotting bodies of Muslim soldiers bloating in the heat, was the collective memory of two generations.

Bennett noted that each man in the room was hanging on his every word. He placed his hands on his hips and spoke forcibly, buoyed by the power of his conviction. "I don't know how much military history you gentlemen have read, but permit me an analogy. I'm reminded of the attitude in the German Imperial Navy during World War I. Though sailing in warships of murderous power, many of the Kaiser's admirals never adjusted psychologically to centuries of Rule Britannia. They found it hard to imagine Germany actually defeating the Royal Navy. So the Kaiser's dreadnaughts sortied believing they might lose, while the British never considered anything but defeating them."

Bennett did not realize it immediately, but that short, heartfelt speech was repeated throughout the Royal Saudi Air Force by those who heard it.

Thus, Bennett's "fadeaway plan," as he called it, won acceptance. The king himself still hoped to avoid a full-scale war in the region, for that would only endanger his nation and his throne. But the monarch's advisers—coaxed along by the suave Safad Fatah—agreed to the air plan at length. Satisfied that the spadework had been done, Bennett addressed himself to a final bit of pleading.

That afternoon at tea with Fatah, Bennett had earnestly pressed his case. "Safad, I wish to ask you this favor for me." It was almost the first time Bennett had addressed the minister by his given name. "I have seen with my own eyes"—a favorite Arab phrase—"the effect of an undeclared war. It is said that such declarations are out of date in the late twentieth century. But please consider my request on behalf of Tiger Force and all of your Saudi warriors." He paused, looking Fatah square in the face. "If there is war with Israel, or with any other country, ask the king to issue a declaration of war. Make it formal, make it official, and make it stick."

Fatah blinked, hiding the surprise he felt. It seemed such an unnecessary request. But he trusted the American's judgment. "What reason should I propose to His Majesty?"

"Legal protection for your people under international law. I saw that absence of a declaration at work on my friends, on my country in my lifetime. At least provide your soldiers with access to the international community and legal recourse if there's a full-scale war." Leaning forward in his chair, Bennett concluded, "I'm not confusing a raid or a skirmish with a war. I recognize the legal and practical differences between them. But, Safad, if a real war is worth fighting, it is worth declaring. Will you pass on my thoughts to the king?"

The dignified old Arab said solemnly, "Yes, my friend. He shall hear your words."

12

Colonel Solomon Yatanahu sat in his office, feet unmilitarily propped on his desk, his Nomex flight suit open almost to his navel. He was still perspiring from the forty-minute workout with three of his F-15 pilots. Yatanahu was commander of Balhama Air Base, one of three Israeli airfields near Beersheva. And though he was technically no longer on operational status, the forty-two-year-old officer still liked to compete with the younger men in air combat practice. Prematurely gray with a chiseled face and startling blue eyes, Yatanahu had spent his life in fighter aviation. More than two decades of flying, including combat in three wars and eleven aerial victories, had honed his professional senses to a fine edge.

Yatanahu had come up the hard way, which is to say the *only* way, in the intensely competitive world of the Israeli fighter pilot. In order to lead a fighter squadron, the commanding officer had to maintain his standing in the top three positions in tactics and gunnery. If he slipped from the upper bracket in either category, he was likely to lose his command.

The Israeli Air Force's attitude is pragmatic if nothing else. The operating philosophy is "experience leads." Yatanahu had led missions as a captain with a lieutenant colonel flying section lead in the number three position. And he knew of special-purpose missions led by lieutenants because the junior officers possessed the qualities and experience which made them best-suited for the job. Ironically, perhaps the only air force in history which had come close to the Israeli philosophy was the Luftwaffe during World War II.

Solomon Yatanahu studied the debriefing reports on the Saudi airfield reconnaissance. It had been known for some time that the Saudis had a capable F-20 force, trained by American and British instructors. Given the background of the instructors, it was to be expected that the Tigersharks would put up a good fight. Yatanahu knew as well as anyone that much of the Israeli fighter doctrine had been absorbed from exchange tours with U.S. Navy squadrons. Unlike most Arab air forces, which adopted Soviet-style formations and tactics, the Saudis had flown loose deuce, employing fluid tactics.

Reading the pilots' comments, Yatanahu noted that the biggest problem was simply seeing the F-20. He could well understand it. Yatanahu had been an exchange pilot at Nellis Air Force Base in the 1970s, flying against the F-5Es of the aggressor squadrons in the Nevada desert. The Tiger II could not outperform the F-15 and F-16 in most regimes, but with enough F-5s on hand, it was almost impossible for other pilots to keep a safe lookout through 360 degrees. The little F-5 was murderously hard to see, and the F-20 was the same size with 70 percent more thrust!

The school solution was to engage the Northrops at long range with radar-guided missiles. The Israelis had more success with the Sparrow than its American designers had, partly because of far greater institutional experience. The *Heyl Ha'Avir* remained on combat status every day of the year. But the Israelis were unconcerned with the artificialities which dogged the Americans. Superb military intelligence allowed the Israelis to engage radar targets beyond visual range with little concern about hitting a friendly.

Even so, Yatanahu knew that the simple weapons work best. Sparrows and other radar missiles were complex and expensive, so the heat-seekers were the weapon of choice. His own experience was typical. Of the eight Syrian and three Egyptian aircraft he had shot down, Yatanahu used Sidewinders or Israeli-built Shafrirs on all but three. Like most fighter pilots, he was emotionally inclined to use his cannon because it was personally more satisfying. "No kill like a gun kill," the Americans always said. But the heat-seekers were accurate and efficient. Though Yatanahu loved to tell about his gun kills, he acknowledged the infrared missile was the champion MiG destroyer.

The colonel knew that the Saudis and their advisers would anticipate the Sparrow option and would work to deprive the Israelis of it. As yet, electronic countermeasures had not been a big factor in air-to-air combat. The F-20s facing his squadrons across the Jordanian border came without radar for the most part. The colonel knew also that there would be a reason. This so-called Tiger Force would seek to engage in close-in maneuvering, the "knife fight" where the radar missile could not be used. He fervently hoped the Israeli scientists and engineers were working on a means to negate the various U.S., French, and Soviet jammers now available to all major Arab air forces.

The politicians in Tel Aviv were maintaining their hard line, so there would be another war. The time had passed for negotiation. Yatanahu did not set policy. But there had to be a better way.

Solomon Yatanahu was an agnostic. He would not openly deny the existence of a god—that was contrary to Israeli military law. But he had doubts. In his lifetime he had seen enough misery inflicted upon innocents—especially children—that he had to question the mercy, and therefore the existence, of a supreme being. He acknowledged that this earth also was a place of much beauty, at least as much in the sky as on the ground, so perhaps—just perhaps—there was some sort of ordered plan.

Long ago Yatanahu had decided that if he were a praying man, he would pray for more wisdom in the world. He considered it insane to pray for anything like peace, particularly in his part of the globe. That was the trick, he decided: not to pray for the absolute best that could happen, but to pray for the best that was *possible*.

DAMASCUS, 15 September—The governments of Syria, Iran, Iraq and Libya issued a joint communique today, demanding that Israel withdraw from occupied Jordan. Though no specific timetable was advanced, the message stated that if "good faith negotiations" were not forthcoming "in due course," a military solution would be employed by the Arab powers.

While not formally parties to the communique, in separate statements the governments of Egypt and Saudi Arabia went on record as supporting the call for Israeli withdrawal from Jordan. The Saudi foreign ministry in Riyadh went even further, adding that prolonged failure at negotiating a settlement to the lingering crisis could result in a declaration of war against Israel.

Bahrain

John Bennett read the article in his air-mailed copy of the London *Times*. He wondered what he might have set in motion following his conversation with Safad Fatah, but the question did not bother him. He had told Bear Barnes, "At least if our guys go to war, they'll be entitled to whatever protection the law allows."

But the Tiger Force CO had little time for philosophizing. He had been busy coordinating RHAW acquisition with Riyadh, obtaining a mixture of American and French electronic "black boxes" for his F-20s. There would not be enough to equip every Tigershark, but at least each flight leader could be so equipped. He knew that if the Israelis came across the border again, they would come in strength with full support—including radio jamming and electronic deception. He also knew the Royal Saudi Air Force had configured several Tornadoes for the same role, with modifications to the E-3s to back up ECM operators.

Overall, Bennett expected the respective electronic warriors to cancel out one another. The air battle would be decided on the basis of the human eye and the human heart. And he would not have it any other way.

Northern Arabia, 16 September, 0905 Hours

Brilliant motes of light flashed across the high plateau, 248 times faster than a supersonic aircraft. Forty-two F-15s, F-16s, Phantoms, and Kfirs—all bearing the blue and white Star of David— were supported by the powerful airborne jammers of other aircraft orbiting across the Jordanian border. The attackers' targets were four Tiger Force fields—those considered to pose the greatest threat to Israeli frontiers after the initial clash two weeks before.

The *Heyl Ha'Avir* plan was a classic. It relied upon simplicity, speed, and as much surprise as possible. From Wadi al Qalībah to the New Badanah strip farther east, the Israeli aircrews had been carefully briefed on times, routes, and altitudes to each Saudi field. Unlike most Israeli blitzes, this one had not been rehearsed as thoroughly as possible, but the timing and heavy radio and radar jamming were enough to encourage mission planners for a good chance of success.

Leaving the Jordanian-Saudi border, most of the Israeli jets were twelve to fifteen minutes from their targets. Monitoring Saudi radar frequencies revealed which operating bands were most likely to be used, and therefore it was possible to cloud the screens with hundreds of false targets. The "snow" on radar scopes washed out the true blips, most of which were below the ground-based radar horizon anyway. Similarly, voice communications circuits were jammed by electronic noise which made extended conversation nearly impossible.

Ed Lawrence had Black Squadron at Orange Base that morning, doubling up with Ahnas Menaf's unit. The policy was to rotate the various squadrons between different bases to prevent the Israelis from gaining a clear picture of the air defense net. The two COs were in the operations shack when the low-frequency walkie-talkie circuit came alive.

"Attention all bases, attention all bases. Unidentified aircraft crossed the border southbound about two minutes ago. Mirror signals indicate crossing on a broad front at low level. Suspect Israeli aircraft inbound."

Lawrence cast a glance at his former student. In two seconds they were both out the door, sprinting for their planes. Lawrence punched the button to activate the siren and the duty flight immediately started engines. Already parked at the downwind end of the runway, the four Tigersharks were airborne in sixty-eight seconds, scrambling for altitude. Twelve more F-20s were started and taxiing in minutes, led by Lawrence. But he feared what was likely to come. Setting a fast pace for his flight, he taxied past two fighters parked on the ramp for maintenance. Then he pushed the thought from his mind.

According to prebriefed plan, the four flights fanned out at staggered altitudes in an arc from west through north to northeast. If bogeys were inbound, they would almost certainly arrive from those quadrants. Lawrence checked his wingman's spread as he leveled off at 18,500 feet. He checked his watch. Four and a half minutes had elapsed.

Menaf's duty flight, first in the air, made first contact. Through scratchy voice radio Lawrence detected the flight leader's report: "Many bogeys at low level northeast of the field. Am engaging. Out."

Moments later there were half-discerned calls of bandit sightings, frantic warnings, and G-muffled cries for breaks. Looking to his right, Lawrence saw an ephemeral flash on the desert floor and crisscrossing missile trails. After a moment's reflection he led his wingman in a turn back toward the field. He estimated that by arriving at 12,000 to 14,000 feet in the next few minutes he could interrupt the bombers' roll-in.

The exec had called it correctly, but he was a shade late. The Israelis had maintained a sandblower mission profile, hugging the ground until within four miles of the field. Then the Kfirs popped up to get a look at their target, selected their dive headings, and rolled in. The first two were down the chute as Lawrence and Badir headed for the second section from the right side.

"Black Lead, bandits astern, three miles." It was Khalil, leading the second section.

"You take 'em, Three," Lawrence replied. The response was garbled but Lawrence had to assume it was acknowledgement.

The unexpected appearance of Saudi fighters airborne over their own field was a nasty surprise to the Kfirs. The delta-winged fighter-bombers, an Israeli upgrade of the French Mirage, were caught at a disadvantage. Pulling in behind the second Kfir, Lawrence had a good missile tone at one mile. The Israeli jinked violently in his dive, but refused to abort the attack.

When the tone in his earphones told him the port Sidewinder was tracking, Lawrence pressed the trigger. At only fifteen degrees angle off the tail, the AIM-9 homed on its target and connected. The missile tried to rendezvous on the jet's tailpipe, but because of the evasive maneuvers the 'winder's proximity-fused warhead exploded 15 feet away. The fragments were flung outward, penetrating the target's empennage and slicing through fuel and hydraulic lines. Lawrence had a clear view of his victim arcing crazily into the bottom half of a loop, bombs still aboard. There was no ejection from the fuel-fed fireball.

Pulling up, Lawrence rolled into a hard climbing reversal to look for Badir. The redheaded flier glanced through the top of his canopy and caught sight of the wingman's F-20 spiraling upward, engaged in a vertical rolling scissors with an F-16. Lawrence felt an immediate sense of dread—where there was one Falcon there would surely be another. The second Kfir seemed to have disappeared.

Lighting his afterburner, Lawrence accelerated quickly. He was passing through 550 knots at 18,000 feet when he caught a glint of sunlight at eleven o'clock high. He padlocked the glint, turning to put it on his nose. *Damn*, he thought, *that 16's almost too small to see at three miles*. He wondered if the Israeli saw him.

Suddenly Lawrence heard Badir's muted call, topping out of his spiral with the first F-16 while pitching down to regain lost energy. Simultaneously the Falcon to Lawrence's left front fired a Sidewinder at him. It was the first time the exec had to cope with a forward-quarter air-to-air missile, but his simulator training at Bahrain had prepared him for this moment. With careful timing, he snapped the stick hard back and left, helping with left rudder. His abrupt upward spiral was more than the AIM-9's small wings could duplicate, and the missile exploded beyond lethal range.

Breathing heavily from the effort, Lawrence regained visual contact with the two Falcons. Both broke sharply away, the glow of their afterburners visible in the morning sky. Lawrence turned to try a Sidewinder shot, but got no tone. He heard Badir call "Snake!" and saw the white wake of the missile, but it could not track at that distance.

The Israelis had made one pass at the field, and though only the first two Kfirs had bombed, they did their job. Lawrence's victim had crashed near the northern boundary and the second evidently had pulled out to avoid its partner's fate. The fight was over in two minutes, and the F-20s began landing by sections under cover of the flight with most fuel remaining.

One hangar was partially destroyed and there were bomb craters in the runway. The latter would be repaired in hours by Saudi workers with access to gravel and steel plating stacked along the edge of the runway. No center hits had been scored on the landing strip itself, but Lawrence's heart sank as he taxied past the smoldering remains of the two grounded Tigersharks. He recalled feeling less grief over pilots who succumbed to carelessness or bad luck.

Only that night, lying in the bunk in his trailer, did it occur to Lawrence that he had achieved a lifelong goal. The Kfir had been his fifth kill in aerial combat—he was a fighter ace. But he could not tell anyone back home about it, and that knowledge robbed him of easy sleep.

Hā'll, 1210 Hours

The reports were in by noon. All four of the F-20 fields targeted by the Israelis had been hit, but Orange Base and one other got off lightly. The defenders had been late scrambling from New Badanah, and were caught by the F-16 escorts at 9,000 feet. Too involved with the Falcons to intercept the Phantoms, White Squadron's two flights fought at a disadvantage and lost three in exchange for one kill. Overall, the Israelis lost six aircraft to seven F-20s. But two fields were out of commission until major repairs could be made.

Bennett discussed the day's events with Bear Barnes at the new Tiger Force HQ near Hā'il. "I talked to the British air attaché in Riyadh this afternoon," Bennett said. "He seems better connected than our embassy people. Looks like the Israelis decided to preempt possible air strikes from Saudi Arabia before taking on the Syrians and Iraqis."

Bear agreed. "So they're going to fight after all. I sort of thought the Israelis might pull out of Jordan. I mean, they're overextended. They can't hold all of Jordan, the West Bank, and part of Lebanon, too. So why push a fight now when they still have time to prepare?"

"My guess is, their government just doesn't think it can survive by ceding territory back to the Arabs. That limits their options. I agree with you, Bear. They *are* overextended. It's a serious strategic error, but it's not the first time politicians have screwed up things for the military in a country."

Barnes finished his coffee. He wished he had a Coors. "Word from the rumor mill is that the Arabs are starting a big offensive in a couple of weeks. I wonder if the Israelis got wind of it and that prompted these strikes. Seems logical—they'd want to secure their southern flank."

Bennett perked up. "I haven't heard that. Where'd you get it?"

Barnes looked around to make sure no one overheard him. "I was in Saudi Air Force HQ yesterday—you know, about the ECM gear. Heard two colonels discussing contingency plans with a Brit, apparently showing what big shots they were. One of them hinted at October ninth. Not very good security—"

Bennett felt an electric shock. Claudia. He had not thought of her in the past two days. But hearing the date of her birthday brought back a rush of painful memories.

"Skipper? You all right?" Barnes grasped Bennett's forearm in a powerful hand.

"What? Yeah, Bear, I'm okay."

"You sort of drifted off the scope there for a minute."

"I was just thinking." With alarm, Barnes noted that the CO's left hand trembled visibly. Bennett glanced away, clearly embarrassed. The big Marine squeezed the arm.

Bennett ignored the tacit message. "Well, I guess we should go over the fadeaway plan again."

"No need, boss. Devil and the troops have all the details. We sent that stuff by courier to avoid any oral transmission. All we need to do is phone or teletype two words and the plan goes into effect."

"Devil . . . I wonder how he's doing up there."

"Hell, I reckon he's happier than a hog in slop. He bagged himself another one, you know. Probably painted the fifth star on his helmet before the turbine blades stopped turning."

Bennett regarded his operations officer. "Tell me something. Do you ever wish you were flying with these kids? Would you rather be in a squadron than running the ops office?"

Barnes leaned back, regarding his digital wristwatch. "Well, to be honest, no. If I was younger, say, the age I was in Nam, you bet. I was like every other MiG-hungry stud in an F-4. Couldn't wait to tie into some gomer up in Route Pack Six. But now . . ." He chuckled softly. "I'm honest enough to admit I'm not the stick I used to be. Can't be helped; age does that to a guy." He glanced at his boss. "But I'm not telling you anything you don't know."

Bennett sympathized with Barnes and admired his honesty. "We can't all be like Devil. Hell, the Saudis will have to kick him out of the country before he hangs up his helmet. I guess Brad is still strong in the cockpit. He missed Vietnam, you know. Like Tim Ottman—he wanted his shot at combat."

An ironic smile crossed Barnes's face. "What's that saying you mentioned so often? Be careful what you want; it might come true."

"I don't mean to be gloomy, but when I think of Ed and the guys like him, I'm reminded of something attributed to Raoul Lufbery. You may have heard of him. *Lafayette Escadrille* in World War I."

"Yeah, he invented that squirrel-cage maneuver, a defensive circle. What reminded you of him?"

"He's supposed to have said, 'There will be no after-the-war for a fighter pilot.' "

Barnes was intrigued. "What'd he do after the war?"

"Nothing. He was KIA in 1918."

Hovda Air Base, 1215 Hours

The debrief was orderly but intense. The Israeli aircrews had dispassionately reported what they had seen and done over the four Saudi fields, knowing that intelligence evaluation would confirm their estimates. Meanwhile, other pilots were sitting cockpit alert in the refueled, rearmed Kfirs, poised to launch immediately from the camouflaged blast pens and dispersal pads.

Despite the outward calm, the underlying emotion was puzzlement. Even with heavy electronic countermeasures, the strike aircraft had met alerted, airborne interceptors. How had the Saudis reacted so quickly in the face of Israeli jamming and deception? Especially since countermeasures had been instituted on an irregular basis days before to "desensitize" the defenders.

Lieutenant Colonel David Ran, veteran of the 1973 war, had led his Kfirs against Orange Base. His bombs, and those of his wingman, had cratered the perimeter of the runway and destroyed two grounded F-20s. But he had lost his number three man to a Tigershark and number four had been prevented from bombing.

"I tell you, they knew we were coming," Ran insisted, speaking to the intelligence officer, bespectacled twenty-six-year-old Captain Danny Peled. "They were up in force and had enough altitude to intercept with an advantage."

"Could it have been a standing patrol?" asked Peled.

"No. We only saw two aircraft on the field, and the number of interceptors was too large for a standing combat air patrol. Somehow our jamming must have broken down."

"We've had no report of that, sir. But there will be a full account in the mission summary." The report from Hovda would go to Air Force headquarters for compilation with the other units' accounts, after which a summary would be issued.

Ran's wingman handed him a cold glass of lemonade. "Come on, David. Let's get changed. I think Ari can use some cheering up. He feels badly about not bombing."

The CO stood silent for a moment. He thought of the old adage: No battle plan survives contact with the enemy. But damn! The mission should not have met as much opposition as it did. "All right. He's probably upset about Ephraim. Well, I am too. But it couldn't be helped. Ari wouldn't have done any good to press his dive with an F-20 locked at his six o'clock."

The intelligence officer was scribbling at his notepad as most of the pilots filed out. Ran took a detour to Peled's desk. Leaning on the top, the Kfir leader said, "I want every available detail on the mission as soon as possible. In my office tomorrow."

"Yes, sir." This was not the time to address the CO by his given name. "I believe we'll have data on the SAM batteries tonight."

"Good." Saudi Hawk surface-to-air missiles, plus those purchased from Britain and France, had taken a toll of the attackers. A Phantom and a Kfir had been shot down despite Israeli jamming. There was little opportunity to counter the simple electro-optical aiming systems adapted to the U.S.-made Hawks or the passive infrared guidance of the European weapons. Ran turned to go. "Oh, one more thing. Don't contact Ephraim's family yet. I'll do that myself."

Waiting outside was David Ran's wingman. Lieutenant Asher Menuhim stretched his arms, rolling his shoulders. Sometimes it was just good to be alive. Merely to stand on your own two feet and breathe God's pure air. When Ran emerged, moving at his usual four-miles-per-hour stride, Asher fell in beside him. As they paced along together Asher remarked, "David, I've been wondering about something. It's this whole series of strikes."

"What about it, Asher?"

"I wonder if it's good doctrine. We knocked out two airfields for perhaps a few days. But we've taken losses we never used to take. It's obvious that the Saudis are definitely more proficient."

"Yes, they are." Ran thought of his A-4 squadron's losses the first day of the Yom Kippur War. No, the Arabs aren't always pushovers.

"Well," Asher continued, "I wonder if we shouldn't conserve our resources for our own defense." He broke step slightly, wanting to stop and talk.

Ran slowed imperceptibly, leaving his wingman two steps behind. "You know the procedure, Asher. We don't make policy, we just carry it out." He was lapsing into his commanding officer tone of voice. It said, *Tread lightly*.

"Yes, I understand that. But do the politicians? Look, I don't mind dying. But I don't like the idea of dying for a political whim."

Ran stopped cold and glared at his wingman. "What's the matter with you? We're going to be fighting for our survival in a few days. You know and I know, and probably the ice cream vendor down the street knows. What choice do we have?"

"I just can't help thinking there's another way. We're never going to be loved by the Arabs. I know that. But maybe . . ."

Ran's voice cut off the thought like honed steel. "Damn it, Asher, I don't want to talk about it. I didn't make this world, and neither did anybody I know. It was decided for us long before you or I were born. All I know is this." He held up a finger before the younger pilot's face. "We have one spot on this earth, just this one. There are millions of people around us who would cheerfully cut the throat of each man, woman, and child in Israel. We have two choices, Asher. Only two. We can fight, or we can die. We can't reason with them or argue the moral subtleties. We can answer only to ourselves. Nobody else is going to look out for us. Not the Americans, not anybody. So, Asher. When it comes down to a choice of fighting or dying, I choose to fight."

The two men stood face to face for several seconds. Asher's face was red beneath his tan, and he made a conscious effort to unclench his fists. Then his CO clapped him on the arm.

"See what you've done? You've turned me into an orator. That's the longest speech I've made in years." He smiled broadly. "Come. Let's see if we can cheer up poor Ari. Drinks on me."

Asher allowed himself to be pulled along. David was right; there's no room for doubt in a warrior's heart. But he could not shake the feeling. Something terrible was coming.

Hā'Il, 17 September, 1500 Hours

Ed Lawrence poked his head inside John Bennett's office. Rapping on the doorsill, the exec asked, "Skipper, can we talk?"

Bennett looked up from his paperwork. "Sure. Come on in."

Lawrence stepped inside, closed the door behind him, and sat down in the vacant chair. "We got trouble, John." Bennett leaned back, folding his arms behind his head. He expected another supply problem or a bureaucratic snag. "Black Squadron gunned a parachute yesterday."

Bennett's easy posture evaporated. "That's for sure? No possible mistake?"

Lawrence vigorously shook his head. "Negative. We have the HUD tape. The pilot doesn't even claim it was accidental." The videotape showing the view through each plane's head-up display was intended as a debriefing tool. Whatever the pilot saw when he fired his guns or launched a missile was recorded for later analysis.

Bennett expelled a long breath. It spoke of infinite sadness. He looked at his friend. "All right. Who?"

"Ahmed Salim. Good stick, good kid from Class One. He was just cleared for flight lead. No disciplinary problems at all."

Spreading his hands, Bennett asked, "Then why'd he do it?"

"Well, you know we lost Karasi in that hassle. Salim was real close to him. Apparently they grew up together. Karasi was jumped by two F-16s at low level and got clobbered with twenty mike-mike. He ejected okay but he was only about 800 feet off the deck. The Israeli was close astern and pulled up directly over the chute. The 16 probably couldn't do anything else, but it collapsed the canopy and Karasi went in with a streamer."

"And Salim saw this happen?"

"Yeah. His wingman took on the other 16 and Salim went for the leader—did a good job and bagged him. When the pilot punched out, Salim honked around and hosed him." Sensing Bennett's impending outrage, Lawrence was quick to add, "The wingie told me the Israeli probably didn't mean to collapse Karasi's chute, but Salim thought it was intentional. He figured he was within his rights."

"Have you talked to Salim yet?"

Lawrence scratched his pockmarked face. "Yes. He seems kind of sorry now, but he's still shook about Karasi."

Bennett shook his head. "Damn it!" He stood up and paced his office. "I won't have my pilots killing defenseless men in parachutes— especially over *our* territory. We've discussed this in the military ethics portion of preflight. It's not just morality, Ed. There are practical aspects as well. . . ."

"Sure, I know. You start gunning chutes and you open your own people to retaliation, and there's always the chance of mistaken identity. Either way, we could lose pilots we'd otherwise save or at least have them survive as prisoners."

Bennett's gray eyes bored into Lawrence. "What do you recommend?"

The exec shrugged. "In this case, heat of combat, retaliation for a perceived enemy offense . . . I'd let it go with a warning."

"That's awfully damn lenient, isn't it?"

"It's pragmatic, John."

Lawrence saw Bennett bite his lip, as if stifling a retort. Lawrence shifted nervously in his chair. In all the years he had known John Bennett, the man seldom had allowed pragmatism to interfere with a personal code of behavior. Privately, Lawrence considered his friend an anachronism, a throwback to the era of single-combat warriors deciding affairs of state in the arena. The twentieth century was alien ground to such men.

At length Bennett said, "From now on, no Tiger Force pilot will even harass an enemy pilot in a chute or on the ground as long as it's in our territory. Violation will result in immediate grounding. I'll reconsider this policy only if the opposition makes a habit of shooting our parachutes, but any change must come from me. Write it up and distribute it to all squadrons."

"Okay. What about Salim?"

Bennett thought for a long moment. "He can keep flying, but he's lost his flight lead. He'll have to requalify."

"John, I don't—"

"That's my decision." Bennett's voice had an uncharacteristic bite.

Lawrence left the office. He felt, as Bennett did, that killing a defeated opponent who could be captured was bad policy. He was less certain he would allow an enemy pilot who ejected over enemy territory to get another jet and come back tomorrow, abler and wiser. Then he put the matter out of mind. Instead, he was more convinced than ever that John Bennett had been born five centuries too late.

Washington, D.C., 7 October

The cabinet meeting had several domestic items on the agenda, but the rapidly deteriorating situation in the Middle East took precedence. The president and Secretary of State each referred to a set of contingency plans drafted against the increasing probability that the major war so long feared and predicted would have to be enacted.

"Ladies and gentlemen," Walter Arnold began. "You have before you a document which has been compiled by White House and State Department staffers and revised by Thurmon and myself. It deals with our possible options amid the very serious situation between Israel and the Arab nations." He glanced at the NSC representatives in attendance, some of whom disagreed with the administration's neutralist Middle East policy. But Arnold had learned that he couldn't please everyone—nobody possibly could. Then, addressing the conferees in general, he said, "I earnestly solicit your comments and suggestions. Take your time. I've set aside the rest of the afternoon."

After several minutes of reading, most cabinet members put down the four-page appraisal and waited for others to speak. A couple of individuals, however, quickly penned notes to themselves. At length Secretary of Defense Ben Wake spoke up.

"Mr. President, my opinion has not changed significantly since discussing this with Thurmon last month." The two secretaries, never intimates, regarded one another cautiously. "I'm in full agreement with this thinking as far as it goes," Wake continued. "I share your opinion that we should not commit ourselves to a course of action which probably would earn further enmity from the Muslim world. Toward that end, an even-handed, neutral approach makes sense.

"However," the Secretary of Defense persisted, "I think we must have a clearer idea of our possible military posture in the region in the event of hostilities. This paper only provides for recall of nonessential diplomatic personnel from combatant nations and contingency plans for a crisis evacuation by air or sealift."

Arnold, though a strong advocate of the position paper, played moderator at most cabinet meetings. He threw the challenge to the Secretary of State for comment. "Thurmon? Your thoughts."

Thurmon Wilson leaned forward to look down the table at Wake. "Ben, there's more to it than that. Right there on page one, we state that rules of engagement now standing will remain in effect. Our people in the area are fully permitted to defend themselves. My God, your people and the Joint Chiefs have agreed we shouldn't jump in militarily but we have the right to a presence. So what's your objection?"

Wake waved a placating hand. "Yes, yes. I note that feature in the second paragraph. But as I said before, we can't simply wander into this thing with optimism and good intentions. We have ships in the Mediterranean and North Arabian Sea. We have Air Force units flying in and out of many of these places. And, I hasten to add, we have some U.S. citizens still under contract to the Saudi government in what amounts to a combat role. Now, I recognize the benefits of maintaining a regional presence and of keeping communications open through all possible avenues. But do we really want our people in a position to get shot at? Another *Stark* or *Vincennes* incident is a very real possibility. The domestic reaction alone could be . . . well, decisive."

Everyone knew what the Secretary of Defense meant. The election was a month off.

"All right," the president responded. "Ben's framed the big question. Do we pull our forces out of the region in deference to the political situation here? Or do we stay put, maintain a presence, and risk the possibility of getting involved in the shooting? It's no easy choice, and there are advantages and disadvantages to each in this evaluation." He flipped the paper.

"Mr. President." Secretary of Commerce Lawrence Janowitz spoke up. He was a short, stocky financier in his mid-fifties, an old political crony of Arnold's who could be counted upon to speak his mind.

"Yes, Larry."

"I don't like the idea of being seen as running for cover when trouble brews up. We might invite problems for ourselves by pulling out as well as by staying in the Middle East."

"That's exactly my point, Larry." Wake's voice was slightly higher than normal, his words nearly colliding with each other. "We need a clear-cut policy stated up front, before we have to choose from any number of possible actions. We need a starting point, that's all I'm saying."

"Well, how about a compromise starting point?" Janowitz replied. "Reduce our naval and air forces in the area to those levels necessary to remind the locals that we can get involved if necessary—even though we don't plan to. At the same time we would be limiting the possible exposure of American servicemen to hostile action, but we're close enough to meet the evacuation criteria listed in the paper."

The president suppressed a smile. Trust Larry to find a bargaining stance that would appeal to both sides. Arnold glanced around. "Comments, anyone?" He looked directly at Wake.

"Yes, that's all right with me. But with reduced force levels in-theater our mutual support will be degraded. I would urge that we pull our people well back, beyond the likely range of hostile action—even by accident. At least that way we'll avoid most chances for mishap. As Larry says, we can jump in with strategic airlift or carrier aviation on very short notice, if need be."

"Sounds good." Arnold was pleased that a consensus was emerging.

"One other thing, though," Wake interjected. "We can't pull back our people in the Saudi F-20 squadrons like we can move our own ships and aircraft. Has there been any idea of what to do about those fliers still under contract?"

Arnold and Wilson exchanged a quick look. The president said, "Thurmon and I have discussed this matter. It's a ticklish point. The Saudi foreign minister has made it plain to State that he wants the U.S. and British advisers in this capacity to remain. Thurmon and I agree that to withdraw them would risk our current relationship with Riyadh, which remains fairly good. At least, it's the best contact we have with any Arab nation right now.

"Very well," the president continued. "We'll discuss particulars about ship and aircraft dispositions tomorrow with the Joint Chiefs of Staff. Let's move on to the next item. . . ."

PART ★ IV

And the stern joy that warriors
feel in foemen worthy of their
steel.

Sir Walter Scott

"The Lady of the Lake," Canto V

13

DAY ONE: 9 OCTOBER
Golan Heights, 0325 Hours

THE JIHAD AGAINST ISRAEL BEGAN IN THE PREDAWN. And it was led not by Soviet T-72 tanks or supersonic MiGs, but by a twenty-three-year-old Iranian zealot named Omar Razlavi.

Omar was legendary to the crusaders engaged in the holy war. He had come to prominence midway through the hard-fought bitter war with Iraq when, as a teenager recruited to fill the Ayatollah's ranks, he found his niche in life. At five feet five and 118 pounds, the boy was ideally suited to wriggling through barbed-wire entanglements, probing for enemy mines. The life expectancy of sappers often was measured in hours—sometimes in minutes—but Omar Razlavi thrived. He outlived his comrades by orders of magnitude until finally his division, which suffered 120 percent casualties in his first eight months—was renamed in his honor.

Moving out from his sandbagged trench south of Mount Hermon, Razlavi was armed with a plastic knife to probe for mines and a knapsack of fifty white-flagged stakes to mark them. Scrambling across the ground on all fours, ferretlike in his agility, the youngster felt completely at home. He had been doing this work for years and accepted as an article of faith that he was immortal. A grimy headband with a religious slogan testified to his devotion.

The Razlavi Division had moved into place east of Al-Kuneitra during darkness over the previous several nights, relieving the Syrian unit which usually held that portion of the front. It was considered a signal honor to lead the assault on the Golan, but the Razlavi Division expected no less. Most of the Iranian soldiers awaiting the jump-off signal fully expected to die in the next several hours; their imams had told them as much. But the Muslim priests also had promised that paradise awaited.

With infinite calm, Omar Razlavi probed the earth before him. His plastic knife, unable to detonate a magnetic mine, struck something solid. The metal outline of instant death. It was a sensation Razlavi had experienced thousands of times. He had long since lost count of how many Soviet-, French-, American-, and Israeli-manufactured mines he had located. He inserted a wooden stake with its white cloth next to the mine and continued forward, probing as he crept along. Behind him, his platoon leader watched through night-vision glasses, noting the path to follow as the hour of attack approached.

■ ■ ■

NEARLY 500 METERS TO THE WEST, ANOTHER SET OF night goggles was in use. The Israeli sergeant carefully scanned left and right, taking in the green-tinted imagery of the Litton glasses. Catching a movement, he swung on the location and stabilized the device. After what seemed an interminable wait, the motion repeated itself. There . . . emerging from behind a discarded spool of barbed wire. The human form edged along the ground with surprising economy of motion.

Picking up his field phone, the sergeant called his command post. The sleepy young lieutenant who answered was mildly upset at being disturbed. He listened to the NCO's professionally terse report and consulted the area's topographical chart on the wall. With a routine phrase, the officer ordered the sergeant to take routine measures. These probes had gone on before, but now there was a way to halt them.

In eight minutes Omar Razlavi had reached the position shown on the lieutenant's map. The noncom opened the access to an electrical panel, flipped a switch, and the circuit closed.

Omar Razlavi's frail body was hurled into the air by the force of the explosion. The garish splotch of light ripped the night air and the Iranian platoon leader instinctively reeled away from his glass. The white light of the explosion strobed in the scope, temporarily ruining his night vision.

He knew that, at long last, Omar sat at the right hand of Allah.

From the Al Biqa—the Bekaa Valley—which runs a hundred miles along the Syrian-Lebanese border—south to Mt. Hebron in the Golan, and on to Jordan, Araby massed its legions. Some thirty divisions of infantry, mechanized, and armored formations—plus supporting air, artillery, and special forces—were poised to strike. Including logistics troops, nearly two million men were engaged in the enterprise which began with crushing, single-minded violence.

Ninety minutes before dawn the Arab army began to move. It rolled forward behind a shattering barrage of artillery, rockets, and low-flying helicopter gunships. And though the Israelis were not caught by surprise this October, the strength and volume of the offensive destroyed any lingering sense of smugness in Tel Aviv. The hard-eyed men in Damascus, Baghdad, and Tehran had worked more than three years for this moment, and they had chosen their time carefully.

With more contempt than concern, the Muslim leaders had assessed the American government's reaction would be determined by a desire for neutrality. To back either side would invite severe criticism from the other—and harsher considerations from the Arab world. Thus, the most attractive course would be the middle road. Imams and generals alike agreed that the president's cherished role as mediator would work to their benefit. And they would be proven right.

Washington issued declarations of concern, repeating the oft-quoted offer to serve as "the lightning rod of reconciliation," in Walter Arnold's own words. But nobody on either side expressed an interest in arbitration. This was a fight to the finish, pure and simple.

Balhama Air Base, 0600 Hours

"Well, boys, we're in it now." Colonel Solomon Yatanahu addressed his grim-faced F-15 pilots in the auditorium. "We'll give you all the support we possibly can. Our maintenance and ordnance crews have shaved every possible second off your turnaround times. We should be able to generate maximum sortie rates as long as fuel, spare parts, and weapons hold out." Yatanahu did not need to mention that all three items soon could be in short supply. If this war went beyond the second week without resupply, Israel would be in very poor shape.

Upon concluding the briefing, the base commander returned to his office. Inwardly he was furious at the government's obstinacy.

Yatanahu had railed his frustration time and again, most often to his wife. "The idiots! All they care about is where they stand in the opinion polls. They've spread us throughout most of Jordan, where we haven't a hope of holding that much territory, and once war comes we'll be forced to withdraw to shorter lines." He had known he would be proven correct; now one look at the map showed the situation. A two-pronged Arab assault down the road from Damascus to Jerusalem and from the Iraqi border toward the holy city could cut off thousands of Israeli troops.

Yatanahu sat down at his desk and called for his aide, Lieutenant Yoni Ben-Nun. "Yoni, we're going to have our hands full. Set up a cot for me in the rear office. Then collect the signals from Air Force HQ. We're likely to be concentrating on the Bekaa at first, but if the Saudis and Egyptians jump in, we'll be spread awfully thin. I want constant updates on all enemy forces—especially the northern F-20 squadrons."

Hâ'll, 1910 Hours

John Bennett wandered alone outside the Tiger Force advanced headquarters. He enjoyed the solitude of the desert night, picking out constellations in the crystal-clear air. For most of his flying career he had seen the stars as they really were, viewed from above 30,000 feet. Beyond the natural haze and man-made pollution which covered so much of the earth, they represented a reassuring constant in his life.

Walking a hundred yards from the half-buried command center, Bennett sat down and wrapped his arms around his knees. He mused to himself that never would he have believed he would come to this place in this capacity.

I'm an aerial warlord in charge of ten squadrons of eager young Arabs who soon may become actively engaged in a holy war against

Israel. How did that happen? What set of circumstances conspired to bring me to this situation? What god of irony gave me Claudia at this time in my life, then took her from me and committed me to a war against her historic people?

Bennett recognized the onset of a melancholy mood which he seldom allowed. He concentrated on facts, not conjecture.

Face it, Bennett. You wanted this, you worked for it, and you cherished it. No, it wasn't luck or circumstance that brought you here.

Be careful what you want. It might come true.

All his professional life Bennett had heard the catchphrase, "I'd rather be lucky than good." But he had never believed it. Instead, he was convinced that you made your own luck most of the time. What others attributed to fortune, Bennett believed was 90 percent hard work.

Well, old Pirate, that may be true upstairs. But how to reconcile hard work with finding the right woman? You've been lucky—if that's the right word—twice in your life. You found two good women over twenty years apart. They both gave you happiness and they're both gone. You've come out ahead, John. Finding happiness once in a lifetime is rare enough. Twice hardly seems possible. But nobody promised it would last.

He leaned his head on his arms and breathed deeply. The desert air felt good in his lungs. Then he said one word to the night.

"Claudia . . ."

Later that evening General Mohammad Abd Maila gave a briefing to Tiger Force at Hā'il. Brad Williamson and Geoff Hampton already were there with Red and White Squadrons. The Arab commanders or executive officers of each of the other F-20 units attended, including delegates from the two Jordanian squadrons. Maintenance, communications, and ordnance supervisors also sat in.

Bennett was pleased that Maila had been chosen as liaison between the Royal Saudi Air Force and Tiger Force. The American and the Arab had developed a close professional relationship over the past few years, for temperamentally they had much in common. A former F-5 pilot, Maila had completed two advanced courses in the United States during his career, which qualified him for higher pay and the attendant prestige. However, he seemed unaffected by his elevated status, remaining wholly mission-oriented. He was, Bennett thought, a true warrior.

"Gentlemen," Maila began in British-accented English, "I am here to answer some of the questions you must be asking. And I want to set a brief picture of what you may expect in the coming days.

"As you know, His Majesty has made good his commitment to see Jordan returned to its rightful owners and to the Arab alliance goal of securing the West Bank for permanent Palestinian settlement. By stating these limited goals at the beginning of hostilities, we hope to ease global concern and strengthen our case.

"The Saudi government does not seek the destruction of Israel. It has been made plain that our armed forces will not participate in activities aimed at occupying Israeli soil, and that was a precondition of His Majesty's commitment to the alliance. Under these carefully defined circumstances, our goal is beyond question."

Turning to the map behind him, the general said, "The Egyptians are moving armored and mechanized infantry forces eastward in the Sinai. At present this is to force the Israelis to commit troops to defend this front, thus preventing their employment elsewhere.

"We have a similar role here in Arabia. The difference is, we shall use our air arm to accomplish the same purpose. Colonel Bennett and his staff devised a contingency plan long ago, when the F-20 force was being organized. Colonel, please proceed."

Bennett walked to the front of the room. Without consulting the notes in his pocket, he began his presentation. It had been imprinted in his mind for three years.

"Many of you have heard us discuss portions of what we call the fadeaway plan. It is based upon two principles: goading the opposition and economy of force.

"The Israelis have run recon flights over several of our forward fields, and they attacked four of them, as you well know. Two bases were badly damaged but now are back to a limited operational status. The timing of the raids indicated that the Israelis were confident that hostilities would very soon occur. They didn't want to have to deal with their southern flank at the same time as the main threat out of Syria and Lebanon.

"So the object is to give them a reason to come after us. Just running counter-air operations against our northern fields is well within their current capacity, and all we would accomplish is about a one-to-one exchange rate. That means attrition warfare, grinding them down a bit at a time. It could work over a prolonged period—assuming they had little or no resupply. But to accomplish *our* goal, it has to be done at a condensed period in time and space."

Bennett moistened his lips. He was coming to the crucial part of his plan. "The Syrian Air Force, and to a lesser extent the Iraqis, are involved in supporting their ground forces. Riyadh indicates that the Egyptians will conduct offensive sweeps over Sinai, requiring Israeli attention on their western flank. This leaves us to play the main role in drawing the bulk of their air force into battle—on our terms.

"A bit of philosophy, gentlemen. I believe that the air weapon is the most fragile of all. Tiger Force is a prime example. It's taken us nearly four years to bring the F-20 squadrons to their current combat-ready status, and we've done it faster than anybody else ever has. It's been a combination of streamlined training, rigid pilot selection, and a relatively inexpensive, easily maintained aircraft. But even the few losses we've sustained have not been replaced in kind.

"The same applies to the Israelis. They cannot put an equally competent, experienced pilot in the next available cockpit after losing one of their first-line aviators. Thus, the experience level is degraded with each loss.

"If we can force the Israelis to come out and fight us over our own territory, we gain a double advantage. We're fighting close to our bases, and we keep anybody who ejects. The Israelis will lose not only their KIAs, but most of those who bail out."

Bennett thought back to the long-ago War College class and the treatise he had written—the paper which had brought him to the attention of Safad Fatah.

Only airpower can defeat airpower. And in the Middle East, with no weather to hide in, without forests and towns to conceal one's troops, everyone is vulnerable from the air.

Looking around the room, Bennett was confident his air arm could do the job. He saw Ahnas Menaf, skipper of Green Squadron, stylishly sporting a green scarf. He noted Rajid Hamir had sent his exec, preferring to remain with Orange Squadron. The acts were typical of each young Saudi. Ahnas leading from the most visible position, confident and assured; Rajid accomplishing the same results in the opposite manner.

Bennett briefly thought of Ed Lawrence, moving tonight with Black Squadron to a second-line base for two days. *They're living like supersonic gypsies,* Bennett thought. *Devil must be enjoying himself. At least I hope so; this is the biggest thing he has to look forward to for the rest of his life.*

DAY TWO
Over the Mediterranean, 2200 Hours

The U.S. Air Force Boeing E-3 made a gentle turn, taking a heading west-northwest toward its base on Crete. The huge radar disk mounted atop the fuselage, capable of detecting targets almost 500 miles away, was secured, its mission completed. The vast array of monitors remained in operation, however, to detect electronic emissions of any kind.

Previously the U.S. Air Force had kept the sophisticated airborne warning and control systems aircraft in Saudi Arabia. In fact, it had been a political sore point for two U.S. administrations, since the Israeli lobby protested loudly. But with Arabia's declaration of war on Israel, in support of regaining Jordan and the West Bank, it was not feasible to keep the AWACS planes in Arabia.

Normally, constant monitoring flights were made by the converted Boeing 707s, collecting valuable intelligence from almost every nation in the region. But this October evening six fast, low-flying jets temporarily went undetected by any radar. Their mission plan had taken into consideration the E-3's routine schedule, noted several days before.

The Six British-built Panavia Tornadoes, each bearing the green and white cockade insignia of Arabia, penetrated Israeli airspace from three directions. Flying at low level, in the dark, their navigation had to be precise if the plan was to succeed. And it very nearly did.

Mission planners had timed each two-plane section's approach to coincide exactly for weapons release: one section from seaward into Tel Aviv, two more from east and northeast over Jerusalem. But the wide-ranging western section had missed a turning point by fifty seconds and was late popping up to identify its target.

The nature of the three targets could not be ignored in Tel Aviv. In less than three hours the picture was clear to the Israeli leadership, and orders were hastily transmitted to air force headquarters:

> Destroy Saudi bases earliest time possible. Highest priority. Prepare contingency plan for air raids on Mecca and Riyadh.

DAY THREE

New York

Avrim Ran stepped down from the rostrum amid a scattered chorus of shouts and catcalls. The Israeli ambassador to the United Nations had cut short his prepared speech to the General Assembly, for clearly the mood of the international body was against him. His face flushed, fists clenched, he crumpled his text, stared straight ahead, and walked from the hall.

Ran had intended to cite the Arab assault upon occupied Jordan when he prepared his speech the day before. But the news from Tel Aviv and Jerusalem during the night had changed the complexion of his address.

Avrim Ran went straight to his office, locked the door, and sat by himself. He felt humiliated, embarrassed, and angry. But most of all, he imagined the grim smile he knew must cross his younger brother's face. David Ran had never believed in the power of diplomacy. Avrim had set his life and his career to the pursuit of peace through negotiation. Now, it appeared David had been proven right. Only military force could retrieve the situation. The thought galled the ambassador.

Pulling the telex from his file once more, Ran reread the starkly objective report which still was less than twelve hours old. The Wailing Wall destroyed and the Knesset damaged. How were such things possible?

Despite the emotions seething within him, Ran knew that the Arab outrage was calculated in its objective. The television news early this morning contained vivid images: the crumbled stones of the Wailing Wall open to Israeli cameramen anxious to show the world what the Jewish State now faced. No scenes were permitted of the Knesset.

Ambassador Ran was enough of a realist to know that air strikes

against military facilities were more important than cultural or
political targets. But wondered what his brother would think of the
retaliation orders which were certain to follow.

"The fools! The goddam idiots! Not even those imbecile politicians can be this insane!" Lieutenant Colonel David Ran bran-
dished the warning order alerting his squadron for strikes against
Mecca and Riyadh. "It's playing straight into the Saudis' hands.
Don't they realize that?"

Ran vented his anger at the desk, at the walls of his office, and
peripherally at the two flight commanders standing before him. His
face was flushed and the veins stood out in his forehead and
temples.

"Sir, maybe headquarters can get the order rescinded." It was
Major Yarom Sarig, the senior flight commander, second in command of Ran's Kfir squadron.

"That's already been tried," Ran snapped. "The Knesset is
running scared right now. The damage was minimal but you know
politicians. They're hellfire orators when they send somebody else to
get shot at. But let a couple of bombs fall near them and they start
thinking about their own skins."

The political fallout in Israel was beyond all magnitude of the
actual damage inflicted. When the six Saudi Tornadoes struck
within minutes of one another, the full spectrum of the nation's
vulnerability lay exposed: political, cultural, and military. Most
of the military professionals recognized that loss of the sacred
Wailing Wall was trivial in practical terms, even less so than
targeting of the legislative assembly. But the Saudis had struck
a nerve. David Ran bitterly wondered what hard-eyed intellect was
behind it.

At length the squadron CO calmed down. He heaved a sigh which spoke volumes. He was physically drained and mentally spent. Both flight commanders recognized the symptoms; they had only to look in the mirror to see the same strain on their own faces. They had been flying multiple sorties for three days, with no letup in sight.

"Well, I have to say one thing," Ran declared. "The Saudis did a professional job on this mission. It's now apparent that they sent in the first two Tornadoes to focus our attention on Jerusalem while the other four went after the wall and the Knesset. Their electronics coverage and deception tactics across the Jordanian border were well conducted. We can't assume they are anything but first-class opponents."

Captain Uzi Nadel, the second flight commander, spoke up. "Excuse me, sir, but isn't it true that we shot down two Tornadoes? That's a thirty percent loss rate on this mission."

Ran lanced the captain with a frosty glare. "Wouldn't you trade two aircraft for a shot at an enemy's primary political and cultural centers, with a major airfield thrown in?" He let the question dangle momentarily. "Of course you would! It's partly our fault that they succeeded as much as they did, anyway."

"How is that, sir?" Nadel asked.

"We've known for the past few years that the Saudis were buying Tornadoes from Britain. We know the performance and ordnance capabilities of those aircraft as well as the designers. It's basic doctrine to evaluate the threat based upon what the enemy is *capable* of doing, not what you *expect* him to do."

The captain knew his CO was right. The twin-engine, two-seat Tornado, built by a consortium of British, German, and Italian firms, was one of the world's premiere strike aircraft. It regularly won NATO bombing competitions, and with a two-man crew it was capable of delivering precision weapons at low level in any weather. "Do we know how they conducted the strike, sir?"

"Pretty much, based on known capabilities." Ran's voice was flat, almost toneless. "Their Tornadoes are configured for the French AS.30 missile, directed by the Atlis laser pod. This system gives at least a ten-kilometer standoff launch capability with accuracy of under two meters. Apparently both missiles launched at the Wailing Wall scored hits, but it was risky from their viewpoint. They passed within two hundred meters of the Dome of the Rock."

The two officers instantly grasped the significance of that fact. The Dome of the Rock is a mosque covering the site where Muhammad was said to have ascended to heaven and therefore is the oldest monument in Islam. But the site also is sacred to Jews. Abraham, patriarch of the Hebrews, prepared to sacrifice his son Isaac on the same spot. The Wailing Wall, also called the Western Wall, formed part of the 60-foot-high perimeter around the Dome, but now most of its 160-foot length was reduced to rubble.

Sarig spoke up. "Sir, is it known why the missiles launched at the Knesset fell short?"

"Supposition. We know that one Tornado was shot down during its approach. The second was hit, apparently after launch. Evidently that hit caused the laser operator to flinch off-target just before impact. The AS.30 struck about fifty meters short of the building but there was still a lot of damage." The missile's 528-pound warhead, impacting at nearly 1,500 feet per second, was capable of penetrating two feet of concrete. Blast damage alone would have been considerable. "Anyway," Ran continued, "we still have to plan for the Mecca and Riyadh strikes."

"We're going after Muslim shrines, then?"

"No, I don't think so. My guess is the government wants to present a high moral tone to the world, so we won't retaliate that way. If that were the case, we could use the upgraded Jerichos. But the Saudis have surface-to-surface missiles from China and since nobody can defend against them, nobody is likely to use them."

"Then what is our target, sir?"

"I don't know yet. Evidently we'll be told when Tel Aviv condescends to let us in on it." Ran's voice dripped bitter sarcasm. "Meanwhile, pass the word to the maintenance and armament sections. And get Asher in here to start work on mission profiles and planning. That's all."

The two flight commanders had been dismissed, leaving the CO to rub his temples with his fingertips, closing his eyes. David Ran, warrior, prepared himself for an unnecessary mission from which he quite probably would not return.

14

DAY FOUR

Hã'll

JOHN BENNETT AND BEAR BARNES CHECKED THE TIGER Force status board, pleased to note that aircraft availability was running at more than 90 percent full-mission capable going into the crucial test. There were ample stocks of fuel and ordnance, including Sparrow radar-guided missiles. The two-seat Tigersharks attached to each squadron were ready with radar installed. The General Electric APG-67 system was capable of detecting a five-meter-square target 85 percent of the time at more than forty miles, and this day the F-20s would employ their Sparrow option.

Bennett asked his operations officer about coordination with other Saudi units.

"We're all set," Barnes replied. "The schedule has been passed by discrete land line to the F-5 and F-15 squadrons, which will move to the northeastern bases. We've confirmed authentication codes with every unit, and the Eagle drivers understand they're not supposed to engage. They're only Sparrow shooters today."

Bennett concurred. With F-15s on both sides, the Saudis did not want any of their $35 million Eagles shot down by F-5 or F-20 pilots. Instead, the Eagle's outstanding long-range Sparrow capability was to be used as a preliminary means of breaking up the anticipated Israeli strikes. Bennett was less enthusiastic than the Saudis themselves about the prospects for scoring many kills with radar missiles, but that was beside the point. He knew that "the great white hope," as the AIM-7 was called, would force the Israelis to concentrate on evading the initial shots. That would give the Northrops time to position for an advantage when the close-in, cut-and-thrust dogfighting began.

Barnes was smiling to himself for no apparent reason.

"What's so funny?" Bennett asked.

"Oh, I was just thinking of what Tim Ottman used to say. You remember? He said he'd just as soon have a cardboard tube filled with a smoke generator to get the opposition's attention. It'd be a lot cheaper than a radar missile and accomplish the same thing."

Bennett chuckled aloud. It was a reassuring sound; Bear had not heard the CO laugh since Claudia died.

"Yeah, I remember. And that's from a thousand-hour Eagle driver. I just hope none of our 15s gets buck fever and piles in. The way the Tiger Force honchos are keyed up, not to mention the F-5 troops, I wouldn't want to get within visual range of an Eagle today."

Bennett recalled the briefing from the night before. The Israelis would come with everything: F-15s, F-16s, Phantoms, and Kfirs.

Bennett's word on aircraft recognition: "If it isn't built in Haw-
thorne, California, shoot it!" It shaped up as Northrop against nearly
everything in the Israeli inventory.

Rubbing his back, Barnes straightened up from the table. "You
know, Skipper, this is going to be one hellacious donnybrook. There
will be bogeys all around the clock, heat-seekers and radar missiles, heavy ECM from both sides. It's going to be a jet-propelled
Dawn Patrol." He grinned. "I'm almost sorry I won't see it."

Bennett did not respond for several seconds. Then, softly, he
replied, "I used to feel that way. But I think a lot of good drivers are
going to die pretty soon. The desert's going to be littered with
smoking piles that once were beautiful flying machines." He raised
his gaze to Bear's face. "You know something? I'm *glad* I won't see
it." He noted the concern on the ops officer's face, and understood.
"Oh, don't mistake me, Bear. I'm not having second thoughts. After
all, it's my plan. But whoever was behind Claudia's killing, it
wasn't any of the guys in cockpits over there. No, I'm just glad I
won't have to watch it, that's all."

Bennett turned to the situation map in the briefing room. The
forward lines were revised every two or three hours, according to
field reports and photographic reconnaissance. It was obvious that
the Israeli Army, overextended into Jordan, had been unable to hold
its ground in the face of the massive, violent assault. The units in
danger of being encircled had made a reasonably orderly withdrawal
toward the West Bank, fighting hard all the way. Low-flying jets
with the Star of David had inflicted heavy losses on Arab troop
columns, and antitank helicopters made sizable dents in enemy
armored columns.

But from Amman to Al-'Aqabah, Israeli units had been forced to
pull back in the previous three days. Those not actually in contact
often were left in precarious positions, one or even both flanks
exposed by the withdrawal of adjacent regiments. Fighting had
stabilized on the East Bank of the River Jordan, mainly helped by

Israeli armor and airpower. But nearly half the *Heyl Ha'Avir* tactical aircraft had been siphoned off for the massive retaliatory strikes ordered by Tel Aviv. The air force professionals recognized it as a blunder. And so did a young paratroop captain fighting near Amman.

Amman

Captain Levi Bar-El had had no time to think of his fixation on the American John Bennett lately. The intelligence officer had been fully occupied identifying nearby Syrian and Iranian units, interrogating occasional prisoners. Other than that, it was a constant routine of filling in small pieces of the overall puzzle, making some order out of near-total chaos.

Bar-El was leading a recon ground patrol that afternoon, searching a gully south of the Jordanian capital. He was aware of the jets almost constantly overhead, but he paid them little attention. Israeli infantry were accustomed to having friendly aircraft around, and Bar-El's unit had only suffered two attacks from enemy aircraft: Syrian MiG-21s which strafed the area before being run off by F-16s, and Iraqi Mirages which bombed and rocketed.

The point man in the patrol knelt at the bend of a ravine, scanning the area ahead. Bar-El had just placed the handset back on his radioman's harness when a movement caught the patrol leader's attention. Hefting his Galil rifle, Bar-El stood up and walked four paces to his left. He intently searched the scrub brush topping a small sand dune, signaling his corporal to spread out to the right.

Abruptly three Syrian commandos broke cover near the crest of the dune. Two opened an undisciplined fire with their AK-74 automatic rifles, wounding one of the Israelis. Bar-El's men returned fire with better accuracy, toppling the two in a cloud of noise, dust, and blood.

The third Syrian was visible from the belt up, perhaps twenty-five meters from the captain. Bar-El saw the man retract his right arm to throw a grenade.

Despite its boxy appearance, the Galil rifle is an excellent-handling weapon. With his folding-frame stock extended for proper use, Bar-El instantly mounted the rifle to his shoulder, got a quick glimpse of his front sight settling on the man's pinkish camouflage shirt, and took the slack from the trigger.

The Syrian's hand already was moving forward, loosening the grip on the grenade which arced toward the Israeli officer.

The trigger sear disengaged from the hammer and the Galil bucked in a three-round burst.

The grenade, now well toward its target, was twelve meters from Levi Bar-El, shoulder high.

When the first .223-caliber bullet hit the Syrian's chest, a gout of blood erupted from his shirt. The second and third rounds were wasted, going high. It had been a quick-and-dirty shot, not as well centered as a rifleman would have preferred, but it did the job.

The grenade struck the ground, bouncing once.

Bar-El moved his sights, trying to realign on the soldier, who tumbled sideways and collapsed into a bush.

The grenade exploded knee-high, three meters to Levi Bar-El's left.

DAY FIVE
Hā'Il, 0530 Hours

Operation Fadeaway was based on two elements, a hammer and an anvil. At daybreak Bennett watched his hammer sweep off the runway, Geoff Hampton leading twenty-two fighters from White and Blue Squadrons. They flew northeasterly to an auxiliary strip near the Kuwait border and landed on the single runway. Fuel tanks were topped off and ordnance checked. Then the former RAF flier led a taxiing procession of Tigersharks to the takeoff end of the runway and shut down. Fully fueled and armed, they waited.

The anvil was led by Ed Lawrence from Black Base. Forty F-20Cs from his own squadron, Rajid's Orange, and Ahnas's Green were dispersed along the taxiways and end of the runway. They also waited, as did one twelve-plane Jordanian squadron at Hā'il with Brad Williamson's Red Squadron in reserve. Tiger Force was glad to have the Jordanians—British-trained, experienced, and angry.

Bennett was not sanguine about the prospects for fully coordinating his plan. As a lifelong student of military history, he knew that even the simplest plan could turn to hash in the opening minutes of combat. But he knew that if even most of the elements came together, the Israelis would sustain losses they could not replace in time to make a difference. He checked the status board for the eighth time that morning. The Saudi F-15s had their schedules and the F-5s were deploying northward at that moment.

Everyone on the ground now sat back to wait.

Jerusalem, 0545 Hours

Orbiting the most fought-over city on earth, Colonel Aaron Hali reduced power to the twin F100 engines of his F-15A, settling down to a five-mile-circumference turn at an indicated 285 knots. Below and behind him he could see his squadrons joining up with a discipline born of years of experience. Aircraft in two-plane sections joined into four-plane flights which became building blocks for squadrons. Soon the entire force of seventy bomb-laden attack aircraft and sixty-four fighters headed east, stacked between 8,000 and 14,000 feet above ground level. Behind them, E-2Cs took up station to lend electronic support and early warning.

The large size of the strike force required more fuel for join-up than a normal mission, and the Israeli Air Force had not been able to acquire enough aerial tankers to support such an endeavor. Realistically, it had not been needed very often. The aerial combat arena of the Middle East was small enough to cross in a supersonic aircraft in several minutes; long-range strikes were unusual.

True, the *Heyl Ha'Avir* had demonstrated its superb professionalism on special missions—the 1981 Baghdad nuclear reactor strike and the 1985 precision attack against PLO headquarters in Tunis being best known. This, however, was about as close as Tel Aviv's air arm had come to the massive applications of power which the U.S. Air Force and Navy had launched against North Vietnam during Operation Rolling Thunder from 1965 to 1968.

Today's main target—Hā'il—was 450 miles deep into hostile territory.

John Bennett knew as well as Aaron Hali how much fuel each Israeli pilot would need to fly from sea level, to reach cruising altitude, to descend upon the Tiger Force airfields, and to return to base with perhaps 1,500 pounds remaining. The mission profile, checked and rechecked by planners and the strike leader, allowed for no more than five minutes to attack and three minutes of hard combat in afterburner. Upon withdrawing, anything which forced them to pause, to turn and fight again, would whittle away their safety margin.

Arabia, 0606 Hours

From a hundred hands across the desert came an incessant flashing of sunlight on mirrors. For the Saudi soldiers and nomadic tribesmen recruited into the Tiger Force warning net, this was their sole reason for existence. Many were frightened, a few terrified. The combined noise from so many jet engines bespoke an awesome power bound upon a mission of single-minded violence.

Some of the Saudi radio channels remained usable for a few minutes before they were obliterated by jamming. But enough early calls, plus confirmation from the mirror system, told the defenders what they needed to know. The single key of a radio transmitter issued a micropulse message from the air defense center at Hā'il. The ultra high frequency message contained two words:

Fadeaway. Go.

John Bennett had done everything he could. Now the outcome lay in the lap of the gods and the hands of his fighter pilots.

Black Base, 0608 Hours

Ed Lawrence raised his hand from the cockpit and rotated his finger in a circular motion. The other pilots saw his signal and repeated it down the line, starting their engines. The anvil pilots lifted off the runway in two-plane sections, stringing out in trail as the plan took shape. Each flight leader knew his orbit point and altitude—a designated bearing from Black Base spread northwest to southwest.

Simultaneously Geoff Hampton led twenty-one of his F-20s off the single runway near the Kuwait border, headed west. One plane sustained a last-minute hydraulic leak and ground-aborted, leaving the twenty-four-year-old Saudi pilot nearly in tears. They were starting the war without him.

At other fields, other squadrons were working on their prearranged schedules, some delaying their launches, others scrambling to medium altitude and heading south, away from their bases.

This was the impression Tiger Force wished to give the Israelis. By apparently fading away from the attack, they might entice some of the escorting Israeli fighters deeper into Saudi airspace. Bennett held out little hope for this option, as the *Heyl Ha'Avir* was too professional, too disciplined. But it was worth a try. At the very least, the radar picture emerging in the Israeli E-2s would show a logical reaction—enemy aircraft scrambling to get out from under whatever was coming.

Jordanian-Saudi Border, 0609 Hours

Aaron Hali checked his watch and his map. So far, so good. At designated points his flight leaders would break off right or left to approach their briefed targets. Hali would continue to a point equidistant from most of the Saudi fighter strips en route to Hā'il in order to lend a hand in case of unexpectedly strong opposition. He recalled his parting words with his lifelong friend Solomon Yatanahu, barely an hour before.

"Well, you see the advantage of being a junior colonel. I get to fly the missions while you sit at your desk and run base operations."

Yatanahu mimicked his friend's breezy attitude. "Yes, it's the burden of rank. A beautiful little *sabra* brings me iced tea and lemonade at the push of a button. While you're up there sweating in your boots, adding to the lines on your face from peering into the sun, I'm taking a leisurely lunch. A dog shouldn't have to do what I do."

Hali had looked at the morning sky, craning his neck. "It's a long way from Kibbutz Deganya, isn't it, Sol?"

"Farther in time than I like to imagine." Yatanahu paused a moment. "Aaron, what do you remember best?"

"Ah, the bananas. I never tasted better."

Kibbutz Deganya, near the Sea of Galilee, had been founded in 1911. It was famous in the region for its wheat and bananas and as the boyhood home of Solomon Yatanahu. There were nearly 300 kibbutzes in Israel, and though they represented only 3 percent of the nation's populace, they typically produced 60 percent of the military officers and over half the political leadership. Yatanahu and Hali both were products of that system.

Finally Yatanahu spoke what was on his mind. "This is a no-win mission, Solomon. Even if it accomplishes its goal, it won't change the course of the war. We're barely holding onto the West Bank now. I cringe to think what will happen if we lose as many planes and pilots as we might." The operational analysts had predicted a twenty percent loss rate, assuming everything worked well. Both fliers knew that was unlikely.

Aaron Hali said, "At least headquarters talked the politicians out of the Mecca strike. My God, over six hundred miles one way just to make a point of no military value. What were they thinking?"

"I have no idea, my friend. That's why you and I are fighter pilots, not politicians." Yatanahu wanted to say more, but time was running short. Besides, there were some things one just did not say to a comrade at times like these.

The two men had shaken hands, then walked away.

Colonel Hali shook himself from his sentimental musings. He nudged up his twin throttles a percent, forcing himself to concentrate on his flying. With a mild surprise, he realized he was beginning to lose the sharp edge which had characterized his entire professional life. *Better get a grip on yourself, Aaron. Start daydreaming up here and you'll wake up dead.* He checked his radar screen with the vertical- and horizontal-lined grid. Any time now, the blips would appear. He wondered how soon he would gain a visual on the bogeys that must be deploying.

Hali could not know that Tiger Force and the Royal Saudi Air Force had agreed on the most basic principle of war: concentration. They committed 70 percent of their fighter-interceptors to the campaign in central and northern Arabia, and the combatants now were screeching toward one another at 1.8 times of the speed of sound.

Northern Arabia, 0610 Hours

Lieutenant Colonel Mohammad Agadir checked his order of
battle one more time, though it was hardly necessary. The thirty-
nine-year-old Saudi already knew his battalion's lineup by memory.
The thirty tracked missile launchers had been deployed during the
night over a ninety-mile front with two other battalions arrayed in
depth behind him. His senior NCO had reported that electronic
countermeasures were appearing on the mobile radar vehicles' screens,
and the operators were switching frequencies on a random basis. As
soon as the oncoming Israelis reached optimum range, Agadir would
order three-quarters of his launchers to fire. The remaining 25
percent would wait until the attackers were outbound.

Agadir approved of the plan. Though he had never been in
combat, he benefitted from exchange tours with missileers in Egypt,
Britain, and France. He had hoped for a tour in the United States
but that goal had eluded him. A sober professional, Agadir nonetheless relished the good times his counterparts always seemed to enjoy
in America. They came back full of stories about the people and
places. Some of them still sang cowboy songs their American friends
taught them, though Agadir had trouble following the plot line of
"I'm Walkin' the Floor Over You."

The air defense officer returned his attention to matters at hand.
This plan would ensure that most of his radar-guided missiles, two
per launcher, would be employed against high-flying aircraft. The
Israelis were taking diverse routes and altitudes, but after the
attacks and dogfights many would egress at low level. They would
come within range of his passive heat-seeking and electro-optically
guided weapons.

Agadir tapped his gloved hands in a rhythmic pattern on the
hatch of his command vehicle, recalling another song. He could not
remember the lyrics, but the story had something to do with a young
cowboy who got in a gunfight with another man over a Mexican girl.

Someplace called El Paso, which apparently was in a vast wasteland. Well, Agadir knew about that sort of place. He remembered many years ago the wisdom of his old grandfather, who had no idea how prophetically he spoke when he repeated the ancient wisdom, "No man meets a friend in the desert."

Over Arabia, 0611 Hours

Aaron Hali keyed his mike twice, the signal for his first group to break off toward its targeted airfield. It was unnecessary, as the flight leader already had the time down pat, but Hali never took details for granted. He watched the Eagles and Kfirs break away to port, accelerating toward the southeast.

At that moment Hali's radar warning system demanded his attention. Visually and aurally he picked up the emissions of Saudi radars. He knew immediately from the frequency and tone that it was SAM tracking, undoubtedly with the track-on-scan feature which allowed short electronic glimpses of aircraft without constant monitoring. The colonel experienced two seconds of confusion.

"Where did *that* come from? The intel briefing mentioned nothing about SAM batteries this far north!"

Then he knew. Whoever was running the Saudi air defense net was a shrewd bastard. Undoubtedly they had moved portable launchers north of the Tiger Force bases on short notice—probably during the night. Hali ruefully admired the professionalism of the setup. Then he concentrated on dealing with it.

Warning calls came rapidly as pilots saw the missiles lift off, blowing large geysers of dust and sand as the first-stage boosters ignited.

Without looking, Hali knew his suppressors were in their dives, rolling in on the most threatening sites, but there were too many of them. Goddam it! How many were there? The desert before him seemed saturated with the telltale dust clouds of lift-off and the smoky white trails of missile boosters headed toward his formation at a slant range of ten to thirty miles.

The next few minutes were aerial bedlam. Even in the clear air it was difficult to spot the missiles in sustainer stage, lancing upward at twice the speed of sound. But there were so many—no Israeli flier had ever had to deal with such an intense concentration of SAMs.

The orderly, spaced formations became ragged as pilots opened out to loose deuce, flying the "SAM box" which allowed two planes to maneuver independently without drawing a missile toward either one. But with each wrapped-up, mind-blurring turn, with each diving countermove to defeat a missile, the formations began to disperse. Sections became separated from flight leaders, wingmen from section leads. Air discipline—a hallmark of the *Heyl Ha'Avir*— was sorely tested. Some pilots had to take their planes down below 3,000 feet to escape the missile barrage. Then, climbing back to altitude with heavy bomb loads still on board, they bled off energy and became more vulnerable.

Aaron Hali spotted a SAM streaking toward him from almost dead ahead. From long experience, he turned twenty degrees port, to better gauge the threat's closure. At the moment his professional instincts told him it was now or never, he wrapped his Eagle into a hard barrel roll, defeating the SAM's tracking in two planes. He snapped his head to the right, watching the smoke trail flash past him and continue to its inevitable end.

The mission leader also sensed something else. The Saudi fighters would be approaching at this very moment. He knew because that is how he would time it if he were running their show. With his pilots concentrating on evading the SAMs, their mutual support degraded by violent evasive breaks and altitude loss, this would be the perfect time to commit interceptors.

Hali glanced at his radar screen. It showed the tentative traces of Arab jamming, but he could discern blips with the fifty-mile grid.

He hoped most of his other F-15s also acquired long-range targets before both sides' ECM wiped out the radar option. The radio channels were clogged with warning cries; not much chance of alerting his Sparrow shooters. But then he relaxed a bit. They were professionals; they'd take action on their own.

The Israeli strike groups passed through the ninety-mile SAM belt in less than ten minutes. There were dirty gray tendrils in the clear blue sky, and dissipating SAM trails. There also were parachutes, and smoking wrecks on the ground. With the superb visibility from his F-15 cockpit, Hali took in the situation. It would be a few minutes before his squadrons reformed, but he estimated four to six planes had gone down. It was a small loss rate considering some 135 missiles had been launched, but any loss was irreplaceable. Hali looked again to his screen, hit the autoacquisition switch, and locked up one of the radar blips. Then he pressed the trigger, sending an AIM-7 off the number one station at ten miles.

0613 Hours

Major Abdullah Ben Nir glanced to either side, admiring the excellent view from his F-15. He keyed his microphone, uttered a terse order, and returned his attention to his radar scope. The Israeli jamming was taking effect; his two flights would have to shoot fast. The Saudi squadron commander designated his target and pressed the trigger, firing his first Sparrow at twelve miles. He anticipated the built-in delay but the AIM-7 never appeared. Its rocket motor had failed to ignite.

Cursing to himself, Ben Nir double-checked his switchology, confirmed lock-on, and pressed the trigger again. This time his weapon functioned properly. The radar-equipped F-20s also fired their two sparrows, then prepared for the coming "knife fight."

Airpower historians later would describe it as the largest radar missile shootout ever. Nobody would ever know for certain, but it was reliably estimated in staff studies—in Riyadh, Tel Aviv, London, Washington, and Moscow—that over the next few minutes some eighty Sparrows were fired, slightly more by the Saudis than Israelis. Since ECM efforts already were in progress, many of the missiles were decoyed or diverted. Others were evaded by hard maneuvering which further split up leaders and wingmen. Four Israeli aircraft were knocked out of the air or too badly damaged to continue. Seven Saudi planes were lost in the exchange. Major Ben Nir knew his orders were to disengage as soon as he'd expended his AIM-7s, but he found the opportunity too much to pass up. Rocking his wings, he led his wingman and second section into the fringes of the fight he knew would be developing.

0614 Hours

In the second flight of Black Squadron, Lieutenant Mohammad Assad caught sight of the white smoke trail headed for his F-20. Hurtling toward him with an inhuman intelligence at nearly Mach 4, the big Raytheon missile seemed to eat up the miles. With pounding heart, Assad executed the barrel roll maneuver he had been taught for such cases. He loaded six Gs on the wings of his Tigershark, completing the maneuver three seconds too early.

Timing is crucial to defeating an airborne missile. Too late a countermove allows no latitude at all. Too early, and the missile has time for a mid-course correction. Assad had a glimpse of the Sparrow compensating for his turn out of plane, and yanked the stick hard over. He knew as he initiated the maneuver that it was too late.

The AIM-7 smashed into the Northrop just behind the port wing. A violent explosion blew the fighter inverted at 200 feet over the rocky terrain. Instinctively, Assad pushed the stick full over in an attempt to right the aircraft. *Never quit trying.* From inverted, he looked through the top of his canopy in the last seconds of his life and watched his homeland rush up to greet his stricken aircraft. Like a canister of napalm, a large fireball scarred the desert landscape, marking the end of Mohammad Assad, citizen of Saudi Arabia, fighter pilot, and martyr at age twenty-one.

ED LAWRENCE CAUGHT THE ORANGE-BLACK FIREBALL in his peripheral vision, then led his anvil force into the Israelis. He saw the F-15s, having expended most of their Sparrows, close to visual range, lowering their noses and meeting his three squadrons head-on. There were bogeys all around the clock, and what remained of the formations moments before was shredded as the opposing forces swept through one another at 1,100 knots closure. They each pulled into abrupt, mind-blurring climbing turns to bring weapons to bear. But two Saudi flights kept going.

Devil flashed through the initial line of Israeli fighters, passing up the option for a head-on Sidewinder shot. The percentages were too low at that rate of closure. Instead, at high speed he raced on west. He knew the second line of Israeli jets would be about five miles behind the Sparrow shooters. From 500 feet above the terrain, his four sections pulled up to attack the second group as the first line of Israelis desperately reversed to assist. But most were too closely engaged with the pilots of Black, Orange, and Green Squadrons. Lawrence knew, having occupied the Israelis on his anvil, that Geoff Hampton's hammer would be swinging downward just about now.

Twenty-five miles southeast of the main combat, orbiting behind Orange Base, were two Tornadoes. Both were specially fitted for electronic warfare, the ECM pods on the hardpoints under their variable-sweep wings. Both also carried electronic counter-counter-measure avionics attempting to neutralize the Israeli jamming, but this met with limited success. The radar portion of the combat was limited to the early phase, and now it was eyeball to eyeball.

Ed Lawrence had told his pilots that the battle would be decided by human anatomy: eyes, guts, heads, and hands. He was right.

0615 Hours

Geoff Hampton looked down at the "furball" of milling fighters 4,500 feet below him. He deployed his two squadrons, sending Brad Williamson's Red around to the north to hook in behind the main Israeli force, while leading White straight into the fight.

Hampton had never been in aerial combat. His twenty-two years of flying had included twelve on active duty with the RAF and four as a contracted Jaguar pilot in Oman. The remainder of his career had been spent in clandestine activities in Africa and the Middle East, affording a wide variety of experience. Now he moistened his lips beneath his oxygen mask, anticipating the ultimate test of his life.

Rolling over, Hampton called, "White Lead is in."

He began stalking a lone Eagle on the fringe of the furball. It was sound doctrine—avoid the center of the fight, where an opponent may appear at any quarter and surprise you. Don't go "tits up" if you can help it—far better to avoid inverted attitudes and retain better orientation. Hampton accepted this tenet, despite the fact that his extensive aerobatics background had made him as comfortable inverted as upright. But above all, he wanted to maintain what the Yanks call "situational awareness." Know what the hell is happening in the three miles of airspace around you.

Hampton pressed his attack on the Eagle from its nine o'clock position. The Israeli saw him at two miles and made a hard left turn into the attack. Hampton leveled his wings, pulling the F-20 into an eighty-degree climb and passed the lead to his wingman, Lieutenant Quabis Mendat. With the nose well up, Hampton kicked rudder and brought the Northrop around to a nose-low attitude in position to support Mendat. But it was not necessary.

Few things are as terrifying for a fighter pilot as to turn as hard as his aircraft will sustain, the airframe at its structural limits under heavy buffet, and see behind him an opponent who cannot be pushed out of his radius of turn. The Israeli captain watched in awe as the F-20C out-turned him, its nose beginning to pull inside his own turn radius. When he saw the underside of the Northrop's fuselage, an icy hand clutched his stomach—a terrible certainty that the pilot behind him was able to track him in the gunsight. The Israeli's turn into Hampton had set him up for a six o'clock pass by the wingman, whom he had not seen.

With his neck twisted to scan behind him, the twenty-seven-year-old Israeli's head weighed nearly a hundred pounds. His neck muscles strained to sustain the five-G load which his entry airspeed allowed in a maximum-banked turn. Momentarily he thought of reversing the turn, but he knew that would gain a few seconds respite at best. At worst it would get him killed sooner.

He thought of the other option. He could pull the yellow-and-black-striped handle between his knees and catapult himself out of the fight, into the Arabian desert. He could live to see his family again.

Or he could sustain his turn, knowing that if the Saudi behind him didn't shoot in another few seconds, the Eagle's surprising maneuverability would begin to stabilize the combat.

He decided to fight.

In that instant he saw the bright flashes from the F-20's nose, and his life ended as 12 of the nearly 200 rounds in the burst raked the top of his aircraft, smashing the canopy, cockpit, and seat.

Brad Williamson took his flight into the combat from the north-northeast, gaining a favorable initial position on four F-16s. The Falcons were covering some Phantoms, which boldly dived to the deck and proceeded to their target at 200 feet. Williamson sent his second flight after the bombers and locked horns with the nearest F-16.

The Israeli saw him coming and pitched up into a climbing turn. Brad was willing to play that game. He admitted to himself that he was not as comfortable turning with a 16—he had 2,000 hours in Falcons—but he would play the vertical game willingly. After two upward-rolling scissors he was gaining the advantage and knew the third evolution would be decisive. The trick was energy management. The former Thunderbird knew the F-16 could not fly as slowly as his own airplane in the pure vertical. When the Israeli reached minimum controllable airspeed, he would have to nose over. The Tigershark, however, could go to zero airspeed and hammerhead-turn back on top of him.

With his neck craned back, Williamson carefully watched the dancing F-16, suspended in infinity through the top of his canopy. There was no up or down, left or right; only motion relative to one another. Then the American saw the movement he needed. The F-16 abruptly pitched over and nosed down to regain airspeed. Instantly Williamson stomped right rudder, forcing the nose to slice down and around, emerging from a sixty-degree dive above and behind the brown-and-tan-camouflaged Falcon. Williamson got a good missile tone, closed to less than one mile, and pressed the trigger.

The port Sidewinder flashed off the rail and corkscrewed slightly as it sensed its target. The F-16 had gained enough momentum to begin an evasive turn but it was not enough. The AIM-9 sliced off the Falcon's tail and the pilot ejected.

Williamson let out a howl of exultation. Briefly he pondered the chance of buying that Israeli driver a drink this evening. What a kick to hear it from that guy's viewpoint! He glanced down again, taking bearings on where his opponent would land, and began to circle the likely spot.

"Red Lead! Break right! Break . . ."

Williamson's instincts began to take over. In automatic response to his wingman's call, he slammed the stick hard over to begin evading whatever Red Two had seen. He felt a heavy lurch, heard an impossibly loud *bang*, and vaguely felt the onset of searing heat. Then Brad Williamson died.

Red Two looked down at the aerial debris. He could hardly believe what he had just witnessed. The F-16 he had been fighting zoom-climbed from Brad's bellyside in a turn and collided. In an instant both aircraft were windblown smoke and shards of metal. The Saudi shook himself, glancing around the clock, and detected friendlies out at three o'clock. He bent the throttle to join them.

AT THIS POINT THE FIGHT HAD BEEN IN PROGRESS FOR six minutes. Since most jet combats seldom last more than two minutes, it was several eternities in duration. But Ed Lawrence knew that time was almost impossible to measure in combat. He recalled an F-4 pilot who dueled with a MiG-17 over Vietnam and returned swearing the fight had lasted four to five minutes. The mission tape proved it was barely forty seconds.

Lawrence and Badir had jumped a flight of Kfirs and destroyed two. The fight now was dispersed over an area measuring thirty to fifty miles on a side, and the intensity of combat was diminishing. Black Lead's flight reformed and trolled the perimeter of the arena, looking for additional bogeys.

During a momentary pause in the jamming, Lawrence heard a

call from Ahnas Menaf with Green Squadron: "Bogeys pulling away northward. Am pursuing. Out."

There was also a short transmission from Orange, though the call sign was garbled. Lawrence figured that Rajid was patrolling the nearby fields. *Good lad. Always does the right thing.*

Central Arabia, 0630 Hours

Aaron Hali knew that things had turned to hash around him. Orbiting north of Hā'il, waiting to provide withdrawal support for part of the strike force, he knew there had been heavy losses on both sides and doubted that more than two flights would reach the target, still more than a hundred miles away. He checked his fuel state—ample but getting low—and looked around for his wingman. The boy was right there, spread out to two miles.

Hali's Nomex flight suit was soaked in sweat and his arms felt heavy. He had been through the toughest fight of his life: two engagements with F-20s. He out-turned one, which he caught at a depleted energy state, and was going for a Sidewinder shot when two more dropped out of nowhere and forced him to break tracking. There had followed the damnedest set-to he had ever experienced.

In the confusion Hali surprised another Tigershark and killed it with a 'winder.

Never had he seen Arab aircraft flown so competently and aggressively. *But then*, he mused, *why not? They held most of the cards—fighting over their own territory close to their own bases, flush with fuel.*

He called on mission frequency and ordered the withdrawal northward. He would remain on station with his flight a few more minutes to provide a rear guard.

■   ■   ■

MAJOR ABDULLAH BEN NIR WAS FRUSTRATED. HE HAD gained visual sightings on several Israeli aircraft and had a good shot at a Phantom. But he had fired too soon and the F-4 had evaded the missile. To make matters worse, the McDonnell Douglas fighter-bomber—essentially a generation older than its Eagle relative— had disappeared in the shadow of a ridgeline.

Ben Nir realized he had stretched the limit of his orders and then some. He was farther north than he should have been in the first place, and it was time to think about returning to base. He began a turn into the sun, wondering how the "wall of missiles" tactic had worked against the Israelis.

CAPTAIN HASNI KHALIL'S HEART WAS POUNDING IN his chest. He knew he would never be able to relate the proper order of events he had just experienced. The past five minutes were a wild kaleidoscope of spiraling, turning fighters, smoky missile trails, and brownish black smoke rings in the air, and plumes on the ground. He shuddered involuntarily at the memory of two near-misses: once with a Kfir and once with another F-20. He was rattled, upset with himself for not getting a kill. But it was good to be alive.

Khalil scanned the horizon. He prepared to patrol Orange Base when he caught a glint in the distance. He padlocked the speck and accelerated toward it. In a few moments he was visibly overtaking. It was a large aircraft, definitely not a Tigershark.

Turning in his seat to check his wingman's position, Khalil bobbed the nose of his fighter up and down. Though he could not see the bogey, Khalil's wingman repeated the motion and clicked his radio button to acknowledge.

Khalil arced in behind the bogey, slowly overtaking. He wondered why it was flying at basic cruise power. As he got closer he made out four of them—all F-15s. He knew that no friendly Eagles were to be in the area after the initial missile exchange. These four were heading parallel to the Kuwaiti border. Well, if they were Israelis they'd probably be conserving fuel, flying at altitude in a moderately fast cruise.

Keying his mike, Khalil transmitted on B channel. He wondered if he could get through; jamming still was persistent. He tried twice and got no reply. *Maybe we'll get close enough to look at their paint,* he thought.

The F-15s began a lazy turn to the left, Khalil noted, which simplified his intercept geometry. He continued his approach from below and slightly to port. At two miles Khalil squinted, hoping to make out the markings but it was still too far.

"TWO BOGEYS EIGHT O'CLOCK LOW! BREAK LEFT!"

Major Ben Nir reacted instantly to his wingman's warning. He looked left to see the specks of two small aircraft over his shoulder and loaded more than six Gs on his airframe. He nearly blacked out, forgetting to contract his diaphram and abdominal muscles to aid his G-suit.

KHALIL'S PULSE JUMPED. "THEY'RE ENGAGING! COVER me!"

Favorably positioned, the lead F-20 crossed behind the closest Eagle and cut the corner on the leader. Khalil rolled in trail, got a high-pitched steady tone in his earphones, and pressed the trigger. "Snake! Watch the shot!"

The AIM-9 hurtled toward the F-15's tail but exploded well below the target. *Damn,* Khalil cursed inwardly, *another fuse failure.* He prepared to reattack when he saw the third Eagle in planform as it pulled up. The green-and-white roundels on the wings stood out clearly.

"Knock it off, knock it off! The Eagles are friendly!"

. . .

IN HIS COCKPIT, MAJOR BEN NIR WAS EXTREMELY BUSY. FIRE AND warning lights came on across the board. He had felt the near-miss and knew that fragments of the warhead had punctured the belly. He was rapidly losing primary hydraulic pressure.

The wingman slid under his leader, assessing the damage. There were dozens of holes from the blast—several large ones. "You're venting a lot of hydraulic oil and some fuel. There's smoke from the left engine. How does it feel, sir?"

Ben Nir scanned his instruments again. The Eagle has a large hydraulic reservoir but the gauges told a grim tale; PC-1 was near zero and the second system, PC-2, was fading. That only left the utility system. "I want to get clear of the border," Ben Nir said. "I can make it farther south."

Above the stricken F-15, Khalil watched with bitter frustration. The sinking feeling in his stomach threatened to reverse itself and spew up his breakfast.

The Eagle completed its turn and rolled wings-level when Ben Nir called again. "PC-2 is falling off . . . utility looks weak. Controls are getting stiff."

"Get out, Major. Eject while you still have control." The wingman's voice had risen an octave.

Ben Nir swallowed hard, focused his attention, and replied, "Negative. I want to get farther from the border." The Code called for self-control, studied indifference to danger.

The minutes dragged by. The Eagle's increasingly erratic flight betrayed its imminent doom, but the pilot remained committed to his decision. The wingman called again. "Major, you *must* eject right now. You're—"

"Ahhh . . . I've . . . I've just . . ." The modulated voice was gone.

Abdullah Ben Nir never finished the transmission. As his utility hydraulic system failed, the controls locked. The big slabs of the unit horizontal tail dropped with a decisive *thunk* into the full-down position. The violent pitching movement was impossible to duplicate in simulation—no pilot could ever be prepared for it.

As the nose snapped viciously through the horizon, aerodynamic forces in excess of thirty negative Gs smashed the pilot upward out of his seat, against the canopy. Ben Nir blacked out instantly, never realizing what happened. But his wingman saw the entire ghastly evolution. He would never forget the incredible sight of his squadron leader splayed like an insect on a glass slide despite the fittings meant to keep him secured to his seat.

The F-15 nosed into the bottom of an outside loop, but solid earth interrupted its arcing path. A fireball marked the end of one more life this day.

Hā'il, 0632 Hours

Bennett had attempted to follow the progress of the battle from the operations center. He knew it was futile, as the combat was too disjointed, spread over too much ground and hundreds of miles of sky.

Climbing atop the camouflaged command and communications center, the chief of Tiger Force surveyed the area. Smoke still drifted from bomb holes and dust was swept up in eddies of wind. He looked toward the runways. There appeared to be a cluster of bomb hits near the approach end of the nearest strip, but he could not tell about the parallel runway. Bennett had laid out the field with parallel runways just for this purpose. On conventional airfields, with crossed runways, it was simple to shut down the facility by bombing the intersection.

Six Phantoms had gotten though to Hā'il. Two fell to SAMs and antiaircraft guns but four pressed in to deliver their ordnance. At last one hangar was destroyed, and one fuel tank had been leveled. Fortunately, it contained little JP4 at the time.

Bennett breathed deeply. *Well, it looks like the base got off light.* Then came the scarlet thread of anxiety. *Wonder how the boys are doing. . . .*

Northern Arabia, 0653 Hours

Colonel Aaron Hali finally turned northward. He had seen Israeli aircraft pass below him singly and in pairs, but not one four-plane flight. It appeared the battle was over, and he wondered if Solomon Yatanahu had listened in on the morning's events. Hali looked forward to debriefing with his old friend. Time permitting, they would get drunk together.

Continuing his scan through the turn, Hali saw nothing. He heard calls from pilots ahead of him, crossing the SAM belt again. *My God, how many missiles do the Saudis have?* He could not imagine how they retained any after the godawful barrage they had unleashed—was it possible?—less than an hour ago.

"Bogeys six o'clock high!"

"More out to the east, Lead. Three and four o'clock."

"I'm in!"

"Cover me, Benny, there's Tigersharks up here."

"Where did they come from?"

Colonel Hali wracked his Eagle into as hard a turn as his airspeed allowed. The last call bothered him—it was unnecessary, contributing nothing. That seldom happened in the *Heyl Ha'Avir.*

Feeling his G-suit compress about his abdomen and thighs, Hali sustained a maximum-rate turn into the unexpected threat, seeing two Northrops pass to port. He noted twin motes of light at their tails. Tigersharks had only one engine.

"They're F-5s! All Eagles, all Eagles, this is Aaron. These are F-5s. Out."

Hali stole a glance at his fuel gauges. He knew that he would be lucky to walk home from this one.

The Jordanian portion of the hammer was well timed. Those Israeli pilots able to disengage from the anvil had begun climbs to optimum cruising altitude, flying profiles for greatest range. The F-15 carried bags of fuel, affording it exceptionally long "legs." But repeated combats, using afterburner, were not part of the equation. Any additional full-power usage would quickly erode the fuel reserve to dangerous levels. A thirty-minute reserve built into the mission plan would not accommodate five more minutes banging in and out of afterburner—especially at lower altitudes.

Those two-plane sections closest to the mission commander had no choice. They unhesitatingly turned to engage, willing to take one more enemy with them before they were shot down or flamed out. The others had a fifty-fifty chance—accelerate away, trading fuel for distance and the chance of a Sidewinder up the tailpipe, or accept battle.

High over Arabia Deserta, grim choices were made in F-15 and F-16 cockpits. In a few minutes only windblown smoke and drifting parachutes remained to tell the tale.

15

JOHN BENNETT RACED HIS JEEP FROM REVETMENT TO revetment, occasionally swerving to avoid cheering mechanics and exultant pilots. He noted with professional concern that few of the men were refueling or rearming the aircraft immediately upon return. He grabbed a maintenance supervisor, shouted a few words, and depressed the clutch. Shifting into low, he resumed his initial review of the returning Tiger Force pilots.

From his own combat experience, Bennett knew what the young Saudis were feeling. It would be hours before the adrenaline abated and hypertension drained away. Then an inner calmness would wash over them, and many would lie awake.

Grateful and proud, they also would remember the men they had killed this day. Most would realize that the enemy were men very much like themselves, skilled, dedicated adversaries. In the heat of combat one saw only airplanes, not men. Somehow it was always a shock for a fighter pilot to realize there often was a dead body in the wreckage of the airplane he had just destroyed.

Seeing Rajid Hamir climbing down from his F-20, Bennett braked to an abrupt halt. He saw the young squadron commander run down the line and scramble up the ladder of Orange Five, his exec. They exchanged a few terse words, then Rajid dropped back to the ground. He began to unzip his G-suit when he was hoisted upon the shoulders of his pilots and mechanics. Once again the chant rose. "Ra-jid, Ra-jid!" But this time the young man seemed more withdrawn.

Bennett pressed his way through the crowd, ordering the armorers and mechs to return to work. The eight-plane standing patrol would have to be reinforced soon.

Rajid saw his mentor coming and asked to be put down. Bennett reached for the Saudi's hand and pressed it firmly. "How'd it go, Rajid?"

The young CO mussed his sweaty hair and rubbed the lines on his face left by his oxygen mask. "It was a tremendous fight, sir. We hit them just after the Sparrows fired. The timing was good. After that, I cannot tell you very much. It was . . ." he searched for the English word, "a madhouse up there. But we did well, I believe."

"How'd *you* do, son?" Bennett realized he had never before used that term with one of his pilots.

Rajid rubbed his forehead. "I got an F-15 before he saw me and then another in a rolling scissors. After that I went for a guns pass on a 16 but only damaged him." Rajid gulped water from a canteen offered by a mech. "After that I took my flight and two loners to patrol our case. We were ordered back here to refuel and rearm."

Bennett patted his shoulder. "That was smart thinking, Rajid. I'm afraid we may have lost Ahnas. He isn't back yet."

"That was what I heard on Green's channel. I checked with my exec, and he thought Ahnas went north to chase the Israelis. Ahnas is a better pilot than I am, Colonel Bennett. He always was, since we were students together. I wonder—if he didn't make it—"

Bennett cut off the boy's doubts. "Rajid, listen to me." His voice was cold and unemotional. "If Ahnas went glory-hunting with his flight, he committed a mortal sin. Yes, he's a good pilot. One of the best. But hot hands aren't enough. He should have used his head, too."

Rajid said, "I had better check my people, sir. We have had losses."

"Of course, son. Go ahead. I'm coordinating the search and rescue efforts from here. We'll know more this evening."

Balhama Air Base, 0730 Hours

The flight line was arrayed with serious, quiet maintenance personnel and staff officers. The Israeli Eagles landed by ones and twos, taxiing to their dispersal areas, where mechanics and armorers immediately went to work. In some cases the big fighters were fully serviced before the fatigued pilots climbed stiffly from the high cockpits.

Colonel Solomon Yatanahu stalked down the line, looking for the mission commander's aircraft. Not seeing it, he turned around and jogged back to one of the flight commanders. The captain stood between the twin tails, inspecting battle damage inflicted by a 20mm shell. Yatanahu called up to him.

"Hey, Benjamin!" The captain looked down at the base CO.

"Oh, hello, Colonel."

"Aaron?"

The captain slowly shook his head, then returned to his inspection of the shell hole.

Hovda Air Base, 0732 Hours

Lieutenant Colonel David Ran ripped the helmet from his head and lofted it in a high arc over the side of his cockpit. One of the enlisted men caught it. The Kfir squadron commander sat for several seconds with his gloved hand rubbing his temples.

The crew chief put the ladder in place but decided against climbing to assist the pilot. He knew when the CO was in one of his moods.

At length Ran unplugged and unsnapped himself from the cockpit. Some of his intense anger had dissipated, and he felt the onset of a growing numbness. He wanted to return to his billet and sleep, but he knew there was much to do before he could indulge in that luxury. Climbing down the yellow ladder, he accepted his helmet from the mechanic and walked alone toward the operations shack. One of the maintenance officers trotted over to him.

"Colonel, we're missing three planes so far and—"

"Not now, damn it." With a slicing wave of his hand, Ran continued walking in brooding silence.

Hā'Il, 1840 Hours

John Bennett and Ed Lawrence sat in the dining hall of the command center. They occupied a corner by themselves, enjoying one another's company as much as debriefing.

"I have the preliminary figures from Bear," Bennett said. Digging a sheet of paper from his pocket, he toted up the score. "Looks like our guys claimed about thirty kills, plus whatever the Eagles bagged and the F-5s got in the end run. We should have the figures from the SAM battalions tomorrow. Meanwhile, it looks like we lost twenty-two, including Brad in a mid-air."

Lawrence tapped his fingers on the metal tabletop. "Wonder how many of the Israeli drivers jumped when they ran dry?"

"Don't know yet, Devil. Several of them undoubtedly came down in Jordan. It'll take the Saudi Army a while to scoop 'em up and count the wrecks. Bear is preparing a tentative report to Riyadh. It'll include all this data plus our preliminary analysis on ECM and rescue operations. The helo guys are out now and will continue through tomorrow."

Lawrence said, "I lost two planes and one pilot. The first went down when an AIM-7 hit him. The other lost a turning contest with a 16—apparently our guy overloaded himself and blacked out. Got hosed and ejected. He was lucky, but I'm going to have a word with him."

"What did you guys claim?" Bennett glanced at Bear's notes. "Eight or nine?"

"Eight confirmed, plus another probable," Lawrence said. "Badir and I each got a Kfir climbing back to altitude after the SAM break. Then we latched onto a section of F-16s. We must have fought 'em for three or four minutes. Damnedest fight I ever was in. Finally nailed one but the wingie got away."

Lawrence leaned forward, his blue eyes animated. "You know, Pirate, I felt invincible in the F-8. Nobody ever got a clear win over me after I got out of the training squadron. Not even you. But in this 20 . . ." The redhead whistled softly. "In the Tigershark, I'm immortal. I tell you, no lie, G.I. As long as I play my game and keep my eyeballs moving, ain't nobody can take me. And I've been up against the best."

Bennett chuckled inwardly, recognizing the same world-class ego in his friend which he had once possessed in himself. "Well, Jesus, Ed. I should hope you're that good. I mean, you only have seven thousand hours and one war up on the rest of these sports."

The exec waved a deprecating hand. "No, no. I mean it. Look, it's like I'm the world champion chess player. I don't have to fear any other grand master. Whatever he shows me, it's a move I've seen before or a strategy I've used myself."

"Okay, I won't dent your fighter pilot ego. But for Pete's sake, Devil, remember you're pushing forty-eight years old. You can't keep this up forever."

Lawrence gulped the last of his iced tea. Crunching the ice cube, he shook his head. "Won't have to. Hell, I'll probably be KIA before this is over. Not through any fault of my own, of course. That's a statistical impossibility. But late one dark and stormy night, Allah might tap old Devil on the shoulder and ask me to help organize things in Paradise."

Bennett looked his friend straight in the face. "That's not the worst thing that could happen to you, is it?"

Lawrence returned the gaze. "No, it sure isn't, pardner."

"You know, I never mentioned this, but Claudia asked me about you and what you might do when this is all over." He smiled a grim, bittersweet smile. "She thought maybe we could adopt you and try to make you a useful citizen in society."

"Bless her heart. I almost believe that girl could have saved me." Lawrence paused, unsure of his ground. He had not heard Bennett mention Claudia's name since she was killed. "You still miss her a lot?"

Bennett closed his eyes for a moment. "Sometimes it's like she never existed for me. I mean, it's hard to believe I ever found her. Like she was just a pleasant dream. Other times . . . God, I can hardly stand it." His voice dropped an octave.

"Whoever it was that killed her, I hope they're paying for it now."

Lawrence touched his friend's arm. "After what happened today, maybe they are."

DAY SIX
Tel Aviv, 1120 Hours

Modi Aharon, a paratroop lieutenant colonel, opened a dirty knapsack and deposited the contents on the table. "These were on the prisoner," he said, "and we picked up these items from Saudi patrol members." The paratrooper handed the two piles of personal effects to the intelligence officer.

"Thank you, Modi. As usual, you have been very thorough." Chaim Geller thumbed through the documents. Then he picked up a standard rescue mirror. "Where did you say you found this Saudi patrol?"

Pointing to a map coordinate, the lieutenant colonel said, "About here, just south of the Jordanian border. We wouldn't have seen them if they hadn't shot at our scout helicopter. We already had the prisoner aboard and one of our own pilots. The gunship escort made one pass, then we landed to pick up documents. One of the bodies had this mirror and a signal book."

Geller rubbed his chin. "Now why would a Saudi foot patrol be up in that area, and why would only one of the men have a rescue mirror? You'd think each member would be equipped with this type of emergency gear." He turned to the paratrooper. "Which is the signal book?"

"Bottom of the stack, sir."

"Hmmm. I'll have our linguists get right on it. Something is peculiar here, Modi. We'll have the answer soon enough." He laid down the document. "Now, where is our hotshot Saudi fighter pilot?"

"Outside in the hallway. We're giving him small quantities of water. He's partially dehydrated and the medics don't want to overdo it."

The intel chief said, "Now would be a good time to talk to him. His resistance will be down after a day and a half in the desert."

They walked around the corner to where a medic and two paratroopers stood watching the young flier. His face was sunburned and he lay on a bench with his knees elevated, sucking on a handkerchief containing ice cubes.

"Good afternoon, Lieutenant," Geller said, glancing at the Saudi's rank insignia. "I trust you're feeling better. What is your name and unit?" English would be their common language.

The Saudi sat upright. "I am Lieutenant Menas Abd Halif, Royal Saudi Air Defense Force."

"Yes, Lieutenant, I know your air force. But what is your squadron?"

"I am not obliged to tell you, sir. Our nations are at war and I am a member of the Saudi armed forces which have lawfully declared war against Israel."

"Come now, Lieutenant Halif. You needn't be coy with us. We know you are an F-20 pilot with the so-called Tiger Force. We know about your leaders, Colonel Bennett and Lieutenant Colonel Lawrence. We know you trained at Bahrain. We're merely filling in the necessary forms." He waved a sheaf of blank papers in the air. It had worked several times before, but this was a new war against a new enemy.

The Saudi pilot made no reply, so Geller pressed on. "We also know that your squadron leader, Captain Menaf, led your flight northward to pursue some of our aircraft, and was trapped by our withdrawal force of fighters."

The lieutenant's face revealed surprise. Then the curtain descended, expressionless. *They've intercepted our radio calls*, Halif thought. *Just as Colonel Lawrence warned.*

The Saudi looked up at Geller. "What I do not know, sir, is who you are. What is your authority?"

Geller was momentarily surprised. For the first time in his life, the intelligence officer looked into the face of an enemy and saw reflected there an equal.

Hovda Air Base, 2019 Hours

The combined staffs from each Israeli base which launched planes on the Saudi strike prepared a joint mission summary that night. Working late, the eight planners and intelligence officers finally had completed their work. They were tired, anxious, and some were discouraged.

Major Zev Lapido from Balhama snapped his notebook shut with a crisp movement. "We have to give them credit. The Saudis set this up extremely well. The only fault I see here is the F-20 flight which chased some of our planes north to the border."

Lieutenant Colonel Shimon Weiler, a former Mirage pilot, pounded his fist on the table. "Damn it! Anybody could see this coming. We were suckered, to use the American phrase. And what did we accomplish? We moved some sand dunes, that's about all. In exchange for over forty planes and at least three helicopters. Not to mention the boys out there. . . ."

The colonel directing the debrief, Reuven Yeier, wanted to regain control. "Gentlemen, please. Let's remember we were *ordered* on this mission." He looked around the room. "We can take this as a lesson learned and avoid similar mistakes in the future."

"Damn it, Reuven, that's no good." Weiler snapped at his superior, uncaring for the breach of decorum. "The point is, this never should have happened. We were led down the path. The Saudis knew the government would order retaliation for their raids on Jerusalem and the Knesset. Next, we were drawn over the mobile SAMs, then the Sparrow volley, and the F-20s jumped our boys while most of them were still dodging missiles. Finally the Jordanian F-5s cut them off." He picked up a sheaf of pilot reports. "Look at these! Our pilots never even saw the F-5s until too late. They came out of the sun without radar warning due to enemy ECM. God in heaven!"

Colonel Yeier retained his composure. "We knew the Saudis had accepted many of the Jordanians, who have a high standard of training. And we knew the radar jamming would be better than any we've faced before. After all, the Soviets don't like to show their hand by giving the Syrians all their first-line equipment."

A captain from Hovda spoke up. "I think we're missing the point. We're crying over what's past. I believe we should be more concerned with retrieving more of our pilots from Arabia."

"Ezer, nobody in this room disagrees with you." The colonel's tone was calm and reassuring. "We're doing absolutely everything we can. But remember, our helicopters must fly over Arab-occupied Jordan into Saudi airspace to reach those sites. We have already lost three helos and their crews." He looked around the room, making his point with his eyes. "From now on we need to conserve our planes and pilots for the most effective use. That message is going to Tel Aviv this very night. I don't think there will be a repeat of this folly."

With that, he walked out the door.

Watching him go, the Mirage pilot said, "From now on, I wonder if we *can* hold what we have."

Ed Lawrence wandered into the debriefing room, drawn by the noise and chatter. Despite the hour, he noted with pleasure that morale remained at a peak. Thirteen of the Tiger Force pilots who had been shot down were recovered. Those returned to Hā'il were greeted with a combination of hearty hugs and good-natured ribbing.

In the corner, several Black Squadron pilots were singing the organization's theme song.

> *He set up in the front quarter*
> *At a fairly respectable range.*
> *Hit the disappear switch, rolled out at Deep Six*
> *And the Fox Fifteen went down in flames.*

Lawrence walked over to join them in the hoarse shouting which passed for singing.

DAY 10

Near Jericho, 1220 Hours

The mirage from the midday heat shimmered in the distance as the binoculars focused on the West Bank. General Hassan Gamail rotated the knob and set the mil scale along the Israeli-held front. His Zeiss binoculars were a prized possession. He had carried them since 1984 when the Iraqi chief of staff had presented them to the new regimental commander. Gamail had proven himself an accomplished soldier at every command level, and despite his country's military stalemate with Iran, his career had flourished. He had outlived many of his contemporaries.

The Iraqi corps commander carefully tucked away the valuable German glasses and edged back from the sandbagged emplacement.

Motioning to his driver, he scrambled into his command car and gave directions to the nearby divisional headquarters.

With two infantry divisions and a reinforced motor rifle division under his command, the veteran soldier believed he could make an option work for him. He needed to arrange supporting arms on short notice—artillery and air. But if he was correct, the opening he saw developing could turn this war around. It was Day Ten, and if Gamail's plan worked there would not be a Day Twenty. But first he had to talk to the combined headquarters in Damascus. This would require coordination on three fronts.

Hā'il, 1455 Hours

John Bennett tapped the map with his pencil. "You know, Bear, this war should be winding down pretty soon. The Arabs have control of most of Jordan again and the Israelis only hold this part of the West Bank anymore." He pointed to the slight bulge eastward toward the River Jordan.

"What still surprises me is that the Arabs stuck to their plan so well." The ex-Marine rubbed his neck; he had gotten sunburned two days before. "Once the Israelis began to pull back to shorten their lines, I figured the Syrians and that bunch might try to press right through to Tel Aviv."

Bennett glanced around. He did not want to be overheard. "There have been rumors to that effect all along, but since the Egyptians and Saudis have declined to back that move, the campaign seems to be living up to its press. The Arabs are playing this one smart for a change. By defining their mission and stating it to the world, they gained a hell of a lot of support. It'd be contrary to their interests to invade Israeli territory."

Bear flashed a huge smile. "Bring the boys home by Christmas? Seems I've heard that one before."

"Don't be so goddam cheerful," Bennett said with mock earnestness. "The day this shooting match ends, you and I are out of a job."

The big flier said, "Yeah, I know. But somehow being unemployed doesn't bother me much anymore. I guess the main thing we have to worry about is the State Department. They know we're here. Probably know what we're doing."

"Well, don't sweat it, Bear. If necessary, we can dig up a sea lawyer to muddy the waters. After all, we're not in the same boat as the contract maintenance folks, or even the military attachés. We're working directly for the king of Saudi Arabia. State isn't going to rock the boat after that. If anything, the diplomats will be falling all over themselves to return to business as usual in Riyadh. If things do get tight, I think we can count on Safad to smooth things over."

Bennett turned from the wall map and picked up a clipboard with operations reports. "I see the Saudis approved your rotation plan for the northern bases. Are the two Jordanian outfits flying from Green and Blue Bases now?"

"Affirmative. And Black is supposed to rotate back here with Orange in a couple days. Now that it's about over, I guess Devil and Rajid and the guys will look forward to some R and R in Bahrain or Riyadh."

"Some of them will, but I don't know about Ed. He's having a real good time. He bagged another one a couple days ago and he won't be satisfied unless he gets the last kill with the last missile in this war." Bennett flipped the chart cover shut. "Besides, there's no kind of R and R Devil would enjoy in any Muslim country."

"I guess you're right. But what about the young tigers? I'd imagine Rajid is anxious to see his boy again. The kid must be . . . what, almost two years old?"

"Not quite two." For the first time in days, Bennett thought of his own son, and of his granddaughter. *God, I'm ready to go home. We've proved our point.* "Things still quiet along the border?"

Barnes leaned back on the table, one leg dangling. "Pretty much. Some of the boys are saying the Israelis are afraid to come back in force after the big shootout, and I lit into a couple of them. I was polite, you understand, but firm. I guess we've both seen that kind of overconfidence backfire on a pilot."

"Damn right, Bear. These kids need to understand the Israelis haven't been back because there's no reason for it. Hell, from their viewpoint there was no good military reason in the first place. The fact that the politicians panicked and ordered their air force south just means our plan goaded them into our hands." He thought for a moment. "There must be some mighty upset Israeli drivers up around Tel Aviv this week. I wouldn't blame 'em for dumping napalm on the Knesset."

Bear consulted his notes. "Tiger Force is deploying standing patrols along the Jordanian-Saudi border, alternating with F-5s. I figure since the radar signature is identical for each type, the Israelis will have to assume all patrols are F-20s. At least, as long as the guys keep zip-lip."

"Remind me to hire you as an ops officer sometime, Barnes. You show real promise. Now, I'm going to log some ACM with a couple of the guys. Is 001 ready?"

"Right where you parked her last time, boss."

Balhama Air Base, 1458 Hours

Colonel Solomon Yatanahu checked the communications from *Heyl Ha'Avir* headquarters again. He had informed the air staff that he wanted to consolidate his remaining Eagles into two squadrons instead of the usual three. Attrition had made the ordinary administrative division unwieldly. Now the base commander wanted to pool all his aircraft and assign them to pilots from the same squadrons in order to maintain maximum possible coordination in the air. He proposed putting up four-plane flights from two squadrons at a time, keeping the pilots of his third squadron on rotation.

Yatanahu was reading the availability reports when his adjutant, Lieutenant Yoni Ben-Nun, entered the office. "Excuse me, Colonel. We've just had a bit of good news."

The fighter ace turned around. "I could stand some good news, Yoni. What is it?"

Ben-Nun waved a teletype form. "Word from the International Red Cross. Aaron—er, Colonel Hali—he's a prisoner of the Saudis. He injured his back on ejection but apparently he's all right otherwise."

Yatanahu, like many Israeli pilots, was not devoutly religious. But he closed his eyes and said a short, heartfelt prayer of thanksgiving.

The aide saw the relief on his superior's face. "Evidently several other pilots were captured, too. We probably won't know full details until a cease-fire is arranged."

"Well, that may be quite a while, Yoni. I just saw the kill-loss ratio from the first week. We're destroying eight to ten enemy aircraft for each loss in air combat. It's not as good as it used to be."

The captain said, "We knew the Syrians were working hard to improve in the past three years. And the Iraqis have a lot of institutional experience from fighting Iran. Even the Iranians have produced a few top fliers. You recall that memo about their ace F-14 pilot who claimed sixteen kills against Iraq during the 1980–88 war. But—"

"I know," the colonel interrupted. "The Saudis. We may be lucky to break even against them. They and the Jordanians are very good."

Feeling defensive, Ben-Nun interjected, "But there have been only a handful of engagements, sir. We were fighting over their territory, close to their bases. My God, the Hā'il strike was a nine-hundred mile round trip. And the F-20 is so small. It's very hard to see. Many of our pilots never even—"

Yatanahu waved a hand. "Yes, yes. I know all the pertinent arguments, Yoni. And each one of your points is valid. But we shouldn't have expected a pushover. Intelligence reported the Tigershark pilots were flying a *minimum* forty hours per month, often sixty. With the quality of their instructors, a fine airplane, and three and a half years, they were bound to build a first-class air force." The colonel looked sharply at his aide. "You remember your basic military doctrine? Never, never assume enemy actions based upon what he is *likely* to do. Assume the worst case he is *capable* of forcing upon you and proceed accordingly."

"Yes, sir."

"All right. Enough philosophy. What else do you have for me today?"

Consulting his clipboard, Ben-Nun pulled out a notification of the next day's scheduled operations. "The army is moving some units from the West Bank to reinforce the northern front, where the Syrians are massing. We have to maintain standing patrols over the withdrawal area before daylight and maintain cockpit alert with every serviceable aircraft not assigned to fly."

Yatanahu glanced at the order and initialed it. "Very well. What do you make of this, Yoni?"

The aide hated it when his CO played military professor. "Sir, I suspect a deception. The Syrians already control all of Lebanon. The stated Arab goal in this war is to drive us from Jordan and the West Bank. If they follow von Clausewitz, they'll concentrate at the decisive point—the West Bank. This activity in Lebanon could be meant to draw us off."

"Excellent!" The colonel clapped his aide on the shoulder. "It so happens I agree with you. It also appears the government wants to seize some Lebanese territory as a bargaining chip to retain a presence on the West Bank if we're forced out."

The young captain asked in a low voice, "Colonel, can we hold the West Bank? If we have to pull back—"

"I know, Yoni, I know. There'll be hell to pay."

DAY THIRTEEN

CAIRO (Exclusive to Middle Eastern News Service)— Egyptian forces entered the thirteen-day-old Arab-Israeli war this evening, driving a two-pronged assault into the previously inactive Sinai front. The attack, apparently largely unexpected in Tel Aviv, is directed along the coast to the Gaza Strip as far as Ashqelon in the north. The southern flank seems aimed for Sedom on the shore of the Dead Sea. Reports indicate that favorable defensive terrain has slowed the Egyptian column in the hills near Dimona.

Egypt's abrupt entry into the war came some six hours after an Iraqi assault upon an exposed portion of the Israeli lines on the West Bank. Low-flying jets reportedly spread smoke and chemical curtains ahead of a regimental-sized heliborne force which landed in the Israeli rear, cutting off the defenders from immediate aid. Though casualties among the Soviet-built Hip and Hind helicopters seem to be heavy, the follow-up infantry assault—allegedly supported by mustard gas from artillery—gained "considerable ground," according to Baghdad sources.

The present Cairo government has been far more sympathetic to the Muslim alliance of Iran, Iraq, Syria, and Libya than its predecessor. Following the death of President Khalid Amad and many of his cabinet ministers in a still-unsolved air crash five years ago, Egypt has edged ever closer to an outright alliance with the hard-line Arab states. But sources in the capitol still expressed surprise at the size and scale of the Egyptian army offensive.

Military observers in the Middle East have noted over the past two weeks that Israel's Jordanian front lines were overextended in the face of so strong an assault from Lebanon southward. The Iraqi attack should not have come as a complete surprise, say some analysts, since the corps which launched the combined-arms assault was known to be capable of such action. The corps commander, General Hassan Gamail, reportedly gained such experience during the eight-year war with Iran.

Western military attachés, queried about the new development, expressed doubt that Israel could sustain its present position in Jordan.

Without actually stating its aim, the Arab coalition seems to have abandoned its avowed goal of merely expelling Israel from occupied Jordan and the West Bank, said one diplomat. That same concern has been expressed in statements from Geneva, Paris, Washington and the United Nations.

DAY FOURTEEN
New York, 0100 Hours

The Soviet ambassador's heels clicked on the concrete, echoing in the Second Avenue subway station. Twenty paces behind him two security agents kept pace with the fast-walking diplomat. Several blocks to the north was the United Nations Building.

Anatoli Servenoff was one of the few old men left in the upper strata of the Soviet hierarchy. A new clique finally had replaced most of the World War II generation, but a few remained because of influence or ability. The United Nations ambassador had both.

As a twenty-four-year-old, Servenoff had been a petty bureaucrat in the Ukraine when the Germans struck in 1941. He had saved himself from liquidation—the usual fate of Communist Party members—by offering to cooperate in locating and exterminating every Jew in his district. He had worked hard and effectively for two years before making a dash for Soviet lines. Taking with him information and marginally useful documents, Servenoff had ingratiated himself with his superiors, who commended him for his espionage work among the Nazi barbarians. By 1945 he was a security commissar, still rounding up "unreliable" elements among the Jewish population.

The prospect of speaking directly and privately to the Israeli ambassador to the United Nations was distasteful to Servenoff. There was a metallic tinge in the Russian's mouth, and he spat several times trying to dislodge the bitter saliva. But the Soviet ambassador, like many of his Kremlin colleagues, was a master of expressionless demeanor. Secretary of State Thurmon Wilson had once remarked, "They may be a nation of chess players but their negotiating face would do credit to a master poker player."

Servenoff glanced around to satisfy himself that nobody was within earshot. He had been directed by Moscow to present his message to the Israelis without a chance of being recorded or overheard. One hundred yards ahead, approaching from the opposite direction, he recognized the Israeli ambassador, Avrim Ran. As if on signal, the Israeli bodyguards stopped when the Soviets halted. The two diplomats continued walking toward one another, each with hands in his pockets.

Neither man extended a hand in greeting.

Ran stared unblinking at the Soviet. He knew Servenoff's life story, knew that this man could be relied upon at Politburo meetings to push for harsher treatment of Soviet Jews. Western efforts to increase Jewish emigration from Russia drew mixed reaction from Servenoff. On the one hand, he wished every Jew gone from the Soviet Union—even the "good" Jews who abounded in Russian life and the Communist hierarchy. On the other hand, a lifetime of harassing, prosecuting, and deporting Jews had become ingrained habit.

Without preamble the Soviet diplomat spoke in near-perfect English. "Ambassador Ran, my government has directed me to convey to you in the most forceful terms the following: Because of our long fraternal relationship with the oppressed Arab peoples, Soviet friendship and assistance for them is a cornerstone of our Middle East policy." He swallowed but the metallic taste lingered. "We have viewed with alarm over the past twenty years the possession by your country of nuclear weaponry. Our intelligence is unassailable." He was sorely tempted to add that much of the information came from inside Israel. Some people would do anything to contact relatives still in Russia.

"We know that Israel has approximately one hundred such weapons." This with a faint smile. But the Soviet was slightly disappointed when Ran gave no sign of surprise.

"Mr. Ambassador." Ran's voice was even, controlled. "What has this to do with current events in my nation? After all, your client states have invaded Israel."

Servenoff never tired of sloganeering. "After your own illegal invasion of Jordan, and the cruelties practiced upon the Palestinian peoples displaced from their homeland, the Arabs are united in opposition to Israel's military arrogance. We Soviets have no desire to see war come again to your region, but we will supply our Arab friends with whatever weapons are necessary for their legitimate defense. This is the message I deliver to you." He held up a stubby finger. "If you Jews—" He halted from force of diplomatic habit. "If you use atomic weapons against the Arab states, the Soviet Union will immediately provide nuclear-armed artillery shells which could reach almost anywhere in your country. I tell you in candor that these weapons are in position at this very minute."

The Russian glared at Ran for a long moment. The Israeli made no comment. Then, without another word, Servenoff turned on his heel and walked briskly toward his waiting men.

Washington, D. C., 2015 Hours

That night Avrim Ran flew to Washington for an emergency meeting with Tel Aviv's ambassador to the United States and the chief military attaché. Already a motion condemning the Arab invasion of Israel had been defeated in the Security Council by the Soviet veto. However, Ran now held no illusions about the power of diplomacy. He intended to help press the Arnold Administration as hard as possible to intervene in some form.

Ran told his dinner companions about the Soviet decree. They dined in Mordechai Weissman's apartment, free to converse without distraction from other Israeli embassy personnel. But Ran was visibly shaken. "I think they mean it, Mordechai. This doesn't sound like a bluff."

The diplomats turned to General Lom Olmert. They asked his opinion.

"I don't see that we have any choice," Olmert said. "If we do not employ our nuclear force, we'll go under in a week—two at the absolute most. On the other hand, if we issue a pronouncement, threatening their use, that may provoke the Soviets into carrying out a preemptive strike."

Ambassador Weissman said, "Then it's over for us, one way or the other."

Olmert shook his head and sipped some wine. "I'm inclined to believe the nuclear option should be played without announcement.

It increases the shock value and forces the Arabs into a defensive mindset."

"What might the Americans do to help?" asked Ran.

"First, I doubt this administration wants to get directly involved. Particularly when Servenoff's threat becomes known. Even then, it's probably too late." He shrugged. "We are as we have always been—on our own."

Avrim Ran leaned forward, hands clasped under his chin. "I must say, General, that seems a remarkably detached evaluation."

Lom Olmert looked frankly at the diplomat. "Mr. Ambassador, if I'm not objective, you should fire me on the spot." He took another sip of wine. "There's one aspect we've not addressed. Are the Soviets really going to turn over nuclear weapons to the Arabs? Just consider that prospect from Moscow's viewpoint. Atomic artillery in the hands of Muslim fanatics—heirs to the Ayatollah. There's an American fleet in the Mediterranean. What if the Syrians or anyone else fired at those ships?" He paused for emphasis. "No, gentlemen. I do not think the Russians will be so stupid."

Weissman spoke in a near-whisper. "But Lom, what if you're wrong?"

"Then we're finished anyway. You know, I've fought in three wars and I've seen hundreds of dead men. Not a single one ever complained about being killed by a bomb instead of a bullet."

DAY FIFTEEN
Belhama Air Base, 1730 Hours

Solomon Yatanahu faced his pilots and maintenance and intelligence officers in the briefing room. It was evening, and the past two days had whittled down his Eagle force even further. Everyone looked tired, the ground officers as well as the fliers. Attrition had set in; the Darwinian principle applied to supersonic aircraft and proud-tired young men.

"Boys, you know the situation." Yatanahu tapped the map. "These three armored columns are on a converging course. If they merge, we've lost." One glance showed that the projected axes of the Arab thrusts would meet at Tel Aviv. *The enemy is going for the jugular*, Yatanahu mused. *They've read von Clausewitz. They're concentrating on the* Schwerpunkt—*the decisive point*.

The base commander continued. "The Arabs have changed tactics for this new thrust. They're continuing to move tanks and troops under an umbrella of mobile SAMs, but they're concentrating their fighters better. Coordination between SAMs, anti-aircraft artillery, and fighters means a near-continuous air defense net. We can't get our strike planes at their armor without exposing them to interception." He bit his lip. "In honesty, we've lost aerial supremacy. Now we're fighting for local superiority over our own territory."

Those words rang with a deadened peal; not since 1948 had such a condition existed within Israel's borders. Few of the men in the room had even been born then. They had grown up with certain natural laws. The sun rose in the east. Water ran downhill. Israel owned the sky. Now it was as if the laws of nature had been suspended.

Yatanahu asked the senior intelligence officer for his projection. Major Eliazar Maimonides shuffled his papers and began. "We have run these figures with every variation that occurs to us. But the fact is, we have no more than two days to effect a change The median is one-point-eight days—call it thirty-three hours from midnight. By then, any one or all of three things can happen."

Maimonides looked at his notes. "Either we'll be out of fuel or out of sufficient planes to put up a worthwhile strike. Or the first tanks will reach Tel Aviv." He glanced up for a moment. "We're still outshooting them over eight to one in the air, without recent

F-20 engagements, and we have enough twenty-millimeter ammunition to last. But missiles and fuel are going fast."

"Solomon." It was Major Yehudi Ne'eman, the senior squadron commander. He was thirty-two years old but right now he looked about forty-five. He had shot down six Arab aircraft in the past two days, and landed a crippled F-15 when nobody would have blamed him for ejecting. "It's obvious we need to break the pattern, try a different approach. We have to get into their second echelon."

Yatanahu agreed. "Precisely, but the Arabs also know the importance of their backup formations. They are what sustain the drive. That's no doubt why they allocate their strongest fighters to patrol those areas." He cleared his throat, not wanting to leave anything unsaid. "We're at parity with the Saudi F-20s, trading them essentially one for one. But it's no good, we can't afford that kind of exchange rate. We're forced to back off from the deeper strikes and concentrate over the battle front."

Maimonides interjected. "Gentlemen, we do have some things on our side. We're definitely superior at night, and what strikes we've flown in darkness have been pretty successful. Also, our decoy measures against the surface missiles are taking effect."

Though he couldn't explain details to anyone likely to be captured, the major was pleased with the latter ploy. It had been his idea. When Soviet-made SS-20 surface-to-surface rockets began dropping on and near Israeli airfields, the Syrians needed spotting reports to gauge their accuracy. Israeli intelligence, already onto most of the clandestine spotters, scooped them up and sent false corrections and optimistic results. It seemed to be working, but some SS-20s still found their mark. Meanwhile, Arab fighter-bombers were freed to concentrate on the front lines.

Mildly irritated, Ne'eman, the heavy-eyed F-15 skipper, pressed his point. "All right, that's fine. But what do we do tomorrow morning? We're faced with a vicious circle. We must stop the armored thrusts, but we can't do that without engaging their fighters. Our losses already are near-prohibitive, as you noted."

The pilot and everyone else knew that the loss of 265 Israeli aircraft had forced the *Heyl Ha'Avir* into a defensive posture. More shot-down pilots were being saved over friendly territory, but their planes were gone forever.

Yatanahu explained the results of the tactical panel's evaluation. But he also knew that a backup plan was being considered.

16

DAY SIXTEEN

Hā'il, 1500 Hours

BENNETT FACED THE THREE REMAINING TIGER FORCE
instructors. He had called Ed Lawrence and Geoff Hampton to join
him in a discussion with Bear Barnes, and they occupied the bunk
and one chair in his billet.

"Guys, I want to let you know my thoughts on this new development. When we signed on, it was to defend Saudi airspace against
any intruder. We've done that—first with the South Yemenis and
now with the Israelis." He glanced at Devil's helmet, stacked in a

corner with the rest of the IP's flight gear. There were nine stars now—three yellow, six blue.

"This is just my personal opinion. It doesn't have to reflect your own." He bit his lip in concentration. When he looked up he said, "I'm leaving. I'll stay two more days to wrap up administration and coordination. After that, I'm going home." He did not elaborate.

Geoff Hampton said, "John, I wonder what the effect would be if any of us stay on." He glanced at the others. "We're not actively engaged over Israeli territory—just the odd interception in South Jordan. That shouldn't pose any problems, should it?" The Briton was still considering his options.

"No, I don't think so," Bennett replied. "My reasons are . . . well, they're personal." From the expression on Lawrence's face, Bennett knew his friend had surmised the reason. *Claudia's too closely involved with the Israelis in his mind,* Devil thought.

Bennett continued. "Bear will remain at least as long as I do to run the ops office. Ed, are you and Geoff still going to Bahrain?"

The redhead replied, "Affirmative. I need to coordinate a resupply of Sidewinders and spares. Geoff is due for R and R." He looked at the mustached flier. "What'll it be, pardner? Monte Carlo or Rome?"

"Believe I'll try my luck at the gaming tables, old man. Used to be a croupier in my line back some generations." He smiled under his regulation mustache. Then his face turned serious. "I'm for packing it in, too. I've had a good run here, wouldn't have missed it for anything. But I feel it's time for a change."

"Very well." Bennett stood up. "I'll be in touch by phone when you get to Bahrain. Ed, you and Geoff might as well take my bird to Tiger Base. My 001 is due for an annual. That'll leave your two fighters for use here." He raised a cautionary finger. "But don't you dare scratch my pet. She's been good to me and I may want to take her home."

Lawrence waited for the others to leave before talking to Bennett. "Pirate, I'm staying. This isn't over yet, and I'd sort of like to stick around for the finish." He glanced at the floor. "I raised these kids from pups. I couldn't leave them now. Not while there's still some flying to be done." Bennett knew his exec meant, *While there's still some fighting to be done.* Ed Lawrence had long since passed the point where merely flying—even flying supersonic fighters—satisfied him. The aircraft had become an extension of himself, of his purpose. And his purpose was combat.

That's the difference between us, Bennett thought. *I look at a Tigershark and see freedom. Devil looks at the same airplane and sees a weapon.*

Bennett patted his friend on the shoulder. "I figured you'd want to stay. Just keep checking six, will you?" Bennett had the unnerving impression he might never see Lawrence again.

"Always have. Don't worry, Pirate. We'll get all the guys together in a year or so for the first Tiger Force reunion. Maybe the king will foot the bill." They made plans to meet on the flight line before Lawrence took off.

LATER THAT AFTERNOON BENNETT STOOD BEFORE THE situation chart in the briefing room. It was updated twice daily by the Saudi intelligence officers attached to Tiger Force. With professional detachment, Bennett evaluated the developing blitzkrieg against Israel. In the manner of all staff studies, friendly forces were blue, opposition red. The blue arrows thrusting inward from Sinai, from the north, and particularly from the east threatened to slice Israel into pieces.

It was now two days since the combined power of Syria, Iran, Iraq, and Egypt had smashed into Israeli territory behind artillery barrages, air strikes, armored columns, and mustard gas. Though he lacked precise details, Bennett knew that many—perhaps most—of the Israeli airfields were within range of enemy artillery. As the *Heyl Ha'Avir* consolidated its squadrons on the decreasing number of operational fields, two factors would work against them. Maintenance facilities, ramp space, and accommodations would become overloaded. And the planes bunched on available fields were more vulnerable to shelling or air attack. It was a descending spiral of options which seemed to lead inevitably to defeat.

Bennett pondered the turbulent history of Israel. Since her birth in 1948, the Jewish State had lived with the ever-present threat of destruction. She had survived against impossible odds because of superior organization and combat skill. Now that the Arabs had matched Israeli resolve, their vastly superior numbers were wearing down Tel Aviv's fighting edge. Not even American support—crucial to Israel's existence—could reverse the situation. And this time there was no U.S. aid. Washington, acting in its own best interest, lacked the willingness or resolve to jump in.

The Tiger Force leader acknowledged his ambivalence toward Israel's peril. *They're undoubtedly the ones behind Claudia's death,* he thought, *and for that they deserve extinction.* But he recognized that "they" did not include the nation's entire population, nor the military personnel who would continue to die in this expanded war.

Bennett also felt mixed emotions about his allies. To an extent he felt betrayed by the duplicity of the Muslim states which had reneged on their pledge of reclaiming only Jordan and the West Bank. The opportunists had seen the chance to carry their crusade much farther than announced. True, the Saudis were not participating directly, for the king had remained true to the letter of his declaration. But neither had the House of Saud spoken against the invasion.

Well, what could the Saudis do, anyway? Bennett found himself engaged in a mental debate which neither part of his psyche was winning. *The royal family will be lucky to survive on the throne after this is all over, that's for sure.*

To hell with it. There are no clear answers. It's time to go home.

Absorbed in his thoughts, Bennett suddenly became aware of Bear Barnes standing next to him. The ex-Marine asked, "Doing more homework, boss?"

"The irony just struck me," Bennett said. "Most of our European allies long ago abdicated the responsibility for their own defense— the most elemental duty of any government. The Israelis have fought their own battles for over two generations and now they're on the ropes."

Barnes gave a wry smile. "That's an odd sentiment for the leader of an Arab air force. Besides, you know damn well Israel couldn't stay afloat without U.S. aid and weapons. They barely repay half of what they receive."

"Yeah, I know. But at least they fight. They call a spade a spade. There's seldom any doubt about their position. Hell, some of our so-called friends around the world take billions of dollars in aid and vote against us in the U.N. Or they look the other way when some assassin or terrorist sneaks through their country en route to somewhere else."

Barnes shrugged his big shoulders. "Well, what's the option?"

Bennett looked at the map again. His gaze fell on the port city of Haifa. "Did you ever hear of a contingency plan called Pharaoh?"

"No, don't think so."

"I studied it at War College," Bennett explained. "It was a scenario in which U.S. naval forces attempted to rescue the survivors of an Israeli collapse. The logistics people estimated that maybe a quarter-million Israelis—mainly women and children—could be recovered by sea. I wonder if they've dusted off that study and delivered it to Com Sixth Fleet." He glanced at the two carrier battle groups plotted in the Mediterranean and thought of Dave Edmonds, a rear admiral now. With a start, Bennett realized he had not thought of his friend in months. Maybe Dave was riding one of the carriers out there.

Barnes whistled softly. "I don't see how they could pull it off, John. Not on that scale. It'd be tough enough in peacetime, but under fire? Man, they'd lose more than they saved just getting from the beach to the ships."

"Probably so." He tapped Bear on the chest with the back of his hand. "Let's see Devil and Geoff tuck their wheels in the well."

Forty minutes later Bennett and Barnes stood near the runway and watched 001's engine run up to 80 percent military power. Bennett could tell when Lawrence released the brakes, then heard the afterburner cut in. Instead of pulling up to climb for altitude, the sleek little fighter remained near the runway, retracting its landing gear in level flight. Then, abruptly, the F-20B rolled inverted and passed the two onlookers at 20 feet, wings rocking in farewell. It was a prideful, foolish piece of flying—something only Devil would do. Bennett shaded his eyes from the sun as the nose came up sharply, angling into the sky under negative G.

Watching the Tigershark disappear from sight, Bennett realized he probably never would see his jet airborne again. He might get one last flight in 001 before he headed home.

Bear Barnes wondered why Bennett stood watching for so long. The two-seater had disappeared from view two minutes before. Finally he tapped the CO's arm. "Come on, Skipper. Let's go to chow. Dinner's ready."

With a last look eastward, Bennett fell in step with the fast-walking Marine.

Balhama Air Base, 1618 Hours

Colonel Solomon Yatanahu shifted the piles of documents on his desk. Most of his files and official materials were boxed and ready for transportation or quick destruction. Though the Beersheba airfield complex remained operational, the three bases would come under Arab artillery fire before long—probably in just a matter of hours.

As a professional without illusions, Yatanahu recognized that Israel finally had lost air supremacy. Now it was mainly a matter of aerial parity, but inevitably the margin was slipping. The fighter ace knew that his Eagle pilots were claiming 40 percent of their kills with gunfire these days. It would not be lost upon the Arab fliers, who would recognize that a decreasing stock of air-to-air missiles required the cannon option. The mechanics and armorers were working eighteen-hour days routinely, but still sortie rates were declining. There simply was not enough time to properly maintain the remaining aircraft.

The intercom buzzed and Yatanahu picked up the phone. "Priority message for you, Colonel." Yoni Ben-Nun's voice betrayed the strain he felt, and the base commander marveled at his own stamina. He had heard infantry officers comment on the seeming contradiction: the old men still were going strong when the nineteen-year-olds were asleep on their feet. In truth, he knew the reason: experience in pacing oneself, applying full effort only to priority matters. The youngsters tried to do everything at full speed until fatigue overtook them.

The colonel pressed the lighted key and spoke into the desk speaker. "Yatanahu here."

The voice on the other end was familiar. "Solomon, this is Seth. My authenticator follows. . . ." The Israeli Air Force director of operations read an alpha-numeric sequence which told Yatanahu to stand by for a special courier.

"I acknowledge. Courier en route?"

"That is correct." There was a pause. Yatanahu thought the connection may have been lost. Then the DO said, "Good bye, Sol." Then the line went dead.

Yatanahu notified his staff that a special courier would arrive within thirty minutes. The officer was to be brought to base head-quarters immediately.

Then the colonel studied his situation chart. He saw the red arrows penetrating Israel from the south in two prongs, either side of Beersheba. He noted the arrows from the north and west as well. He knew the blue arrow aimed northeastward at the Golan Heights represented a determined counterattack the night before. Supported by artillery, helicopters, and special forces, it had succeeded long enough to silence several enemy artillery batteries but the Arab riposte had been too strong. Israel had lost the Golan.

Twenty-two minutes later an air force intelligence officer was escorted to Yatanahu's office. The courier, a lieutenant colonel, presented his identification and a second authenticator sequence which completed the original. Then, locked in the office with no witness save the base commander, the courier presented his message on the special-purpose form.

Solomon Yatanahu read the message twice, noting the details printed below. It merely said, "Initiate Jehovah." The remainder was a list of times, coordinates, and desired aircraft.

The base commander felt a surprising calm. He completed the double-check of authenticators and confirmation of orders received and understood. Then he dismissed the courier and picked up his phone. "Yoni. Give me six sections, two Eagles each. Full armament, including Sidewinders and Sparrows. I'll provide takeoff times for you, and I'll conduct the briefing myself."

He listened to the aide's complaints about limited aircraft availability and interference with scheduled missions. "There's no room for argument, Yoni." His voice was calm, matter-of-fact. "This assignment supersedes all others."

Then Yatanahu sat down and pulled a sealed document from his safe. He would have to coordinate with the pilots from Hovda, but that was all right. No specifics would be discussed by phone or radio—merely rendezvous points and times. The final briefings would be conducted face to face. Yatanahu looked at his watch—

1635 hours. It would be a nocturnal mission, which was according to doctrine.

Leaning back with his eyes closed, the colonel allowed his mind to retrace the world of his youth. It had been a difficult existence on Kibbutz Deganya, but the hard farm life was the best he could imagine for an active boy. He thought of Aaron Hali, fortunately out of it now, a prisoner of the Saudis. Aaron was right—the Deganya bananas were the best anywhere.

The day before, Yatanahu had learned that Deganya had been overrun by an Iranian division. Most of the inhabitants were dead, missing, or presumed dead. He imagined the rage which the youthful Persians must have unleased upon the community. He also thought of Kibbutz Sha'arhagolan on the southern edge of the Golan Heights. Captured twice and retaken once in the past few days, it lay in ruins. Nobody seemed to know how many of its inhabitants might remain alive.

Yatanahu's blue eyes snapped open. He thought he might fly one of the Eagles himself this evening. It would be pure pleasure. Then his professionalism overtook him. *No, Solomon, that's not your job. It's for the youngsters this time.* But he remained hard-eyed, certain of his task.

Jehovah. Good. It's about time.

Hā'il, 2025 Hours

John Bennett climbed the ladder to the roof of the command center, spread with sand and artificial shrubbery. The concrete structure was half buried with only eight feet visible above ground, but it afforded a decent view of the area.

Bennett sat down and pulled a mint from the pack in his shirt pocket. In a few minutes he would return to his small room and complete packing his bags. He would hop a ride with one of the

Jordanians in an F-5F in the morning and be in Riyadh in time to book an airline seat to Rome the following day. A stop at Saudi Air Force headquarters to check out, then he would be on his way home.

Home. Not long ago he had planned on making a new home with Claudia. That dream had ended violently. Meanwhile, there still could be some good years ahead with Paul and his family. Angelina was over three now, and she had been without her granddaddy for too long. John Bennett, warrior, decided to spoil her as no granddaughter had ever been spoiled.

He stood up to go, then an arcing line of white light caught his attention out to the northwest. At first he thought it might be a shooting star, but it was rising, not falling.

Balhama Air Base

The six sorties had departed on staggered schedules to reach their targets simultaneously. First off, at 1915, had been Major David Ran with his two F-15 escorts. The pilots assigned to each target had briefed together and knew the procedures so each mission could be flown under minimal communications. Ran's two Eagles checked in with terse calls on the discrete frequency and set up in trail, one on either quarter at staggered altitudes. Their radar search pattern was planned for irregular intervals, alternating quadrants.

Ran's initial leg took him northeast to Bar Yehuda on the western shore of the Dead Sea, allowing good radar identification of the hook on the opposite shore. Then it was straight southeast nearly 400 nautical miles, radar off but ECM activated.

Another Kfir and four reconnaissance Phantoms, which possessed a strike capability, also launched that evening. The night was clear, not requiring infrared goggles for the pilots. Since the Israelis were intimately familiar with the geography surrounding their borders, navigation was not difficult.

Ran penetrated Saudi airspace at low level. Rarely topping 500 feet, he streaked along the desert at 400 knots, navigating mostly by dead reckoning. As he approached his target he would accelerate more. The trick was a fast run-in—one pass in and out.

On the centerline was a special-purpose bomb cradle weighing 70 pounds. The silver-and-orange weapon it carried weighed 760 pounds, measuring nearly twelve feet long and thirteen inches in diameter. Ran, always a methodical pilot, rechecked his precombat list. There had been no opposition thus far, and he had heard nothing from his two F-15s. So far, so good.

Ran's gloved hand engaged the master armament switch, then checked the settings marked FUSING and YIELD. The indicators showed IMPACT and 400, respectively. The latter was adjustable from 100 to 500. The automatic release sequence was timed so the intervalometer would induce weapon separation in a few seconds after pitch-up from the 3,000-foot desert floor.

When his elapsed time showed five minutes remaining to target, Ran pushed his throttle to the stop, selecting afterburner. In minutes he was making nearly Mach 1. Despite the speed and altitude, he felt calm and controlled in the dim red light of his cockpit. He had practiced for this mission many times. But one aspect was different. When the operations order came through listing the two Kfir targets, Ran had exercised his rank. He wanted this sortie for himself, and relegated the adjacent assignment to the captain selected for the mission.

A crisp call came through Ran's headset. "Jehovah Four, Eagle Seven. All clear. Will meet you as briefed. Out." Ran keyed his mike twice in acknowledgment. The F-15s would withdraw along an alternate route to avoid retracing the ingress. If all worked as planned, the three jets would rendezvous along a course back toward the Red Sea. David Ran was now on his own.

■ ■ ■

JOHN BENNETT STOOD IMMOBILE ATOP HIS COMMAND post. Another missile lifted off, then another. Three launches in a few seconds. There had been no advance warning. He wondered if it was a jittery antiaircraft unit. He decided to stay and watch a little longer. Airbase defense was the realm of the Saudi lieutenant colonel.

TO HIS RIGHT, AT ABOUT TWO O'CLOCK, DAVID RAN was startled by the ignition of a rocket booster some twenty miles away. He watched the tail of the SAM as it arced high into the dark sky, then began to turn and come down toward him. He glanced at his electronics panel and noted his RHAW and ECM gear were activated. Then he saw two more missiles rise from the dark and follow the trajectory of the first.

The French-designed countermeasures package in the Kfir worked on two independent but related strategies. It attempted to deceive the SAMs' radar guidance, while affecting the fusing of the missile warhead by electronically picturing the target aircraft as closer than it actually was. The black box picked up the radar tracking signals and in milliseconds fed them back to the Saudi fire-control radar. The Israeli watched the missile arcing down and, when the red light pulsed on his warning panel, he started a hard right climbing turn into the missile. He wrapped up the delta-winged bomber in a high-G barrel roll to the right. Completing the roll over the top, he saw the SAM explode harmlessly beyond a range of 350 feet.

Though his night vision was degraded by the blast, Ran resumed his high-speed dash toward the target. The second missile passed well behind him, and he evaded the third with a less violent maneuver.

Two miles out, David Ran yanked back on his control stick and arced the Kfir into a zoom climb. Pulling into the pure vertical, he held that attitude momentarily. He felt the lurch of weapon separation, then continued the arcing pull-up until he was inverted.

Topping out of his four-mile-high Immelmann, Ran pulled the nose down through the horizon before rolling right-side up and diving away to the north.

The Israeli's aiming point was midway between Hā'il's two runways, 800 yards apart. The Kfir pilot knew from long practice that he had made a good release, and he was confident the weapon would land within 200 yards of either runway.

BENNETT SENSED MORE THAN SAW THE JET DESCRIBE its startling pull-up and arc over the top. He picked up the tiny fast-moving mote of light which was the American-built J79 engine in afterburner.

Involuntarily, he shivered and wrapped his arms about himself. The dream came rushing back—the elevated platform, the jet exhaust in the night sky, the bomb which must now be on its way. He knew to a mortal certainty that the fast jet now diving away to the northwest was a delta wing.

Five minutes, Bennett said to himself. *If it's ground burst it'll be a bit more.*

He sat down and waited.

The bomb, released at 530 miles per hour, immediately deployed its Kevlar drogue chute and two seconds later was drifting downward at 35 miles per hour. From release it would take almost six minutes to reach the ground. By that time the Kfir's headlong plunge would take David Ran 60 miles away.

The Israeli weapon was similar to the American B61 Mod 5, with a permissive action link safety system. All models of this type are one-point safe, meaning that in an accidental detonation in its high-explosive components, the probability of a yield greater than four pounds of TNT is not over one in one million.

Though the bomb weighed over 700 pounds, it contained less HE than an eight-inch artillery shell. Its nose shrouded a package of electronic safety, arming and fusing devices. In the middle of the casing stood two geometric solids—a sphere and a cylinder—composed of the lightest and heaviest elements in the universe. Their architecture resembled a fifty-pound globe on an eighty-pound pedestal, the cylinder resting in a plastic foam structure and the sphere covered with wires.

BENNETT SAT WITH HIS ARMS FOLDED ABOUT HIS KNEES. He had time to think of the course of his life, and he was glad of that. One of his friends, a Marine lieutenant colonel, had said that dying should be neither too fast nor too slow. Now Bennett knew what the officer meant. One wanted time to ponder it—but not too much time.

How did I get here? Bennett mused. *What sequence of events set me on the path that led to the middle of the Arabian desert this night?* He hugged his knees, drawn up under his chin, and then he remembered.

He had been sitting in this same posture that wonderful day at Jacksonville Naval Air Station the first time he saw a Navy airplane up close. His uncle, recently returned from combat, had taken the ten-year-old enthusiast out to the flight line to watch pilots practice carrier landings. The hour that young John Bennett sat alongside the runway, legs drawn up to his chest, had passed like seconds.

Uncle Phil, Bennett thought. *It began with him.* A tall, glamorous fighter ace wearing wings of gold who indulged a nephew's passion. The boy had only seen him fly two or three times, but the image lingered: one of the original pilots of the team known as the Blue Angels, looping and rolling in gloss-blue Hellcats the next year. Then Korea, and Uncle Phil didn't return.

But the mold had been formed. John Bennett followed his idol into naval aviation and seldom had cause to regret the choice. It had been a wonderful career, with all but two of twenty years spent in the cockpit. That seldom was possible anymore. Bennett reflected on his carrier deployments—the Mediterranean cruises with fabulous liberty ports, and even his four combat tours in the Tonkin Gulf. Vietnam had been fraught with pain and frustration, but combat flying had its own challenges and rewards as well.

Bennett remembered his backseat ride in Dave Edmonds's Phantom. Dave had been one of the aggressive, experienced F-8 pilots transitioned to F-4s to impart air combat knowledge to the Phantom community. After an extremely low practice mission, Bennett had climbed from the rear seat on unsteady legs. "That was just a might low, Dave. If an engine had coughed we'd be dead."

His friend had shrugged fatalistically. "Beats the hell out of cancer."

Well, Bennett reflected, *at least now I'm not going to die of cancer, or drift along with Alzheimer's or be a burden to anyone. It's not so bad . . . not so bad.*

THE FUSION WEAPON DRIFTED DOWNWARD. IN ANOTHER three minutes its electronic fuse circuit would close on impact with the ground, detonating a ring of high explosive surrounding a hollow sphere precisely machined from eight pounds of South African plutonium, together composing the bomb's round primary stage. Though only one-fifth the diameter of "Fat Man," this arrangement of perfect geometry and rare matter differed little from the architecture of the twenty-kiloton bomb that flattened Nagasaki half a century before. That weapon had missed by a mile. This thermonuclear device, with twenty times the yield, would land within 600 feet of its aiming point fifty percent of the time.

Bennett remembered that during his retirement ceremony at Miramar, somebody had asked him the inevitable question: What did he most enjoy about the Navy? And he had given the usual answer—the people. It was a cliché, but it was true.

Certainly the hardware had been a big factor. Nobody was more devoted to the F-8 than Bennett had been, and in the past few years the Tigershark had become the icon of his soul. But sharing a life in the air with other men of similar motivation had been the genuine reward: Dave Edmonds, Ed Lawrence, Masher Malloy, and so many more.

There had been others, of course. Bennett thought of Elizabeth and how he missed her those long years after the drunk driver took her from him. He thought with satisfaction that he had provided for Paul's future, and the future of little Angelina, whom he would never hold again.

And he thought of Claudia.

THE IMPACT-INITIATED DETONATION COMMAND PASSED through a series of stolen American timing switches and ignited forty pounds of plastic-bonded PBX 9404 high explosive in 32 places. The detonation wave raced through the HE lenses at 29,300 feet per second and interacted with embedded lenses of slightly slower-burning explosive, turning from convex to concave to match the curvature of the surrounded plutonium ball.

After ignition the high explosive burned concentrically, imploding the subcritical sphere of South African Pu-239 inward upon itself, symetrically crushing the seven-inch ball to the size of a small fist. Nanoseconds—billionths of a second—after the mass of fuel went supercritical, a stream of neutrons shot into the plutonium ball to initiate the rapid chain-reaction that is nuclear fission. The freed neutrons then fissioned other nuclei to produce more neutrons and more energy. Billions of plutonium nuclei were split in half a microsecond, unleashing the energy that bound together their 94 protons and 145 neutrons—energy equal to nearly forty kilotons.

X-rays from the fission trigger reaction super-heated the plastic foam surrounding the cylindrical secondary stage into a plasma momentarily denser than lead. The process fused twelve pounds of lithium deuteride into helium, releasing some 200 kilotons—the power of 200,000 tons of TNT—and billions of fast neutrons. These high-speed particles were absorbed by a sixty-pound mantel of U-235 around the core of lithium deuteride, producing over 160 kilotons more of explosive energy from the fission of billions of uranium nuclei. The 400 kilotons generated by this fission-fusion-fission bomb theoretically could be produced with one-third as much nuclear fuel. But the assembly was blown apart before all the fuel was used.

BENNETT'S THOUGHTS TURNED TO TIGER FORCE. HE wondered whether the IPs would hold reunions in later years. He hoped so, for reasons at once egotistical and sentimental. As long as Tiger Force was remembered, *he* would be remembered. But he hoped the fliers would cling to one another as well. Maybe the Saudis would participate—his few hundred sons. Bennett thought of Rajid. *Gosh, I hope he makes it through this. At least he's away from here. He deserves to make it. Good little guy.*

Then, thinking of his best pupil the way any good teacher would, John Bennett died.

FIRST CAME THE LIGHT—VISIBLE, ULTRAVIOLET, AND gamma rays. Microseconds later came the heat, infrared radiation from the fireball caused when air absorbs such energy. X-rays emitted by this explosive release were absorbed within a microsecond— a millionth of one second—by the dry, hot air, creating a vivid pinkish-orange fireball with hints of yellow-green. Temperatures inside the fireball—a little sun blooming on the desert floor— reached 30 million degrees or more. It rose as it expanded, like a mile-wide hot-air balloon, changing to reddish then, within a minute, becoming too cool to be seen. Around the fireball formed a blast wave of compressed air that raged from the fireball at thousands of feet per second.

Two thousand feet from ground zero, this moving wall of air struck objects with 190 pounds per square inch of pressure over the normal atmospheric pressure of 15 pounds at sea level. At that distance, the rapidly-rising mushroom cloud of radioactive soil and weapons debris generated winds of 2,000 miles per hour. Even an earthquake-proof structure of reinforced concrete can be flattened by only 30 pounds per square inch of overpressure.

Within the fireball, all matter was ionized. Before lifting away from the ground, the fireball scooped out a 150-foot deep crater in the dry earth of Arabia Deserta, 700 feet across. Ground shock cracked the base of both runways and the blast wave swept away all above-ground structures, vehicles, aircraft, and crews.

The surging, roiling mushroom cloud spread out along the tropopause at 45,000 feet, carrying glass-like radioactive beads and human aspirations several miles downwind.

DAY SEVENTEEN
New York

Avrim Ran stepped to the rostrum to address the United Nations General Assembly. This time no delegates walked out.

"Last night, the Israeli Air Force launched six special missions against selected targets in Lebanon, Syria, Libya, Iraq, Egypt, and Saudi Arabia. Five of these targets were destroyed. Two of our aircraft did not return."

Avrim Ran carried in his pocket the telex from Tel Aviv. Lieutenant Colonel David Ran was missing in action. But the ambassador continued reading his prepared speech in a flat, emotionless voice.

"We call upon the Arab states to withdraw from Israeli territory. We propose a seventy-two hour cease-fire in order to disengage the combatant forces, after which time the government of Israel is willing to participate in negotiations to designate the West Bank of the Jordan as a Palestinian homeland." He paused for emphasis. "Should this opportunity pass, then the Israeli armed forces will continue to employ nuclear weapons, including on our own soil if necessary."

Ambassador Ran folded his paper and walked from the stage. Not a word was exchanged, but he looked the Soviet ambassador square in the face as he passed.

The military attachés in Washington were abuzz with rumor and speculation. Everyone expressed surprise at Ran's disclosure; it was unlike the Israelis to admit any of their planes had failed to reach its target and another never made it home. But there were a few who knew something else. The wreckage of two Mirages shot down over Arab-occupied territory had been closely examined. The aircraft were found to be repainted over the original South African colors. This led to speculation that Pretoria may have provided some of its own rumored nukes to Israel. There was limited knowledge that the *Heyl Ha'Avir* had a close relationship with the South African Air Force— pilot exchanges, resupply of common aircraft, and air-to-air missiles.

Thus, although Israel had expended some of her own atomic arsenal, she might have an undetermined number of additional bombs. Naturally, Tel Aviv did nothing to refute that speculation.

NEW YORK—In a rare gesture, the United States abstained today in a United Nations Security Council vote, allowing to pass a Soviet and Arab-sponsored resolution condemning Israel for use of nuclear weapons two days ago.

However, diplomatic sources indicated that the unusually strongly worded resolution—which carries no force of action—may have been part of a compromise package leading to disengagement of the warring nations. Those sources said that American and Soviet leaders were "terrified" of the prospects for a wider nuclear conflict. Earlier reports of Russian commitments to radical Muslim regimes for a Soviet nuclear umbrella could not be confirmed, but some Arab delegates stated in private that Moscow's military promises had not been kept "in full."

Secretary General Pedro Ortiz of Spain conceded, however, that Israeli nuclear strikes had brought the two-week-old war to a standstill. He announced that Arab forces are to begin withdrawing from Israeli territory over the next two days under a U.N. plan which will include American and Soviet observers.

Meanwhile, military and scientific authorities have been attempting to evaluate the effect of the five nuclear blasts which shattered Arab troop, supply, and communications targets. Most are estimated at 100-kiloton yields with localized damage from air bursts over the targets.

By far the worst effects are noted in central Arabia, where a ground burst on a Saudi airfield produced effects described as "enormously bad." Experts predict the region may be radioactive for years, though most of the nuclides descended locally owing to light winds in the area.

One moderate Arab diplomat described the Saudis as "livid with rage," since Riyadh had limited its participation to air support and a few units in southern Jordan. In contrast, no atomic attack was launched against Iran, which played a major role in the war against Israel from the beginning. Informed speculation held that the distance was too great for fighter-bombers to penetrate layers of Arab air defenses. Other authorities, noting Israel possesses long-range Jericho missiles, believe the initial attacks were warnings of a second wave to be launched in the event the war continued. Military experts note that neither side can defend against missiles, and that Israel—perhaps 24 hours from collapse—had nothing to lose in that event.

Israeli ambassador Avrim Ran told a news conference that no Arab troops should remain in Israel within 72 hours. In exchange, Tel Aviv will cede the West Bank to U.N. control while acknowledging the "loss" of Jordan as the long-awaited Palestinian homeland.

17

SIX YEARS LATER
Tempe, Arizona

THE DOORBELL RANG IN THE HOUSE ON MILL AVENUE. The young father shouted "I'll get it" and walked briskly through the living room. He opened the door to see a well-built man in his late thirties, leaning on a cane. The visitor had a dark tan, and his curly black hair was flecked with premature gray.

"Mr. Paul Bennett?" the visitor asked.

"Yes."

"I phoned you yesterday, from the airport."

Paul opened the screen door. "Oh, yes. Of course, Mr. . . . ."

"Levi Bar-El." The visitor extended his hand.

"Mr. Bar-El. Please come in." Paul stepped back and bumped into his daughter. "Be careful, Angelina." The girl was nine years old with light brown hair and big gray eyes. Uncertain of what to make of the stranger, she retreated to the corner to join her younger brother, Edward.

Paul showed Bar-El to the sofa, careful to seat him where his left leg would not be cramped. Paul assumed the Israeli had been injured in the war, as he had mentioned research for a book when he phoned.

After giving Bar-El an iced tea, Paul Bennett asked, "What may I do for you? I assume you want to know about my father."

Levi Bar-El sipped his tea and nodded. His gaze took in the dining room and Mrs. Bennett's silverware. Then his scan stopped at the mantle. He leaned forward, staring at a green figurine. It was a pregnant woman.

Momentarily distracted, Bar-El recovered quickly. Turning to Paul, he said, "Actually, Mr. Bennett, I know a great deal about your father. I thought I might be able to tell you a few things about him."

For most of the afternoon the former intelligence officer described the inner workings of Tiger Force. Some of the names were familiar to Paul. Bar-El had talked to Peter Saint-Martin and Geoff Hampton in London, where he had signed a contract with a publisher for a history of the war. They in turn had led him to some of the Americans.

The most helpful IP was Congressman Tim Ottman of New York. Though few of his constituents knew anything about Tiger Force, they admired the second-term representative for his candor and his humor. He had stolen more than one tense press conference with an elaborate display of skill with an old yellow yo-yo. However, House staffers knew Tim Ottman to be exceptionally well informed on tactical airpower. A few regarded this as normal for a former Air

Force pilot, but others wondered about his sense of urgency in procuring a mix of simple, reliable aircraft and complex, expensive ones.

Not all Tiger Force IPs were anxious to talk to an Israeli officer. But some were professionally curious, and others bore no grudge. Paul Bennett himself was mildly surprised to find he liked the disabled Israeli, and questioned him closely.

Paul asked about the remaining Saudi F-20 pilots. He knew that many had perished in the explosion at Hā'il or from the radiation effects thereafter. While not telling all he knew, Bar-El said that some still were in the program and two or three had been promoted to seniority beyond their years. Paul already knew that Lieutenant Colonel Rajid Hamir was headed for the top. They kept in touch by mail and by phone.

Seattle

The next day Levi Bar-El took an airliner to Seattle and rented a car at Seattle-Tacoma International Airport. He had phoned Ed Lawrence from Phoenix to confirm the meeting. Actually, Devil already knew of the Israeli's interest in Tiger Force and looked forward to the meeting with cautious anticipation.

Ed and Nancy Lawrence lived on twenty acres near Renton, where they raised Arabian horses and llamas. Peter Saint-Martin and Tim Ottman had said that Devil surprised everyone who knew him by settling down to a happy married life, and the irony was not lost upon them. Like John Bennett, they had expected the Tiger Force exec to die in an F-20 or, failing that, to drift away as an aerial beachcomber.

No one was more surprised than Lawrence himself. A lifelong bachelor, he had met Nancy Mays on a Boeing 737 to Phoenix. An uncommonly pretty brunette, she had startling green eyes and a genuine curiosity about flying that captivated him. But her interest should have been no surprise—she was captain of the airliner, and they talked shop at length.

Two years later they married and built a home on Lawrence's property near Renton. In addition to their animals they maintained a Champion Citabria in a small hangar on their private airstrip. It was a trim little aircraft, sporting a red-and-white color scheme. Lawrence had intended to paint three yellow and six blue stars below the left window, but Nancy refused to allow it.

From a lifetime of globe-trotting the Lawrences were content to remain at home with their son, John B. The boy was almost three now and already had more flight time than some private pilots. Ed and Nancy Lawrence always made it to the Tiger Force reunions, but his attendance had dropped off at the Tailhook and Red River Rat gatherings. He was mildly surprised to find he preferred staying home.

It was mid-afternoon when Levi Bar-El finally found the farm, "Devil's Den." Nancy greeted him and led him to the hangar, where Lawrence was pulling unauthorized maintenance on the Citabria's Lycoming engine. Bar-El followed Nancy inside, appreciatively noting her shapely figure. She wore designer jeans and a faded blue T-shirt with some sort of black-and-white naval insignia on the front. Nancy introduced the Israeli, made him at ease, and returned to the house.

Lawrence had weathered the years in good form, Bar-El thought. The red hair was lightly streaked with gray, but the bright blue eyes and dazzling white smile seemed to erase ten or more of the aviator's 54 years. They sat and talked cautiously at first, feeling out one anothers' attitudes.

At length Lawrence motioned outside and suggested they sit by the fence in the evening's low sun. The Israeli leaned his back against the rails, easing the load on his bad leg. He noticed some llamas and horses in the pasture, but paid them scant attention.

Lawrence was describing his pilot training philosophy when Bar-El let out a shout. It was more of surprise than pain. Lawrence saw the cause and laughed aloud, in spite of himself. When Bar-El turned, he was eyeball to eyeball with a magnificent stud llama. The animal had curiously stuck his nose in the back of Bar-El's neck.

"He's just mooching," Lawrence explained. "Wants to see if you have anything to eat." He waved his orange ballcap at the black-and-white animal, who raised its head and gurgled. "Damn it, Rambo, get away. You're the biggest chowhound in three states."

Distracted, Bar-El took in the livestock again. "You make a living with these creatures, Mr. Lawrence?"

The aviator shrugged and laughed. "Yeah, pretty good. Rambo here would go for about forty thousand dollars if we wanted to sell him. But he's like an overgrown pet. Llamas seem to go with Arabian horses and Nancy likes to ride. I prefer the llamas myself, but I enjoy the horses, too." He looked around. "That one over there"—he pointed to a dappled gray-and-white mare—"is our prize breeder. Aren't you, Inshallah?" He whistled and the animal pricked up her ears.

Bar-El turned to Lawrence. "Her name is Inshallah?"

"Sure, it's Arabic. But then you know all about that, I suppose."

Bar-El thought to himself, *Life is strange. A former mercenary enemy of my country entertains me with his Arabian horses and South American pack animals. Who would believe it?*

At length Lawrence asked the question which had been on his mind through all the intervening years. Bar-El had anticipated it, and he was ready.

Emphasizing that he could not reveal sources, the Israeli said, "We learned a few months after Claudia Meyers's death that the operation was planned by the Iranians, who hired another party to contract the Lebanese mercenaries. Apparently Tehran was concerned about possible hostilities with the Saudis and wanted to eliminate the head of Tiger Force."

"I'll be damned. To tell you the truth, John and I figured it was you people or the South Yemenis."

"Mr. Lawrence, I would have to deny I ever said this. But we knew that you and the Saudi government also were concerned about Iran." Bar-El's mouth tightened in an ironic smile. "I can tell you now that your name also was on Tehran's list but you kept so busy flying that they never had an opportunity to get you."

The expression on the redhead's face told Bar-El that the American knew the report was accurate.

Finally Lawrence asked about any surviving Israeli fighter pilots from the air battles over Arabia and Jordan. He said that he would like to buy some of them whatever they drank.

Bar-El said, "Well, I cannot mention any names but you might contact the office of our air attaché in Washington. I believe he could investigate." In fact, the current attaché was a lieutenant colonel who had been shot down by an F-20 and was rescued by helicopter after the Hā'il strike. "I also know of two others who might be willing to meet you. Both are retired colonels. One was base commander at Balhama during the war. The other is partially paralyzed from back injuries sustained in ejecting from his F-15. They are both fine men—real warriors." Bar-El was tempted to mention their names. Instead, he added, "The attaché would put you in touch with them if he is permitted to do so."

Lawrence had one last question. "What about the two losses during the nuclear strikes? What happened?"

Bar-El was cautious. He had been cleared to write an unusually detailed account of some aspects of the war, but he did not wish to offend his host's sensibilities. Still, he decided to reveal more than he had planned to.

"A Phantom was shot down en route to its target in Syria. Evidently there was an antiaircraft battery which unexpectedly showed up along the flight path. We don't know what happened to the weapon, as far as I am aware. I guess the Soviet advisers probably got it." He paused, pondering the likely options. "We don't think they would have wanted the Syrians to obtain fissionable material."

"Okay. What about the other?"

Bar-El shrugged. "That one is still a mystery. Probably it always will be. It never rejoined its fighter escorts after reaching its target." He decided not to mention the target. "We estimate it was shot down during its egress, but the unit responsible must have been wiped out in the aftermath of the attack. We know of no claims submitted for destruction of a Kfir that night."

FEW TIGER FORCE PILOTS CAME TO PROMINENCE FOL-lowing the war. Most shunned publicity and others preferred to do their talking at reunions.

The most famous veteran of Tiger Force may be seen in the Royal Saudi Air Force Museum six days a week. Mounted on an elevated platform in the rotunda is an F-20B. It forms the center-piece for the area and is the first exhibit one sees upon entering the museum.

The paint is faded on 001 from exposure to the desert sun and its markings are not as bright as they once were. But visitors walking past the sleek Northrop may count the victory stars painted on the fuselage—one for each kill by Tiger Force. And some pause to read the name on the canopy rail, testimony of a king's promise to a warrior.

About the Author

A former managing editor of *The Hook*, the journal of carrier aviation, Barrett Tillman's writing has won awards from the American Aviation Historical Society and the Air Force Historical Foundation. He coauthored *On Yankee Station*, a definitive history of the naval air war over Vietnam, with Cdr. John B. Nichols, USN (Ret.) Mr. Tillman currently lives in Athena, Oregon.